The All Jamaican Library

The All Jamaican Library

Thomas MacDermot

MINT EDITIONS

The All Jamaican Library features work first published between 1903–1909.

This edition published by Mint Editions 2023.

ISBN 9781513211657 | E-ISBN 9781513210452

Published by Mint Editions®

MINT EDITIONS

minteditionbooks.com

Publishing Director: Katie Connolly
Design: Ponderosa Pine Design
Production and Project Management: Micaela Clark
Typesetting: Westchester Publishing Services

Contents

Becka's Buckra Baby
  Thomas MacDermot

      Madonna   13

I. The Father of Noel   15

II. Noel Herself   19

III. Becka   25

IV. "Becka's Buckra Baby"   31

Maroon Medicine:
  E.A. Dodd

      Preface   41

      Maroon Medicine   43

      Paccy Rum   50

      The Red Cock   58

      The Courting of the Dudes   69

Marguerite: A Story of the Earthquake
  W.A. Campbell

I   83

II   85

III   87

IV	89
V	93
VI	95
VII	97
VIII	99
IX	101
X	104
XI	107
XII	111
XIII	114
XIV	117
XV	120
XVI	122

ONE BROWN GIRL AND ¼
THOMAS MACDERMOT

THE "UNUSUAL" PREFACE   127

I.   Liberta Passley and some of her ways and meanings.
Old Peter as owned by Liberta—His rebellious hair
and clothes—What Liberta wrote on her tablets—The
arithmetic of humanity—Mrs. Cariton's understanding
of it.—Whence Liberta's name came—Liberta
No. I—The Doctor's Dictum—"The Princess" and

Waiting Time—"Hell in a House"—How Aunt
Henrietta's "Kingdom" fell.   133

II.   Enter some other people, Ada Smith and a casual
      Harold—"The Unfair Treatment of some Jamaicans"—
      Captain Burn's words and Liberta's thoughts—Liberta's
      "disease"—The Reader who did not comprehend—And the
      Listener who did—Ada explains why—Noel as Referee.   157

III. Mrs. Gyrton and the afflictions of some other Mudfish—
      The Father who was Resurrected—Theories of Taxes—
      The Prince of Wales and the Secret of Raphael White—
      Governors and Collectors—"Coughing up Taxes"—
      Marriage and Money—Mr. Grant's Proposal and His
      Views on a Wife.   175

IV.   The Slaying and Eating of the Last Fowl—The Pouring
      Forth of Debate—Into Theological Mazes—Prayer—
      The Devil and the Carpenter—A Final Surprize.   193

V.   Between the jaws of the Meffalas—Fidelia, the
      Coromantee—The smiting of John Meffala on the
      mouth—The Sot at Midnight—The Order of the
      supple-jack—The tragic work-seeker—Through
      wine to truth—A misinterpreted meeting.   207

VI.   Pic-nicking on the Mountain-tops—And on the
      Plain—Dragons of the Past—In the Tropical
      Moonlight—The Reader and her Audience of one—
      Miss Vera and her Story.   238

VII. The Letter addressed by a Lady—Harold Entertains
      Ada—The Beauty and Her Beast—"I do Love You"—
      Two Interpretations—When One Receives and
      Gives a Shock.   258

VIII. When a Young Woman Knows Her Own Mind—
      And a Young Man Does Not—The Figure Beside
      The Carnations—Ada Meets a Colonial Secretary.   265

IX. A Duel: Harold vs. Noel—Love, Creator and
Creature—Responsibilities—What Percival Road
Held in the Starlight—The Cross Roads' Pause in Life—
What Noel Remembered: and What She Forgot—
Calling a Beautiful Body to the Bar of Judgment.   276

X. Human Fingerposts Up and Down—The Sinner by
the Wayside—"God's Best Dog" smells Sin—Into the
Silence—After Church With Meffala and Ada—
A Minute in Oblivion.   288

XI. When Bachelors are Merry—High Jinks, Musical and
Otherwise—Something That "Stank Of Lawley"—
George announces an Interruption, and a Lady—What
Harold Expected on one side of a Door—And What
He Found on The Other Side.   304

XII. In Which Everything Depends On Noel—When One
Decides By Refusing To Decide—The Way Harold
Did It—The Way Noel Did It.   315

XIII. The Yielding Of Weakness—Ada in Noel's Room—
Phantoms and Realities Today on The Hills—
Tomorrow on the Plains.   324

XIV. Tells The Beginning of a Soul Hunt—The Trail Of a
Woman's Soul—Noel Follows It—The Last Step On
Life's Staircase—Liberia Tries to Pick The Meffala
Lock—How Cariton Unconsciously Did Something
Important—The Major Sees Behind the White
Sepulchre of Decency.   330

XV. Tells How The Major Handled Meffala, Junior—
And Continues a Hunt—With Digressions.   342

XVI. In Which we Leave the Soul Hunters—And Study
the Soul At Close Quarters—Under Coralilla Bowers
—A Crisis, via A Bad Coin Plays an Important Part—
Ada's Theological Convictions—Cold Water In a Glass

and Elsewhere—An Attempted Deal in Gold
Bangles—Peeping In at the Cottage Window—
And after.   346

XVII.   Gleaning in the Wake of The Hunt—Liberta's Review
and Foreview for Ada's Benefit—The Major's Counter-
view Unexpressed—Rumours True And Untrue—
Meffala Returns to Oblivion—And We Leave The
Major at a Black Moment.   360

BECKA'S BUCKRA BABY

Madonna

The Night on the Town has fallen,
    And the Gar Lamps, few and far,
Out-flame like the picket fires
    On the rim of a lonely war.

The lights of the Town, Madonna,
    Are the eyes of a Soul's despair;
The streets are the thoughts, Madonna,
    That are dreary and dark and bare.

The lights that the World affords us,
    Though we win where they burn their best
Reveal but the pain, the hurry,
    The stir of a street's unrest.

And we turn from the street's confusion,
    From the toil and the City's pain,
From all that the heart desires.
    And all that the hand can gain:

For what if we win it or lose it,
    The praise that the World bestows,
It fades like a flower gathered,
    It dies like a withering rose.

Ah, the calm of God, Madonna,
    It is far from the streets away,
And seeking that calm. Madonna,
    The hearts of thy children stray.

Thomas MacDermot
Jamaica.

I

The Father of Noel

All the rough world passed by,
All that it could not try,
When it weighed act with act,
And balanced fact with fact.

Noel Maud Bronvola, this was her name, and she could hardly ever remember repeating it to another in full without hearing the following comment expressed, or seeing it suppressed in the eyes that regarded her:—

"Noel, for a girl?" And then her mother was want to reply:

"Yes, her father would have it so. She was born on Christmas Day."

Everyone, who knew him, or nearly everyone, had said that Jack Bronvola was a peculiar man; and they were not slow to tell his peculiarities in detail, if you cared to hear them.

He gained a position in business while still a young man which meant for him in a decade or two, a fortune equal to any in the Island. That position he resigned a month or two after Noel's birth, because he considered the policy that he was called upon to execute, was unjust and cruel. Men generally find good reasons for not resigning £1,000 a year, steadily increasing to thrice that amount; and a man who does otherwise must justly be considered peculiar.

He was a man whose ability no one ever cared to dispute; and his family connections were influential and far reaching. Other positions scarcely less good were something more than open to him; but they had their objections, as he saw matters, and the end was, that he secured a post under Government which was worth barely £300, to start with.

Still the way lay clear before him for ascent. His ability soon told, and his prospects of early promotion grew bright. But unkind Fortune again interfered, and brought another opportunity for the exercise of that peculiar mind of Bronvola's.

Among his subs was a youngster whose father was a Magnate of the largest dimensions, literally and in a proprietorial sense, and of a power and influence not below those of any man between sea and sea through all Jamaica. All of which did not prevent the Magnate's youngster being a scoundrel of the first water. He drank, to the confusion of office work, and Bronvola rated him; he gambled, and this peculiar man both warned him and watched him. When it came to embezzlement, Bronvola put his hand out and crushed the young fool—like a fly.

So directly and carefully did he move, and with a determination so composed and unshakably firm, that, willing as the Authorities, or some of them, might have been, in view of the Magnate's, greatness, to let the quarry break the net and escape, they dared not allow it; and so prison doors received the Magnate's son on the day when they received the son of old Christie Downley, Parade and Sollas Market higgler, convicted of burglary in a Kingston suburb and of carrying off a watch and £5.

"Both thieves," said Bronvola and was satisfied.

Yet common-sense told him, and, as he knew it would, Time ultimately proved it true to him, that he on this day struck dead his chance of promotion. The Magnate's arm might be too short to save. It was quite long enough to destroy; and his hate was as long as his life. Bronvola, a man of serene soul, met his hate without a tremor; and lived without bitterness towards the Governors who feared the Magnate more than they feared God.

Noel was only twelve when her father died. For many years she knew of Jamaica only what Kingston, reveals; yet she loved the Island, and this intense love was wonderful; for Kingston is in ugliness past all endurance, and in wickedness beyond all imagination. Her father had been posted in the City and there he died in the full tide of his days, his life laid down unshrinkingly to redeem that of his daughter.

Noel lay sick of Diphtheria and was dying when her father saved her life and lost his own by sucking the breathing tube clear of the deadly fungus. He did it calmly, quietly, without outward sign that the heroic resolve he had taken was more than ordinary.

"It probably means death," the Doctor said, warning thus a man who he knew required no warning.

"I know," replied Bronvola, and did the deed of salvation for her and of death for himself.

Noel, still weak and wan from the struggle with the Mortal Foe, had at the very last when the end came for her Father, clung to him with a kiss that seemed to drive the two lives into one, like two flames commingling. She was too truly his daughter, and his mother had been too truly his helpmate and too thoroughly understood him, to thank him, or to praise that last great sacrifice. The wife joined hands with the Doctor and did all that skill and knowledge could to give the victory and life to the man who had dared to meet and face Death at the moment when His prey seemed irrevocably his own; but never once had she spoken what she thought and felt concerning that deed of self-sacrifice and supreme daring. Between father and mother and daughter there was the communion of souls. Words were not needed.

When Noel gave him that last, long, lingering, passionate kiss, her words were the simplest she could utter. She said,

"Goodbye, Father." But the eyes that poured their gaze on his spoke as the pure Angels of God speak, naked life to naked life; and the eyes of the dying man spoke back to her in full understanding, and with the deep, untroubled peace and flawless trust of the Soul that has been true to the Light.

So out into the Unknown passed the life of John Bronvola; and in the great heart of a girl there remained abiding the priceless resolution to follow worthily after that Soul into which her own had twice flown, at the mystic borders of Life and Death; to follow worthily and well, through things temporal and transitory, to pass with his untroubled peace, into things unseen and eternal. A priceless deed, that deed of Bronvola; never publicly acclaimed by pen or pulpit, known to men and women fewer than one counts fingers on a hand; but to reach to and through the great distance of years, and to be felt in lives innumerable.

The last struggle had quivered into quietude and perfect rest; the last, faint gasp of life on the hitherward side of the Vail was hushed and ended; the Widow wept softly as she prayed; and, from the lingering by the dead, an anxious Nurse strove to lead Noel away, dreading lest, weak as she was, Death should turn ere he left that house of Life and strike her also—it was then that perhaps by some sudden touch of God's hand upon his brain the old Clergyman who stood with these women in the Chamber of Death spoke the words "Greater love hath no man than this, that a man lay down his life for his friend." This he said, not knowing what manner of death Bronvola had died: but pointing these latest born of the Children of Sorrow to "a hill named Calvary." But surely it did not put them further from the Saviour of the World that mother and daughter were brought by the sublimely simple and pathetic words into the presence of a nearer sacrifice.

So passed Jack Bronvola, a man whom the world termed eccentric and peculiar, and very correctly so; for eccentricity is relative, and depends on where we place the centre; and peculiarity is relative and depends on what we make the standard.

The money that he left his wife and only child, gave them decent support, since he owned the house in which he passed from this life; but it allowed little to be laid out in the luxury of travelling, and thus it was destiny for Noel to pass her girlhood in Kingston. They had not many friends, the Bronvolas. A man who begins with £300 and ends with £1,000 will have no lack of friends. And he who has his £300 and sticks to it all through, will not be without some friends; but the man who has £1,000 and descends to £300; then with his own hand bars a re-ascent, that man will have few friends, indeed; a sordid bit of fact this.

II

Noel Herself

"Mixed———
In spite of the mortal screen."

Jack, his wife and Noel were very happy, almost perfectly so, till it pleased God to take the father; then the mother and the daughter went forward again, less happy in that he was no longer with them in the flesh; but all in all to each other, and sufficient.

And so year after year passed away, and there came for the two in due portion the sorrows, the pain, the anxieties, and the labour that fill up human life. But, till her girl was seventeen, the Mother could say with truth and gratitude that Noel had never grieved her heart. She had her father's strong, steady temper. Like him, she would get to reasons and neglect appearances, if they had no worthy justification. Like him, the currents of her mind swept from the first in that deep and resistless flow that broke neither into bitterness nor anger. And, to train such a heart, her mother was exactly the mother needed. Like the deep of the star sown sky, with its wide spaces and with the snow-white cloud drift, above plains where in the calm hush the buds are swelling into blossom—about the daughter's life the influence of the mother dwelt; and her girl's growth was like that of the lilies that toil not neither do they spin.

She had ways, had Noel, that a stranger prying into the home, would have pronounced odd; but to the two whose hearts dwelt there they were but sweet and natural.

Her father's Study remained as he had left it, with his books and pictures where he had set them; and there the many treasures he had been fond of assembling round him, cunning bits of woodwork, curiously grained stones, specimens of rare seeds, all were still kept in the places they had occupied when, in the midst of them all, sat Jack Bronvola, before and after office hours, writing, thinking or talking to his wife, or to his little eleven year old daughter.

Noel took charge of the Study after his death; she kept the key; her fingers alone dusted and replaced the table ornaments; and the books were removed from the big shelves by her arms only. Here she often came and sat for hours; sometimes with her mother beside her, and sometimes alone so far as a bodily presence went. On the table, day after, day she placed fresh flowers, and there they glowed, a flame from the invisible Spirit of Life that moves in the earth's dust and ashes, and changes death into life, the seed into the plant and from the murk of the clay calls the beauty of the flower. On the dead man's table the flowers, varying with the varying season, but daily renewed by unfailing love, burnt like the fires that in some Temples of God are never allowed to quench themselves in darkness, but speak the thought of Him that never fails, though the generations fail and pass; and to that thought types the Mystery that is from everlasting to everlasting.

Often when mother and daughter sat in the early darkness of night—on the vine-covered verandah, the house lamps burning low behind them, and the big stars above, answering with their steady light, to the gas glitter that the town showed here and there to illumine her darkness—while to the noises that street and lane flung up were returned the reaches of abiding silence—often then Noel would place a second chair, her father's, beside her mother's, and leaving it empty, go back to her own, to talk, or sing, or listen; just as of old they had done, when they were three, and when the second rocking chair was not empty where it stood. At such hours He was again with them.

The great thoughts of Great Poets, of the students of Life, the Novelist, the Philosopher, the Prophet, these came and went in their talk, casting no shame, imposing no insignificance on the ordinary affairs of their immediate lives, of the house, the town, the school, of friends and acquaintances; the beggars that came to the gate, the noise that rose from the streets—mention of which mingled also with their evening talks. All themes seemed to meet and interblend without jar or collision; as why should they not; and as they will whenever we win to Nature's way, and lay aside man's affectation and convention—since every bit is part of the Whole, and the beggar feeding his life with his crust is an integral bit of a discussion of the Immortality of the Soul and of the Infinite. Life is the garment woven from hem to hem, without seam.

But Nature has her work to do with us and she does it, while flesh and blood endure, and in seed time and in harvest; and when, at sixteen, Noel closed such books as we learn from in the Schools, there was arising, that within her that came to lead her to the larger pages of the great Book of Life. That other learning was to begin for her, and to lead her further than it is the general lot of women to go; and as it brings truth that is far more valuable when gained, so is it learning far more dangerous in the gaining.

She stood erect at sixteen in a beauty that showed nor spot nor wrinkle. Truth and purity, and the fearlessness these two create, dwelt in the clearness of her brown eyes. The true proportion of all the face, from the fine, full forehead to the dainty but firm chin, flung the beholder into no need of resting admiration on any one feature. Complete and entire as it was, the beauty before him conquered his admiration at once; and in beholding Noel one never said:

"What beautiful eyes; what perfect lips"—but,

"What a beautiful girl." "What a Life."

She had what is rare with the West Indian, white, black or brown, features in all but perfect proportion; for the West Indian girl, often good-looking, is seldom beautiful, if in beauty we demand as an essential fine proportion of form and feature. She had, what must be said to be rare in all women, a spirit akin to Nature's calm, and of that strength so unconscious, so full, set towards great issues, and working them out amid the ordinary and commonplace, without fret or jar, or sense of indignity.

Such a girl goes forth to be tried and tested by Life, and by the World's rough hands,—to win only a fool's reward—riches, position, praise from the lips of men, power; or, with these or without them, to receive honour, the praise that does not tabernacle in words, and the life eternal. Her fall, if she fall, shall be deep as Hell. If she endure, she indeed shall stand redeemed while yet in the flesh; and but a little lower than the angels that see God.

Noel's first contact with outside life came when she left school. The Clergyman who had been her father's friend asked her to become a Sunday School Teacher. Most commonplace of beginnings; but to be made great or insignificant as the soul is in the man or the woman. Life palpitates round a class in a City Sunday School; and through her class Noel entered the streets of the City of Humanity.

In her group of small black girls she began to touch Life, the Sores of Reality. Everyone of the half dozen existences that the school brought to her feet, led her away in a different direction It is not only when the road ascends Life's sunny slopes that the interest of variation begins. Variety lies also below, in the shadow, on the lowlands of Poverty; the apparent sameness and monotony there are an appearance only; reality lies beneath these, a different thing to its covering.

And so a year passed; and Noel at seventeen was beginning to be talked of by many in Kingston; with admiration by some, with wonder by others. She was to all appearance a lonely girl, often seen by herself; in fact seldom otherwise; and that this should be the case with one so beautiful and so manifestly gifted made most men, and specially most women, marvel.

Sometimes she went about with her Mother; very occasionally she was seen with a friend; but for the most part she was alone, whether walking or driving. She was known in the lanes where her scholars lived; and on the country roads beyond Kingston, where she was wont to travel great distances alone. Yet she was unfriendly to no one. She gave none the feeling that she wished definitely to avoid man or woman; and perhaps the explanation of her proneness to be alone was that she never felt alone.

To her it was the most natural thing possible to sit by herself in the Study, or on the Verandah; to take her way through the City; or to roam along a quiet road, fully occupied with her thoughts and observations; with these about her as friends, and with a sense of fellowship and remembrance, she did not live a life dependent on words, and so showed in contrast with our modern life which is a great waste of Speech with oases of Silence.

"Alone, Miss Bronvola?" a young man would say to her sometimes, in surprize.

"But I do not feel alone," she would reply, telling the simple truth.

Still, inevitably, she had to make friends; and one day she said;

"Mother, I am making a friend."

"Making? So the process is not complete?" said her mother, smiling.

"No, Mother, it is not. But you know who it is," and she told her mother his name.

"Your father was his father's friend," said her mother; and that for the present was the end of the matter.

But on an evening, a month later, while they both sat on the Verandah, to which Noel had just returned from playing dreamy, haunting music on the hall piano, a visitor came. It was the Young Man.

"This is my friend, Mother," said Noel, who had gone forward to receive him in the Drawing Room: and thus the door was opened to many such evenings; and so that night the vacant chair was filled; but when her Friend left, though her Mother bade her goodnight and went to bed, Noel returned and sat for a long time beside her Father's chair on the Verandah, with a spirit within her that was deeply, though vaguely, moved. But it was of her Father she thought; not of the Young Man, of whom she was making a friend. Thought of her Father was generally an atmosphere of her soul, rather than a distinct effort. But on this night her spirit was strangely stirred.

For long she sat in silence and perfectly still; then rising and leaning over the Verandah's Vine-crowded rail she watched the street till it grew utterly empty, as the City sank towards midnight's deeper silence and rest.

She came back and sat again beside her Father's empty chair, leaning her head on its arm. Closing her eyes, she tried to fancy she felt his hand resting on her hair and caressing it. Seldom did she feel him not so sufficiently with her, but that it was needless to invoke him by the effort definite and direct: but tonight the yearning for more than spiritual communion; the longing to feel his hand of flesh and blood as once she had felt it; to see his brown eyes, fixed up on her, lighting slowly into smiles; to rise and kiss him; to hear him speak—the longing, moved her soul through and through; and it grew to an agony that was unendurable.

She loosened her hair; and it fell in long length, a dark flood about her white, tense face. The Moon, unclouded, rising above the trees poured its beams over those fine waves of hair that framed the face so full of strong, healthy life and beauty. She looked up with eyes bright with unshed tears. The eyes he had loved; the hair he had fondled; the eyes into which he had so often smiled; the lips which he had kissed; all the life of this beautiful creature that he had given, seemed beckoning him to return to her; to return to her from the land of the Spiritual and Unseen,—once again to put on Mortality; once again to inhabit flesh and blood. The call of a Soul yet in the body for a return of the Soul that has lain down the flesh and passed to the immortal. The call so terrible because so futile. The hour when the unreason of the flesh triumphs, and to its triumph itself brings defeat. Rushing to the very brink of the depth it hears only the echo of its cry returned from the abyss of Night. While Horror and Despair creep out upon it, ready to strike it from that dizzy edge. For there indeed Despair and Horror face the Soul in their most hideous shapes; like survivals of primeval monsters, no longer encountered where men live and move; but which, frightful in appearance and deadly in power, still make their lair among the flame-scarred crags and cliffs of desolate heights, regions all but never trodden by the foot of man. There on the sudden they meet the infrequent Intruder; and in the moment of that terrible meeting strike him dead.

Noel rose at length, and taking a Lamp went into the Study, and there her Father seemed to welcome her She took down book after book that he had used, reading the lines underscored here and there. Every now and then a sentence flashed like a sun-smiten jewel; and through the influence of these thoughts he seemed to come; gently leading her back from that mood so dangerous, so horrifying, when the flesh demands with fury what the flesh can never more have; leading her back to the paths that the spirit finds and treads from life to life through death. Her wildness sank; the agony of longing receded; and he who in that agony had seemed dying away from her into a far distance, now, in the calm and ebb of her passion, returned: in part, she was comforted.

Flung abroad from the old Church Tower, the single stroke proclaiming that the first hour of a new day was completed, rolled loudly and heavily over the sleeping City. It found Noel once again Mistress of her Soul.

III

BECKA

"When Thou rememberest of what toys
We make our joys."

Over that part of the fence which was mended with kerosene tins, cut open and nailed flat to hide the holes in the boards, Mrs. Gyrton looked into her sister Rosabella's yard, and spoke her mind; of which a bit ran thus:

"Which it is not, Rosabella, becausen you have pickney dat is good as buckra to look at, an' its Poopa is a buckra out-an'-out—not becausen of dat,—you fe lick down me chicken."

Rosabella sat at her door nursing her baby; and she answered with the feeling of a General who knows he has the strongest position, and that the Other Man must excite himself a great deal, and fail in the end. She said:

"You can't done fe talk, noh—you nigger woman is——"

"Nigger woman," interrupted Mrs. Gyrton with such indignation as made her almost grind her teeth, for she was a passionate woman. "Nigger! Oh, Lord, me God, what is dis? Me dead Mooma, me Poopa, dat Buckra put in a lockup, an' to dis day I don't know weh him deh, if him dead else him live—don't Rosabella an' I born one way? If I nigger, you nigger. What more nigger I can nigger dan you?"

Rosabella went on looking at her baby as it tugged at her breast.

"You can't ebber tink say, causen you got baby fe Buckra you whiter dan me, you own born sister; one Teeta, one Mooma. You kyant fool so. You kyant fool so, Rosabella."

"Well," said Rosabella returning to the chicken, "why you can't keep you chicken out a me yard?"

"Fe who yard?" demanded Mrs. Gyrton. Former battles had taught her to note with very great nicety the words Rosabella employed.

"Fe who yard? Weh you get yard; eider money fe buy yard?"

"For I an' Mista Stanley, of course," replied Rosa with dignity.

"Well, I tank God, an Big Missis who did teach me to be servant at Big House, dat I don't get pickney nearly white. I is a married woman."

"Married to a Carpenter," sneered Rosabella.

"I married doh, an' you lib in sin; an' hell da hot fe you."

"You is dah talk after what Buckra tell you," said Rosa disdainfully. "Weh you husban' is?"

"You know him gone look work in a Colon," said Mrs. Gyrton, a sudden touch of deprecation softening her voice; but her sister was implacable.

"I know he is a drunkard man; an' dat him lazy wuss dan man ebber lazy since man stan up an' shake himself. I know him is a tief—"

"Tek you d——mout off him," broke in the wife, "Causen I speak an tell you not fe kill me chicken you raise pon dis piece of an abusen."

"I know seh," pursued the relentless one, "I hear de two a' you jam and blarse', and blarse' and jam, till dog outside stan a you gate mout an' howl, an' rooster start cackle and crow."

"You got's no right fe lick down me chicken," persisted the Carpenter's mate doggedly. As regarded the Carpenter she knew the case was hopeless; but she stood on her undoubted rights as regarded the Chicken, and behind an entrenchment of undisputed fact.

Rosabella was quiet a minute, then she said;

"Well, an' I woulden lick it, if it would satisfy fe walk bout de yard an' pick up what him fine'. But when it come to jump pon me drawing room table, I mus' lick him; an' I wish to King it was him neck I bruck, an' not him leg lonely, when I fire de piece of wood at him."

"An' suppose I did lick down you *maugre* dog when it come slap in a me kitchen, and tief out me bit and fippance tripe I just buy."

"Dat you nebber see," returned Rosa, gathering her things together for a retreat; she noted something which as yet was unseen by her sister. That person all unconscious of developments in her rear burst out:

"See him too jam well"—but as Rosabella vanished, Mrs. Gyrton turned, for the gate of her yard had opened, and a white girl came across.

The face was a delightful one to contemplate at any time, as was the graceful young figure, lithe and erect: but the Girl seemed particularly attractive amid the sordid surroundings of that poor yard and beside the temper-furrowed and the harsh time roughened countenance of Mrs. Gyrton. The white girl with her finely moulded features, in her dress of simple white relieved by pink, appeared in the midst of the unlovely commonplace of that Kingston Slum like an Angel of the Ideal. It was Noel.

"I have come only for a minute, Mrs. Gyrton," she began brightly, "to wish you a Merry Christmas. It is the day after tomorrow, you know; and I won't see you before the day comes. I have brought this for Rebecca. Can I see her?"

Rebecca was out, and Mrs. Gyrton said so.

"Well," replied Noel, "that may be all the better. It is a doll, and I wish it to be quite a surprise. You must keep it wrapped up as it is, and give it to her on Christmas morning itself. Here it is; I will open it and show it to you at once. Then you must keep it wrapped and tied for Becka, till Christmas Day."

Mrs. Gyrton promised solemnly; and after a minute or two Noel departed. She was Rebecca's Sunday School Teacher, and her very good friend.

Mrs. Gyrton, after seeing her ceremoniously to the gate, and carefully closing that rather shaky framework, came across to the weak place in the fence, and called:

"Bella, Bella."

Her sister appeared; and the Carpenter's wife enquired anxiously:

"You tink seh she hear me when I did jam you jus' now?"

"I can't tell," said Rosabella languidly; and then with woman's readiness to be unpleasant to woman, she added; "but she did bound to hear you; de way you halla it."

"I wish to Master she don't," said Mrs. Gyrton. "It all come troo you, Bella" she added.

But now Rosabella was weary of battle, and only asked:

"What dat she give you?"

"It is fe Becka."

"A what?"

"China Baby, me lub."

"Oh, Dolly," said Bella; for dolly it is in Whiteman's phraseology and "China Baby" in the saying of the Black; Bella affected, as a matter of course the Whiteman's style.

"How it stan?" she enquired.

Mrs. Gyrten on this promptly untied the string and displayed the doll, saying as she did so:

"She beg me quite hard not to open it, neider gib it to Becka till Christmas Day; an' I pramise her particular on de matter."

The two examined the Doll carefully and with curiousity. Blended with Rosabella's curiosity, was the more directly practical desire to decide whether such a doll would be good enough for her atom of coloured humanity when it was old enough to have dolls.

But in Mrs. Gyrton the mood was more reflective and philosophic. She said:—

"Bella, what you tink? Backra dont hab time to trow way; wen dem sit down good, good, and mek ting like 'a dis? It is white man and white woman got little or nutting to do."

Bella, busy with excursions into the Future, merely grunted; and indeed nothing beyond a grunt was needed in response to a remark embodying a truth so patent to the Negro at least; namely, that it is the lot of the Whiteman to play and enjoy himself, and of the Blackman to work and do only that which is useful. For in the West Indies, where the refrain of every White author is "the negro won't work," it is amusing to note that the opinion of the said Negro is set in just the opposite direction. "Blackmen," he says, "are born to work; but Backras to please themselves"; and again, he says: "It is only Backra got time to sit down an do nutting—and who get money all de same."

Mrs. Gyrton's reflections next took a moral and religious turn.

"You know, seh, Rosabella, I dont tink Backra should make likeness of live Pickney so. Why, me King, dis China Baby you might tink it was da got alk. Him got han, him got eye; him can move dem; him got shoes; him to got stocking. Big Massa gib dem true true, pickney, what de debil deh mus' go mek up play play one for. I bet you if it was Nigger shorance so Big Massa would a' open him han so box fe we head off. But Backra a' Young Massa; and Nigger a' servant boy. All de same, I tell you, dem can tek it too far; an one a dis day Backra *will* tek it too far: and you will see a piece of a trouble. Me Master, but what dem Whiteman lef' to do now? save and except build road and drive buggy go slap a heaven."

"It is a good dolly," said Rosabella, who had now reached the end of her thoughts on the matter of the Doll's value, and desired in thus expressing her opinion to convey the patent fact that she, and not her sister, was competent to pronounce on such a thing as "a dolly."

The Carpenter's Wife, still full of forebodings of the trouble in store for the "shorance Backra" who "went too far with Big Massa," failed to perceive the intention of Rosabella's remark; but, with the sadness of the Author who feels his best thoughts are not getting fairplay, she muttered the rest of her comments, doing her duty to the world by expressing them, but dismally certain that Rosabella was paying no attention whatever.

"But de hard ting is dis," she continued, "when Big Massa get mad an' bex wid dem shorance Backra, and him tek him Volcano, else him

Hurricane, else him Comic (Comet) an' mek to bruck dem up and sweep dem out, him nebber stop to tink say Blackman deh all bout me foot an' dat Blackman is not man fe do nonebody any harm; but de which and de way Big Massa bex him lick down eb'ry bit, black oh, white oh, brown oh; an' dat's how poor black people in Jamaica can't get on."

Taking the doll she wrapped it in its paper covering. Entering her dirty, shabby, little house she laid the parcel on the table beside a china ornament, now chipped and broken, which long ago the Carpenter had bought to help furnish the house; for they were an ambitious couple in the days when they first launched on the somewhat treacherous seas of matrimony.

The parcel lay there waiting Becka's coming; beside it was the little girl's Bible, and a cup containing a few grains of the corn to which the Chicken, whose leg Bella had that day broken, was treated on state occasions.

Mrs. Gyrton gat her outside and continued to starch clothes.

Meantime where was Becka? And who was she?

A small black creature of nine Augusts, she was Mrs. Gyrton's only child; the only child she had ever borne; a fact that was often emphasized by Bella and other enemies of the Carpenter's wife, when, in wordy battles, the contention was, on Mrs. Gyrton's part, that she, as a married woman, was set on high above her fellows; and, on their side, that she was after all only an imitator of white people's ways; and a failure at that.

"You is a one-pickney-an-no more woman," was Rosabella's bitter taunt towards her sister; to be followed by the triumphant argument, that it was always and ever thus that Big Massa taught Black women the folly of "marrying like Backra."

Each returning Sunday saw Becka blossom out into neatness and the glory of a clean dress; but she was a ragged little figure from Monday to Saturday. Her dress roughly made of a coarse blue cloth, was allowed to become very dirty. Buttons deserted their posts, and here and there the blue cloth itself was rent and torn, showing beneath the outer dress an under garment made of calico, that had once been white.

All through the day of this story Becka had been carrying water by the bucketful for her mother. Their yard had a pipe; but the pipe just then gave no water. The Water Commissioners desired a payment of Rates in arrears. Mrs. Gyrton could pay no arrears; and thereupon her pipe was locked off from the main.

Under such circumstances, the Law threatens that man with dire penalties who, having still his pipe with water therein, and seeing his brother in need, gives to the thirsty soul to drink. But it is perhaps as well that, threats notwithstanding, there are persons who will transgress the sacred law of the Kingston Water Commissioners; and from some of these, rich people unmindful of their duty to other rich people, Becka's mother got water, transporting it by means of her little daughter, who, carrying the full bucket on her head, had tramped the morning hours away.

Then it was her duty to assist her mother hang out the wash clothes; to do which she had to lug from place to place a chair, wooden, very old and without a back; for with her dirty bare feet planted on the very bosom of Mother Earth, she was altogether too short to reach the clothes line; so she climbed up and stood on the chair as she arranged the wet shirts and the trousers and the jackets in the places where they should be, fastening each piece with a wooden clip, to hold it against the breeze's persistent and mischievous attempts to fling it down on the dirty yard.

Hours of this brought the afternoon; and then once more, obedient to directions from her mother, Becka resumed her bucket and set out to carry more water.

She was away on this errand when her Sunday School Teacher came to the yard; and little did she think, as she loitered just then, resting on the rough board beneh beside the water-pipe, that by so doing she was missing the sight of her much beloved Miss Noel.

Gushing from the clean brass of the pipe, and splashing into the overflowing bucket and brimming, with bubble all afloat, over the grey tin side, pleasant was the sight and the sound of the tumbling water; pleasantly ran the soft murmur of the passing breeze in the leafy trees of the Garden near by, where, round and clean and sweet-looking showed the boles of the handsome Palms; and pleasantly, as the sunbeams found them out, shone, in rich, brave, glow, the Crotons ranged along the green grass lawn.

The tired little mortal sat and watched and listened and rested many minutes; meanwhile, at Becka's home Miss Noel came and went.

IV

"Becka's Buckra Baby"

The swift mysterious instincts

* * * *

The fated and fatal moments

B ecka," said her Mother, when Becka had returned to the yard, "Miss Noel did come fe see you; and she bring you a China Baby. It is you Christmas, and she beg me quite hard not fe show you it till Monday; neider to tell you bout it; but Saturday done already; tomorrow Sunday come; next day Christmas. It come already, so I going ghee you it now, now; but you mind me, if she ax you a' Sunday School tomorrow you must talk circumspect, and dont tell no lie pon me; but mek her to understand I not going ghee you it till Monday 'cording as I promise and she tell me; for I promise her very particular."

"Yes, Mam," said Becka almost choking with the sudden joy of the thing.

"Look in a de hall, on de table. It wrap up in piece a brown paper and it tie wid green string. When you eat you dinner done, tek it."

"Yes, Mam," said Becka.

She emptied her bucket, took the little tin plate with her dinner and obediently eat the boiled banana, rice and salt fish, that she found thereon.

"Wash you plate, mind," said her Mother, catching her eye as the last morsel of food disappeared; and Becka, washing the plate, placed it to drain.

"Tek you China Baby den," said the Mother with a touch of the ceremonious. Becka took it.

Then for a whole hour she was blissfully and completely happy.

Touched by some softer feeling, her mother left her entirely alone. Rosabella came to the fence, by and by, and the Carpenter's Wife cracked a joke with her.

"Rosabella, we got backra baby, too, now, Becka got white baby same as you."

"Praps she we' have one fe true, time to come," said Aunt Rosabella graciously.

"Who can tell," assented the mother of Rebecca; "but I trus' she will marry same as Backra do, an' same as me."

Rosabella only laughed.

It was getting dark when Becka's Mother called her.

"You mus' go downtown, Becka. Mrs. Paterson tell me bout a shop out a' Sollas weh dem got some salt pork cheaper dan anyways in Kingston. It is nighst de corner a' you left han a de market. One Chinaman keep it; so you can't loss it. Something do de pork, and him da sell it fe little and nutting. It eat all right dem tell me; and so I going sen you buy a half pound; and being as you is dere you can walk go in a market and buy me some scallion and a breadfruit; and see you get it nuff."

"Yes, Mam"; and Becka forthwith got her basket.

"And, look, yah," said Mrs. Gyrton then, "dont tek you baby, bimeby it go bruk, an' Miss Noel fine' out seh I gib it you before Monday."

Becka would gladly have appealed against this decision, had she dared; but she dared not.

"An' when you come back, if I dont yah, put what you buy weh dog cant eat it in de kitchen and go a' you bed. I got to go a' Mrs. Smart to go see if she we' pay me fe de washing, and it deh chock up by Half-way Tree; so I may be well and late."

"Yes, Ma'm," said Becka monotonously, but with delight piercing suddenly, like a ray of light, into her sombre little heart. She saw that after all it was quite possible to take the doll.

Forth Becka went on her journey, empty basket in hand, the pink of propriety before her Mother's eyes. But she went up the road not down.

Hurrying along, she chose a spot where the interval between the gas lamps was longer than usual, and where it was in consequence darker than elsewhere. Quickly then she hid herself behind a clump of bush, and waited.

People went and came, unconscious of the small eyes that scanned their passing with attentiveness.

At length Mrs. Gyrton, wash clothes in hand, went by, bound for Half-way Tree. She had passed quite out of sight ere Becka crept forth. Back to the yard, she went, opened the door at the back, and a minute later had her precious "backra baby" in her loving embrace.

With the Christmas holiday so near at hand, the streets, always crowded on Saturday nights, were more than usually packed; and

Sollas Square was the centre of the densest grouping and onflowing of buyers and sellers. But, amid the noise, the dirt and the bustle, Becka was quite at home.

She made her way to the Chinaman's shop. In that, attracted by the fame of the cheap pork a crowd had gathered, and a good natured struggle proceeded among those anxious for a place before the Counter. For a time Becka declined the combat, and while awaiting a chance to edge in, played with her Doll.

"You tief," said a voice behind her, sudden, loud and rough. She turned and finding a big lout of a Boy idling by the barrels near the door, she "sucked her teeth" at him.

"Come, I going tek it away," proceeded the lout, menacingly. "You little brute, you tief it from some one who employ you."

"You is a liard," responded Becka, indignant, and ready for battle. She "cut her eyes" to show contempt and fearlessness.

"Tief! Oh," mocked the Lout. "Who tief China Baby?"

"You tell a false," cried Becka angrily. "Miss Noel gib me it for me Christmas."

"An' Christmas dont come yet," pursued her tormentor; "and what Mies Noel would gib ting like you China Baby."

"You fast long mout naygar," answered Becka with spirit, hastening, after the manner of her sex, to defend by attacking. "What business you got with my baby?"

A Market Woman turned at this juncture, attracted by the contention. She was resting her headload near by, while she tied up "change" in a handkerchief.

"Don't noyance de chile," she remonstrated. "You boy got nutting to do but use you mout. Buy what you want, me gal, and go you ways; if you follow answer boy nonsense you got fe walk a long road; an' special dese Kingston boy," she continued, "dem don't got a piece self of manners. Got's nutting to do but mock country people, an' walk roun' and roun' da 'noyance somebody."

Becka, following her champion's advice, pushed her way to the Counter, and in due time was served with the half pound of pork that she wanted, and with a box of matches that was "brata."

By that time both the Boy and Market Woman had disappeared.

Becka's next business took her to the Market itself; and there, plunged into the multitude of buyers and sellers, and wriggling her way from stall to stall, she sought diligently till she found the Breadfruit and the Scallion that experience told her would be grateful to the judgment of her Mother.

This completed the business of the evening; and left Becka free to take such pleasure as she could take. She had not a farthing to spend; but sight and sound were free to all; and to Becka the streets were as good as a Theatre.

Staring curiously into the passing cars, and mooing very slowly along the picturesquely lighted stalls, on which glittered bright tin-ware, or glowed brown buns, brown cakes, or white bread curiously plaited, she feasted eye and ear to the full.

A Street Preacher at one corner was laying himself out to describe Hell; and Becka listened to him with great interest, till a man in the crowd spoilt everything by vexing the Preacher.

"Captain," he called, "*you* don't know what Hell is like."

"The hotness," persisted the Preacher, hoping to talk down the interrupter, "the hotness of Hell, my friends—"

"Talk foolishness," said the Critic, angry the more at being overlooked, "wha you know bout place hot. I wish I could catch you on a Steamer and mek you feed furnace one night, one single night, ole man; den you would know more bout Hell and Hot."

The Critic was a Stoker, and being a man acquainted with the Realities, his gorge rose at the feeble colouring painted by this well intentioned but incapable Artist now before him.

"Brothers," said the Stoker's, Victim, "and Sisters," he added as an after thought, his eye falling on Becka, "We will now sing a hymn." He was a man, slow and patient, but not without craft, and some desire to retaliate.

"Well, sing," grumbled the Stoker, hurrying up speech before the oncoming roar of sound drowned his voice. "Sing you hymn dem; but don't talk bout Hell and Hot, when you don't know."

"Whiter than Snow" was the melody that then rose to heaven. Truly that Stoker would have taken some washing.

Becka moved on, to be attracted presently by a long and bitter disputation which proceeded at the stand of a Peppermint Seller. The matter at issue was three farthings worth of candy; but the Seller wielded a style of description and narrative that far outran, in the graphic art, the Preacher's feeble attempts; and it was a real pleasure to hear her tell the story of how the man at whom she now pointed the finger of scorn, had attempted to get her "gill worth" of peppermint "for little or nutting."

The man, poor worm, replied only just enough to inspire further castigation; and Becka lingering, listened, hugely interested, and even oblivious for whole minutes to her Buckra Baby.

Then someone jostled her; and, turning at the minute sharply she realized that the Lout had snatched at her doll. He seized it and ran up street crying:

"You tief it; you tief it. Who tief China Baby?"

Becka dashed after him, her whole soul so racked and strained that she hardly saw the horses and the buses round her; even the Electric Cars with their big head lights, their loud wheel rush and harsh sounding bells crashed by her, unregarded! She called out passionately:

"Gib me, me backra baby. Gib me, me baby," but the basket weighed her down and the Boy easily kept ahead.

So, block after block, he teazed her; and a group of people who waited at a cross street might have seen the whole of the proceedings from first to last, though in fact they noticed neither the Boy nor the Child, till the former, tired of the sport, pitched the doll with a quick toss out into mid street, where it fell across the tram line.

Then a cry of warning, blending into one of horror, rose; for, blind to all else but the fallen doll, and to every circumstance of danger, Becka ran across to the line at the very moment that a Car on the down line rushed there with a noise of harshly loud wheels The strong, intense blaze of light flung before it marked her out, like the eye of a monster searching for its prey. For the fraction of a second, the eager child's figure stood out in appalling glory, and those watching saw that of the Motorman as he strove wildly to apply the brake.

From the side of the street a White Girl, standing there with a young man, ran forward to reach Becka. Her companion, crying sharply:

"Miss Noel, it is madness," seized her arm at the same instant.

Her Will thrust his words away, as granite beats through a puff of spray; but as he realized that speech was vain he tightened his hold on her arm, till he felt her impulse recoil, curbed by the physical check. His grasp and not his words stayed her gallant motion.

Then she turned on him with eyes that blazed a deep anger such as he had never met before. Her beautiful face quivered with strength of feeling.

In the swift instant of her pause and look the terrible death of Becka was over.

Too small to be crushed, the doll lay safe and sound on the bricks where it had been tossed, except that in falling a hand had been snapped away.

Becka was a mass of quivering, bloody flesh.

The crowd swooped down on the scene at once, and word went up:

"Dead. Quite dead. A little black child."

The White Girl with eyes averted from her friend's face, waited tensely till the death was announced. Her one swift glance a minute before, which read for her the approaching catastrophe and led to her quick leap to save the child, had not revealed the identity of the victim. Noel had not recognised Becka. If the child, thought of as a stranger, was dead, nothing more could be done by her.

She turned to the young man beside her:

"I wish you to leave me," she said in a cutting tone.

"I?" he asked, astonished. "Have I offended you?—I—I—held you. I could not help it."

"You stopped me," she said.

"The danger," he urged, "you did not see it."

"I saw the danger," she replied, quietly, but in anger.

"I was too rough," he said penitently. "I hurt your arm; but I had to hold you tight to stop you."

"You stopped me," was her reply to that.

"I prevented you killing yourself," he returned with a touch of impatience.

"The child was killed," she answered.

"You could not have saved her." He spoke like one applying cold Fact and plain Common Sense to Fancy if not Fantasy.

"There was a chance." The girl said, "I would have tried."

"And have been killed."

"A life for a life," she said; and she in her turn was now impatient. "Goodnight."

He would have been a wise man to have left her then, at once, with not a word further: for in truth she needed solitude. But how few are the young men who are wise. He persisted and cast himself over the precipice.

"Your life against hers," he answered hotly and angrily; "a child like that; and you. My dear Miss Noel, don't be unreasonable. I apologise for touching you; but it was the only way to stop you."

"I should not have been stopped," said the Girl, so quietly that apart from the blood of the child on the street, you might have thought she jested. But she was in deadly earnest.

THOMAS MACDERMOT

"You mean that? You should not have been stopped?" he exclaimed. "You are quite unreasonable."

"We will not argue it," she said, with a deepened cadence of intensity.

"But it was a most serious thing."

"It matters, because it was so serious," she answered at once.

"You did not see—You did not understand."

"I saw everything. I understood, and I could have stopped myself had I wished to. No one else should have stopped me." She repeated her "Goodnight," and turned very slightly from him.

He flushed; looked at her, and a ugly flame of the hate born of a miscomprehension of motive flashed momentarily in his eyes. It is the Hate most uncompromising, most deadly. Then it sank and he said, pleading:

"Don't be unjust, Miss Noel." Then after a pause "Don't be unreasonable." Then almost with humility, "I did it for the best."

She did not answer.

"At any rate," he said, "let me wait till your car comes."

"I would prefer you to leave me, now."

Then, he lifted his hat and left her, conscious in a dim way that his dream was over.

The first man attracted by this girl's soul had made his failure to enter into communion with her spirit.

And Noel! She stood alone, waiting for her car, filled with the strongest indignation; a girl so beautiful in her young womanhood, so erect and strong in her youth, that even apart from the charm of her finely moulded features, the firm but lovely lips, the complexion delicately clear, eyes, brown, bright, and of perfect vision, hair dark and wavy, her truly proportioned form, she had a charm potent to attract and influence any spirit that could respond to Beauty, Purity and Grace.

She was one of those women about whom the Spirit of Life seems a penetrating, a pervading, almost a visible influence; so that, it is really by an after thought that you note the beautiful face and the graceful form.

Noel did not know that the little mangled body had any special claim on her interest. She was ignorant for the present of the tragedy induced by her Christmas gift; but she quivered to the last fibre of her being at the thought that the sacrifice her *willing* heart, in that moment of high realization, had leapt to make, had been crudely and roughly pushed back from the very foot of the Altar.

And late that night when Becka's Mother and her Aunt Rosabella were wailing their dead; and waiting for the morning that they might send and tell Miss Noel of their trouble, Noel, in her dainty bedroom, sat wide awake in the darkness at the window. She looked out into the night, watching the stars burning in their far off homes, and looking from them to the City's feeble fires; and she could not sleep, nor could she rest.

And, behold, her thought was not that she had escaped by her friend's ready hand frightful mutilation; but that they were ever divided as friends because by his hand she had been restrained from giving her life for another.

It was her destiny to cross the years and to enter Womanhood; but had her choice that night been fulfilled her splendid life would have been spilt in red drops on the threshold; or flung, on lintelland doorpost, a crimson Passover mark to wave back the Angel of Death from a life that he had claimed.

To Youth is excess of thought and of emotion; and to Youth, from the angle of an older world, and a world that claims to be wiser, unreason, even absurdity is charged in its, actions and impulses of nobility. But who will say that this girl was unreasonable who, full of life's happiest, fullest pulse, leapt to obey an instinct that had been given to her, deepest of any in her nature.

But the episode of "Becka's Buckra Baby," which we have now watched to its conclusion, came not to end but, for good or for evil, to begin the Life of Noel, a girl unlike and yet most deeply like other girls; to an attention to whose fortunes the reader may some day be called by the present writer Meantime let us leave her, recovering strength and composure, in the hours of darkness leading out to the Dawn, during the moments when her soul swayed and shook as, with the tremor of deep currents, vibrates an ocean full to the shore-lip, brooded over by Night and Silence, and watched by Stars, large, strong and serene.

THE END OF THE EPISODE

MAROON MEDICINE

Preface

In the four short stories that are now set forth to the Public,—I have in no way touched upon the Social Problems I might say Problem,— which, as a rule, engross the attention of writers who deal with life in Tropical Countries. On the contrary, I have avoided all such deep questions, and have attempted merely to portray the lighter and more pleasant side of the labouring class in the hills. The stories, indeed, are scarcely more than sketches, but sketches, from life, and as such may have some value.

I have tried to instil into this little book, the spirit, so gay and careless of the people I have encountered, and their simple cuteness. Mr. Watson, however, is hardly an ordinary type, and has been made up from two or three characters. Some people may object to the two love letters in the story, "The Courting of the Dudes," as being too well expressed and civilized, but it may be remarked that they were composed very much after the manner and matter of two or three letters that had been actually written and which I had the good fortune to read.

E.A. Dodd,
Jamaica

Maroon Medicine

I t was just one of the cottages that you see scattered all over Jamaica; possessing four walls made of plaster and lathes, and a thatched roof—the whole enclosing two rooms, dignified by the names, of bed-room and hall. From one corner stretched a small barbecue, which again at one corner fed a small, "Kick-um-buck" tank, covered over with rough logs to prevent people falling in. All around, for the space of about half an acre, grew in picturesque medley, coffee bushes, yams, breadfruit trees, orange trees, the products of the lower mountains in the Parish of Manchester. A couple of fowls scratched around the house, and a hungry-looking pig messed about his little railed in pen.

It had rained in the night, but the morning had broken exceeding fresh and fair, warm yet cool, with a bright beauty that I cannot believe could have been surpassed anywhere. It may be that the pig felt something of this, or it may be that he knew that his morning meal was nearly ready, but undoubtedly he felt happy and showed it in little unmusical squeals. His master sat at the edge of the barbecue, chopping up into a box with his cutlass, steadily and with attention, a few small canes. Having finished chopping all except one choice bit which he reserved for his own consumption, he rose and went to the pen, where he put the box before the pig. He then proceeded to chew his own piece of cane, with a certain amount of intelligent repose on his face.

This face of his was long and of a neutral brown, with the bony chin going in sharply up to the neck. The man had a wide and mobile mouth, with a quaint twitch at one side, two small twinkling eyes and a bald and sloping forehead under his hat of plaited thatch.

It was a perfect morning in the end of November, yet to judge from the slight frown which crept up and marred the repose of Mr. Watson's face, one could not think the latter was in sympathy with nature's peace. The reason was simple, Mr. Watson had very little ready money; and Christmas was coming, and he felt aggrieved with himself and his wits, which were not in the habit of failing him. His thoughts ran in this groove:

"An a what me got fe Chris'mas bar dis little maugre pig? Me cawfee no sell well, and me premento don bear, a what me got? Me we have to do sompin?"

His musing was suddenly interrupted by the approach of a neighbour, who was walking through to his ground, and who stopped to salute him.

"Hi, mornin' Miser Watson!"

"Mornin', Coz! How you do?"

"So, so, sah, a not too well an' a not too bad, you a feed you pig, sah."

Mr. Watson turned carelessly and twitched the few scraggy hairs that formed his whiskers, with a gesture peculiar to him.

"Yes, sah, me a feed him, but a wha de use? I buy him back dis tree weeks from Miser White at James Hall, and I gie'm yam pealin! cocoa head, banana an' all sort o' ting, an look pon him now, h'no ah piece fatter than when I buy him. Well (with emphasis) as you might seh, a doan pay much fe him, but it tan like a not goin get no more fe him."

"Hi, but a wha do de pig den?" said the neighbour sympathetically. "Him really ought fe fat. Aldo some of dem, a so dey tan. I remember dis man Joe Crawford got a pig; well when he buy him, h' not too fat so h'n get plenty o feedin', cane, cocoa head an' I don know what; an' him feed that pig fe true, but you believe me sah, dat pig was no fatter at de end of tree monts dan when he got him fus' time. Mus a same way wid dis."

Mr. Watson looked with a philosophical calm at the pig.

"Well, it may be. Ah same way wid some man; you wi see some o' dem eat, eat, an eat and yet dem never get fat, dey tin all de time."

"You speak true, sah, a same way wi some men."

After a pause the neighbour hitched his bankra better on his shoulder and said:

"Yes, sah, ah jus' a walk trew to me groun' go look somepin for me wife."

"You welcome, you welcome," said Mr. Watson hospitably, "a no hear you wife sick? A fe true?"

"Yes sah. It true! night before las' she tek in wid a single pain in de stomach, de pain hol' her dat way. Well she go to bed, an' ah tek dis bush dem call 'Piobba' and a bwoil it down and mek some tea, gie 'er but it doan any good, den ah mek some oder tea out o'dis other bush; 'Vervain,' an' gie 'er dat, but dat also doan do any good; and all dis time de pain dat bad. Well yesterday about sun hot, Mrs. Weekly advise me try some soda and nut oil mix wid a little water and I do so, and since then she feel a little better and could walk bout de yard in the evenin'. Yes sah she really sick but she not too bad dis morning."

During this speech Mr. Watson showed his sympathy in a few well chosen sounds and affirmatives which cannot be reproduced by any combination of letters.

"Ah glad fe hear she better. Some of dese teas is really wonaful. To be sure some doctors good. I woan seh dey not, but mos' time you go to dem, you jus' wase you money. Dis bush or dat is all I want."

"You right, Miser Watson, you quite right," agreed the other heartily, "Some doctors no wut a grass louse, aldo dis Doctor Pratt him really good." Then moving on, "Well ah gone, Miser Watson."

"Yes, sah."

Mr. Watson sent him on his journey with a wave of his hand and then resumed the reflective chewing of his cane. I may remark here that the man's ground was five miles away, but there is nothing strange in this; for the Jamaica Peasant will travel up to ten or twelve miles to get some fresh piece of land to till and work as a ground. Every two or three years he throws up one piece and takes another fresh bit.

After his friend's departure Mr. Watson's face took on an even more reflective look; and for half an hour he lolled in deepest thought; then straightening with a brightened face, he walked into his house, and emerged with his jacket on, having been without it before.

His face now was the calm inscrutable and cunning face of Mr. George Watson of Every Garden. This was the name of his place, but how it had arisen, and what was its origin, Mr. Watson himself did not know.

He left the house and yard now in charge of a little ragged girl, his daughter, and took one of those paths, which fed the main road like tributaries of a river. Coming out on this, he walked for about three miles, when he came into a village, consisting of two or three rival shops which sold various, assorted articles, from very weak rum to a drawing book, and a couple of professional houses of shoemakers and blacksmith. At one of the former he bought a sixpence worth of soda, and between the three, two dozen pint bottles, saying in sort of excuse that Mrs. Smith (who made bread) had asked him to buy the former for her, and as regards the latter, he was speculating in bottles, and was going to sell to a man from Kingston. He also gave out that he was going up to the Mile Gully Mountains to invest in ginger.

Having bought what he wanted, and having refreshed his mind with a little light conversation, he left and went home where he was busy all day mixing in the privacy of his half-tumbled down kitchen, some vile-looking stuff.

It was perhaps between four and five next morning when Mr. Watson started for the Mile Gully Mountains "to invest in Ginger," driving his donkey, yclept Alice, before him. The hampers contained the two dozen bottles he had bought the day before, a dozen on either side, empty no longer—also some little provision for his journey—a gill bammy, a little pork already boiled, some yams and some oranges. His house he had locked up, but the pig and the cultivation around he had left on the charge of his neighbour and daughter. This latter by the way being driven from under the paternal roof, had taken up her abode for the time being with her aunt (?) She was not Mr. Watson's only child, having three brothers and a sister alive. These, however, having come to the conclusion that their father was not perfect, in his ideas regarding obedience in his children, had severally run away to other yards, a common enough practice in Jamaica. Needless to say, Mr. Watson did not go after them. His was a philosophical soul and he in no way regretted not having to feed three hungry children. He would not have received them back; and his children knew it.

By the time the sun had risen and another perfect day had begun, Mr. Watson had passed Mandeville and was nearing Williamsfield. On reaching the latter place, he stopped near the Railway Station under the shade of an overhanging roof of a front house, and sitting down proceeded to assuage his hunger with half the bammy, half the pork, and half the oranges. The yam was destined to be roasted and eaten higher up when he had come to the end of his journey.

After half an hour's rest, Mr. Watson rose, stretched himself, and started again with a touch and a word to Alice.

From here onwards his road led higher and higher, and at about mid day he entered the district he was bound for. At one or two houses near the road, he enquired his way to the yard of Mr. Hezekiah Brooks. This Brooks had once travelled his way and had partaken of Mr. Watson's hospitality, the latter putting him up for a couple of days. He undoubtedly would now in his turn be glad to put up his former host. After about half an hour's walk, Mr. Watson came to the Brooks yard and found the gentleman of the house at home, who welcomed him and expressed his delight at seeing him again. Mr. Brooks was a small brown man, a carpenter by trade, of not much force of character, yet kindly and good-natured.

"Ah really glad fe see you, Miser Watson. Don mention it, sah. Jus' tie you donkey to dat tree and sted dis way. Me no ha much as regards house and place to sleep ina, but weh me hav, you welcome to."

Over some roasted yam and boiled saltfish the little man took upon himself to find out why Mr. Watson had come up that way.

"Excuse me, sah, and I doan mean nutten by it, but ah curious to know whey you travel dis way fur. You mus' be going buy and speculate?"

Mr. Watson resting easily against the side of the kitchen twitched his whisker:

"Well you guess right enough, Miser Brooks, I am goin' fe speculate, Ah did notice dat our way, well dem doan grow ginger or nutten to speak of, an' de backra ladies dem, dey always a want ginger. So I tink if I buy some up dis way an' tek it down, a might a mek a little pon me bargin." Mr. Brooks looked at him.

"Yes, sah, you might a really mek sompting pon it. Me neber tink o' dat, or me might ah try it before. You mus' be going carry it, de ginger in a bottle, me notice you got plenty o'bottle."

Mr. Watson ate his saltfish and remarked indifferently:

"Oh de bottle only got a little Maroon Medicine in dem. It such a good thing for sickness dat I tink dat as a coming up here wey dey doan know it and colds is plenty ah could ah sell a little here or dere."

Mr. Brooks got so interested that he stopped eating.

"Weh you call it, sah, Maroon Medicine? Me no hear 'bout it before. A wah it good for?"

Mr. Watson took a bite out of his roast yam.

"Well, down our side, dey use it for all sort o' sickness, but specially for boile, and stomach ache and cold wid fever. A see plenty o' people cure wid it."

"Me would a really like fe try it"; said Mr. Brooks. "Me daughter, Susan yah, often trouble wid stomach ache. How you sell it sah?"

"Well, as it mek out a somptin' dear enough, me sell it at shilling a bottle, but as you is a fren' a would a gie it to you for sixpence."

"But it's really good, Miser Watson?" asked Mr. Brooks.

"Well it is not for me to praise me own ting, aldo in dis case it really not mine, for I didn't mek it, a Maroon mek it for me, but of all de medicine and fever bush I know, none cure you so quick as dis. But of course if you doan want it, well den doan buy it."

Mr. Brooks hastened to assure his friend that he meant nothing by his remark.

"A only want fe know, Miser Watson, and me tink me wi tek a bottle, sah."

Mr. Watson sold a bottle to Mr. Brooks and the latter promptly made Susan take a small dose, which undoubtedly had a certain medicinal effect by night.

Towards five o'clock in the afternoon the two men took their way to the popular rumshop in the neighbourhood, Mr. Watson wisely leaving all medicine behind, trusting to Mr. Brooks to advertise him. The little man was of a loquacious turn of mind and that evening certainly lived up to Mr. Watson's trust. Over a glass of weak rum and water he told in graphic terms how he had given Susan one dose not two hours ago, and already.

"It hab a wonaful affeck!"

Mr. Watson when questioned about it gave polite but modest answers, only asserting that he had got an old Maroon to make it up for him, the latter assuring him that they used it a lot among his people and he, Mr. Watson, had indeed found it good. Towards half past seven Mr. Brooks and his guest returned home where they found Susan emitting groans at intervals and rather sick. Mr. Watson comforted her and her father by assuring them that she would feel much better by morning and that the medicine always made one feel sick at first.

Next morning Susan was much better and radiant at having taken such a "wonaful" medicine. She had no pain and said she had a great appetite. Her father was delighted and Mr. Watson felt cheerful himself, having had up to now certain doubts about the after effects of his medicine. He sold six bottles that day, taking over ginger and home made ropes in part payment, where the buyer did not have sufficient cash. They went out again to the shop in the evening, and Mr. Watson found himself being rapidly advertised. He was asked several times how it was made and what of, but he refused to tell saying that he had promised the Maroon not to. Various guesses were made at its composition which produced a desire in every person to taste it, and by the end of a week Mr. Watson had sold every bottle, and he found himself regretting he had not brought more with him. Most of the people who had taken it felt much better for having done so. Making the most of his job, he loaded his donkey once more and started for home, giving out that he was going for more medicine which he would sell more cheaply this time. He reached home after another half day's travelling and found after selling his ginger etc., he had realized one pound five shillings on his adventure. Not being satisfied he made more medicine, and after Christmas sold to an appreciative market on the Mile Gully Mountains.

In conclusion I should say that soon after Mr. Watson had left the Mile Gully district the second time, some slanderous and evil reports got abroad about him, and the numerous buyers of his "Maroon Medicine" were heard to say that "dey wish dey could a catch dat—man agen, dey would a gie him medicine fe true!"

Paccy Rum

I t was about three o'clock in the afternoon—the hour when the sun seems brightest and hottest in the tropics. Along the heavy grey sand of the beach were ranged a number of black canoes, some high up from the sea,—these had come in from early morning—others which had just been beached still on the wet shore. On the horizon, the sails of a few late fishing boats could just be seen appearing on their way back from their fish pots. They would reach White Bay, as the bend in the shore was called, in about an hour's time. The gunnels of the boats which had last come in, were thickly lined with women and girls, buying fish from the fishermen, and making a loud clamour over the business. The atmosphere about was heavy with the strong raw smell of fish, in all states, live fish, dead fish, fish boiling, fish roasting, and fish being cleaned. The sea was dazzling with a thousand lights, glittering on the moving wave tops, especially in the west and more directly under the sun; out in the Southeast and far away under the low lying and purple hills, it was a rich blue, and nearer, but in the same direction, a tender green. From the bay and following the shore was a long line of cocoanut palms bending over towards the water and looking top-heavy, with their heavy masses of boughs Separated from these and so near the canoes which were selling fish, that the rush of the foam almost reached the roots, were a couple of palms affording at their curved bases seats which were generally occupied. Under the shade of one of these palms a middle sized man with a long bony face and small eyes and large "weh-fe-do" hat, was barganing with a woman for two small mullet. The woman had bought a string of fish—of which the mullet formed a part, for sixpence a few hours ago, and was now trying to get the man to pay "quatty" or penny-half-penny for about the eighth part.

"Oh, but Miser Watson, you can see dem wut quatty! Dem wut more if it come to dat, but sake ah you, you can tek dem fe quatty!"

Mr. Watson slowly stroked his whiskers and wrinkled up his eyes to shut out the glare which was on the sea.

"Well, Miss Jane, you seh dem wut quatty, and I tink dem wut gill, and if dats what you goin ask all de time fe dem, ah wi hav to guh look elsewhere."

The woman looked at the fish and at Mr. Watson's face undecidedly, then bending over her tray:

"Mek ah tie up me fish den, you want too much fe you money, sah!"

Mr. Watson shouldered his "bankra" and turned to go with such final decision in his movement that it made the woman say hurriedly:— "Alright, Miser Watson, see you fish yah!" Mr. Watson turned and putting down his "bankra," took the fish calmly and gave the woman her gill, which she received with a deep sigh, that would have deceived no one:

"Lard but it cheap! Dem tek advantage of a poor ooman!"

Putting up the fish carefully, Mr. Watson shouldered his bankra again and turned away with a, "Well ah gone, Miss Jane," to which the woman accorded a gracious, "Yes sah!" in a tone of voice whose kindliness one did not expect from her former bargaining.

Quitting the canoes and people Mr. Watson walked a little way up the beach, then turned at right angles on his left, up a path which after a minute, brought him out on the main road. For about a mile he walked along inland when, coming round a bend in the road, he entered a small village. Though small, it was, however, of some importance as one could easily see, for it had a Market, a Post Office and a Police Station. Through the gate of the Station Yard he turned in and walked up to a Constable who was sitting in shirt sleeves on the piazza of the house. The station with its yard, like all other Police Stations in the Island, was scrupulously clean and well-kept; and there was the usual air of neatness and respectability about the whole that spoke well for the discipline of "the Force."

"You come back quick!" said the constable to Mr. Watson as the latter approached him.

"Yes sah, me nuh top no time down ah de beach. Ahjus buy me two little fish dem an come back fe me bundle and donkey to start fe de mountin."

"Well see you bundle deh!" said the constable pointing to a corner in the piazza where a shallow open box lay filled to overflowing with coloured cloths, handkerchiefs, etc., and bound round with a thatch rope. Mr. Watson entered the piazza and putting down the bankra, untied the rope and proceeded to pack the upper clothes more neatly. Having arranged them, he put a piece of oil skin over all and strapped the whole again.

"What you going do wid dem stuff?" asked the constable with a smile, as Mr. Watson finished his repacking. Mr. Watson turned and looked thoughtfully at the constable:

"Well, sah, ah doan know what ah goin do wid dem rightly. Ah may keep dem, ah may sell dem, well den of course you wun know bout dat," here the constable laughed and said, "you speak true, I wun know bout dat."

"Because," proceeded Mr. Watson gravely, "ah no got no license, but to tell you de troot, corporal, ah doan know rightly what ah goin do wid dem."

"Well ah doan tink I wi know me-self, bar you tell me!" answered the Constable who was not a Corporal by the way, but just an ordinary policeman.

"Oh I wi tell you alright, when ah come down agen!" answered Mr. Watson as he lifted his box out to where a donkey was tied under a lignumvitæ tree. He strapped, or rather roped the box on the donkey's back, which also bore the burden of two hampers, then came back for his bankra.

"Ah no hear that some man or other did da sell rum widout a license up your way?" said the constable, as Mr. Watson gathered up his guiding rope and prepared to start:

Mr. Watson rubbed the side of his face slowly, and answered as if in deep thought. "Now you remin' me corporal; ah did hear bout it, not up my way to be sure, but down ah Mary Town. But I neber hab anyting to do wid such wickedness, so ah carn tell you fe true as I neber come into contack wid dem. Well, ah goin, corporal!" he added as the Constable did not say anything more.

"Yes sah," answered the Policeman with a grunt.

Giving the donkey a fillip with the rope, Mr. Watson started and was soon out of sight of the village and on the road leading up to the hills where his home lay. Shortly after he had left the station yard, the Constable with whom he had been talking, wont into an inner room of the station house and remarked to the real Corporal who was sitting at a desk writing.

"Him no got any rum this time, Corporal! I did really tink me'd ah catch him." The Corporal turned round, "I did tink so meself. Did you look in his box properly?" The Constable nodded "well, Corporal, ah raise up all de clort dem and ah see no sign of it. But you tink a man would ah leave his box wid rum slap ina de station piazza? Him no fool!"

"Fac! It is a fac!" answered the Corporal musingly. "Him mus' ah hear dat we are on the look out and tek warning; nex' time ah goin search him properly doh."

"You right, Corporal!" answered the other, "Him wi sure got some dat time. But, Lard him cunning sah."

Meanwhile, Mr. Watson, not entirely unconscious that he was being talked about, was wending his way slowly up the steep beginning of a long hill. By sunset he had got over the more arduous and bigger part of his journey, and by about eight or nine o'clock he entered his own yard. He unloaded the donkey and gave her over to the charge of his daughter, a girl of about fifteen years, who, taking her, gave her drink and tied her out in a grassy patch. Mr. Watson put up everything carefully, taking a special care over six large quart bottles which he had found wrapped up in some clothes at the bottom of the box. The very boldness of his action in leaving his box with six bottles of rum at the station had brought him safely through the hands of the police. Then he went to bed after a hot dinner of bread-kind and salt fish.

During the earlier part of the next day Mr. Watson took it easy, resting doubtless after the weary journey of yesterday. Towards the latter part of the afternoon, however, he went out to the village of Beersheba which was near his place, and stayed there two or three hours. He seemed to have gone there with some purpose, for next day he had plenty of visitors, who first examined his cloth and handkerchiefs, then bought according to their liking. He also managed to exchange his six quart bottles for silver coin at a price double what he paid for them. By evening he had got rid of all his cloth and stuffs and was plainly satisfied with the results of his undertaking. "Dem Constable ah watch me fe true, Lorita" said he to his daughter in the privacy of their kitchen as he sat smoking his dirty-looking clay pipe.

"Dem search you box no sah?" answered Lorita with eager interest stopping for a minute in her work of pealing some sweet potatoes.

"Yes chile! Dem raise up all de elort dem at de side wen ah down at de Bay. Dem neber really look clean true it, because dem neber dream dat ah would ah leave rum slap ina de station, but dem look in a dey." Lorita laughed out loud with the noisy into nation peculiar to her race, and said:

"Lard but you fool dem sah!" Mr. Watson even permitted a feeble sort of grin to pass over his face which showed he was very much pleased with himself, for he never went so far as to laugh and seldom to smile.

"Wen you going down agen sah?" asked Lorita after a pause.

"Tree week from yesterday to come," answered her father. "But ah wi have to tink out some odder way of hiding de rum, or dem we sure catch me nex time."

"You no can tek pass true somebody yard or some oder road, no mek dem see you?" asked Lorita, plumping the potatoes into the big iron black pot.

"No me chile, dem ah look out fe me and dem would ah certain fin' me, aldo ah might ah risk it, and try mek ah fool dem same time. Ah really might ah try it," said Mr. Watson gazing thoughtfully with half-closed eyes out at his donkey which was browsing on some Spanish Needle near the coffee bushes. "But," he added, "ah not trying it agen, bar dis one time. Ah doan seh ah doan mek some money out ah it, but it too risky, it too risky. You can fool dem Constarb today, an' you can fool dem to-marra, but dem wi catch you sometime. You carn fool dem all de time. So ah only going try dis once more." Lorita gazed with some admiration at her father after this truly profound and philosophic speech and grunted in affirmative approval.

"You right, sah, you really right. Me always ah tink dem going ketch you."

Mr. Watson continued to himself. "Yea, sah, me really mus fool dem dis time, or else not, me wi know Panish Town inside, and learn how fe eat carnmeal. Dem planth'n roas' yet, Lorita?"

ABOUT THREE WEEKS LATER MR. WATSON again took his way down to the plains, and about four o'clock in the afternoon having accomplished a little transaction of his own at a Sugar Estate, was wending his way back home. His donkey was heavily laden with hampers containing stuff of a weighty nature, and in the outskirts of the village near White Bay, he stopped to adjust the hampers and body ropes more easily. He then continued at a brisker rate through the village, past the shops and market, till he approached the gate of the Police Station Yard. Here he slowed down and in an indifferent and leisurely manner, walked past the gate. He had not gone two yards past however, when he was stopped by a shout from the same Constable that had taken charge of his baggage before. "Miser Watson!" Mr. Watson stopped and turned.

"Miser Watson! A word with you sah! Bring you donkey in too!"

Mister Watson led the donkey back and turned within the station yard where he was met by the Constable and the Corporal.

"Marning, Miser Watson!"

"Marnin' Corporal! Marning Sargent!"

The Corporal then addressed him. "Sarry fe stop you, Mister Watson but some people ah seh some tings, bout you, dat you ah sell rum widout license, so as it is my jurisdiction and duty, ah wi have to search your hamper, jus' fe prove dem is arlright."

Mr. Watson at this speech, looked at the Corporal, as if he did not understand him, then, stroking his hand on the side of his face, he said slowly:

"Dat I ah sell rum widout a license?" Then after a pause, he led the donkey forward and said gloomily as if overcome by the wickedness of people. "You no can search him."

The two proceeded to search the hampers while Mr. Watson stood silently by with a look of cold impassive dignity on his face. The Constables quickly took off the "cruckcuss bag," or bag of sack-cloth that covered the contents of the hampers. They then saw that each hamper contained two kerosene tins, covered over at the tops with a piece of cloth tied down tightly. They removed one of these pieces of cloth and saw to their disgust nothing but thick "wet sugar" which filled the pan almost to the brim. They tried the other three and found them just the same, full of wet sugar. The Corporal tried to hide his disappointment and disgust under a cloak of outward good humour.

"People will tell lie Miser Watson," said he, "an ah really lose me drink dis time. Pan sugar is really better to trade in dan rum doh, an ah sorry fe hab to trouble you."

Mr. Watson waited in silence till they had tied back the cloth and put in the bags, then he began:—

"Well, Sargent, you hab you duty, and you tink it right, maybe dat you should ah stop an hones' man ina him way, to go hol' him donkey and search him like any common tief slap ina de public. But I doan tink it right." Mr. Watson's voice rose higher, "I' doan tink it right. Seh help me, if ah doan tink you treat me like any common dirty tief dat dem haul go ah Spanish Town. If dat—"

"Go on you way and doan mek a noise in de yard," said the Corporal, angry at his failure to find rum and the hypocritical defence of Mr. Watson. "Go out de yard."

"Ah goin, ah goin!" said Mr. Watson moving out. "You tink ah would ah stay yah in dis place, weh dem mek me out a criminal; an hones man got no place ina dis yard."

With this parting shot Mr. Watson and his donkey took their way out and went again on their journey home. Long after dusk he reached his yard, where he found Lorita anxiously looking out for him.

"As ah no see you come by sunset, an it ah get late," said she, "me seh dem mus' ah really catch you dis time, sah. Me really anxious fe you." She helped him unload the donkey and move the hampers inside the kitchen, then gave the beast a little water and tied her out for the night. Returning to the kitchen she filled her father's plate with bread kind roasted and boiled, yams, cocoas and plantain, the whole flavoured with pork and country pepper.

Mr. Watson made a hearty dinner and during the meal gave an account of his meeting with the Constables, and how he fooled them, to his daughter, who listened with much interest.

"An den, as ah come to de station yard gate, ah tek time walk slower fe mek dem tink ah warn go pass widout dem see me, as if ah no care. De Corporal and de Sargen' tan up inside an watch me dem really not any Corporal and Sargent but so. I call dem—an' as ah could ah get bout one yard pas' de gate, de Coporal cry out loud:

"Miser Watson, Miser Watson, ah warn see you. Bring in you donkey come too ina de yard."

"Well, when ah hear dat ah turn roun' as if suprise, and lead de donkey ina de yard."

"You no feel frighten, sah?" asked Lorita as her father paused to put a big piece of "nager" yam in his mouth. Mr. Watson masticated for a few seconds before answering:

"Well, ah doan seh ah doan feel kine o' funny when ah hear me name call sharp, but of course ah doan mek dem see it, but jus' lead me donkey in quiet, an tell dem marnin'. Well den, dem tek off de baig quick fe true; an as dem see de kerosene tin, dem eye jump, and dem whip off de clort quick as anyting."

Mr. Watson paused again to take in some more food and give power to the climax of his tale.

"An what dem seh when dem see de sugar?" asked Lorita eagerly.

"Dem neber seh scarcely a ting," answered her father, "dem so disappoint. Dem could ah only smile an' look like dem torm fool bud. Dey neber would ah guess in dis word dat rum could ah ina wet sugar ina paccy. But you tink de paccy doan fit de kerosene sweet!"

"Weh you get dem sah?" asked Lorita, "down ah White Bay?"

"No me chile," answered Mr. Watson, "ah get dem higher up de beach, at a place dem call it, Lef River Hole, where dem grow like Premento grow yah almos'. Ah fill dem firs' wid de rum and stop up de hole tight, den put dem in de kerosene tin an' fill up de tin wid de pan sugar. Dem could ah neber fine it out."

Mr. Watson by this time had come to the end of his dinner, and he handed over the plate to Lorita, who washed it and put it up in its place on a shelf with a couple of pans and cracked mugs. Her father who was tired and sleepy then went to bed, Lorita following his example, and they were both soon sleeping, if not the sleep of the just, yet the sleep of undisturbed consciences.

The Red Cock

Chapter I

Wherever two or more roads meet in Jamaica, there is, as is doubtless true for other parts of the world, generally to be found one or more shops. Sometimes the situation is important enough to demand first one shop, then a village, then a town, then perhaps a large city according to the development of the country. Jamaica has not yet got many towns however, and the one shop usually become two or three with a couple of other houses around, and is then called a village. In this state it generally remains, and probably will remain for many more years. Beerthsheba belonged to this class, but it had to show as a sign of some advancement, a Post Office; and the Tax Collector came at his times to receive taxes there. It lay in the southern part of the Parish of Manchester and had roads leading from it to Mandeville and Vere and St. Elizabeth; from which it will be seen that it had a good position.

About four or five years ago it was celebrating with much noise and fervour the 1st of August. Very few, if any of those who celebrated remembered why it was a public holiday, or brought that forward in their enthusiasm; still they were recognizing it with games and sports. About a hundred yards from the shop, in a field which formed a sort of surburban part of the village, the annual Cricket Match between Beerthsheba and Smithfield was going on, and was being played with much spirit. The pitch consisted of a long naked piece of land; all its grass having been rubbed off by continual running upon, and it was very red and very dirty. As the players went too and fro they gradually par took of its redness in their clothes and socks (for most played in their socks alone). It took a lot however to tint the original colours of some of the socks, these being very brilliant in hue—purple, and yellow, and red. These facts did not detract from the enjoyment of the game, and the pitch was certainly more level with the grass off. The spectators, other than the men of the team now batting, were chiefly women and girls selling bread and cakes and ginger beer. The absence of the men was due in a measure to the fact, that there was a game cock fight just about to begin outside the saddler's shop, and there thirty or forty men were collected round two who had a cock each in their hands. Game cock fighting happened now to be very much in vogue, and like all other transitory amusements had a good deal of enthusiasm behind it. The present fight was between Mr. Joe Robinson's "High Licker" and Mr. James Bolton's "Harkaway," and the stakes were £2 a side. These stakes were formed from twenty shares of two shillings each, ten of which had been taken by an owner of one cock, the rest being divided among ten other shareholders. Thus either cock had eleven enthusiastic backers, not counting the interested spectators who indulged in independent bets and shouting. The referees were two shopkeepers, and men of standing, as one could easily perceive from their dress and high dignity of bearing. Among those nearest the cocks, which was long and grave, a shareholder in the company which favoured Mr. Robinson. He took great interest in the proceedings, but did not grow loudly excited as the others did. His name was Mr. William Watson of Every Garden, this being the name of his place. Suddenly the chief shopkeeper raised his hand,—

"Let them fly," said he and the owners raising their birds flung them at one another. Mr. Robinson's bird was smaller than the other, but looked more game to experienced eyes. Either fowl had had its spurs cut off and a sharp long piece of steel substituted, clumsily, in their place to produce a more deadly battle. The cocks now began to spar in earnest and various opinions were passed and good humoured remarks:—

"Hi! Miser Robinson! You fowl good, you know. Him little but h'n trong."

"Come on now, I wi' bet you five poun' dat de red cock beat; yes me son, five poun'!"

"Five poun', Lard me Massa, ah since when Charlie get five poun. H'n mus' ah tief it from old Fader Dennis!"

"Choh no man!" said another, "He mus' a going married to dat yaller giurl from Queentown. I no hear she got money."

"Shut you mout, you impudent chap you!"

"Hi! Miser Watson, ah bet you a sixpence 'gainst you raw-bone jackass dat de yaller cock beat!"

There was some laughter at this, but Mr. Watson disdained to answer. He only scratched his side whisker.

"Hi, de yellow cock ah gie de oder all him looking for! Mises Robinson, I gie you quatty fer you cock!"

"Quatty and gill!" yelled another. Here a shout went up:—"Fus blood, for Miser Bolton Harkaway!"

"Hah, what ah tell you, I know deyaller cock would ah win!"

"Cho, man, him doan win yet You wi soon see him favour John-crow when h'n going dead."

The odds now were in Bolton's favor and the red cock seemed indeed goin to lose, when suddenly he began to attack with fury and jumping up high, came down with a cruel slash across the head of Harkaway, blinding him in one eye. A great shout went up:—

"De red cock beat! De red cock beat!"

"Him doan beat!"

"Him do beat; you no see him wun get up!"

"H'm no beat, ah tell you!"

"Ah wha ah tell you! Han up me sixpence!"

"Han up which sixpence? Ah owe you any sixpence!"

"Doan mek ah get angry yah, today! Did you not gie de sixpence you bet wit me to George Bent to hol', and den tek it weh when you see ah going win?"

"Oh man de bet off!"

"De bet off what! You is a d—m wutless scoundrel!"

"Ah who you ah call all de wutless scoundrel? Jus' call me so agen!"

"You *is* a scoundrel!"

The one struck the other and a scuffle ensued. They came apart and took on an awful appearance of most deadly hatred. One feared for their lives.

"Now you jus' strike me agen!"

"Strike you wha! You strike me fus?"

"Jus' strike me! You jus' hit me!"

"Well you jus' hit me fus', and I wi' show you what you want!"

It ended in each requesting the other to hit him, but as the other refused to do such a rude and unchristian act, the quarrel evaporated gradually. During this the yellow cock had fallen, and refused to get up though urged by his owner to do so. The referees then adjudged the victory to Mr. Robinson's High Licker. As soon as the red cock had beaten the other to the ground, it might have been observed that his eleven backers had showed in round the stakes holder, and when victory was declared, hastily took their money from him and also their rival company's. Plenty of vigorous language was being shouted on all sides, as the losers tried to get out their bets and the winners urged their rights. By one of those powerful unwritten laws which hold all the world over, Mr. Robinson had to stand drinks for the defeated company and everybody adjourned to the most popular of the rum shops, which by the way, belonged to one of the referees. Here for two or three hours, plenty of shouting, argument in very curious English, and some quarelling which ended in words for the most part, went on. The negro does not as a rule need much rum to make him tipsy, for a very little affects him. He seldom however gets really very drunk, or intoxicated to that extent that he cannot go home without help. This is true for the country parts, where the lack of ready money, perhaps has something to do with the soberness of the people. Nearly every shop outside the towns in Jamaica sells rum and other intoxicants, but this does not mean that there is an excess of drinking among individual parties, but rather that nearly everybody takes a drink now and then. After an half hour's convivality, Mr. Robinson who was rather cautious as regards all his money affairs, took his cock and started for home accompanied by his wife and Mr. Watson whose home also lay in the same direction.

"You going home soon," said Mr. Watson, to Mr. Robinson, "You not going join in de spoart at de shop?"

"No sah, no port for me, ah win me money fair, ah wah ah going spen, it for? ah hab one drink, dat's all ah want more?"

"Tell me"; he added half angrily and half drunkenly to Mr. Watson.

"Tell me sah, you tink a man should ha' spen' and wase h'm money pon de ting dem call rum and get drunk like a beas. Dem is a fool."

"You speak true sah," said Mr., Watson soothingly, "Dem is a fool." "But sah, when ah see you fowl beat, ah really glad. Him is de bes' bird bout."

"Him good, him really good," agreed Mr. Robinson, whose ager passed away at once, excessive amiability taking its place.

"Did you see how h'm rise up and slash de oder cross de head? Me heart leap till ah tink it going pop, when ah seem gie dat blow.

Mr. Watson eyed the bird with grave admiration. "Wunderful, sah, wunderful."

"An' how much," with a diferential air that flattered Mr. Robinson, "would you be askin' for a cock like dat sah?"

Mr. Robinson looked at him as if he did not understand.

"An' how much would ah ask fe him?" he repeated.

"But him not fe sale. You tink ah would ah sell dis fowl; ah woulden sell him, not even if ah ah dead fe hungry, an me belly swell out like dem little maugre pig. Ah bring up dis cock from de berry eggshell, and ah watch him and see him grow to dis size and den ah going sell him?"

"No sah, you don understan me," said Mr. Watson, hastening to pacify the other; "ah don mean to ask you how much you would ah sell him for, but what, jis out of curiousness, you tink him wut? Ah no hear dis man Thomas Simit seh him would ah gie ten shillin' fe him?"

"Ah know, ah know," said Mr. Robinson, "h'm offer me dat already, h'n na sell."

"Me hab a little money from me tobacco and premento," said Mr. Watson musingly, "if ah could get a real good bud like dat, ah would ah buy him. Doh ah mus' seh dem is a risky ting to keep. Dem may boat, and den agen dey may lose an' you no know when dem going sick."

"My fowl na going sick!" said Mr. Robinson as if in protest to some remark against his cock.

From these casual remarks, Mr. Watson gradually led up to the direct question of asking Mr. Robinson to sell him his fowl, and he was in full persuasion when they came to the meeting of the two paths which led from the public road to their respective homes. Finding Mr. Robinson obdurate and quite opposed to any business, Mr. Watson scratched his right whisker philosophically and said goodbye.

"Well as you wun do any business Miser Robinson and ah doan seh you wrong, I mus go me way. Evenin'! Sah, evenin'! Miss Ann!" this to Mrs. Robinson who had been walking as a wife should about ten yards behind her husband.

"I wish you a good evenin' sah!"

It was dusk when after a couple of minutes walk from where he had separated from the other two, Mr. Watson entered his own yard. His daughter a ragged girl of about twelve had preceded him, and had stirred up the fire in the rotten shaky looking kitchen to greater vigour by the addition of some wood. The walls of the kitchen were of plaster white washed outside, but lacking this dressing inside. The inside however, to make up for the coating of white-wash had taken to itself several coatings of soot and was very black and dirty especially near the fire corners. From the rafters of the thatched roof, hung bundles of tobacco leaves which were being cured in an atmosphere of peculiar smell, born of smoke and other odours. It is easy to recognise this smell, when on a pleasant summer evening, a man will pass on the road smoking his "donkey rope." The seat of honour, a polished block of wood, stood near the fire, and around were various odds and ends, old pans, cocoa heads, a donkey's pack saddle, etc. This roomwas Mr. Watson's study, dining hall, pantry and kitchen. When Mr. Watson entered and took his accustomed seat, the girl was stirring a pot of red peas soup, and a little boy of grave long face, inherited doubtless from his father, was sitting in one corner eagerly awaiting his dinner.

"You feed de pig yet Josiah?" asked Mr. Watson of this little boy.

"Yes sah, me feed him dun dis long time."

"Ah want you go wid me to de groun' tomorrow to help me carry some potatoh slip," said Mr. Watson; "ah doan wan mek de season pass."

"Me have fe go up to Cedar Valley to morrer go bruk premento sah!" said Josiah in his shrill young voice.

"Hi fe true," said Mr. Watson. "I nuh fuhget. You tell Miser Torn dat you wun tek fipence a day?"

"Yes sah, but him seh sah, dat if ah doan wan de fipence, ah fe stay way sah."

Mr. Watson gave a grunt and was silent. The soup was now ready and the girl poured it into three receptacles, a blue soup plate with a yellow border, which as being the only soup plate belonged to Mr. Watson naturally, a cracked mug which the girl kept for herself, and a tin pannikin which the boy eagerly accepted. They had pewter spoons however of the same pattern, design and size. After finishing his soup and some roasted potatoes the boy departed to his bed, which was a sort of bench in the hall of the house proper. On his leaving the kitchen, his father began a conversation with his daughter:—

"Lorita, ah offer Miser Robinson eleven shilling for his cock dis evenin' an he wun tek it."

Lorita who was a thin featured and sharp looking girl looked at her father then laughed. "Him mus a fool."

Mr. Watson fingered the few hairs that formed his right whisker: "You speak true, Lorita h'n is a fool. When a man see eleven shillin' in h'n han' h'n should a sell. You no know when time mongoose goin' tek you fowl or h'n may dead or h'n even walk way."

Mr. Watson then lowered his voice and proceeded to whisper cautiously, "Stop you laughing Lorita and listen to me. Ah been tell all o' dem dis evenin' dat ah goin to me Uncle a Santa Cruz tomorrow, so dey won know. Ah going start ina morning soon an' you mus come down Thursday night (It was now Monday) to de Bay cross roads whey I wi meet you. You certain you know whey fe do? Eh?" Lorita nodded.

"Ah know fe certain sah, ah could ah walk bout dat yard ina blackes' night."

"Well ah speak to you enuf to mek you unerstan an' you ought to do it right. But ah wi tell you over agen."

Mr. Watson kept on whispering loudly and earnestly to Lorita for about half an hour, then both went to bed in their palatial family house.

Chapter II

ON THURSDAY MORNING ABOUT SEVEN o'clock, Mr. Robinson having rubbed the sleepiness out of his eyes by a vigorous application of water to his face,—this was generally as far as the bath went with him—strolled leisurely round to the back of his house to look at his fowl. To his astonishment he found the door of the coop open and its occupant absent; thinking however that his wife had loosed the cock to have a run, he went back to quarrel with her, for he had, given her no permission to do any such thing. He learnt from her, however, that she was innocent of the charge, neither was anyone of his children guilty. His feeling then became one of terror and anxiety, and he and his household looked long and eagerly for the cock. The news spread quickly among the neighbouring yards, that Mr. Robinson's Red Cock was gone, and by about ten o'clock it became apparent that the fowl had been stolen.

Mr. Robinson now was frantic and his language would have been interesting to the thief if he had been around.

"Ah wish to Gawd Awmighty dat ah could ah hol de man dat tief me fowl. Me Gawd, ah would ah kill him! Ah would ah tear h'n inside out. But whah sort o' man dem hab bout yah dat h'n should ah come slap ina me yard ah night and tek out me fowl. De dam blarsted tief!"

Having given up all hope that his fowl had strayed, Mr. Robinson put on his coat and set out for the nearest Police Station, which was about four miles away. He took sometime to walk the distance, as he stopped several time to relate the news to sympathizing friends, and give candidly his opinion of the thief's character.

On arriving at the station, he told his story to the Corporal in charge, and gave a minute description of the fowl, leaving out, however, the fact that it was a game cock. The reason for the latter reticence being that game cock fighting was not allowed by the law. The Corporal told him that he would have the description of the cock sent around through the *Police Gazette*, but said that as Mr. Robinson did not suspect anyone in particular, there was nothing much more to be done.

"You certain that you got no suspicion 'gainst any man at all?" he asked.

"No sah, me no got any suspicion," answered Mr. Robinson gloomily. "Dem is all a tief."

"But if ah hav' fe spen ebery penny ah got, ah wi punish him," he added vindictively. He then tried at the neighbouring shop to find consolation in a couple of glasses of weak rum and water, but the rum only helped to inflame his passions and he returned home very angry and sullen. His way, when coming to his yard, took him very near Mr. Watson's home, and in passing he might have noticed Lorita fast asleep under a banana tree in some coffee bush. He might have noticed too that she looked very tired, but these little things went unseen to his clouded intellect and he certainly would not, even if he *had* noticed her weariness, dreamt of associating it with the absence of his fowl.

About this very time or a little earlier, Mr. Watson and his "raw-bone jackass," Alice, entered the yard of his uncle "Old Father Matney," after a walk from the bottom of the Manchester Hills. Father Matney's yard was some miles southeast of the village of Santa Cruz, and Mr. Watson and his donkey were rather tired, for the road leading up from the Savannas into the Santa Cruz Mountains is a monotonous and wearying climb, over stiff and numerous little hills. When Mr. Watson entered the yard of his uncle (he was supposed by some to be his father), he found the old gentleman asleep under a mango tree with a bible open in his hands. Father Matney had been rather a wild fellow in his younger days, so to make up for lost time, had taken enthusiastically to religion in his old age. At present his inclinations tended toward Seventh Day Adventism, but he had not become a regular convert and his mind was still open to any taking ideas that might come along. He welcomed his nephew cordially and gave him breakfast which his daughter, a good looking woman of a sort of yellow colour, dished up for them. The name of this woman was Eliza Matney, and she had that peculiar yellow colour of skin which is seen chiefly in the people of the Savannas and hot plains of the Southern and Southwestern parts of the Island.

"You bring anything fe me Willyam?" said Mr. Matney after the donkey had been unloaded and tied out and they were eating their breakfast. Mr. Watson finished swallowing some boiled potato before answering.

"Well sah ah doan bring nutten much, but knowing dat provision is scace down dis way, ah bring you a couple o' yampi an' cocoh."

"Tenk you me son, tenk you," said the old man, "The blessing of de Lord fall pon you, for you tink bout de ole man an you len to de Lord."

Mr. Watson chewed his yam modestly:—

"Well sah, me doan go to Church ofen, an de collection man dem, doan ofen see me money, an ah swear and all de res' o'it, but ah do tink pon me relations sometime."

"Well Willyam," replied the old man who liked yampie, "so far you bad enuf, but when you gie to me, de poor ole man, you lenin' to de Lord, you lenin to de Lord, an de Lord will repay you, for h'n seh so and h'n hab to."

"Ah notice you hab a cock wid you," changing the subject abruptly. "What you goin do wid it?"

"Ah buy it cheap from a man up ah Plowden," answered Willyam, "ah did hav' de money an it so cheap dat ah buy it for a shillin!"

"Shillin?" said Mr. Matney, "It cheap, an a game cock to?"

"You right sah," said Mr. Watson "ah game cock, an because ah game cock ah buy it. I bring him fe try a fight wid de cock bout yah."

"Cock fightn Willyam?" said Mr. Matney, "you going in fe dat, you wi lose money, an' besides its sinful. Aldo you is a young man an you mus hab you way. When you is my age, well den you wi tink more about gettin you soul ready for de great day. But me no hear dat dem doan allow it by law. Dat dem can punish you."

"Dem doan allow it fe true!" agreed Mr. Watson, "But if dem doan know, how can dey punish you?"

"Well de station is far enuf away," said Mr. Matney, "an ah doan suppose dey wi catch you. But dese tings is sinful, Willyam! Bery sinful."

Mr. Watson did not think it worth while to take up the question of its sinfulness, and went on eating without making a reply. However, Mr. Matney finding his nephew unwilling to discuss cock fighting from a religious point of view, limited himself to the financial and social sides of the sport. For an old man who was supposed to be wrapped up in the pursuit of religion, he showed a surprisingly keen knowledge of his neighbours affairs, what sort of cocks they had, and the latest fights that had come off.

"It really curious, Willyam," remarked Mr. Matney, "dat as you comin' to see me you should a buy a game cock, an you no know dat dem ah fight cock up yab. It really curious."

"You speak true sah"; said Mr. Watson gravely, "it really curious."

"All tings is in the han of de Lord," said Mr. Matney without intending any irreverence.

Mr. Watson learnt from Matney and Eliza that a certain Philip Brown living two miles away, had a cock that had beaten nearly every other cock in the district. It would be easy to get up a fight between the two cocks, for Brown was keen on the sport and had won plenty of money on his. Mr. Matney seemed doubtful about the advisability of fighting such a good cock without trying theirs first, but Mr. Watson assured him that his cock was quite capable of beating any cock around, and he was going to Mr. Brown's in the morning to arrange the combat.

Next morning Mr. Watson found Mr. Brown quite willing to have the fight, and it was arranged that a duel, with a bet of ten shillings a side, should come off at Ole Matney's yard between the two cocks that day.

At noon then of the next day, Mr. Brown with his fowl and small party of backers went to Mr. Matney's yard where they found awaiting them, Mr. Watson with his fowl and his backers. After a few preliminaries such as placing the stakes in the hands of some worthy man and appointing two judges, a ring was formed round Mr. Watson and Mr. Brown and the fight began. During the fight a man who had but lately come from Manchester was struck with the resemblance between Mr. Watson's cock and a fowl, which he said belong to one Mr. Robinson who lived near Beersheba. "Ah neber see two fowl favour so"; said he, "Aldo ah do see a difference. But dem do favour fe true."

"You right, Marse John," said Mr. Watson heartily, "Ah know Miser Robinson fowl eben more dan ah know dis, an ah neber see such a likeness. Same so de oder one red!"

"De berry same!" said Marse John, "only fe you cock little smaller!"

"Ah tink so meself," agreed Mr. Watson. "Him little smaller."

The fight took place with less noise than at Beersheba, but it was longer and more game. After about ten minutes, severe sparring however, Mr. Watson's red cock first wounded and then completely de feated the other and his owner was richer by ten shillings.

After the shouting had stopped and some hostile arguments had passed off, Mr. Watson and Mr. Matney brought out some glasses, some rum and some water; and everybody had a drink in the red cock's honour. Mr. Matney, who had a strong belief in the idea that all things little or great that profited him, were the work of Providence, and that anything that was unfortunate was the work of Satan, was especially joyful and even took a drop of rum in excess of good fellowship. Mr. Brown and his party finally took their departure about an hour later, taking with them however, an open challenge to anybody in the district, who having a cock might like to fight.

As the result of this challenge, no less than four fights came off during then ext two or three weeks, of which Mr. Watson's cock won three, and his Master we will not say owner—gained £2 in all. It is to be feared that Mr. Matney's soul did not benefit by Mr. Watson's stay, and he had, for several lapses in sinfulness, to make up by many outward signs of remorse and much bible reading.

At the end of the third week however, Mr. Watson sent Eliza Matney's little boy to Lorita at Every Garden with some tobacco and a message, and two days after the boy had come back, he departed himself from his uncle's yard. He went away at an exceedingly early hour of the morning, near midnight in fact, and by some strange coincidence met Lorita at the foot of the Manchester hills on his way to Alligator Pond at about two o'clock in the morning. Lorita did not stop to talk, however, but started off back home at a very quick walk, while her father went on in a leisurely manner to the bay. Two days later he returned home and found all the neighbourhood excited over the curious way in which Mr. Robinson's red cock had come back to his coop after a disappearance of three weeks about. Mr. Robinson himself did not know what to make of it, and meeting Mr. Watson on the day of the latter's return, expressed his opinions:—"Well Miser Watson, such a ting sah! Fus' ah lose him an ah sure somebody tief him, and den when ah ah look after to fin' de tief, de fowl come back. De only ting sah, is dat eider some man tief it an' put it back because h'm frighten o' me, or dat it some o' dem blarsted obeahman tricks."

Mr. Watson stroked his whisker thoughtfully:—"Well den ah doan tink it's obeahman Miser Robinson, from what I understan; but rader dat it's some tief, who mus' ah tek it weh and as you seh, h'm so frighten dat it put h'n back. But dayse wickedness sah!"

The Courting of the Dudes

Chapter I

"Heh, heh, heh eh. . .! Doan bodder me son! But coo Thomas nuh! But Lar! Dayse trouzez and de gaiters—jus ah boasy! You ah go courting, nuh Thomas?"

Thomas for answer made a quick grab at the small barefooted boy who thus impertinently addressed him; failing to hold him however as the latter had been expecting the grab and easily escaped. Thomas in the glory of Sunday clothes did not think it worth while to go after him so merely remarked in tones that were not very vindictive:—

"Alright Hezekiah, you jus' wait yah till ah come back from chutch! Ah gie you arl you looking for. You too bloomin' farce."

Hezekiah at this merely laughed a shrill young laugh and followed his brother out of the yard,—at a respectable distance however. Thomas's get up was certainly one to evoke attention if not admiration in all other people. His shoes beginning from the bottom were of the fashionable colour brown, and of a peculiar and stylish cut, being a sort of cross between a shoe and boot. They were not high, nor yet low, buttoned by two rows of four buttons each, yet also laced with broad brown laces. Just above the shoes, sufficiently high to give a glimpse of a purple sock, came the end of a remarkably fine pair of light coloured gaiters, tailor made of corduroy and fastened with large buttons. The light colour of the gaiters was in fine contrast to a pair of dark brown trousers, which appeared also to advantage against the brilliant hues of a sash which looked like silk, but which, it was to be feared, was only coloured cotton or cretonne. Above this encincture shone out in dazzling splendour a full expanse of white shirt, with silver studs all complete. The coat which bounded this snowy bosom, was of a bright blue shade with a large handkerchief hanging half-way out of the breast pocket, hiding the end of a silver chain which passed from the first button hole and had several large and ornate charms hanging to it. His hat, a new stylish felt, bought only a week ago, rested lightly on the "brush top" of his head, which was held a little stiffly by a high collar girt, at its base by a red and green necktie. The tie was kept well in place by a necktie clip of ornate and chaste design, bought of a Syrian peddlar. As jewelry, other than the charms of his watch chain, Thomas had two silver rings on a little finger, one of which had its value enhanced by a large red stone cut like a seal. He carried an orange stick or rather cane nicely varnished in his hand, and had as a finishing touch to a masterly and most effective get-up, a gorgeous ginger lily in his button hole. Thomas was undoubtedly *the* Dude of the district.

They,—for Hezekiah was also going to church and was also dressed in Sunday clothes, which unlike those of his brother consisted simply of a blue suit and cap,—proceeded along in silence following a path which led over a stone wall into the pasture of a property or pen, through this pasture then over another stonewall and into the public road. Thomas did not walk too quickly for the day was warm, and the heat might take a bit of the polish off his appearance. To prevent any risk however to his collar, he stuffed his handkerchief round his neck between the skin and collar during his journey through the pasture; coming out on the highway he removed the handkerchief back again into its former elegant position.

As he and Hezekiah came into the road the first person they met was Mr. George Green, a teacher, riding on a young and rather small horse. Teachers in Jamaica generally ride, and it is strange how one can easily single one of that class from a crowd without any foreknowledge that he be a teacher. There is a mixed air of respectability, some bumptiousness, some self-assurance, some timidity, some importance, that always gives them away. Mr. Green in his way, was also a bit of a dude, not so flashy or bright as Thomas, but as befitted a older man and a teacher, more given to dress that showed solidity and dignity in its foundations. On this occasion he sported a pair of leather leggings, black and shiny, a rather dark suit with its coat cut long, and a collar, the lowness of which was due to the thickness and shortness of the neck it encircled.

Mr. Green greeted them with an affable and slightly condescending smile:—"Goodmorning Thomas! Morning Hezekiah!"

Thomas answered with a rather absent-minded "mornin' sah!" for the sight of Mr. Green riding so stylishly and with such dignity to church had set him thinking about his chances in love against such a rival, for be it known, Thomas and the teacher were rivals for the hand of fair (meaning comely) Miss Annabel Gibson who could not make up her mind which to choose. Thomas had the advantage of seeing her, far more often than Mr. Green whose duties kept him busy, and although up to now she had seemed gracious to him, still she had not refused altogether the advances of the other, and the position and comfortable salary of the teacher often obtruded themselves on his mind and made him gloomy. For some little way along the road his mind was thus melancholy, but the cheerful salutations of aquaintances that he met bound for church, added to the brightness of the morning, gradually dispelled his gloom, and by the time the church had come in sight round a corner of the road, he was feeling quite good-humoured. Besides was he not going to have the privilege of walking home with Miss Annabel after church!

Mr. Green had gone on ahead, presenting by the help of a martingale as well as a curb and snaffle bit on the mouth of the horse, a stylish and spirited appearance.

When Thomas had walked through the gates of the church yard, past the church and up to the schoolhouse he found Mr. Green talking to Miss Annabel, and her mother Mrs. Gibson under a mango tree.

He was neither surprised nor dismayed however, for he felt that off his horse the teacher was not such a terrible foe, so he took off his hat gracefully and shook hands rather bashfully with Mrs. Gibson and Miss Annabel. Mrs. Gibson who was dressed in a much starched print gown that stuck out around in stiff folds, accorded him a kindly, "How you do dis morning Thomas?" and Miss Annabel who looked charming in a white dress trimmed with bright blue ribbons and girt at the waist with a belt, also of a blue ribbon, gave him a gracious "mornin' Thomas." Thomas felt that he had not got himself up for nothing.

As they had a few minutes to wait before the service would begin, they remained under the mango tree for the time chatting; or rather the teacher and Mrs. Gibson chatted, the younger two being self-conscious were silent enough.

"How is Mr. Gibson?" asked Mr. Green of Miss Gibson. "I doun see him in attendant anywhere."

"No sah," answered Mrs. Gibson, "H'n not yah today; H'n not feeling too well dis morning; H'n nuh really what you would ah call sick, but jus' enuf to no mek him warn go a church."

"Perhaps doh," said the teacher looking about him, "The mornin' is so bright and warm, it might have do him good—Been effecatious."

"You speak true sah. It might ha ha really do him good," said Mrs. Gibson, "but h'n jus 'tan so but h'n doan feel incline."

"Well however, de family well represent," said Mr. Green gallantly, an Miss Ann look so agreeable dis mornin'.

At this Mrs. Gibson said, "Hi Misar Green!" while Miss Ann turned her head away with a bashful giggle. Thomas did not appreciate the teacher's compliments but he made the best of it and grinned too.

The bell-ringing had now come to a stop so they all went into the church to take their seats, being joined at the door by Annabel's sister, Susan, who had been talking to somether people.

The Gibsons occupied a pew on the gallery upstairs, and Thomas took a seat in a pew not far off, but the teacher being a man of some consequence in the church had a seat downstairs in the body of the church.

The service went on as most services do in the country parts, with plenty of late arrivals coming in every now and then. The young men and young women in Jamaica of the lower class do not consider that boots are worth anything in style or appearance unless they (the boots) creak exceedingly loudly, so the reason of any young man coming in late is probably to show off his clothes and boots.

After service, Thomas and the two Miss Gibsons stayed in for Sunday School which of course Mr. Green attended, being indeed one of the class instructors. When the Sunday School had finished, Thomas and the two girls started for the Gibsons' residence, Mr. Green having first bidden farewell, squeezing Miss Annabel's hand tenderly on the act.

The three walked along the road back, the way Thomas came, for the girls' house lay in somewhat the same direction as Thomas', save that they would not go through the pasture.

The order and manner in which Thomas and the girls walked home was rather peculiar and not to appearances and foreign eyes, the most sociable. Instead of the three walking side by side, they walked separately; Thomas keeping to one side of the road and the two girls to the other. The girls did most of the talking and giggling, though Thomas every now and then would break in with a facetious remark from across the road. They reached Mr. Gibson's place after what seemed a short walk to Thomas, and had a cheerful lunch of bread and sugar and water. Then Thomas went home feeling somewhat satisfied, but not entirely so.

Chapter II

ON THE WEDNESDAY AFTER THE Sunday Miss Annabel received two letters from the Post Office at Beersheba. She did not open them at once, because it so happened that though she was a well brought up girl, she was unable to read, and she wanted the addresses read out in all their importance first. Her sister Susan who also could not read was as much excited over them as herself, and the two giggled and guessed to their hearts-content. It is not impossible that both knew intuitively whom the epistles came from.

However, during the middle of the day they went over to the neighbouring yard of a certain Mr. Richard Timsin a kind hearted man, who having had a much better education in his youth than those of his rank, was looked upon as the scholar of the district, and usually called upon to transact any literary business, such as letter-reading and letter writing of his neighbours. This Mr. Timson was rather a character in his way. As a boy and young man he went to the Mico in Kingston, and after that took up teaching on his own account. Not finding this to pay, however, he went to Colon and was also in the stoker line on board a ship for a short time. After a time when only about thirty years of age he got tired of moving about and returned to his home in the country and took up life again as a labourer and settler. He had a higher sense of honour than possessed by his fellows, and was kind-hearted and cute, though a bit of a rogue.

Mr. Timson had just finished his breakfast when the girls entered the yard, and was sitting with his back against his kitchen wall picking his teeth.

"Mornin' Miser Timsin,!" said the girls approaching. "Mornin' Miss Ann! Mornin' Miss Sue!" answered Mr. Timsin pleasantly. You come to see me?

"Yes sah!" answered Ann shyly. "Me come fe ask if you could ah read two letter fe me; dat ah get dis mornin'."

"Ah love letter?" asked Mr. Timsin looking up at them with a smile.

"Me no know sah!" answered Ann with a giggle. "How me fe know what kind o' letter dey is, if ah doun read dem."

"Where de letter?" asked Mr. Timson.

Ann produced them and gave them to him. Mr. Timson looked at them with interest. The addresses were in widely different styles of hard writing. One was written in a quick ornate manner, with large flowing capitals and plenty of flourishes; the other in a small manner with very little flourish. Mr. Timson read out both addresses carefully and slowly, though they were just the same:—

Miss Annabel Gibson,
Happy Home,
Beersheba P.O.

Finishing the reading he rose; "Come chile, mek we go in the Hall. Love letter not fe read out a doors!" So saying he entered the Hall which with the bedroom made the House, followed by the girls He took a seat in a stiff home-made mahogany chair and gave the girls a bench. Having put on his spectacles as necessary part of the insignia of a scholar, Mr. Timson opened the letter with the large ornate writing and began to read out slowly and carefully:—

> Beersheba School,
> 12 Aug. 1900—
>
> Dear Annabel,
>   As I take up my pen to write you these lines, I feel inmesurably the limitation of the body, which cannot express what my heart feels for you. Do you love me? If so tell me quickly that my mind might rest—for I cannot sleep night or day—my mind is so fix on you. I would like to see you face to face that I might have then throw off the burden if I know you love me. Will you be at the Picnic at White Hall on Saturday? I will be there and hope to see your dear face and hear that you love me. I hope your father is recovered, and that you are well. You do not know how my whole mind and physic.

When Mr. Timsin got to "physic" he stopped. Physic! Physic!" he said thoughtfully, "what you mean? De man ah talk bout him Physic as if hn ah tek medicine. You know what him mean Miss Ann? Miss Ann twisted her handkerchief:—"Me no know sah."

Mr. Timsin read it out again; "Physic! But stop!" it suddenly dawned on him, "oh fe true, him mean physique, which means de body or constitution. You understand?" The girls nodded and he went on.

> You do not know how my whole mind and physique fix on you, and my spirit is crying for you. *Do, do* come to me. I am coming to a close. Give my best regards to your parents, and please accept 100 kisses from me, who is and always will be
> Your loving and dear well wisher,
> George Green

"Well, Miss Ann," said Mr. Timsin, looking at the letter as he finished. "Dat ah proper love letter! You going tek him?"

Miss Ann held out her hand for the letter:—

"H'n too foolish!" said she. "Tenk you sah, Gimme dat and read de oder."

Mr. Timsin handed her the letter and opening the other unfolded the sheet and read as follows:—

> Lang Syne
> 13 Aug., 1900

Dear Ann,

When I was with you on Sunday, I meant to have tell you of my love for you, but when it come to the front all courage leave me. How weak we are in the presence of that whom we love! How can I make you know how much I love you? From when we was young and going to school I love you up to now. Sometime I think you love me a little, and then again my heart ready to sink. Tell me darling, do you love me. The ring is round and has no end, so is my love for you. Are you going to the Picnic at White Bay on Saturday? I shall be there (D. V.), and shall get my answer from your dear mouth. I cannot stay here if you don't love me, so please don't send me away. Give my regards to your mother and father and receive my love and kisses.

> Your loving one,
> Thos. Bonito

Mr. Timsin read out the name of the writer with a kind of pompous flourish, then looked at the letter again as if admiring the writing. "Well, ah doan know how you feel, Miss Ann," he said, after a little pause, "but I like dis letter better than the other. But it not my business. Which one you going tek?" he asked with a smile.

"Tek wha?" answered Miss Ann loudly, "me going tek any o' dem? Dem too fool. Weh me got fe do wid love letter and such ting. Gimme de letter sah?" Hereupon Miss Ann began to laugh and giggle, which showed she was rather pleased to receive two love letters.

"Well it not my business"; said Mr. Timsin giving her the letter, "but to tell you the truth and I can deny it, if I was you I would ah tek Thomas, ah know him from a chile and you know him too an' h'n would ah suit you bes. But of course you wi please youself and ih not my business."

"Me like Thomas better meself"; said Susan. "De teacher too high an' mighty fe me."

Ann was silent and gave no opinion, simply tugged at her dress and laughed. After a little she rose. "Come Susan!" said she, "mek me goh." Turning to Mr. Timsin, "me tenk you sah fe read de letter. It really kind o' you."

"Oh, no trouble at all," said Mr. Timsen, "me always like fe read love letter, an of course I'm not the wan to say anything 'bout them."

"Tenk you sah," said Ann gratefully moving with Susan out through the door.

As they went into the yard Mr. Timsin shouted after them. "Miss Ann, you going to the Picnic?"

"Me na know sah," answered back Miss Ann. "Dem too foolish."

Mr. Timsin smiled at the answer as he sat in his chair, and it was really a charming smile so full of kindliness, good humour and wisdom.

"Ah well," he muttered to himself with a sigh as he rose.

"Dem is young. I hope she wi tek Thomas." But he added, "Ah really write that letter of Thomas well. De teacher nowhere with me."

SATURDAY THE DAY OF THE Picnic broke cloudless and exceeding fair, and for its appointed time kept bright and warm with the bright warmness that the black man loves. Everybody was in good spirits, and Mr. Honeyman who was giving the picnic seemed to be going to get a lot of money. The picnic entrance fee for grownups 6d., for children 3d., had been advertised all around and promised to be a success, for by three o'clock, an hour after it opened, plenty of people were on the grounds, which had been lent by the owner of White Hall to Mr. Honeyman. The sports had now commenced, for be it known, a picnic is not a picnic without the sports. These sports generally consisted of Foot Races, Obstacle Races, Jumping, High Jump and Low Jump, sometimes Horse Races, and other interesting and manly events. You pay a small entrance fee, and if you win the race or event, you get a prize provided by the giver of the picnic.

In this picnic of Mr. Honeyman's there were quite a number of events and the prizes were such as to excite intense desire aud envy of the young men and women, for of course there were a couple of events for girls, races, etc. The prizes were of great variety, White Shirts, Coloured Shirts, Belts, Watches, Knives, Needle Cases etc.; but the prize was undoubtedly a pig, a live pig; and the event for which the pig was prize was the most interesting and exciting, and yet most simple. All one had to do was to pay a sixpence for entering, then try and catch the pig by its greased tail; the first person that caught it properly and firmly got the pig.

At half past three the Gibsons arrived, and were met at the gate by Thomas who insisted on paying for Susan and Ann's tickets, so gaining a point from the teacher who had not arrived yet. Miss Ann who looked even more charming than usual, gave Thomas a shy smile that might have meant anything. As a matter of fact Miss Ann had not made up her mind yet which to take. She liked Thomas much better than the teacher, but the latter's dignity of position and comfortable circumstances still influenced her mind. Thomas who was going to partake in some of the sports, had left his gaiters at home, and was now wearing brilliant blue stockings, with brown shoes. The three passed through the gate, into the grounds and stood up watching a foot race which was being run. Just as the race was ended in a tremendous burst of cheers and noise, Mr. Green rode up to them looking most important and affable on his young and small horse which was prancing and curvetting in a stylish way. When he saw Thomas with the girls, his face darkened a little, but it cleared almost at once, and dismounting he was gallant graciousness itself. "I am very glad you have managed to come and shed your pleasant influence on the scene today Miss Ann!" said he, "I don't know how I come so late. The reports of the school that I was writing, bas delayed me."

The next foot race was one in which Thomas was going in for, so he left Ann and Susan in Mr. Green's charge and went off to do his best. During the race, Mr. Green carried off the girls to have ice cream and cakes, and when Thomas amidst tremendous clamour won the race, and a watch at the same time, the girls were absent eating their cakes. Putting on his shoes again he took the watch, and after a little looking, found them. Mr. Green received him with a condescending and affable smile. "I am glad you have obtained the victory Thomas!" and Ann said shyly. "Ah glad you win Thomas," and asked to see the watch.

Thomas was more than proud.

"You deserve a drink for that race," said Mr. Green. "What will you tek, a syrup or a kola?"

Thomas who did not see why he should not benefit at the teacher's expense, answered readily:—

"Me tink me wi tek a kola, tank you sah!"

Mr. Green ordered a kola and Thomas drunk it off one breath.

When the girls had finished their ice cream and cakes, Mr. Green paid up, rattling the loose money in his pocket incidentally as he put his hand in, and they all went out to see and enjoy what was going on. "You na going in for de next race Sue," asked Thomas.

Susan nodded, "Yes, Me believe me going. Ah really tink ah might ah try."

"You doan bring you entrance money yet?" said Thomas.

"No said Susan, "me doan bring it yet."

"Dats alright den," said Thomas, "I wi pay fe it."

"Tenk you Thomas," said Susan. "It kine o' you an' ah mus' really try fe win."

So when the next race came on, Susan having her entrance money paid, took her place with the other girls, to run. The distance to run was shorter than that for the boys and men And the girls did almost as quick running as the men. Urged on by Thomas and Ann's shouts, Susan ran as hard as she could but she was a little short-winded and only come in third. She got a small prize however, so she was not much disappointed.

"You warn fe eat less," said Ann, with a sister's frankness, "you too stout."

"Too stout wha?" said Susan, "as ah jus' going win, me breat kine o fail me and I have fe go slower mek ah only get third."

Several interesting events then took place and all were enjoying themselves. At about half-past four Mr. Honeyman announced in a loud voice that the pig race would now come off, and would everybody join in please—only 6d an entry.

After some hesitation several young men entered, including Thomas who saw in the pig perhaps an addition to the property he might possess with Ann.

When Mr. Honeyman had got ten entries and no more seem to be coming, he cleared the ground and prepared to let go the pig. First of all however, he placed the ten young men in a line, and at a distance of ten yards at right angles to opposite the middle man, he placed the pig. Mr. Green who stood near the man and near the pig was to give the signal. Everybody and everything was ready, so lifting up his hand, Mr. Green said, "one! Two! Three!" and dropped a handkerchief. Immediately Mr. Honeyman let go the pig and immediately the young men started after it. The pig was not exactly fat and rather in good training being lean and muscular, and long and narrow, with a well greased tail. Now the fun and excitement began. The pig first of all, ran away from the men, then being headed, ran this way and that. One or two grabbed the tail, but couldn't grasp it firmly, and away the pig bolted, in and out among the spectators. Here and there it ran, twisting this way and that, squealing and causing some tumbles as people jumped and got out of the way. Thomas kept well after the pig, but did not try after its tail, knowing that it would be too greasy at first. After about five minutes of intense enjoyment to the crowd, the thing happened which finally decided Miss Ann in her choice of husband and gave Thomas a pig and a wife. The pig had come by this time round to its original position and was getting a little bit tired and going slower, was hard pressed indeed, for three young men were almost on him. Now it must be mentioned that just near here there was a large stone with a small piece of naked and dirty land, at the edge of which the teacher was standing and looking on with a dignified smile. As the foremost of the young men started forward to grab, the pig, with a last despairing effort, made a bolt to right angles and ran by Mr. Green. Mr. Green in getting out of the way stumbled against the stone and fell heavily on the pig and in the red and dirty patch of ground. At tremendous shout of cheers and laughter went up, especially magnified when it was seen that Thomas taking advantage of the pig being nearly squeezed to death by the teacher, had grabbed the tail firmly and in fact had won the prize. Mr. Green slowly rose to his feet, covered with red dust, all over his face and shirt. He began to smile in a sickly way at first, but as he heard the shouts and laughter on all sides, his face got darker and darker. The black race loves a joke like this.

"Hi, Miser Green, you mus' ah sorry you no enter fur de race. You would ah get de pig," yelled one.

"Hi, no man!" said another, "De pig get him." Everybody was laughing and shouting, including Susan and Ann who shook with enjoyment of the joke. At the moment that the teacher went down, strange to say, Ann knew that she would accept Thomas and could never the teacher. Mr. Green must have felt something of this, for he walked past them without speaking, in a violent rage, and mounting his horse, rode home. Ann saw him go without any regret and it was a beautiful smile that lit her comely black face, when Thomas came up later to receive her words of congratulation.

MARGUERITE:
A STORY OF THE EARTHQUAKE

I

"Stay With Me Marguerite, Still."

—ARNOLD

When George came in he found a letter on his table from Marguerite.

> DEAR GEORGE,
>
> I am feeling very much worse and have had to send for the Doctor.
>
> Try and come to see me as soon as you can.
>
> Yours affectionately,
> MARGY

"Arthur, I will be out for a while, don't keep dinner waiting on me," he said and made all haste to Marguerite's home.

Adjusting his glasses, he positively avoided seeing her mother whom he met right at the right the door, and addressing himself to her sister asked if he might see Margy.

"Certainly, Mr. Hodlin, Margy is, awfully ill; we all thought she was going to die last night, oh, such hot fever! Come this way please," said Miss Dorrit.

George never expected to find her as ill as she was.

"Margy," he said, "what have you been doing with, yourself, dear; you must not get sick like this now. Why, you were to have gone out with me tomorrow night, don't you remember?" She smiled a wan smile in reply but was too weak even to raise her hand. George asked for some ice, and rubbing his hands well with it, began passing them gentler her forehead and face.

"Oh, how different this is to using an ice-bag, George; it is *so* refreshing," she said.

"Good Heavens what is this?" George said to himself, "Margy is really very ill; I never felt such hot fever before; I do wish the Doctor would hurry up and come to see her."

For several months George had been keeping his affection for Marguerite in check, and had been persuading himself that it was a case of "very good friends." His sense of humour was too strong to admit of his entertaining thoughts of marriage on £100 per annum, and he knew that if he, married against his father's ideas of "equality," his allowance of £60 was gone. But the sight of, Margy's pale helpless face caused the tide of his pent-up affection to surge up,; and now he saw the girl so near to death he realized, perhaps for the first time, how much he really loved her. As he chafed her forehead with a woman's gentleness he prayed his prayer that God should spare her life, and vowed his vow in silence.

He stooped and kissed her. "Margy, keep a stout heart little girlie, the Doctor will soon be here now, it is near two o'clock. You must not go and get sick like this, *for don't you know I can't spare you?*" There was a tremor in his voice as he said the lase few words. Margy recognized it too, for she had never heard it before.

"Miss Dorrit," he said to her sister, "you must look after Margy; I never thought she was so ill; when the Doctor comes you must tell him everything; it won't do for her to get sick now."

"Thank you very much for coming, Mr. Hodlin; Margy is better to what she was last night. Well, goodbye, you must come again soon." Dorrit was young in years, but sufficiently wise to see that George's presence had done Margy more good than all their attentions.

George was unusually quiet as he dressed; for Church that Sunday night. Margy's pale face haunted him, and he felt that the love he had scarce admitted to himself had overflowed his soul, and that the old game of an "unfailing friend" was up for good. Margy on her part really loved George; she saw in him a purer, more unselfish and thoughtful man than those her mother had encouraged her to associate with. She had once evert encouraged Margy to be friendly to a Corporal of His Majesty's Army,—one who dropped his h's and sung in the choir of a Non-Conformist Church on Sunday nights—, because he was a white man. Somehow, Margy's mother disliked George as heartily as he did her. Indeed there wets something provoking in the way he spoke to her, and adjusted his glasses and said "quite so. It was his method of showing his dislike of anyone, and irritating it certainly was.

II

G eorge had first met Marguerite at Whiteley's store in Harbour Street, where he made most of his purchases. An acquaintance begun across the counter had developed into a friendship; and discussion at tea-time at Whiteley's ran high against Margy.

"My dear child, Mr. Hodlin was here today you know," Miss Brown would observe. "Margy is very much mistaken if, she thinks he is going to marry *her*. If he did not get married last year when he was in England, it is not likely he is going to marry such as her. In fact I can't understand these girls, my dear."

"George had called for Margy and taken her home from work once or twice; but finding that this rather looked like a coachman courting the servant-maid, he gave it up and asked her to go for drives with him occasionally. He would talk to her of England and America, and show her his beautiful photographs taken while there; once he did ask her if she would like to go to those places, and (so I am told) added, "with me" to the question. Margy had blushed and being a brunette with pretty eyes and long eyelashes, had looked quite charming: but George remembered his salary! On one or two occasions Margy had sought George's opinion on little matters. She had, taken his advice, and' professed the success of it to be perfect.

George never let the opportunity pass to do for her some little good service; if he made her a present it was not done vulgarly; if he took her for a row or drive, she knew and felt herself to be in the care of a gentleman. He saw her nearly everyday, and there gradually grew to exist between them an indefinable yet very certain tie. In his own mind, however, the idea of marriage was not allowed to enter; her society was a pleasure to him which he saw no harm in enjoying. Perhaps he almost viewed the life of a married man as something strange, if not altogether ridiculous.

As the friendship grew, George learnt that Margy's father had left Jamaica when she was quite a girl, and that she had been to work since she was eighteen. Herself and an aunt who worked at Robinson's had to support her mother, two sisters and a little nephew whose father was dead. This little fellow and one sister were being sent to school, and so their joint salary of about £100 a year was taxed to the utmost.

George truly admired and respected Margy, but knew that his honest old dad had views of his own concerning the girl he was to marry; and having no desire to ruffle him, never mentioned Margy's name to him. "What's the use," he would say to himself. "There'll be a bit of a row and fuss. I like Margy; she's a real good little woman; I take a great interest in her and I believe she appreciates my friendship but—"

Thus argued the head above the heart, but that latter organ is not always to be argued with.

III

O n several occasions George had invited Margy to hear Father D.
preach. In spite of her "dread" of the Roman Catholic Church,
Margy used to go, and George would smile a sweet smile of recognition
when he saw her; but it must be said to his discredit that if his father
and family were with him, he used only to take off his hat to her outside
and explain to the "old man's" question that she "was a young lady at
Whiteley's store."

George's visits to Margy's home were very few, for as we have seen,
he disliked her old mother most heartily. She saw in George Hodlin only
a "conceited young man with a lot of education and nonsense" and only
£100 a year salary; while George recognised her to be the vulgar-minded
old creature she was and so kept clear of her. Nevertheless the friendship
grew, and it was rumoured among the women from Whiteley's even
unto Smith's, that Margy was bent on "catching" Mr. Hodlin of the—
Department.

"But my dear child you don't know anything," said Miss Brown.
"You know that chap from Grenada, who has been coming here for the
past few weeks; people say he is very rich but—of course I don't know,
but I see him talking to her quite sweet of late; wonder if George knows
anything of *that*."

"I bet you *I* tell him when he comes in our store," said Miss Pert of
Smith's.

George happened to drop in at, Smith's to buy some trifle he could
not get at Whiteley's.

"Good evening Mr. Hodlin," said Miss Pert.

"I say Mr. Hodlin, I see a very-rich chap from Grenada, one Herr
Tietz, is quite sweet on our friend Margy, so Miss Brown tells me. My
dear sir, he won't have anyone to attend to him but her, and then there
are little tete-a-fetes and so on, *you* know." George took it for granted
that it was quite natural that this chap should like Margy to attend to
him, and perhaps did not care to admit to himself that he did feel a bit
queer at Miss Pert's little piece of information. He blushed a little and
only replied, "Is that so? Wish her luck if he is well off." Miss Pert gave
him a most knowing look.

"Tut Mr. Hodlin, don't tell *me* that now."

George forgot all about Miss Pert's "rich man from Grenada" and went to see Margy, that very evening. She seemed so cheerful and happy when he came in; and after a few minutes he suggested that they should go for a moonlight walk.

"You *do* look nice in that that Margy, come and let me see if I can put it on."

Margy smiled,—that is to say she pressed her lips together and there was a twinkle in her eye,—and dropped both her hands to her side. George then proceeded to fix that hat according to his ideas of art. Of course I am subject to correction, but I am given to understand that the old lady being outside and the piazza not lighted, George was awarded a kiss for his skill; and there being no time limit, and it being I believe almost his first, it was a long one.

Thus George loved Marguerite, but fearing the, wrath of his sire, knew not himself how much he loved her until such time as she lay grievously sick of a fever. If he had been guilty of a foolish or false pride before, or of dilettantism of any sort; he was now resolved that, should God spare her dear life, he would marry Margy sometime next year. He planned plans whereby he would be able to send her to Boston, during the summer, to his, friends Mr. and Mrs. A.H. of Cambridge, and he would follow a couple months after. He already pictured to his mind Washington Street as it is near Canton and the Church of the Holy Cross, and Margy dressed in white saying "I will" in answer to Father J's question.

The thought made him rather careless over his week's work.

IV

The Doctor called to see Margy and pronounced her case to be one of typhoid fever. The lifting of his eyebrows when he looked at the thermometer shewed that it was serious, although he did not say much. He left strict instructions and directions and said he would call early next morning.

The young student of German even took to reading a "Family Doctor" and studied the subject of "fevers" most assiduously. He learned enough to be able to warn Margy's sister against the too early use of beef tea or any stimulant. Margy progressed slowly but surely under Dr. R's treatment, and George's visits too were observed to be of a decidedly remedial effect. For an hour or so every evening he would read and talk to her, and although she was too weak for him to tell her of certain feelings somewhere between his heart and throat, it must not be supposed that Margy did not know all about them. Sometimes he would send her into a sweet sleep by gently stroking her hair, then he would kiss her so softly, and go home feeling as satisfied with himself as if he were a priest who had assisted some soul on its journey to its creator.

Going down to work one morning an idea came to George; it was so simple, so luminous, that he could not help wondering how it was he had not thought of it before. He would just telegraph Mrs. L. of Moneague, telling her to send a conveyance to Ewarton and have lodgings prepared for a young lady; he would buy half a dozen bottles of the best recommended tonics Crosswell's had; and in a few days time Margy would be sent off for a few weeks change in the St. Ann Mountains. He told Margy of it so delicately, and pointed out that, for his sake, she must go and come back to him looking rosy and like her dear little self. Of course, there was no use arguing. George was surprised at his own powers anticipating and clearing up difficulties and objections. He went home and prepared against her departure, a letter containing advice as to exercise and diet, a treatise on fresh air and chills, an enthusiastic account of Moneague, where "the hills are round us and the breezes go o'er the sunlit fields," and sundry matters appertaining to her health and love in general.

The receipt for the amount paid n advance was duly received, and Margy set off by the 7:30 A.M. train for Ewarton. George sent down a bearer with a box containing French wines, Hypophosphites and other tonics, also "a twenty-five page" letter. Margy never realized how disagreeable travelling by rail was as she did that day when the crowded train prevented her reading George's letter before even Spanish Town was reached.

Now that Margy had gone George began to feel very lonely. It was in vain Arthur tried to engage him in conversation on the "situation in India," and George never even quoted Goethe once for several evenings. On Sunday night before going to bed he had been reading, for the twentieth time at least, *Vanity Fair*. He fell asleep thinking much of Marguerite, and dreamed a dream that disturbed his peace of mind not a little. Next morning before going to work he wrote Margy by morning train:—

Monday Morning.

My precious little darling,

Since writing you last evening at about two o'clock, I have been feeling so sad and out of sorts that I could not keep my promise to send you a *precis* of Fr. D's sermon. I do hope my unnamed "sadness" is not, (as Mr. Verity explains Antonio's "sadness"), a case of "coming events cast their shadows before." How silly of me, but you must be patient with me. Before going to bed last night I was reading *Vanity Fair* ("that horrid book" as you call it). I fell asleep and had a most wretched dream; I dreamed that somehow I had met old Thackeray himself and that he was talking to me quite confidentially.

"So I see you too are very much in love with on Miss Marguerite," he said.

"Who told you sir?" I asked, anxious of course to hear what he had to say.

"Who tells me anything, my boy," he replied, smiling and looking me steadily in the face with his dreamy far-off eyes.

"Think you," he went on, his face growing more serious, "that your Marguerite's love will always be the same? Don't you know that one hundred a year cannot insure any woman's love and affection; and as soon as any trouble or misfortune comes along she will forget you and look out for someone better off. You are too young to believe all you hear and read about in novels of love for love's sake." I felt hurt and angry, and told him I believed your love would never fail me, and I was surprised that he, of all men, should so speak. He said he did not mean to be unkind by the knew that I should suffer much when the time came for me to be disillusioned.

Margy dearest, I know it is *only a dream* and you must forgive me for telling you of it; but tell me darling nothing in this world could ever make you go before God's Altar and His Priest and swear to love, honour anyone but your own dearest Gorge. We have known each other so long that you must know all my faults and failings and impossibilities, but nothing will make you *love me less?* Now. . . there. . . don't be angry; tonight *you* must come to me in my dreams.

And part my hair and kiss my brow
And say: *my love why suffer'st thou?*

George then proceeded to remind Margy of what the Doctor said about getting all the fresh air she could, and that she must not forget to take the Hypophosphites before going to bed every night, and so on. He haunted the Post Office on Wednesday waiting for Margy's reply.

When I read your letter,

She wrote.

would you believe me George it made me cry, not tears of anger, but when you feel overwhelmed don't you know the tears you shed?

Margy was not long in associating Miss Pert with the cause of George's 'unnamed sadness'.

"I don't know why these women won't leave innocent people alone, George must have gone to Smith's, and she has been telling him a heap of lies about Mr. Tietz the diamond merchant. This man is worth a million in his personality alone, what could he want with me I should like to know." So thought Marguerite to herself, but determined not to let George, know for a moment that she suspected Miss Pert. She only told him of how kind the people were to her and how delightfully cold it was, that her cheeks were beginning to get rosy, and that she weighed four pounds more than she did a few weeks ago.

I could never,

She went on.

love any other but you. You are the first I have ever. loved and you know it. When true love has once been planted it can never be rooted up. I know it is so in *my* case; no power in this world could ever make me love you less *and you know it* George.

In her own simple way she assured him that the man, be he never so rich, was not inexistence who could tear her love away from him.

"Amen," said George kissing the letter. Thus did Margy protest strongly against the things spoken of her by dear departed Thackeray.

V

Margy returned to Kingston in January but being still weak, George would not hear of her going back to work; and so made her take another month's leave. She felt rather disappointed that he did not spend the evening with her on the day she returned, instead of going to Mrs.—'s ball; where we are given to understand by the indefatigable reporter of the "Gatherer," "a large number of the elite of Kingston and St. Andrew was present."

On Monday morning—January fourteenth—George had called to see Margy on some pretext or other, before going to work. He gave her many a "last kiss which never was the last," and telling her to take care of herself, had strolled down to his Office with an extra pleased countenance. At about twenty-five minutes past three, his chief had called him to show Sir——(one of the "distinguished visitors" who came out on the "Kingston"), some pet system he was always airing to strangers,—after first informing them of his distant relationship to Sir——, the famous Birmingham manufacturer—. George had brought the necessary books, and the official had commenced a dissertation on the several advantages of this method of his.

"Tick!" The clock struck the hour:—half past three:—the faithful minute-hand was slowing moving on, . . . "Oh God! What is that?"

A terrific report, like a sudden clap of thunder you hear when the sun shines bright and hides the lightning; a great noise as of cannon discharged continuously; a sudden blow under your feet; then the earth began to rock, and a yellow dust darkened the sky; and men saw gape open before them the chasm of death and feared lest, at the next moment, the~ might be hurled in.

"My God! This is San Francisco over again," George muttered, as he grasped the arm of a brother clerk.

"Your mother and father? Marguerite?"

The question flashed into his soul; by a tremendous effort of mind he staved it back.

"Is the earth going to cave asunder and Kingston perish like Port Royal?" George thought to himself, as the second shock followed on the first. Wrenching itself from the grasp of the upper floor which it supported, a massive wall reared and flung itself down a few feet from where George was standing. He could hear the crash, but could scarce see an inch in front of him. Springing through the nearest window, he alighted a few inches from the mangled form of a man in the throes of his last agony. When George gained Harbour Street, an almost death-like stillness met him. There were the ruins; and men and women lay beneath them! Should he remain and render any assistance he could?

"Your mother! Marguerite!" Swifter, more distinct than at first flashed the thought into his mind.

The "Empire" Restaurant on Har-bour Street, and the Chemists' stores in King Street had already caught fire. What was he to do? Stop, and see if he could save a single life before the flames could claim it? An unutterable sense of his own uselessness crushed, almost awed him; he was not a surgeon, and he could not even dress a wound, but he might. . . The sight of one unfortunate, who to escape the fire, had broken his own arm, put an end to his uncertainty. What if his own mother, if Marguerite lay. . . ?

The thought was not allowed to complete itself. In ten minutes time, George had reached Margy's home. He saw her mother standing at the gate.

"Margy's safe," she shouted to him as she saw him coming up the Street. George could have kissed the old woman a kiss of gratitude for her thoughtfulness. He dashed into the room where Margy was lying in a half-fainting condition. She recognised him and flung herself into his arms.

"Thank God, thank God," he muttered, as the tears, (such tears as we shed once a lifetime) came to his eyes and choked him.

"Margy, I must be going to mother's," he tried to say.

"You'll come back, won't you darling?"

"*Of course*," he replied and rushed to the door.

"Have you seen anything of Aunt R.," cried out Margy's mother to him.

"No, but I'll be back in a few minutes," he answered.

As soon as George reached the foot of the street where he lived, he could see that his home was destroyed. What thoughts filled his heart, and the hearts of thousands of sons and brothers and husbands, when they caught the first sight of their ruined homes, and knew not if mother, sister, wife were alive to meet them!

Let us throw the veil over George and his family whom he found, by the mercies of God, alive and praying for him.

VI

"The woes I saw with these sad eyne."

—Virgil

It was near five o'clock before George could return to Margy. He was met by her sister and nephew; the poor children were in a flood of tears, having seen or heard nothing of their aunt. George, of course, offered to go downtown and make all inquiry.

After spending a few minutes alone with Margy he set out on a search. Approach to Robinson's store was simply a matter of utter impossibility. All Harbour Street from King to Church Streets was in flames: The delicate fabrics of the drygoods stores, and the inflamable stuffs at the ironmongeries had caught fire, and over eight acres of buildings were already burning. George enquired of a few persons he met if they could say what has become of Robinson's clerks—no one could give him any definite information; but the opinion was generally expressed that they had all, escaped before the fire had swept over the store. The best thing to do was to go to the hospital; she might have got injured, and have been taken there. Following in the track of a cart, laden with the dying and wounded, George reached the hospital at dusk. The air was heavy with the smell of fresh drawn blood; the ground was strewn with mangled bodies; a man half roasted alive met George's gaze as he entered. There was no time to enquire or ask questions; he must get to work to examine the features of a couple hundred persons before he could conscientiously say that he had searched for Margy's aunt. At the end of a two-hour search he was compelled to give up. Fresh arrivals of the injured came pouring in, and yet no trace of the poor woman could be found. George returned to Margy's, and telling her of his fruitless endeavour, said he would make an attempt to go on board the "Port Kingston" where hundreds had sought refuge for the night.

The "Kingston" had however been forced to put out into the stream, having caught fire some three times; and as a boat could not be had at any price, George had to postpone that search until next morning.

On his way he met Mr. H. of the Rifle Corps and two of his little party of stout-hearted young fellows, who asked him to give a hand in removing some bodies from a ruin in Narrow Lane. When he returned, after a couple hours' work, he heard that Margy and her family had left their home to take refuge at a friend's place where there was much open space. He hastened down and found them under a tree,—Margy shivering with fever and ague.

"George, you won't leave us tonight will you? I don't know what I'll do without you. Mother has almost lost her head, and if we have anymore shocks I don't know how I'll stand it." George made no reply, but carefully wrapped Margy in his warm overcoat, sat down beside her and drew her close to him.

"Do you feel warmer now dearest?" he asked "You must try to go to sleep;—there—make yourself comfortable!" He took off his coat and spreading it on the bench, put her in a comfortable position, and began chafing her, hands as he, had done a couple months before. She fell into a light sleep, and as he looked at her pale thin face, it filled him with inexpressible feelings of love and longing and anxiety what if this exposure to the night air and this awful trying tax on her nerves should bring on a serious relapse. He decided not to leave her a moment, but to remain by her the whole night to see that she should not get chilled at any rate. Another shock and the prayers and shouts of the fear-stricken thousands awoke Margy from er light sleep. George remembered that he had left his mother about six hours ago, and that she must be very anxious for him.

"Margy," he said, "I want just to run round and see if my folks are all right. I have not seen them since four o'clock. I won't be long."

"Oh George, do make haste and come back; you'll stay with me tonight, won't you?"

George rushed home to his mother and explained that he had been trying to get some information about someone who was missing: "We who are alive, and without even a scratch, surely owe it as a duty to do all we can for the suffering and anxious ones, mother, so if you are all safe I must be going downtown again," he said, and set off for Margy's.

Shall we say that George, in spite of his, anxiety and losses, felt almost happy' on that night of the fourteenth of January? His heart overflowed with thankfulness that all his family were safe; and the thought that his own Margy was alive, and needed his care and attention more than anything else, filled him with a secret joy and exultation. Was he not going to sit by her all that night, and show her how very dearly he loved her? How the words rang in his ears—"George stay with me."

The day was not far off when he should recall those words, and the memory of them, should be very bitter!

THOMAS MACDERMOT

VII

The presence, of a man who did not pray aloud, when the earth trembled, but who spoke words of assurance without bravado, had a wonderful effect on the women including even Margy's mother, (and it was sometime before she referred to him as "that Mister—George Hodlin.")

That awful night wore slowly on; Nature seemed so innocent, so unconscious of the terrible work she had done; the wondrous stars, strong and serene, came out and sang their evening hymn, while yet the roar could be heard in the Park of the fire, as it tore over the business section of Kingston, and devoured warehouse, store and wharf.

George kept the cold bight air from chilling Margy, and before dawn took her, back to her home. Although not very badly damaged, it was not to, be expected that they could remain in it; so it was decided that they should remove, as soon as possible, to the house of a friend who lived out of the city. George made a fire, and they prepared coffee in the yard. A strange glow filled his heart as he took that cup of coffee from Margy, and commenced packing, her things. He felt that she was now his *very own*; he was sure his friends in America, would secure him a good position there, and Margy would be his wife in a few months' time. By day-break George set out to look for Margy's aunt for whom he had searched without success the evening before. From seven o'clock till eleven he enquired on board the "Port Kingston" searched the hospitals some three times for her. All enquiry was in vain. Robinson's store was a mass of ruins; the fire had taken what the earthquake had left, and no one had seen or heard anything of her. George had to go and tell Margy and her family the sad news, that their aunt was dead, and that no trace could even be found of her body.

God rest her soul!

It was a severe trial to the young man, but he stood the ordeal well; and broke the awful news with a sympathy and manly tenderness that made them all cling to him as to a brother. By about five o'clock the removal from Kingston had been effected. At four George had been requisitioned for special duty, and it was not until near eleven that he saw Marguerite again. It was a long walk from King Street to where she was stopping on the Old Hope Road; but how holy those duties and that two mile walk seemed to him. On his way up he met Father H.

and a Salvation Army Captain, who had spent all day at the hospital. He found Margy slightly feverish, and distressed and disgusted at the loud conversation, mingled occasionally with the still louder prayers, that was going on.

Oh how golden was the silence that followed on George's arrival! He had of course made up his mind to sit up and watch by her; but fatigue completely overpowered him, and in a few minutes he had fallen into a deep sleep. Margy looked at bis worn-out face as it lay in her lap, and admired the young man for his purity, his unselfish sympathetic heart; and loved him for himself. It was near four in the morning before he woke, feeling a bit ashamed of himself, but refreshed for the duties of the day.

George had to start work downtown before seven in the morning, and worked without break till near six in the evenings. But never had arduous and trying duties seemed so light so holy to him; he only thought of the hour when he would see Margy, and so did the work of two men without a murmur. A lonely walk of more than four miles through the dark streets of Kingston followed each day's toil: his own thoughts of the future, and the fantastic forms of the trees he passed near midnight on his way home, his only companions.

VIII

"Veni, Vidi, Vici."

—Caesar

N ow, the securing of a tent in those days, was a matter that would tax the skill of a party-politician and the guile of a third-form schoolboy.

"I say, Arthur, I want a tent; how do you advise to set about it?" George asked one morning. Arthur smiled through half-closed eyes, as a brilliant plan for relieving the Kingston General Commissioners of a tent come to his head.

"Leave it to me, my son; I'll enter the camp of the Philistines and spoil'em in less than five minutes."

At ten next morning, on his way to the Victoria Market in a bus, Arthur was informed by his garrulous busman that the tents were being distributed indiscriminately since the previous day; Arthur realized that this would make the task all the more difficult. In a few minutes they reached the corner of King and Harbour Streets; and to say that both Arthur and even the popular Kingston "Sam Weller" were surprised at the crowd. which surged from the waterfront even into Harbour Street, was putting it mildly. The nearer he got to his goal, the less Arthur's chance of getting a tent that morning seemed. "Josiah" began to clank his bell and to exhort the multitude to make room for him, in language that was constantly changing' to suit the tastes of the individuals addressed. Now it was, "Hi, hi, mek way, mek way"; then as some pugnacious member of the crowd objected to his peremptory order, he would hurl at him observations such as "you wutless, big-tree naygur, where is you manners? Mek way fe a gem man," or "shut up cockchicken, does your modder know you are hout?"

Someone shouted, "Backra, fe you tent finish, dem yah a fe black naygur; you can't get none yah."

A well-known Commercial College in London advertises that "perseverance means success." "Josiah" had never been to College; but much experience in the art of slipping the policeman at the Railway Station, and taking up an unlawful position in the line of waiting busses; together with an almost daily practice during the Tourist Season in persuading American visitors to Kingston that the cab fares of this city differ little from those in vogue in New York, had taught him the value of perseverance. Arrived at last at one of the gates, Arthur sought admittance from the burly porter.

"You can't come in, sah," he returned sharply.

"D—it, man, rubbish I must get in at once," Arthur replied, slipping a shilling into the hand of the guardian of Relief Stores.

"Pass on, sah," said that fuctionary, who took care to explain to the crowd that "dat backra hav fe do wid de place." Cerberus passed, Arthur, stalking up to a small mountain of closely packed tents, approached a lad who was in attendance.

"Here's a shilling for you boy, I want a tent; quick about it please, I am in a hurry."

"Yes, sir," the boy replied saluting, "I am your man sir; what kind of a tent would you like? A Marquee., or a Bell or a Wall tent?"

"Oh, a good tent."

"All right sir, here's a good pole, and everything you need; will this one suit you sir?"

"Yes," Arthur replied slowly, with the air of a man who accepts an inferior article, which a persuasive druggist's clerk assures him is as good as, or better than the one asked for.

"Pitch it over the rail lad," was Arthur's order to the boy, when he came out by the Temple Lane gate.

The boy obeyed, and before the astonished crowd could grasp the meaning of Arthur's maneuvre, he was driving up Temple Laue with a choice Wall Tent.

"Lawd me God, lookoo yah; weh dis backra get tent a go; and we dey yah from soon a marnin?" shouted a man who had been waiting at almost the same spot for about three hours. A cry of indignation was raised, and one or two of the more exasperated and bold suggested that they should pursue the "backra-man" and spoil him of his prize. His whole journey through the crowd was made lively by vehement curses, and at one stage he was told some interesting information concerning his ancestors that he had never heard before. But "Josiah" was good for several ordinary citizens on foot, be they never so swift or angry.

Arthur handed over the tent to George who erected it for Marguerite the same evening.

IX

"—can aught beguile
Love's watchful eye?—"

—Virgil

During the next few weeks, things gradually improved, and Margy go well and strong enough to go for walks and drives with George; and they loved each other with an exceeding great love. The events of the past few months had shown Margy that beneath the smooth surface of George's calm even supercilious smile, flowed the deep strong current of a pure soul, and a heart tender, true, unfailing. He had opened the great Book of Life, and had mastered the first few lessons well; like the schoolboy does his first four propositions of Euclid.

It chanced that as George was going home on the evening of the fourteenth February, old Scott (a distant relative of Margy's mother), a sort of retired shop-keeper who still II did a little business," hailed him from his shop in the Parade.

"Hodlin, come here a moment." George started at the old fellow's voice, and felt half inclined to pretend not to hear him; but Mr. Scott repeated the call, and George entered the shop.

"I say Hodlin, going up to Miss Margy's tonight? Got a letter here for her from one of those Islands to my care, but I don't know when I'll ever get up so far. Will you take it for me?"

George could not tell, why so simple a reuest should cause his hands to shake so, and the blood to rush to his head; but ere he saw the envelope, blistered with Grenada stamps, some "swift mysterious instinct" had told him in that fated moment from whom it came. I believe he said "yes," took the letter, and Rushed out of the shop.

Now the writer of that letter was a man large as to size and this world's goods, one who believed in the existence of a God whose business it was to see to it that his affairs prospered, and that none of his bargains were unsuccessful. The letter dripped with the splendour of his-wealth and extravagance of expression; commencing with four or five lines of endearing terms, it ended with the assurance that he would be in Jamaica in a few week's time, and fixed a date as the probable time of his marriage with his "adored Marguerite." On the flap of the envelope was printed:

"WILHELM TIETZ & CO."
General Merchants,
Grenada,
British West Indies.

George had heard that name once before! He enclosed it in a covering letter to Margy, telling her that Mr. Scott had asked him to hand it to her, but as he was unable to do so, and as he felt sure she was very anxious to receive it, he sent it by bearer.

* * * *

NOW IT CAME TO PASS that in the year One thousand nine hundred and six and in the fourth month of the year, there. journeyed from the Isle of Grenada a certain rich man,—Otto Tietz by name—This gentleman, the junior partner of the firm of Wilhelm Tietz & Co. was a German by birth, but had received his education in England before settling in our sister colony. He was a rather handsome, healthy-looking man, of generous and affectionate disposition, most thorough in bis business, and impulsive in his loves. While in England he had shewn promise of being the champion boxer of his college, but now that this blue-eyed son of the Fatherland had settled down to business, he might have served as an ideal model for the artist desirous of representing "Peace" and "Commerce."

Although Tietz & Co. were by no means "diamond merchants," nor was Otto worth "a million in his personality alone," these honest merchants, (who sold coffee for the matter of that) conducted a large and very successful business. Otto had combined business with pleasure in his trip to Jamaica and, of course, had seen Marguerite at Whiteley's, to which respectable business-house he had letters of introduction. From such time forth as he shewed Margy some "attention," her mother had wished George Hodlin out of this world into a next, preferably in that one where the souls of the naughty are supposed to roast and fry—it was not however until the day before he left Jamaica that Otto expressed a desire to lay his heart and worldly goods at Margy's feet. A cable summoned him to New York, and ere definite arrangements were made, Herr Otto Tietz sailed for the "Land of the Free" on the Royal Mail steamer. A correspondence followed in which he told her of his undying love (which he sometimes likened unto the fruitful vines and fig trees of Canaan of old); and to these letters did Margy make answer under her mother's surveillance.

It must not then be supposed that; with her mother on the one hand, and a very proper desire to exchange a life of worry and work, for one of every luxury and comfort on the other; Margy did not reply favourably to the epistles of her "ever devoted Otto." But Otto was several thousand miles away, and George Hodlin she saw almost daily, and was learning to love more and more, in spite of the considerations aforesaid.

X

"I Wailed Not, So of Stone Grew I Within."

—Dante

George was not long in learning, from sources reliable or otherwise, all about Margy's relationships with Otto. After two days had passed, he received the following note from Margy : -

Dear George,

Many thanks for your letter of the fourteenth. God knows, if I do marry this man from Grenada what will cause me to do it. *I love you and will ever love you*; it will be no happiness to me; and I do hope the Almighty will have mercy on my soul. I can stand anything, but not the way you wrote me last Thursday. You are better off than I, as in a few weeks from this, (if you have not found her yet), you will love someone just as dearly as you said you loved me; but *she* will never love you more than I do. God bless you is all I ask. I know my life seems wrecked, but God knows the reason. May I ask you to call for your books and overcoat?

Your affectionate,
Margy.

George had not calculated on a reply such as this! He felt that the supreme moment had come: he would go and see her once more, and learn the truth from her own lips. Accordingly he stopped at a barber's, and had a close shave; (he was afraid to shave himself that evening) and put on his evening dress, intending to call for his books and over-coat before going to dine at Constant Spring Hotel.

He met Margy with a cold cynical smile. All trace of gentleness had disappeared from the slightly mocking voice in which he habitually spoke.

"Can it be that *he* does not care?" Margy, thought to herself as George went on speaking to her in a drawl, in which suppressed emotion and bitter satire strove for the mastery.

"Passing the Synagogue this evening, I heard them chanting in Hebrew"; he remarked, as he was about leaving, "I could not help thinking how well adapted your voice is for singing in that language: I suppose, I need hardly ask if you intend to 'trample the Cross.'" George seemed of opinion that Otto was a Jew.

He made the Sign of the Cross, as he uttered the last three revolting words. Margy only replied that Mr. Tietz was a Christian; the bitter question stung her to the quick. George jaw the effect of his words; although he might not avow it, he was still possessed of a ray of hope; nor could he for the moment help a feeling of satisfaction at the thought, that she too might have to suffer in the days to come.

"Well goodnight, I must be at the Hotel by eight."

What would he not have given, as he shook Margy's hand at the gate, (she followed him to the gate) to take her head in his two hands, and kiss her on the lips and eyes as he had done a week ago. It was not without a pang of regret and even shame, that Margy too recalled that moment she had given Otto his first kiss, his first look of love and tenderness. There was a cold emptiness at the pit of George's' stomach; his, knees and hands trembled, as he walked on to meet his car; and he experienced a faint desire to sit under, instead of in it. Next day he received the following letter from Margy:—

My Own Dearest George,
"I am trying to write you today but I am feeling awfully ill, and sad and sick at heart. As I have told you, Mr. T. has promised to do a lot for us all, and he has even bought a house in the country. As you know dearest, we both, aunt R. and I, had to support our people; since R's death, it now stands that I alone must do it. You, I know, are willing, as before, to do all that lies in your power; but that is for me darling. If I even go back to work, my salary can certainly do for me; but what of the others? I can't do better than bow to the Inevitable. May God forgive me for it all. I will not annoy your ears by telling you how much I do love you. God knows! It would not be like this if R. were alive, but He does all things well; and He knows all. You say I am heartless. and that I am only playing with your love. Ah, George! I have not had an easy time of it from my childhood up, and I have had heaps of crying on me lately. Perhaps my time on earth

will soon be ended. I don't know how it will all end, but rest assured, my own dearest George, that through all the changing scenes of life *I'll love you still the same*: nothing will ever change my love for you, and if I am to marry Mr. Tietz, I'll always come to see you somewhere or somehow; how could I exist without seeing that dear sweet face of yours? 'He holds thy hands, He claspeth mine,' so trust 'Him to direct our paths. Whatever He does we must-submit to, but I want you to believe this, that I still love you dearly, and will ever hold your memory dear.

I'll keep your photo in my nearest reach and give it a sweet kiss very often. Oh, George, I could never, never love you less, or feel too proud to speak to you; and who is to tell what is in the future for us? You may yet call me your 'dear little wifey,' eh, darling?"

"Well, I am d—d," said George to himself. "*Too proud to speak to me* if she marries a confounded German pedlar; because he has a buggy, I suppose!" Even a man desperately in love may be permitted to have a lingering sense of humour, and this was really too much for George.

XI

"Can Vows——Allay
A Frantic Lover's Smart?"

—Virgil

George, although he did not absent himself from work, was observed, to be in very bad health, even by the clerk next him who would have had to perform his duties had he gone on leave. One day the huge figure of Father M. was seen rolling up the steps of the Office.

"Goodmorning, George; hav'nt seen you for sometime; how are you?"

"Not too well, Father," George replied.

"George is gone bad, Father," remarked young Scott; "he's going on as bad as a man in love, sir."

"Oh, I say boys you must not allow that." Now Father M. was much beloved among young men, because of his great bulk and overflowing wit, and the clerks of the Office were determined not to let him go before giving them at least one joke.

"Let's see; today's Tuesday; come up to the college and dine with us on Thursday George," said Father M.

"Quite right, sir, keep him out of harm's way," put in young Scott.

"Ah, talking of George in love; ever heard what happened to Adolphus? Well, Adolphus Morgan fell in love with Moriah Moran and 'with a whoop and a yelp he cleared the stoop before her father's bogan.' You know, I call that real art; Adolphus fell in love with Moriah, and the next thing we are told is 'he Cleared the stoop' before, the old man's boots. Well, goodbye, take care of George, boys." So saying the huge priest ran down the steps.

News does not travel slower in Kingston than in most other places where women live; so Margy soon heard that George was unwell, and that Father M. had even called on him at his work. Two days after the priest's visit George received the following from Margy:—

When I heard you were ill, my greatest wish was to go and see your dear face and remain with you for even an hour or two.

Let's hope dearest that the day is not far distant when we will be together all the time. You said when last I saw you, that the Lord had made woman different to men; I can assure you that *if I am brought to marry this man* I'll ever think of you and only you. Should my life be spared twenty years hence I will still *love you even as I do now.* You are very much mistaken, if you think the girl who has to forsake the love of her life does not suffer as keen sorrow as the man who forsakes his first love and marries another girl. I thought of you the whole time today, and I do hope you will be quite well soon; take care of a cold, and don't fret yourself until you actually see me Frau Otto Tietz. Mother has just got a letter from him enclosing fifty pounds, and saying he expects to be in Jamaica in about three weeks' time.

The misfortunes attendant on unsatisfied love have been all pretty well told, from the story of Dido, to Tolstoy's *Anna.* Now, had George's head continued to rule his heart. he might have realised that it was best to regard Margy as lost, and henceforth to seek distraction in his work and studies. "The web of Fate was woven so," and every attempt to escape the inevitable was sure to cause pain, and keen sorrow and anguish of heart.

Nevertheless George boarded an upgoing East Streetcar on the following Saturday night. The cool night air invigorated him, and the chatter of the querulous market-women distracted,—almost pleased,—him. He felt as though he must call a truce; he must see Margy once more as of, old, just as if nothing whatever had happened. He turned over the leaves of his memory and began reading some of the pleasantest records there. There were several misprints he would like corrected, especially at the beginning; but the reading on the whole was very pleasurable, for he had not yet reached toward the end. Lost in his own thoughts, he walked slowly up the road. No sooner had Margy seen him. than she advanced to meet him; George quickened his pace and came very near picking her up and kissing her one long kiss, instead of shaking her hand. Margy's half-smile seemed as sweet as ever; she hid her real feelings under a false cheerfulness which deceived, for a time at any rate, George's critical faculties. The hours passed, quickly by, and George even missed his last car. If we would know how their time was spent we must read the letter he received from Margy two days after.

I spent a sweet day, and last night I slept the sleep of the just and good. I felt so very happy while you were here and so loth to part with you; but I trust the day is not far off when we'll have no occasion to part or go from one another. I hope to God, dearie, that after all these years of friendship, nothing will ever come between to part us. How could I love another as I do you? I could' never be-stow, all the affection I have already given you upon anyone else. It would be no use to be in a lovely house with cushioned chairs, etc., and not be happy. I would be like a bird in a golden cage. I have been wrong, dearest, in all I have done; but if we get married you would not have cause to be jealous of me, as, I would not look at anyone else in the shape of a man with my eyes—(these eyes you so much want to hide). If all goes well, (and I earnestly pray to God that it may), how happily we ought to live together, especially, when I was on the verge of being snatched from my dearly beloved. Oh, dearest, you cannot,—no not even in dreams,—love me more than I do you. I am longing to see your dear face again, although it was only Saturday that I had that pleasure. Can I ever forget the happy, happy time we had together. I am praying to God to interfere on our behalf. He cannot fail us you know, even if earthly ones do. My intuitive powers, however, tell me *I'll be your wife*. Oh how happy that thought alone makes "me!" What of the reality?

George replied to this last note of Margy's less formally than he had written her since February fourteenth. He pointed out to her that, if she were willing to work for about four months more, their joint salaries would be quite sufficient. At the end of that time he would leave for Boston, and as soon as all arrangements were made, he would send for her. He reminded her of his dream and of her reply' to it, and closed with a passionate appeal to her to be true to him, to herself, and to the promises of love and faithfulness she had made in God's name. Perhaps, Margy thought that some of these plans might work less well in America than they did on George's note paper; perhaps too, that feeling which had doubtless prompted her to write the words which caused George to say that he was what I he was not, that is d—d; together with two other of those sins we pray to be delivered from in the Book of Common Prayer; were at work in her head. Who knows but that she already pictured herself ordering the coach-man to drive her to Whiteley's *new* King Street store with fifty pounds in her purse to buy her dresses? Be her inmost thoughts and calculations what they may, this is the letter she wrote George next day:—

> I have read your last letter. You were a bit stiff, I think, but I have forgiven you that, sweetheart; I have offended you so many times and look how good and gentle you have always been to me! I love you from the bottom of my heart and will ever. Do you think I could love anyone more than I do you; or if I marry anyone else he would ever get the love and affection I have given you? I suppose they would have to get what they are entitled to, but such love and affection as I have given and long to give you,—never! Oh, my darling, I earnestly pray God to help us both to be united; just think of tile bliss if we both get married, it would be one continual dream of happiness; all little misunderstandings over, only love to cheer our hearts. I feel as if I cannot be parted from you, for long. I want you to believe me, and not to think it is only a matter. of pen and ink. Now, dearest, be good till we meet again, and let me see that dear sweet smile of yours once more.

But Margy never saw that "dear sweet smile" again. Otto arrived earlier than was expected. He set to work to fix things in order with his usual business thoroughness, and in a few weeks' time, Marguerite was duly made the lawful wife of Herr Otto-Tietz, by one of His, Majesty's Marriage Officers at their country residence in the Santa Cruz Mountains.

XII

"A God, a God Their Severance Ruled."

—ARNOLD

L ike as when a vivid flash of lightning reveals to the night traveller, on a dark mountain road, almost every detail of the country. he is crossing; reveals all and then plunges all into deeper darkness again: even so did the notice in the "Gatherer" of Margy's marriage make George realize the position he had occupied for the past few weeks; and then plunged him into the uncertainty as to what was now in store for him. Within the last few months he had learned to love Margy to a degree he had not thought possible for his disposition; and now that he had lost her, the bitter thought that she -had been playing a game of base deception for so many months, completely overwhelmed him. He was astonished at, and perhaps sorry for, his own physical strength" and powers of endurance; for although in very poor health, he experienced no general breakdown.

George never thought for a moment that his life and conduct, since he could think and act for himself, was other than pleasing to his God; but if we turn to his carelessly-kept diary, we shall now see what was going on in this young man's mind; so far as he, or any man is aware of his own thoughts. An old philosopher says, that "the soul being transported and discomposed, turns its violence upon itself, if not supplied with something to oppose it"; and it would seem that George never forgave himself for yielding to the fear of his father's and friends' disapproval or ridicule; and that the remembrance of his own dilettantism was ever before him. Returning from Benediction on Sunday night he made the following entry in his diary:

St. Joseph's Day.

Thoughts pure in themselves and actions true and well-intentioned, may be made more than worthless if mixed with a selfish pride or vanity. "The Lord is a just and terrible God with a very strong sense of humour"; says Mr. Kipling; and He punishes us in proportion to our inmost consciousness of wrong or pride. In His anger he may relent; but in His humour, there's a sting.

"Will pierce thee to the quick and trouble thee." "Lead Thou me on." Oh God, for the "night is dark and I am far from home."

Then follow a prayer to St. Joseph, and, under different dates, several random entries such as these:

"On trouve au fond de tout le vide, et le neant."

"The Cross is an integral portion of love." Fr. D.

Work, work, work: for continuous occupation alone can stem the tide of thoughts and recollections pleasant in themselves, (seeing that the things they recall are pure) but which *must not* be encouraged for my own honour's sake and for the sake of her whom I love.

Alas! "Vain is the effort to forget."

Easter Day.

I was not always what I was on the nights I prayed for, and no doubt helped to save her life. God saw all the good there was in that, and has amply rewarded me; but He saw also the vanity, and is now punishing me for those strayings from the path of "whatsoever things are nobly serious." It sometimes seems as if, by concentrated study, and by despising the things of the past, I may live in a sort of region of ice: but, from out of the darkness comes a face I once kissed and prayed for; on my forehead I feel the warmth of a kiss;—the ice thaws and—

"Quand donc, quand donc, celera-t-il?"

Is not this discipline to teach me to be charitable and unselfish? My motives may not always have been as pure as I thought them to be; and every step I have taken away from the path of sincerity must be retraced, though my feet be bruised and bleed on climbing again the mountain-side it is so easy to descend. I wish all vain regrettings wiped out, all struggle over in my mind; "no strife to heal, no fears to beat away"; but is peace good for me? "I struggle toward the light", but while yet the night is dark, lead kindly Light.

Trinity Sunday.

My life has been one of pleasant ways, bordered by flowers, and filled with selfish, if pure, joys. After all, this great disappointment and sorrow may be sent to show me that the sovereign grace of life is resignation to the will of that Divine Providence which shapes all our ends, not for our own self-satisfaction or peace, but for the glory of the Eternal, for rendering us plastic clay in His Hands. Pride rules my heart; Pride calls to me to resent in anger and rebellion my lot; Reason, however, shews me that these things may be well for me; but neither Reason nor Pride can avail my soul. By Thy Divine Guidance and Light, teach me to learn to grasp the *true* Christian Philosophy—"he that loseth his life shall gain it."

Here follow Newman's Pilgrim Hymn, and, this entry made on his twenty-fourth birthday:

24th Birthday,
Whit Sunday.

By the mystery of Thy Holy Life and Death, by Thy glorious Resurrection and Ascension, and by the coming of the Holy Ghost; I beseech Thee, keep thou my feet *in this step I am about to take*; and send me, the while, sweet and wholesome thoughts, to nourish and refresh my soul; for Oh! I am very weary!

Thus George soliloquised, and occasionally noted down what he believed to be his own thoughts and feelings concerning himself.

Let us now, however, pass over several months, and go with him, at Arthur's pressing invitation: to a King's House Ball.

XIII

The music had ceased and Arthur, happy and flushed with his last waltz, came up to George. They wandered to the end of the room, and taking up an unconspicuous position, began to watch the gay well-dressed throng of men and women, bent on enjoying themselves, being admired, or impressing the world at large with their own importance. George fell to observing the faces of a few, whose gaiety he knew would fade with the night, and to whom the sunshine of the next day meant a sharp encounter with their ever-present problem of the ways and means of playing the game of the "Half-Way-Tree set."

At a King's House Ball, there are to be found quite a variety of types; from the dignified Officer Commanding the Troops to the youngster, who spends his ten pounds a month on dress, cigars, cocktails, and weekend excursions to Gordon Town; and who is picking up a West-end accent. He gets his entree through his father, who is a Government official with four or five gushing daughters, yet to marry.

There is a tacit understanding among mammas that to go to King's House increases a girl's chances of making a good match; but there are not a few of the young ladies themselves who are beginning to doubt this axiom, after attending a few seasons under the same surname, and looking their very best too.

"There goes the 'Baron,'" said Arthur nudging George, as his glance rested on the satisfying figure of a medium height gentleman, in faultless evening dress. He was walking across the room, head erect, chest well expanded, a picture of solemn dignity.

"I thought so," said Arthur, as the "Baron" reached a little group made up of a lately-arrived West Indian Regiment Colonel and his lady, a military doctor and a judge of the Surpreme Court. Making a lowe obeisance, he gushed in his carefully cultivated basso produndo: "How dye do, Colonel, and you madame; glad to see you out, doctor, and you too, Sir F." Before the usual platitudes of such a meeting had been exchanged, the healer of bodies and the corrector of straying consciences, having no special desire to listen to the "Baron's" neyer-failing flow of talk on literature and art, sauntered away, ruthlessly leaving the Colonel and his wife for his prey. They were within ear-shot of where George and Arthur were standing. The "Baron" was persuading the lady to assist at an entertainment he was organizing in aid of "local charities." He was taking special pains to assure her that it was to be a "distinctly high-class affair"; everything was to be high-class; the music, the songs, and *of course* those who were to take part. She could have every confidence, because the whole matter was in his hands and that of a few personal friends. Her consent obtained, he at once started, without the slightest encouragement, what would seem to be a learned dissertation on, "Art in Jamaica." The Colonel and his wife, who were really cultured people, were not given a chance to venture a remark; the "Baron" kept "pounding" away in such emphatic language that the Colonel, being a man of action, thought it would be a wise move to retreat, and so cut him short with an excuse in the midst of a six-syllable word; and rescuing his better half with his arm; sought repose on one of the lawn's and in a cigar. The "Baron" was left in possession of the field, feeling a bit disappointed that he had lost the opportunity of disseminating all the knowledge he had absorbed in his previous night's reading.

"Did you see that?" said Arthur, nudging his friend.

"I have been watching the encounter from a position of vantage," George replied:

"The silly beggar!—He never knows when he is snubbed." Arthur returned and burst out laughing. The 'Baron' was a gentleman bred and born in Kingston,but he signed his name—Karl von Reuter. On account however of his insistence that he was the sole remaining descendant of the house of 'Reuter,' and therefore entitled to the title, he was referred to, in and out of Kingston, as the 'Baron.'"

"Here comes Sir Francis," George remarked, when, of a sudden, the shrill notes of what seemed to be a laugh filled the air. Both young men looked in the direction of the strange noise, expecting no doubt to come face to face with one of Artemus Ward's hyenas on, vacation leave; but they only beheld the diminutive figure of Mr. Julius Arcamedes Montgomery. This gentleman was born in "that great country of English people on the other side of the Atlantic," and had secured his present lofty position in Jamaica chiefly through the influence of the mighty. For many years he had pursued the policy of being rude to anyone not ail Englishman, or a Government official with at least £600 a year. But times are changed now, and Julius Arcamedes too is a somewhat altered man. It was an anxious moment for George when he saw the distance between His Excellency and Mr. Montgomery growing less and less; for he recalled the occasion when that gentleman had sprung some inches off a chair and described an arc of over two hundred degrees, on the entry, at a public meeting, of a late Governor. The suspense was awful as the young men wondered what new gymnastic feal a sudden meeting with Sir Francis might give rise to. But the joke which a high Church dignitary was imparting to him was too good to allow of divided attention; so George's anxiety for the worthy little gentleman was set at rest.

XIV

"I have had the pleasure of meeting you before, Mr. Hodlin; I heard you lecture at the Institute once," said His Excellency. George flushed crimson, and Arthur thought that it was His Excellency's compliment that brought the blood to his cheek. But it was not. About ten yards from where George stood, was Marguerite, hanging lovingly on Otto's arm, while he smiled proudly and contentedly on everyone, as he stroked his ambrosial beard.

"My God, how lovely, she does look," George, thought to himself, as he saw the tall graceful figure of, the girl! Indeed Margy looked as sweet and happy as any girl in that room; for, like as a tree planted by the water side grows and sends forth blossom and is comely to behold, even so had Marguerite, with a good-natured husband and every other material comfort developed into as charming and lovely a little woman as you could wish for.

"What's wrong, George?" asked Arthur. "You, look as pale as death, and why I old chap, your hands are as cold as ice; what's wrong?"

"I feel awfully ill; I would like to get home at once," he replied. Arthur saw George in a bus, and returned to claim the next waltz with Miss Hattwell and—but "that's another story."

As George was slowly undressing in his room, Carlo, his pet, threw the door open, and entered joyously wagging what of a tail he had.

"Dorglums," he said "us have seen a ghost tonight," Carlo smiled affably.

"Yes, and God knows it hurts more than I thought," he added, wearily throwing himself down on his bed. Seeing; that his master was not disposed for polite conversation, Carlo retired to his virtuous couch under the bed. Poor George lay awake for hours. For the past few months he had succeeded in finding distraction in his work and much hard reading; but the sight of that face he loved so, those eyes into which he had so often smiled, the lips he had kissed and that old half smile, had thawed the ice of his thoughts, and left him a prey to a feverish restlessness. He thought of the night nearly three years ago when, just returned from his six months holiday in Europe and America, fresh in mind and body, he had lectured the grave members of the Institute on "Some English Poets of the Nineteenth Century." He could almost hear his own clear low voice saying: "It is Goethe who speaks of the presentiment of all the Universe which by the harmonious touch of poetry is awakened and unfolded in us." The aged chairman had paid him a fine tribute, and His Excellency had complimented him especially for his remarks on Byron and Cardinal Newman, and had expressed his warm appreciation of the young lecturer's allusion to Oxford and Oriel Dr. Pusey's words came to his mind—"Think back on the time of thy early prayers, thy freshness of mind, and the simplicity of thy heart; picture to thyself thy childhood, and think what thou art now."

The cool night air tempted him to go and sit by the window, and the rising moon offered her services to carry him in thought wherever he wished to go. George very foolishly accepted the offer, and soon found himself once more at Margy's side in his row-boat.

"On such a night as this," he had taken her out for a row, and as the bewitching light of the moon and her half-closed dark eyes stole into his soul, he had recited in her ears the beautiful lines:

> *"Raised are the dripping oars,*
> *Silent the boat; the lake,*
> *Lovely and soft as a dream*
> *Swims in the sheen of the moon.*
> *The mountains stand at its head,*
> *Clear in the pure June night;*
> *But the valleys. are flooded with haze."*

The next moment he was walking with her on the old Hope Road; and as he drew her head close to his shoulder, she had sworn by the self-same moon,—yea and by the God who created it,—that she had never loved, nor could ever love, any man but George Hodlin. She had sealed that oath with a kiss that had temporarily, interfered with the circulation of his blood! The very next day it was that Margy had received the letter from Otto saying when he expected to arrive in Jamaica and fixing the probable date of their marriage. Youth does not easily accommodate itself to the via media; so George thought long and powerfully, trying to find out whether Marguerite had deceived him out-right, or whether she, too was suffering at, that very moment in her husband's arms even as he was suffering. This shews that our young friend did not understand a woman's mind as much as he thought he did, in spite of his acquaintance with the works of Goethe. Carlo's vigorous scratching under the bed awoke George from his humiliating reverie. The last embers of his self-respect were going out, and he felt that the time had come for him to go somewhere, or do something, to recover himself. Arthur came in at this moment and made use of language not altogether fit for publication.

"What, the three stars, are you, a sick man, doing here, sitting up, star-gazing, moon-talking? Why the deuce don't you go to sleep? My son, remember the words of the proverb, 'Quem Deus vult perdere, prius dementat.'"

George threw himself down and answered not a word.

XV

Next morning George found himself at Dr. Goodnough's dispensary in Hanover Street. The good doctor greeted him with his usual kindly smile.

"Well, what can I do for you now?" he asked. George tried to tell, but found it a more difficult task than he had anticipated. The doctor soon set him at his ease however.

"You see, you are really very much run down; heart's action is a bit weak; what you want is to avoid all worry or anxiety: a couple months in Mandeville or the Santa Cruz Mountains would set you alright."

The mention of the Santa Cruz Mountains made George wince. The doctor did not fail to notice it.

"Or," he went on, "what would be best, go for a few months holiday in America, up in the Catskills or the Alleghanies, you know."

"All right, doctor; give me a certificate to that effect, and I'll be off by the next Boston boat." Dr. Goodnough stated that, "Mr. George Hodlin was under his medical care, and would require at least three months rest and change to recuperate."

"Now, my boy"; he said, putting his hand on George's shoulder, as he left his consulting room, "don't give yourself any mental worry; if anything is causing you pain or anxiety, you must try and forget it all and have a good time in America. It will soon, be alright you know."

Twenty minutes talk with Dr. Goodnough is worth many dollars of medicine; and George went down to his work feeling almost gay.

"Very sorry, sir, but I am afraid I'll have to go on three months leave,—Doctor's orders," said George to his chief, as he handed him the medical certificate. The scandilized official slowly read the paper.

"Of course, you know Mr. Hodlin, we can't do without your services now," he reminded George, "If you go on leave, we'll have to employ someone to do the November accounts, and that abstract is not yet written up, and—"

"Alright, sir. Half pay or anything," interrupted George; "but I want to leave the Island on Tuesday next." The leave was duly granted, and Wednesday's Gatherer announced that "Mr. George Hodlin of the—— Department sailed on the S. S. 'Admiral Dewey' yesterday for Boston, where he will spend the winter for the benefit of his health."

George would have given worlds to know what impression this

notice in the "Gatherer" would make on Marguerite, when she read it; but, as I could never hope to enter the august portals of that country-house, and as neither the "maid" nor "John" were present when Herr and Frau Otto Tietz partook of their morning paper, I am unable to tell him.

XVI

C oming out of the Parish Church one Sunday night, his dimpled-cheek finance on his arm, young Scott of the——Department (he who spake to Father M.) met Arthur.

"I say Arthur, where's George."

"George! Why, George is in Worcester Massachusetts."

"What's he doing, working there?"

"Don't you know George is at Holy Cross College? He was received there as a junior some eight months ago; he has yet four years more to serve before he'll be priested."

"What!" returned Scott, "priested!" The worth young gentleman looked at the girl at his side in astonishment; and she smiled a dimpled smile, as an engaged young lady should. The thought of celibacy of the Priesthood evidently crossed his mind and he wondered how men, presumably sane, took such vows.

"What do you think of that dear? George Hodlin, who used to work at our office is training for the Priesthood."

"Oh, my, is that so? He was such a nice fellow," she replied.

After George had served his time as a junior at Holy Cross, taking high honours in Latin and German, the Father Superior wrote the Vicar Apostolic in Jamaica telling him of the success of the young Jamaican and added that if he had many more young men like George Hodlin in the Island, there was room for them in Worcester. George, he said, gave promise to be a true and faithful servant of the Master, and a credit to Holy Mother Church.

* * * *

MANY YEARS AFTER, HERR OTTO Tiez took his wife and eldest boy with him to America on a business trip. One fine morning they boarded a train at Jersey City, on a visit to a friend in Philadelphia. A few stations were passed, and at New Brunswick, a medium height handsome young priest, (recently arrived from Boston to assist at a newly-established mission), got in. Marguerite looked up; their eyes met, and she recognised the Reverend Father George Hodlin. A visible shudder ran over her; the young priest brow contracted for a moment; he took his seat, opened his breviary, and began reading.

Young Master Otto was getting tired of the journey, and had set out to make the acquaintance of his fellow passengers. He had met with indifferent success so far from the old fogies, until he commenced an examination of the priest's cassock and girdle, preparatory to trying a conversation with him. Father Hodlin took his eyes off his book and smiled at the little fellow: Marguerite saw that smile, and saw too that it had lost none of its sweetness!

Soon little Otto was deep in conversation. "Yes," said the priest, "You must be a good boy, and love mother and father."

"And I love *you* too," he replied with a nod, and put his hands on the priest's clean-shaven face.

"Otto," called out his mother, "Come here."

But Otto did not hear; he was too busy questioning his newfound acquaintance. His father repeated the call.

"Your father is calling you, my dear," said Father Hodlin. The child look the priest in his face, put an arm around his neck and kissed him. "I'll soon come back to you, hear!" he said, running up to his father.

But Otto's father prevented him going back, and the little fellow sobbed himself to sleep in his mother's arms.

The priest resumed his reading.

FINIS

ONE BROWN GIRL AND ¼

The "Unusual" Preface

It is unusual to write a preface to a Novel. I admit it. But the unusual is sometimes the necessary, and, then, to avoid it because it is unusual is as odd and irrational, really, as to hob-nob with it on the streets of the daily commonplace. There are a few things of which it is right and proper to remind the reader as one pushes out a venture such as this to traverse the seas of local literature. Thus comes this preface.

In the face of much kind advice to the contrary, appreciated though not followed, the writer has deliberately chosen to publish this story here, and to seek a Jamaican audience rather than an audience abroad. The M.S. has not, so far, been submitted to any publisher outside Jamaica. There are two reasons for this. One is that the chief ambition of the present writer in matters literary is to produce among his fellow Jamaicans, that which Jamaicans will care to read, and may find some small reason for taking pride in as the work of a Son of the Island.

If this ambition is a reprehensible one, I still plead guilty to it, for I am guilty.

The second reason for local publication is that, to fit a local story for publication abroad, as experience teaches one, there must be sacrificed much in local colour, detail and dialect that seems to the unhampered judgement needed to render the picture as conceived by the writer a faithful one.

I clearly understand, of course, that the fullest possible success here, cannot give the reward in money that would accompany even moderate success abroad. I am not so unreasonable as to expect this. But I do expect that, if I have produced something that merits success, Jamaicans can and will support it sufficiently to save its author from loss. If, for once I may confess it, the desire to make as much money as possible has long since lost for me even the small degree of attractiveness it once had. That my labour should return me a decent living wage, allowing enough for my essential needs and permitting me, when occasion calls, to do something for a fellow-being in need; that is what I desire.

The world's tide of eager money-seekers goes past my door, and I hear the sound thereof, and, knowing full well whence these come and whither they go, I am content to remain under my own vine and fig tree and let the tide sweep on. I desire to get from this Novel a reasonable return in money, but to increase the chance of swelling this, I have not thought it well to sacrifice conditions which seem to me to allow best of the working out of the idea from which this story and other stories spring. I say "other stories," for, if the public of Jamaica co-operate by the purchase of this volume, there are other stories to follow along the same channel of publication.

Now I would make it very clear that I ask no one, on the sentimental grounds of patronising a local writer, or supporting local literature, *to pay a shilling for what he or she does not want;* but this I do ask, as the minimum of fairplay to this or to any local independent publication, whether by myself or by another, that those who want to read the book, and that those who read it and like it, buy it.

I emphasize this the more readily because it is of vital concern to all local writers. Only by this minimum of fairplay can there ever be the slightest chance of fostering the growth of an Island literature. All the fine talk in the world, and all the nice expressions of enthusiasm and regard, will avail little, if the enthusiasts do not buy the local publication that they declare so well deserves support.

It costs not a little in money to produce a volume here; at best, one cannot expect a very large sale; few local writers, (and I am not among the few) have leisure for literary work, apart from the bread and butter routine. Such a story as this, therefore, has to be written as occasion serves, in fragments of time rescued from that somewhat trying routine. The writer has had to do the exacting work of passing these pages through the Press without any relaxation of attention to the daily labour for a living wage.

He is only too conscious, that, thus pressed and elbowed, shadowed also by ill-health, he has worked at a disadvantage, and perhaps the kindly reader, bearing this in mind, will treat him, not as that cold abstraction, "an author," but as an erring man and a brother.

It is one thing to write in the golden leisure of a writer who can choose time and place; there the pleasure is well-nigh unalloyed, to the author, whatever it may be to the reader; but it is quite another thing to have to break away from a happy flow of inspiration, to take up the day's routine, or, at the nod of Circumstance, while brain and body are alike drooping with the burden of labour, to sit down and continue, as one best can, the interrupted thread of description or narrative—to be, in fact, the servant of Opportunity instead of the Master, entering at the wide-flung doors.

Without intruding these and other trials to any painful extent on the patience and good nature of the public, it is but fair, not only to the present writer, but to all others who have trod this road before him, or who may follow in his footsteps, to recall the facts. It is so easy to judge and condemn the local writer without pausing to realize the peculiar difficulties that lie in his path.

I have referred to short-comings, and I assure you, gentle reader, that no one realizes more deeply than I do that such there are in these pages; no one will welcome more than will I criticism which shows it has stood for a little in the presence of the difficulties to which I refer above, and has taken stock of them, ere making keen the sword of condemnation or disparagement.

A few words are due to the reading public concerning the story as it stands. It is complete in itself as here printed, but it is also the second part of "The Story of Noel." The first part appeared in 1904, as No. I of THE ALL JAMAICA LIBRARY under the title: "BECKA'S BACKRA BABY." Readers of this story will find it interesting to look through that narrative, though I regret not to be able to say where copies can now be obtained.

In producing "ONE BROWN GIRL AND——" I have been guided by the desire to give the public something that, in price, is well within the reach of almost all. The story contains some ninety-thousand or one hundred thousand words, that is, it is the length of a tolerably long, novel. It is priced at *one shilling per copy*. A smaller edition, on better paper, has been prepared at two shillings per copy; and there is a very small edition at *five shillings*. In this last the number is limited to less than half a hundred.

It would argue ingratitude on my part did I not take this opportunity of expressing appreciation of the very kind manner in which "BECKA'S BACKRA BABY" was received by the public generally, by the Press and by local writers of distinction.

While thanking critics generally, I wish specifically to acknowledge my indebtedness to "The Gleaner" for an appreciative notice; to "The Jamaica Telegraph?" then under the editorship of Mr. R. C. Guy, for pointing out a rather silly remark in reference to Kingston. (This was amended in the second edition). The, now defunct, "Leader," edited by Mr. W. P. Livingstone, also, in the course of a sympathetic and, as I thought, particularly careful notice, very reasonably took exception to certain vagaries in the use of capital letters into which I had strayed unconsciously imitating a style in modern authorship, sometimes technically known as the "Eastern."

I may be allowed to do him the justice of saying that Mr. Livingstone himself, as Editor of the "Gleaner," has the grateful rememberance of many local writers for the sympathy that he showed and the interest he took in their literary efforts.

The kindly commendation of the talented L.A.K. will also remain a pleasant memory, along with similar expressions from Mr. Noel deMontagnac and Madame deMontagnac. In mentioning these individually I must not be thought to forget other kindly and appreciative notices, especially would I now recall the attention paid to the little story by the Trinidad Press.

In dismissing the story of "Becka" I here mention, since in such ventures it is but courtesy to the public to give the fullest possible details, that the first edition, consisting of one thousand copies, sold out completely, leaving so marked a demand for more that the Publishers issued another edition of the same number, and subsequently a third of five hundred. The second edition was pretty well sold out. The third was entirely consumed in the fire that followed the earthquake of 1907.

As regards the present story, I do not wish to even appear to stand between it and the reader's opinion, but there are certain misunderstandings that pursue publications that see the light in small communities. I particularly ask that "One Brown Girl And——." should not be read with any idea that individuals have been selected for representation in its pages. It does not fall within the purpose of the writer to reveal how his work is done; of course I have gone to life for my materials; but if the story is read with the idea that I have deliberately sketched any member of the community in its pages there will be a grave departure from what is really the case, and a distinct offence will be committed against fairplay.

While studying human nature in its local variations, it has been my earnest aim throughout to avoid, on the one hand, anything approaching the above, and on the other the making of easy generalisations concerning sections of the communiry. They will be nearest the truth who regard the Story as based on life, as to the particular individuals created for the purpose of this narrative; but as not at all attempting to hold up the mirror to any living personage, nor yet to imply that any failings and faults betrayed in the characters introduced are necessarily inferred against his or he class. I regard it as a distinct literary offence to so portray individual citizens in such publications as to cause pain.

One word more as to the publishers of this volume, The Jamaica

Times Printery. It should be noted that the work is one which is probably the longest thing of its kind ever attempted in Jamaica. The Printery deserves praise for its courage in attempting it and for carrying it to completion. When the reader notes faults in the execution, he should remind himself of the difficulties encountered and overcome.

Tom Redcam.
14 Penrith Road,
Kingston, Jamaica
26. 6. 09

LIBERTA PASSLEY AND SOME OF HER WAYS AND MEANINGS. OLD
PETER AS OWNED BY LIBERTA—HIS REBELLIOUS HAIR AND
CLOTHES—WHAT LIBERTA WROTE ON HER TABLETS—THE
ARITHMETIC OF HUMANITY—MRS. CARITON'S UNDERSTANDING
OF IT.—WHENCE LIBERTA'S NAME CAME—LIBERTA NO. I—THE
DOCTOR'S DICTUM—"THE PRINCESS" AND WAITING TIME—"HELL
IN A HOUSE"—HOW AUNT HENRIETTA'S "KINGDOM" FELL.

I?" said Liberta Passley, "am the most unhappy woman in Kingston."
She was not speaking aloud, but was silently building up with
unspoken words a tabernacle for her thoughts. She considered now the
very positive assertion in which she had housed this thought, went again
through its very brief and emphatic terms, and then deliberately added
the further words: "and in Jamaica." Thus she pushed a statement, already
extreme, towards the precipice edge of the extravagant; but to Liberta
herself the statement was one of simple level fact; it was in no wise extreme.

Kingston has some seventy-thousand inhabitants; in this goodly
Island of Jamaica there are some seven hundred thousand human beings.
The Registrar-General will convince the enquirer that, in this grand Army
Corps of Humanity, the women considerably out-number the men.
Liberta was quite aware of this and of other facts germane thereto.
She did not belong to the idle-minded of her sex, whose simpers flap
before vacancy as flimsy curtains wave through windows, behind which
are rooms empty of all furniture.

Liberta was all but twenty-five years of age, and at that age in the
Tropics a woman has at her command all the mental and moral resources
she is destined to know at thirty-two, or forty-two either, for the matter of
that. Liberta had in fact been a woman, with a woman's powers of insight
and reflection, for many a year, before the evening on which we begin
to follow her thoughts. Her powers of mind were distinctive and strong;
and of those powers she made full use. Her conclusions, therefore, on any
given subject were not the idle vapourings of a silly girl whose proof of
innocence is still her flawless ignorance, and whose assertions rush with
the blind boldness of cavalry riding hard on a doom they fail to foresee.

Forty thousand women, more or less, were alive that evening in
Kingston: four hundred thousand women, more or less, were alive in all

Jamaica. This Liberta knew. She added to this very accurate knowledge of how life was just then going with not a few of her three hundred ninety-nine thousand, nine hundred ninety-nine sisters. Yet, I repeat, the assertion of her own unhappiness lay in a sincerity deeper than the surface splash or dash of affectation, or the rippling rush of mere irritation. What she said rose from what she felt; and her feeling drew its waters from a deep source, her thoughts welling there, a clear but bitter stream. To her this unique unhappiness of hers was as much a fact as was the white light of the electric bulb glowing then above her head, and etching the shadow of her profile like a black stain on the floor.

Liberta knew Kingston, a city, which like every other city has its palaces of pain, and the residents that suffering has made equals; suffering that finding its way through the flesh and blood, through the nerve and brain common to humanity, makes us pitiful courtiers, all, in the courts of the King whose shadow is Fear. Here misery lies open to the light of day and to the gaze of happier men; there is the misery that burrows to be out of sight; or that pitifully erects its slight fences, its paltry screens, its thin, weak walls, to fend off the glance that the world flings, casually curious, and cruel, not of intent but because, full-bellied and comfortable, it must use its eyes on all within their range as it passes by, well content; even on those meek subjects of the Things That Be, who, since it was clearly ordained before all worlds that they should suffer, ask only that they may be allowed to suffer unobserved and unpitied, and ask the impossible. Calmly and in its positive style, the World takes it for granted that the dislike to having one's joys and sorrows overlooked, lives only in the rich; and it is in vain that the fact stares it in the face that the poor also yearn for seclusion. Woe to the sensitive poor; theirs is a fate, cruel as that of unfenced, oft-trodden commons lying between towns that traffic much, the one with the other. There Mother Earth's kindly impulse to send up her yellow butter-cups and purple vervain is beaten back forever, with crushed bud and mangled leaf dinted into her brown and mother bosom. Few indeed the blades of living green that survive there; fewer still the flowers that blow.

Liberta Passley had a brain strong enough to deny her refuge in those fastnesses that receive and protect the shrieking sisters who cannot bear to know. She was one of the women who must know; and had there come to her now one stout-hearted enough to bid her stand and declare herself, and with skill equal to his courage, she in reply could have painted pictures, vivid and accurate, of that which women of that island and of that city were just then enduring, where in the rear ranks of the great columns of Humanity, the Cossacks of Misfortune harry the lagging and scourge the footsore stragglers. She knew because she had seen.

Round the left corner of the great house that was her home, three blocks away, in a lane, in a dingy house lay a victim whom Death drew to him with the grapnels of slowly strengthening disease. Liberta knew that sufferer, and could have gone direct to her side in less than five minutes. In about the same time, along another street, she could have entered a high, dully bare house on which in driving clouds by day, and by night, in almost impalpable powder, the City dust fell unceasingly. There lived, in this house, a woman who, before the steady pressure of Poverty, was falling back; step by step, to the brink of the precipice of Despair; and this woman was so bitterly intent on the struggle with her enemy, on the daily endeavour to provide enough food for three to eat, that, as she gave ground, inch by inch, she failed to notice how beside her one whom she loved more than life itself was being betrayed to irretrievable shame: by beauty, that gift of the gods so dangerous to the poor. In the war-shaken States of East Europe the more beautiful of the girls are protected from the lust of the Turkish soldiers by being branded on the face with the sign of the cross. It destroys their loveliness. Wherever the poor man's daughter is a beauty, some such protection is needed in a greater or less degree.

Liberta could have conjured up other pictures as sad and as true. She knew where to find the woman who, reared amid things vile, hideous and sordid, had had flung up within her, mysteriously, a soul pure and aspiring, which pushed upward seeking spiritual light with an impulse like that which drives the tender green of the young corn through the dark earth. This woman could not, for lack of knowledge, conceive definitely the things that were better than the moral murk and morass that lay around her; yet she earnestly sighed for things pure, sweet and true. In vain, maimed, dwarfed, distorted, the impulse, crushed back on itself, availed only to support the life of negation and repression. The things that were not to be done she avoided, the things that she would have done she could not reach; the soul starved, virtuous but anæmic. Liberta knew that woman.

Face to face she had met other such women, women of unhappiness and suffering; and over the blood-marked trail of many another whom she had never seen personally, she had often paused. She knew the sort of burrow to which the blood trail led, and how the wounded animal cowered there in its pain and shame.

Yet, knowing all this, Liberta compared herself with them all, these pain-harried creatures, with their pathetic eyes, and trembling hands, and said, "I am more unhappy than any." And she was sincere to her heart's core when she shaped that extreme, positive and intensive assertion. For, reflect, sincerity depends, not on facts, but on our interpretation of facts. Those who do not realize this are ready to hurl the epithet "hypocrite" like a javelin; those who know the truth better, seldom if ever use that term. They stand like a man who has reached the summit and is silent, because he sees what is not yet visible to the noisy folk who are still climbing the slope of the hill.

Liberta's was the emotional standpoint, from that her statement did the truth no wrong. She said that she was the most unhappy woman in Jamaica, and she felt that to be as true as that she was Liberta Passley. After all though we may by analysis demonstrate that there exist for our neighbour all the elements of happiness; and may thereon argue and assure him or her, that he or she must be, and therefore is, happy; yet still the thing itself, this happiness, is as elusive as the principle of life; which a few bold men have manfully attempted to define; which many silly men talk noisily about; but which escapes forever the surgeon's scalpel and the chemist's crucible.

Emotional, I have termed Liberta, and I am aware that you will begin on this to think of her as a weakling. It is a truism that emotionalism is weakness; but in the fair proportion of cases truisms are simply assertions with swollen reputations. Sometimes a truism is as untrue as is a fact. A truism has indeed embedded in it a vein of truth. It contains metal as does the quartz block; but a truism is no more truth than quartz is metal. As regards emotionalism and strength, there is a rigid strength that can never be made plastic; it can only be broken to pieces; and there is a plastic strength that can stiffen into rigidity and endurance, and soften again into pliability. This I know, you will with difficulty find the West Indian who is not emotional; but, if you understand where and how to look, you will easily find West Indians whose strength will give a good account of itself in the stress and strain of the years and in the hour of battle. Ultimately you will, I think, agree with me that Liberta Passley was not a weakling though she was emotional.

The faculty to decide rapidly and definitely and on that decision to act promptly and piercingly; the will and power to endure; the capacity for self-restraint; these are, severally and collectively, evidences of strength and not of weakness. If as we proceed we find them in Liberta, we must acknowledge that she was a strong character not a weak one. To be intensely emotional and yet to be resolute and enduring is one of those wonderful things of which the West Indian temperament is capable. Here stands a finger-post to help you to understand and interpret that character; or to send you far on a wrong road.

But we descend from these heights, and once again alight on Liberta's hard saying. If indeed happiness is but a matter of the presence of this thing and of that thing, then this girl seemed unquestionably happy. In moments the most morose and mean, when most sullen and most suspicious, the world, turning its eye on Liberta, could not but hold that here stood a pleasant sight. Graceful, well-framed and finely featured; lithe, erect, and with a poise of manner completely at her command; in turn charming, impressive and tender, it would truly have been difficult to find anything to complain of in a person so elegant, and in a face that showed intelligence so little shadowed by ill-nature.

Her life, watched steadily from without and day by day with the closest scrutiny, gave little that could reasonably be taken to imply unhappiness. Her home was a mansion, with a mansion's spacious rooms. Built of white stone, solidly and well, and not with dingy brick and in modern hideousness, slightness and economy, the house, large and lofty, stood in its wide yard. In front a fountain flung up tinkling jets of water amid the green of ferns, mosses and broad-leafed calladiums. The centre of everything, glowing like a core of many coloured jewels, the roses took their place. Valiant-hearted and distinguished, these were the famous folk of the garden. At respectful distances stood the lesser flowers. A great and high screen of broad-leafed creepers, growing thick and dense, repelled the dust that rose from the street and in some small degree mastered and muffled the street noises. Waved aside from all this, to the left, many steps in the rear came the whole range of courtyard, with surrounding stables, kitchens, servants' quarters and all the manifold outrooms of a well-equipped mansion. All were built as to the order of one who had not to cramp and save, to eke out means or to coddle space; and all were kept in that solid, clean and thorough state of repair that bespoke an ownership which possessed many things besides this house and this yard. Among those many possessions was money. Old Peter Passley owned the house and the money; and, with very little exaggeration,

Liberta might have been said to own Old Peter Passley who was her father. Now money, as we ought all of us to know by this time, is held to be synonymous with happiness. Yet Liberta who had so much of it at her command, declared that she was the most unhappy girl in Jamaica and was perfectly sincere in the assertion.

If, rendered curious by so baffling a fact, we passed from the outside to the inside of the house and continued our inventory of her possessions there, we could but find our first impression confirmed. For, through these fine rooms, Comfort had passed with light but firm footstep, her cheery hand-maidens following in her train, and fitting all thing there for human life, unhampered by the petty restrictions, imposed by a slender purse. And after her, Luxury, taking counsel with Common Sense, had trodden, adding to comfort grace and to grace beauty. The taste that had adorned this mansion, if here and there slightly exuberant, was at no point seriously indictable as ostentatious, that is as vulgar, for the essence of vulgarity is ostentation.

Still standing before Liberta's assertion as before a dead wall right across our way, puzzled, we ask, must not all this mean happiness to one capable of appreciating it? Liberta appreciated it all thoroughly; amid it all she was a matchless hostess; but still Liberta insisted that she was unhappy. She was sincere, not merely petulant. Now of course, one can be very sincere and very wrong, for we can be very sincere in stating and believing as fact what is not fact, and most of the statements which with the World's delightful fluency, are generally termed "lies," belong to this class. For to believe that what you say is true is so, does not make it so; and, amid the complexities of modern life, one has to learn how to tell the truth, as well as to preserve the wish to tell it. But in Liberta Passley's case, the statement was both sincere and true. She *was* an unhappy girl. As to the degree of her unhappiness, let us not discuss what is so much a matter of controversy. Kind is fact; degree is theory.

We have our fact; Liberta was unhappy, and now, failing to find reason therefor in the surroundings just passed in review, we, prying seekers after explanations, if not after truth, might be inclined to cry "Eureka," when for the first time and on the sudden we came face to face with old Peter standing beside his daughter. The striking difference here was surely a hostile difference. There is neither sense nor manners in despising the dray horse, but it is only too patent a fact that the racer, all mettle, training and spirit, will chafe if put to plough in a yoke with the honest beast.

To many an observer the one link between this sire and daughter was the fact that they were both brown and, wealthy. Then came the divergences and they were prodigious. No insult meant to the dray horse; but he is a thing very different from the racer. No insult meant to the dray horse, but small wonder if the racer frets and fumes and eats its heart out, compelled if it be to time its steps to those of plodding patience. The divergences, I repeat were prodigious between this father and daughter. Liberta suggested education, refinement, culture. Of these valuable things, Old Peter's form and face gave few hints; so few that even the many who delivered panegyrics on him in after dinner speeches intended to precipitate loans, or in newspaper articles intended to repay them, always looked nervously round when they lauded his "love of the learned arts," to see if any unregenerate wretch was allowing a smile to soak through. Kindness of heart was suggested by both faces; but the sire had none of the daughter's beauty of face and form. Placed beside her smooth youth, his rough old physiognomy showed oddly. It was like a hurricane-shaken hill over-looking a pasture beautiful with the growth of young grass. His hair was a rebellious, untidy lot of stiff, obstreperous curls, which had little ambition to grow longer, and none at all to grow straight. Its imperfect submission to the brush and comb was ever and anon being disturbed by Peter's habit of rubbing it about north, south, east, and west, and then, round and round, with his big, broad hand. Liberta had inherited from her mother splendid long, black, Indian-like hair and she managed it to perfection.

On the young face there showed not a line or a furrow. For her the campaign of life was just begun; but Time had attacked the old man ferociously and persistently, and had pushed the attack home again and again. Though the sturdy soul had fought a good fight and still stood stoutly at bay, body and brain carried the scars of battle, scars honourable but not beautiful. The old face was deeply seamed and roughly carved. The foot-marks of many sorrows showed there. Anxiety had pushed its silent but deadly sapping round mouth and eye and whence, in bye-gone years the final assaults had flung themselves home, the wrinkles and furrows still showed, like grass-grown trenches on an old battle-field. Dead spaces on the skin surface spoke of the relaxation of nerve power following on the dissolution of long cherished hopes, of defeated faith. To win what he now possessed, Peter Passley had endured much. And if at the last he owned that for which men envied him, penns, stores, mansions, wide commercial influence and a daughter like Liberta, he had lost that which men always lose by unflinching diligence in businesss; and he had lost other things less easily forgotten. A wife, dearly loved and faithful, the long time companion of a varied career, two sons and a daughter, he had seen them all go down into the grave. The old face at the end of it all showed gnarled, bruised and battered, like the strong trunk of a sound-hearted tree, that has lived through a thousand raging storms, unconquered but not unscathed.

Shrewdness, honesty, sagacity and kindness are very good things in their way; but we are assured are not good enough to compensate for the lack of grammar and drawing room manners; and had Old Peter Passley possessed only £500 instead of, as folks said he did, close on £500,000, he would very speedily have been made to know his place among the superior people, as a common and uneducated old brown man. As it was his deficiencies were termed peculiarities, his lapses from grammar were treated as quotations, and his company was sought after with zeal.

Of Peter's face, Captain Burns, whose acquaintance we will be making in the course of this story, and who was not distinguished for ability to say good things, once said this good thing: "His face suggests good kindly Mother Earth; brown, commonplace, not lovely, but full of life-making secrets and the wonders of fertility."

"Full of money," grunted his companion, a fish that rose to no fancy flies.

"Damn the money," Burns replied. "The old man is a marvel. I stick to my simile." Thus Burns, from the summit of one of his better moments, and in the after-glow of a financial service of an important kind done him by Peter.

But to our fancy Liberta's unhappiness has changed to an elusive form fleeing from us down distant avenues. Our bloodhounds are on its track. Let us pursue our contrasts. Peter, rich enough to wear just what clothes he liked and generally preferring homely stuffs, went about the despair of his tailors; because, on the first feeling of restriction and discomfort, he sent for number Two, to give him ease by altering the work of Number One. Hence no tailor lived who dared use is patronage for advertising purposes. Identification with the hang of this man's clothes would have been enough to ruin any decent tradesman's reputation. The saving grace with Peter was that he always paid cash down and, though he never gave fancy prices, he was a generous employer. Here, as in every other department, he was no higgler, no cutter down of the workman's reward, a fact that, taken in conjunction with the fact that he had become enormously rich, must surely arrest the attention of the reader who happens to know anything about the gentle art of money-making.

But we must choose another opening to discuss the character of Peter, if discuss it we will, for the present it is of his clothes that we speak. Sloven, callous to all bagginess in his raiment, no matter where bagginess came, or how, in coat or trousers, jacket or vest, a hatter of dress suits and stiff shirts, careless of how the leather covered his large feet, so stood Peter Passley, and beside him Liberta, his daughter.

She had been educated in England, and the people there who taught her many things well, had taught her also how to dress well; dress well she did, always. She had not been taught simply the pretty, paltry tricks that are held for a day or a year to be the exemplification of grace and beauty; but she had been taken to the principles of adornment that explain, justify or condemn the fashions of the day. Liberta knew how to stand aside from the prevailing fashion which was also atrocious, and to do so with sufficient tact and adaptation of some of its features to escape ostentatious distinctiveness. But she had learnt, too, and this she never forgot, that each woman is the embodiment of an individuality, and must dress accordingly, and not by the fact that women entirely different are dressing in a particular way.

Men do not deny that Kitchener is a tall man, even when they challenge his generalship; they do not say that Buller was not brave, whatever their opinion of Vaal Krantz. So those who, like Aunt Henrietta, hated Liberta and said so without prevarication or subterfuge; those who hated her but masked their hatred with care and behind the smile and the kiss which women give women whom they fear or suspect; and those who, with or without reservation, admired her, were all at one in agreeing that Liberta dressed to perfection.

"She has the money," said one. "The instinct," said another. "I don't know how she does it," confessed a third, "but she does it well, always. She never has an off time with dress." Which last if not literally true conveyed what the speaker meant to say sufficiently well for her purpose.

It was quite a mistake to conclude that Old Peter's superfluity of naughtiness in dress tried his daughter's nerves in the slightest degree; or that he distressed her by his deficiencies in grammar.

Again, it was quite a mistake to imagine that, Liberta with her refinements of manner and perception, felt stress or strain in the near and intimate relationship with an old man who, as he himself was wont to declare, was not "educated worth a banana." Liberta felt nothing of the sort, and they wasted their time and sympathy, all that tribe of busy bodies, who circulated their pity for the "poor, dear girl, with that father of hers."

Not a single tremor of unhappiness impinged on Liberta's life from the direction of her father, save that which is inseparable from all love, the recurring whisper that warns us of the final parting. So far as her old Dad went, she would have stood up with him before any company in the world, from Royalty round to a street-preaching crowd, content to be there and to have him with her, speaking in his clumsy, ungrammatical way, and setting forth his thoughts slowly and in his curiously commonplace and unemphasized sentences; or silent, the old brown face roughened and wrinkled, giving little token of the strength of will that had from that citadel mastered so many hard circumstances.

This man had begun life as an illiterate boy, in a small out-of-the-way Trelawny village. Now he had wealth and the fame which is worthy fame, of owing no man and of cheating no man; of being kind, but no fool; resolute, but not hard; wise, but not crafty. Little stood in his face to indicate the riches and the true beauty which his life had put forth, just as between harvest and harvest, the brown bosom of Mother Earth, to which Burns compared this man, shows small proof that she can send violets up and fields of tasselled corn.

The life of Peter would, I think, by itself reward us, were we able to tarry to consider it in detail. But we are about merely to skirt it as we proceed to our destinations in other directions.

This was not a man, to travel close beside through life, could render a girl like Liberta unhappy. Had there been no blood link, she would still have seen that in him which would have made her disregard entirely all that which, in the eyes of the People of the Drawing Room, seemed so huge and monstrous. As his daughter, her content with him was so perfect that it was seldom self-conscious.

Not even to herself, still less to other folks, did she find herself called on to defend her father or to offer excuses for him. Only one of the People of the Drawing Room, Mrs. Richard Cariton, had something to remember as a personal experience under this head. Mrs. Richard, ascending from nonentity in England to be wife in Jamaica of the head of an Official Department, was thus made familiar with King's House balls and Society in all its Colonial glory, and in her empty little head

THOMAS MACDERMOT

was a memory of something like a collision with Liberta on this subject, of her father.

In the gushing coo of talk to "her dear Liberta," Mrs. Richard Cariton one day touched on Peter in a new strain:

"Your dear, good, honest, well-meaning father," she said, "sometimes I cannot help pitying you, just a little, tiny bit."

"Why?" Liberta said nothing but the one word.

Incontinently, Mrs. Richard Cariton tumbled down from the mound of false sentimentality which she had ascended to launch her remark. She began now to pile up words incoherently and unconnectedly, to shield her wretched little pate from impending danger; for she thought that Liberta was about to say something very dreadful indeed, and that even the best excuses she could put up would fare as hadly as a summer sunshade gets along in an October downpour. Mrs. Cariton always had felt that some day "her dear Liberta" would say terrible things to her, and now she felt the shadow of trouble fall round her as if the gigantic head of the sphinx had suddenly been thrust between herself and the sun.

Mrs. Cariton was, like several other persons, afraid of Liberta, for the reason that, beneath a manner of smooth and easy grace, and words that only occasionally pointed away from those much trodden roadways that the People consider safe, this girl seldom failed to leave on her intimates the impression that her conformity and style were outward only, and that there was an inner and hidden Liberta Passley, a soul of storm, a flash reserved for emergency, keen as the lightning and swift as death. The Revolutionary was in that soul, and the People felt it, as the mouse feels the presence of a cat not yet in sight.

Had Liberta really lived shut up with the daily mortification on account of her father's shortcomings for which Mrs. Cariton and her friends gave her credit, adding the rider that "she hid it well," had this been true, I say, then indeed this poor Mrs. Cariton, by that unlucky speech, might have called fire from heaven to destroy her; since a copper wire, the thinnest of things and insignificant, will aid a cloud laden with clouds of doom to discharge a bolt of destruction earthward. But as we have said, Liberta was credited with suffering which she did not endure. She knew now what this remark pointed to, and realised intellectually what Mrs. Cariton, and others more sensible or less sensible than Mrs. Cariton, bore about in their minds concerning her and her father, but not in the slightest degree did it touch her emotionally. Had anyone indeed made such a remark to her with the intention of being nasty, she would at once have transfixed the offender for the sake of his or her evil intention, being of that kind who meet war with war, and drive straight at the heart; but save that she would not permit it for decency's sake, the whole concatenation of Mrs. Caritons and their planetary systems might have met and talked on this matter, according to their lights and in sincerity, till they all wearied, without stirring her to anger, to contempt, or even to a smile.

It was a case in which she was absolutely and entirely indifferent to the opinions of other people. And therein was a curious thing, for, being an emotional girl, the opinions of other people, although never allowed by her to drag her to the crucifixion of open mortification, undoubtedly pierced and wounded, as with minute pickles of venom, that inner and intense life, that soul of unrest, that was the very Liberta.

If Liberta now selected a remark or two suitable to scourge the silliness before her, she did it for the woman's own sake, to teach her well that she must not again intrude where her stupidity ceased to be tolerable, and might bring upon her empty pate the punishment which such a head was ill able to endure, and which Liberta thought it a waste of her time to inflict on an object so insignificant. It was not at all because Liberta felt in the least vindictive. She had the desire to save herself in the future from similar intrusions. We nail the mongoose, the would-be stealers of eggs and chickens, widespread on the boards, and other mongoose take the hint and leave our nests alone, for those of other people.

"Would you expect me," Liberta now said to Mrs. Cariton, "would you like me to tell you what I think of your husband, my opinion about your husband?"

"No, dear Liberta," the reply was tremulous. Why, all social Kingston could at once have said.

"Or about his young friend—"

"No, Liberta, Oh, no," it was an interruption this time, and it came hurriedly, to carry off the oncoming name from the speaker's calm lips; for all the world like a hand suddenly snatching and bearing away, unseen, the ball that a player is poising to throw.

"Well," said Liberta, "I will not. Why should people be worried with opinions about which they are not even curious?"

"Thank you, dear Liberta, thank you, thank you very much." Mrs. Cariton prayed, far more sincerely than she ever prayed in church, that this ended the matter.

Liberta let a minute or two pass in silence, then just as Mrs. Cariton was weakly feeling round for a subject far enough from the point of danger, the girl reached over and drew her tablets to her.

Liberta wrote on her tablets with great deliberation, and Mrs. Richard Cariton hung on the action with a strained anxiety that would have been comic to a third party.

This was what Liberta wrote down so very carefully.

2	1
6	8
2	7
9	4
20	20

She handed the tablets to Mrs. Cariton.

"Add those columns up."

Mrs. Cariton's brain was curdling round drops of fear of an unknown evil that kept trickling into her mind like drops of limejuice soaking into milk. She made the total nineteen.

"Add it again" said Liberta.

Mrs. Cariton made the total twenty-two.

"Try again."

"Twenty-one" said the lamentable arithmetician.

"It is twenty," said Liberta, "try again, take the columns one at a time." As if poor Mrs. Cariton had been trying to do anything else.

Mrs. Cariton on a third attempt, made the first column twenty.

"Now the second column, add that."

"It makes twenty too, Liberta."

"Yes."

"The totals are the same."

"Yes."

"Just the same."

"Just the same," repeated Mrs. Cariton, like a schoolgirl, trying to convey the idea that the words brought a new meaning into the discussion.

"There is not a single figure the same in the two columns," pursued Liberta, taking the tablets, leaning forward and pointing to the figures one by one. Mrs. Cariton, looking more than ever like a schoolgirl, followed the pointing pencil with ingratiating eagerness.

"See?" said Liberta presently.

"Yes, Liberta, I see."

"Every figure is different, and yet the—"

"Every figure is different," interrupted Mrs. Cariton, dutifully anxious to show that she was treading close behind Liberta.

"And yet the totals are the same."

"And yet the totals are the same," echoed Mrs. Cariton.

"Which things," said dear Liberta, recovering her tablets, and slowly erasing the figures, carefully, as if that and not what she was about to say was the chief business in hand, "which things are a parable. That is how I do my arithmetic in humanity."

"Yes Liberta," came the humble refrain while Mrs. Cariton, misled by the word "arithmetic," wandered dimly through vague ideas that "humanity" must be a kind of Vulgar Fractions or new Rule of Three, and racked her brain to remember if it came after or before Decimals.

"Two men," resumed Liberta, "may seem very different in detail, and yet be of the same value—the answer to each may be the same twenty. Eh?"

"Yes," said Mrs. Cariton doubtfully, not because she disagreed or doubted, but because she did not understand. Then "Yes," she said with suddenness and great decision, fearing lest Liberta should suspect dissent from her views, whatever they were, and be vexed.

"One man may have an Oxford education, eh? And the other none at all; and yet the one may be as good as the other, eh? You comprehend?"

Liberta was quite aware that she was not being understood there and then; but she considered it probable that enough of her meaning would ultimately glimmer its way into Mrs. Cariton's mind, or at any rate the little woman would certainly repeat what was now said, and someone would interpret its meaning for her. Liberta continued:

"But of course, do not think that the second column of my figures represents your husband, that is, if you think of the first as my father. I would not think of putting the Dad in comparison with any man you can think of in five minutes or in five years for the matter of that. You understand do you not?"

"Yes, Liberta. Oh, yes. I beg your pardon."

"Granted," returned Liberta, with the quiet, rapid unconcern that was often characteristic of her style of speech.

Mrs. Cariton resolved to think all this out very carefully. She felt it would be like sitting down to unravel a very tangled ball of thread. For the present it was enough for her to realise that her dear Liberta had very nearly unleashed against her terrible sayings. She believed and trembled and resolved not to let a worse thing come upon her. So from that day to her the subject of Liberta's father was taboo and taboo and again taboo. When in the circle she ornamented Old Peter was mentioned and the oil of pity for poor dear Liberta was sent round, Mrs. Cariton held her peace; so great over certain minds is the power of the uncomprehended. For, after all, Liberta, on an occasion when she might very well have said a good deal, had actually said very little; only poor Mrs. Cariton cannot to this day understand what the "Arithmetic of Humanity" meant, and she fears the unknown.

In those natures that are endued with the capacity for great patience there is also a capacity for deep and faithful love. Peter, who was phenomenally patient, was a noble lover. His life only had peace when it had a centre at which he could love and be loved. The blood link is a strong love link, and in any case Peter must have loved Liberta as his daughter. But there were details in his life-story that explained his exceptional devotion to her. This man, who, as we have heard, had built up his fortunes from very small beginnings, was quite a young man, when he married and but a little way ascended on the slope of toil. The marriage itself was a bit of a romance. A Jamaican slave and her daughter were sold to an American before Emancipation. They were taken to the States and thus, when in our Island their relatives and friends stood free, these two remained in bondage. It happened as it were by chance that Peter saw the girl and loved her. He spent almost all that he then owned in buying the freedom of the two, not of the girl alone, and brought them to Jamaica. When he stood up to be married he desired that his wife should be baptised and that a new name should be given to her.

The young Minister, fresh from College sprinklings of Latin, and enthusiastic in the sunny light of those morning years of freedom, gave to the graceful, timid girl before him, the great name of Liberta, and spoke fervently thereafter of the freedom wherewith Christ makes us free.

A quiet, slim, little brown girl, was this Liberta, with long Indian-like hair and that innate grace and sinuosity of figure that were afterwards to be the inheritance of her youngest child. True, faithful, and a help–

mate most useful she had proved to Peter as he breasted the rising road of effort, and as dear and necessary to him when they reached the rolling table-lands of Prosperity. In those days she was mistress in their mansion, if she but chose to command it, of more money than could have been directed by any other woman in Jamaica; but she was still the quiet, retiring, little body to whom in her more private moments adhered patches of habits which had belonged to the older and humbler life. She never quite lost the liking for tying her head with a bright coloured kerchief, though it was in the very recesses of her grand house, and when her only companion was her husband, or her most trusted and beloved relatives, that the old habit was allowed to reappear. From the indignant and scornful eyes of Aunt Henrietta it shrivelled out of existence, as a shy and delicate mountain flower fade and dies when plucked and exposed for few minutes in the lowland noons. The old-time "Sir" and "Ma'am" slipped a times into her speech, not because she had a servile soul, but because that had been her manner of speech when habit was forming in the plastic days of youth.

She bore Peter three daughters and on son, each and all fine children to look at; yet one after the other they all died in early childhood, all save the youngest, who was Liberta.

Concerning her, an old Scotch doctor, Peter's lifelong friend, gave them this hard saying; "If you have courage for it, take my word. Send her to England Send her early and keep her long. Then she will live and not die like the rest."

On the face of it the thing seemed monstrous and absurd, or next door to it. What had this pretty little daughter of the Tropics, filled with their sunny softness langour and dreamy lightness to gain from Mother England, rough nurse of strong souls. What but death could the harsh northern climate offer to the little alien maid. And yet, because in the West Indian of every colour and degree the personal element is so great an influence, the doctor being the friend of the father and mother, had his way. The two had grace to believe his true saying for it was true.

So one warm summer Liberta was handed over to Mother England, to grow and to be trained among her sturdy sons and strong-limbed, health-glowing daughters, and so to pass into young womanhood. When she returned to Jamaica, she was nineteen years old; so long had Peter's patience endured.

His friend, the doctor, did not witness the return, he was dead long ere that. The little mother, quietly waiting the passing of the years, day by day persistently presenting the pious prayer that she should be allowed to live on till Liberta came back, and with the bright eyes faith seeing in the distance of the years, shining there like a star in the night, day of the homecoming, the little mother, I say, had fallen also in the years of separation. She died three years before Liberta returned. Thus, ere Liberta came once more to her father's house Peter had been left alone.

Aunt Henrietta had come to him then, and he had learnt that even an empty home had its advantages.

Aunt Henrietta was Peter's sister-in-law; but she was fearfully unlike his wife. The one a small woman had been quiet, unaggressive, good-tempered and kind. The other was large, loud, self-assertive and quarrelsome, a feminine tyrant. If veins of kindness ran through her anger-scarred heart they were like streaks of metal in a country of earthquakes and active volcanoes. They were dangerous to quarry.

This stout, terrible woman had often been a visitor to Peter's house, to stay for months; but Peter had never in those days known what Henrietta really was, because, mild and peaceable as was his wife she stood like a Spartan against anything that threatened to disturb Peter's comfort, and Henrietta soon learnt that she must keep away from certain lines of conduct if she wished to continue to enjoy the Passley hospitality. She, therefore, reserved her talent for being disagreeable for exercise abroad, and gave Peter the benefit of her negative virtues.

But, as we say in Jamaica, "to come see me is one thing, to come live with me is another." Yet even if Peter had known what Henrietta was, could he have declined her services? She who came, as she herself said, "to fulfil a sacred trust, built on a promise to my poor dead sister." So she said, and there was none to contradict her.

So Peter, a man whose homely soul required to absorb love, and who needed absolutely that centre in his life that is called home, entered into an experience with Aunt Henrietta that shook even his deep sense and quiet patience. He had no counsellor on such matters, and no confidant. The man able to beat his way through all difficulties in the hard world of trade and business, and to be resolute and effective among men, was no match for the situation. He was no match for a woman.

"Good thing," he said to himself once or twice "that I have never held with drinking, or I might get to like it too much now, as a kind of ease up."

"The Old Man looks sick and discouraged," men said of him in those days. "Maybe he is breaking up. Maybe he has been hit in some money plunge, that took him beyond even his depth."

One hope glimmered on him through the years ahead. Liberta was coming back; she might deliver him. How he longed for her coming none realised; but long as he did, he would not shorten her stay in England by a single month. It had been planned that she should remain till she was nineteen, and remain she should, and did.

Shrewd always, Peter realised fully that there was much to make the trust he was reposing in Liberta an uncertain factor. To pit a girl of nineteen just out of school against a woman like Aunt Henrietta was to invite a contest as likely to end one way as the other. Then would Liberta even care to battle for her old Dad's peace of mind? From these doubts the old man took refuge in the simple memory that her name was that of his dead wife. Wife, son, daughters, they had all left him. They had all gone down into the grave. This daughter that the years were slowly and steadily bringing towards him could not he said, fail him; but if she did what then? A few more stumbling journeys in the gloom, the gloom that Time only made darker; and then goodnight to Peter.

Meantime Aunt Henrietta established herself in the Passley mansion, more and more firmly, and flourished exceedingly. The misery that a woman of her kind can inflict is tremendous, when she has to operate on a simple human heart like that of Peter's. Peter endured it all dully. In business he felt like a general operating from a base which was more uncomfortable and unsafe than the battle-field. For the rest he tersely described conditions to himself as "hell in a house." And so he waited, wondering more and more if Liberta could break this terrible yoke; if she would try to; and doubting somewhat.

But from the day on which, on shipboard, where he had gone to meet her beyond Port Royal, he took his girl into his arms, his soul had rest. He received a girl who had already learned her life's lesson. His wife was with him again, but it was his wife with a statelier, abler, firmer soul, behind the same absolute loyalty and love.

Aunt Henrietta, embraced Liberta, too, but her impressions were vastly different from those of Peter. I fear it was hate at first sight here. Still the homecoming passed off smoothly, and for a week or two things went on as usual in the Passley's house. Then Liberta, who had surveyed the ground, began the battle.

"I am ready to take over the housekeeping," she said, without preliminary or preparation of any kind that Aunt Henrietta had noticed. "As soon as you are ready to give it up, I am ready to start."

THOMAS MACDERMOT

"On that point, I think you had better consult your Papa, Liberta," was Aunt Henrietta's stiff reply.

"Very well," said Liberta.

At dinner Liberta consulted her Papa.

"Whatever you like, Liberta; whatever Liberta likes, Henrietta," was Peter's response, as he dodged Henrietta's indignant eye.

That night a servant of the Passley's said to his fellows:

"I wish to king dat dis Miss Henrietta mek haste bruk him neck, so finish. Woman so cross I nebber yet encounter wid. Woman so cross nebber yet make since dem mix up dough and bake de first cross cow." He had been a baker ere starting on his career as a butler. "If she could only but tek a short step on dat big stairs so pitchdown, she must dead; him neck mus' pop, him so big and fat."

"Watch dis young lady just cone from over water," said the Cook, older and sager. "Miss Henrietta kingdom going fall. Watch and pray, me brother."

The kingdom fell in this wise. There had been introduced into the house, as Liberta's own particular maid, a charmingly pretty little thing named Ada Pearl Smith. Aunt Henrietta, hating her on sight, took the liberty, and gave herself the pleasure, of trying to make Ada's life miserable.

"Obey me and leave Miss Henrietta alone," was Liberta's direction. Now it was in Ada to obey Liberta, but to leave Aunt Henrietta alone was beyond her ability. A person with a bad temper, accustomed to outbursts, is at the mercy of any cool-witted foe who chooses to apply the torture, and who is not too much in earnest about the matter Ada Smith was just suited to such mischief, and the misery that Aunt Henrietta had intended to impose on her enemy was pretty largely thrown back on her own hands. Ada was too adroit to give anything tangible on which Miss Henrietta could complain to Liberta, but scarcely for a single half-day did she leave the luckless lady alone. She drew her provocations across Aunt Henrietta's feelings as cleverly as the Cowitch Vine makes the passer-by pay for coming too near it. Only a touch, a venomous little dagger-prickle stuck in, the veriest splinter of poison, so minute, that it can hardly be discerned at all, but round it spreads inflammation, and it smarts and stings.

The crisis between Henrietta and Liberta was precipitated by two events. In one Ada was concerned. She had started very properly by bidding Aunt Henrietta ceremonious and apparently most respectful "Goodmornings." These were never replied to, and Ada ceased from good works. The furious Henrietta demanded an explanation of this insult.

"You never replied when I spoke to you, Ma'am," said Ada, reproachfully, "and I thought you did not wish me to speak to you."

"If I did not answer," thundered Aunt Henrietta, carefully avoiding, admitting, that she had not replied, "I did not hear you. Remember your manners in the future when you see me, that is what you have to do."

Ada resumed her ceremonious salutations making them even more ceremonious than they had been at first; but after a day or two, Aunt Henrietta ceased to respond by outward sign or sound. On this Ada again became silent, and was careful to emphasize her silence by staring full at the almost apoplectic face of Miss Henrietta as they passed one another. Down upon Ada then, like a panther on a fat sucking pig, came Aunt Henrietta demanding explanations.

"You did not reply, Miss Henrietta."

"Did I not tell you that you were to speak to me? That I so demanded and commanded. That I so wished it."

"But, Miss Henrietta," returned a perfectly calm and composed Ada, "I thought you had changed your mind, as you did not answer."

Simple words truly, but kindling a very great fire.

"That is a lie," shouted Aunt Henrietta. "A confounded lie, a beastly lie, an abominable lie, *a damn lie*."

"Please Miss Henrietta, I never tell lies, and I will thank you not to damn me."

"I'll teach you," cried the angry woman, losing control of herself. "I'll teach you, you dirty bundle of impertinence—" and she boxed Ada's ears once, twice and would have done so again had Ada not got out of her way. "I'll teach you," repeated Miss Henrietta who was too enraged to shape another sentence just then; but whether she meant she would teach Ada by the force of her blows to tell lies or to refrain from telling them she failed to make clear.

Now this boxing of servants' ears, or the striking of servants in any part of their corporal being is decidedly a dangerous pastime in the West Indies of today, where the rights enjoyed by British citizens are fully appreciated, the sufferer is as likely as not to return the gift with interest. A Colonial Governor in these latitudes, is said on one occasion to have kicked an offending butler for an act of stupidity. The butler, so runs the story, turned the key in the door and then with much zest kicked His Excellency round the room, after which he said: "If Your

Excellency does not tell, I won't." And he did not, till that Governor had moved on.

Sometimes a case of the sort is moved on to the Courts, being hailed as revenue-yielder, and proceedings become costly and annoying, to the other side. Ada was in fact surprised that Aunt Henrietta had dared to lift her hand against the sacred person of one of Her Majesty's lieges, and for a minute or two she was really wildly indignant; but she soon got over that, and set herself to make capital out of the incident in the direction where she was anxious to score. "Here," thought this sagacious girl, "is just what I wanted to take to Miss Liberta." She sank slowly to the ground, weeping copiously and holding her ear so desperately that Miss Henrietta was assailed by a horrible fear that the girl was seriously injured; for she well knew that her hand was no light weight. She was therefore really much panic-stricken when she foamed out:

"Go and tell your Miss Liberta then I am not afraid of a hundred Miss Libertas." With that she swept from the room.

Left alone, Ada Smith dried her tears, went across to the glass, examined her ear with much curiosity, and then without losing any more time sought Miss Liberta's presence, not forgetting to resume her piteous weeping as she entered there.

"Leave it to me," said Liberta, "you shan't be treated like that in this house," and Ada recognised that vengeance breathed through her words, quietly as they were spoken.

"She said she didn't care for a hundred like you Miss Liberta," she added to raise the vengeance a degree higher.

"Did she?" said Liberta. "Go and wash your ear with something cool."

This was the first incident. The second incident from which the final crisis sprang happened in this wise. Aunt Henrietta declined to have breakfast an hour earlier to suit Peter who had to go out early, he had in consequence to face breakfast away from home, a thing he detested.

Liberta went down to the kitchen, countermanded Aunt Henrietta's orders, and gave her own to a Cook only too pleased to receive them.

That evening Aunt and Niece met for the final duel. Liberta sought the occasion. Her *casus belli* was the boxing of Ada. Aunt Henrietta responded with the countermanding of her orders. Her denunciation flowed like a river into which several large and particularly muddy gulleys had emptied all their contents. Unfortunately for her she used this rhetorical flourish; "We must decide who is mistress here once and for all."

"We must," said Ada.

"You will come to no good," said Aunt Henrietta, in solemn digression, making so to speak a flank march and falling on the enemy from the side. "You and your Ada Smith and your friend in the kitchen." She paused to give her words full effect then added; "You are a disgrace to our family."

"We will not quarrel about that," said Liberta very quietly, for she was very angry. Aunt Henrietta, who in a situation like this understood nothing but a quarrel and a violent quarrel, too, burst into loud invective. She desired that all might hear her, upstairs and downstairs and in my lady's chamber. She meant that they should hear. Liberta rose, shut and locked the door. She meant they should not hear.

Losing in this way her opportunity of filling the house with clamour, and the echoing tale of her woes, Aunt Henrietta suddenly dropped her loud tirade and began to sob. Liberta, though her soul raged within her, made no interruption, at length the storm of tears and gurgling sobs abated somewhat. Then Liberta said:

"Crying generally does one in your state good. I am sure that you feel better now."

Aunt Henrietta heaved with a terrible sob, glared at Liberta, buried her head in a handkerchief, and bowed it as far as a fat neck and abnormally ample bosom would allow her to do it. She hoped that she was bringing home to Liberta the enormity of her wickedness in thus rending a human heart.

"When will you care to leave—today or tomorrow?" asked Liberta mildly, but very firmly.

Aunt Henrietta rose to her feet, she as nearly as possible sprang to her feet. Her look spoke of unplumbed depths of tragedy. She said with savage solemnity:

"Liberta, you are a wicked girl. What do you think your dead mother would say to you? What will your father say when I tell him, and I am going to tell him at once."

"What mamma would say," calmly replied Liberta, "if she takes any interest in such small things now, I do not know, and I don't remember her well enough to guess. I know what the Dad will say. Will you go to him at once?"

The challenge was too direct to be evaded, and poor Aunt Henrietta, who was far indeed from feeling sure of Peter, set out with embittered soul and the cry on her lips: "So I am to be turned out now like a dog into the street."

The flood of Henrietta's speech, thick and heavy with her woes, deluged Old Peter in a thrice. It buried him, so to speak, and swept round and over him, so that for a few seconds the old fellow felt as a pebble may be thought to feel that an angry mountain stream is rolling rapidly along after the rains. But presently he recovered his wits, and on the first opportunity, he struck in with his few words:

"I say what Liberta says. Same as Liberta says. You listen to my girl."

"But you don't know what it is all about. You don't know what she has said and done," gasped Aunt Henrietta, and then was smitten into silence by the man's black iniquity; for she had up to then been speaking at large, only, of Liberta's wickedness, of her disrespect for her elders, and her spite towards Aunt Henrietta especially. She had not opened her special case at all. Yet here was her court of appeal handing down a judgment on that special case.

"It don't matter," said the incorrigible old sinner before her. "It don't matter, at all. I say what Liberta says. You listen to my girl."

"Peter," said the victim of injustice in a new voice, and rising from the wreck of her hopes in terrific majesty, "be careful. I am a rude woman, Peter Passley. When I am provoked I tell you I am a rude woman. Don't let me talk to you, Peter. Don't let me tell you what your father was and what your Uncle Joseph was. I am a very rude woman when I am vexed," as if that were a condition into which she had not yet entered. "I beg you don't let me talk to you, Peter. Don't let me forget that I am your sister-in-law."

"Henrietta," said Peter, "listen to Liberta and you get your 'lowance, same as ever," the old man's business acumen and instinct took him straight to the vital spot in the heart of all this storm of hysterical emotion and this foam of rhetoric.

Henrietta stopped in mid career. She *had* been forgetting that allowance altogether, yet it was a very vital factor in her affairs. So she paused and did a little thinking while old Peter murmured soothingly: "Same old 'lowance, Henrietta; same old 'lowance."

"I leave you to your Maker, Peter Passley," at length Henrietta resumed, "and to the last judgment day, and if He is the person I take Him for, you will hear more about your treatment of me then—me, your poor dead wife's only sister."

"But you will send for the 'lowance, Henrietta," said Peter. "Same old 'lowance; send same as usual, Henrietta." He was anxious that there should be peace as far as that went. There was not an ounce of malice in Peter.

"That," said Aunt Henrietta grandly "I must think about, Peter Passley. After what has happened here today, I must think about it. It is true that I would not like to trouble my poor dead sister by not taking the money that she made me promise her so solemnly I would always take, but I must think it over—" but, she burst out "I tell you plain, and I tell you straight, that if you think that you and your allowance will prevent me talking about you and your Liberta, and telling people the kind of girl she is, no, I say no. I will not let you or she saw up my mouth. I am going to talk, I tell you plain; and I am a rude woman, Peter Passley." With that she made her exit.

Peter rose suddenly and followed her; "Henrietta," he called. He spoke emphatically, loudly, and in a new tone of voice, and Henrietta thought that at last she had brought him to his bearings. Her swift, imaginative West Indian mind was already shaping the phrases and terms by which she would fetter anew her chains on the Passley household, never again to be thrown off. Peter should be her slave and Liberta like unto him. But it was not victory that she found on that field.

"Henrietta," said Peter in that loud, new tone, and it struck Henrietta now that it suggested both cruelty and harshness. "Now listen to me, and mind what I say. So help me God, I mean it. You can go and talk me, you sister's husband, all you like. You can talk truth. You can talk lies. I don't care; you get the 'lowance all the same, same old 'lowance, Henrietta, but, Henrietta, the day that I hear that you talk my girl, talk her true or talk her false, I will stop your 'lowance, Henrietta, I will stop it all You will never get a sixpence more from me, not a copper, not for your life: not to save your life. Now take it in well, and understand it well. So help me God, I will do what I say. Just as I say it"; and Henrietta, who knew that he would, wept sorely.

Peter continued, the fountains of speech broken up by emotion:

"And I will be the devil to you Henrietta. I will be the very devil, Henrietta, if you talk Liberta; not only will I stop the 'lowance, but I will be the devil to you, the very devil. So now you know; and so help me God, I mean it."

There was no mistaking that he did mean it. Truly miserable, Henrietta went forth. Pity the woman who hates, but dares not stab. So fell the kingdom of Aunt Henrietta at the Passley's house; and the land had rest from war.

II

ENTER SOME OTHER PEOPLE, ADA SMITH AND A CASUAL HAROLD— "THE UNFAIR TREATMENT OF SOME JAMAICANS"—CAPTAIN BURN'S WORDS AND LIBERTA'S THOUGHTS—LIBERTA'S "DISEASE"—THE READER WHO DID NOT COMPREHEND—AND THE LISTENER WHO DID—ADA EXPLAINS WHY—NOEL AS REFEREE.

L iberta was unhappy. That fact flees before us a black speck on the staring white roadways of theory and surmise; and after it we go, intent on having answer to our query: "why and how this unhappiness?" But, if any reader expects sooner or later an answer exact and definite, after the manner of those given in Cambridge examinations of blessed memory, or that, like the policemen armed with his warrant and overtaking the thief, we shall at length put hand on the shoulder of a palpable, producible, undeniable conclusion, let him forthwith turn him round about and forsake this pursuit. No such reply do I promise. The answer lies deducible from a study of temperament, and that study is of many things the most elusive.

You are reminded of the query behind which we are at present advancing into this story, lest as the roads grow crowded we should either of us lose sight of what is in a way one of the issues of the narrative; but as to the answer, when we have regarded the fleeing fact long enough, and pursued it far enough, the conclusions will be in your hands very much as in the hands of the chemist there is a wine glass full of clear liquid in which certain matter is held in solution. Be yours then the final task of producing a precipitate in any way that you please. I will have my own opinion, but if yours differs therefrom, by all means enjoy and employ your own.

There was no truth in the assumption that Liberta Passley chafed against the ways and manners of the father that heaven had given her. It may even be said with confidence that if an angel, specially comissioned, had come down and offered her a new thing in fathers, something very different from Peter Passley, the daughter would have replied in her quick, careless manner:

"Not at all. Leave the old Dad, I want no one else." Here again she would have said little, when she might have said a great deal; but that was Liberta's way; an intensely emotional person, whom reason had convinced that emotionalism should be ridden roughly with bit and bridle, and whom nature would only succour in this matter with the gift of a strong will, being in no wise ready to transmute the emotion native to this woman's soul so as to make the outward calm and self-command an exact reflection of the inner being Liberta's central self was storm, not that calm which her manner suggested.

As for the old Dad, he praised Liberta to her face and to friend and foe without veil or pretence, and with or without reasonable excuse.

"I am only sorry," he sometimes said, "for one thing, my girl. That I have not another sixty years, so as to have them with you. Ah, if I was only a young man again, Liberta, like when I married your mother, with strength to do everything for you, and with all those years ahead. You should have seen your old Dad then, Daughter. Like a long a great road, Life was before us two going far on up-hill and down-hill, over green pastures and beside roaring rivers. But what is left of me now? In this old trunk, this old tree trunk, my Sweetheart. What is left? Five years, perhaps, or even if it is ten, what are they but the last leaves on the tree. The last sprouts from the root that cannot come to anything."

And then she would come to him in all her grace and sinuous beauty, her exquisitely finished dress in contrast with his baggy clothes, and the smooth, fine features of her youth and strength showing against the father's time-seamed, years roughened face; and her words would rise from her caresses.

"A strong old man like you, for shame to talk so, for shame, you wicked old man. Why, old men like you forget how to die. They have learnt the habit of living so well that they cannot drop it. Every year they live, they spread out and get more roots, and get stronger. It is young people like me that topple over; they have not got into the habit of living, when by comes a wind and over they go, like the trees down at the penn in a storm. The old ones lose a limb or two at the most, it is the young ones that go over all together. We have no roots. We young people, we are the weak ones. The ages of Life are past. Things don't last now. It is the twilight of the world. We young people go over easily. Dad, I will die first."

"God forbid, my girl," the old man would say earnestly, "God forbid, and give us many years together yet; and make death keep his distance." And so did it seem likely to be; for truly, Peter was still a sturdy old fellow, now as of yore the brain thinking straight and true, the body, for the most part, still as ready and pretty much as able as it ever had been, to obey the mind. As for Liberta, death seemed far enough from that life, sound in all appearance through its every fibre.

After Liberta had charmed every doubt from his mind and each fear, she would go from his arms to the piano and play and sing. She always began with the simple touching melodies he had known and loved all his life. "Home Sweet Home," "Auld Lang Syne," "Way Down upon The Swanee River." Then she would take his soul with hers and lead him away into the wonder music of the Masters, Mendelssohn, Mozart, Chopin, or into magic mazes of Wagner.

Yes, father and daughter might have gone together to the world's length, through life's bitterest blasts and have found no point at which they would have chafed each other into unhappiness. Yet was Liberta unhappy. None knew it but Liberta herself, the old Dad least all; and none perhaps of those round could have understood the unhappiness. In far away England, were two women, as different the one from the other as night from day; could they have come to Jamaica, and there have studied the growth of Liberta's soul they might have understood and helped. These had watched her grow up through school-days. They had helped her then, the imperious little girl whom her companions called "The Princess." They had learnt how to work out half of the problem; in Jamaica, they might have solved the other half; besides these two and Liberta herself, no one else held the key to her temperament; and Liberta, for reasons that seemed good to her, formed a resolve that she would admit no one to her inmost confidence. She went forward, a gallant figure, though slight and alone, under skies that to her eye overarched her destiny with threats of darkness, and doom. The two women in England soon faded into the background. Both had their work to engross their attention; and the girl herself, who was much at leisure, soon felt how true it was that a friendship must—from the beginning—be entrusted wholly to written correspondence, or wholly to spoken. Her old teachers loved her still, and she loved them, but they no longer grew into understanding, full and more full, the one of the other.

In Liberta herself we must find, if find we do, the explanation of her unhappiness. After all, this dissertation, therefore, let us return to read some of her thoughts, as she sits in the drawing room of her father's house, where, here and there, the electric bulbs heavily shaded, fling their light in warm strong gushes amid the semi-shadow that floods the rest of the room.

Liberta's thoughts ran thus:—

"Do I show the plague mark anywhere? Is there place or spot with the fatal sign? Tush, my disease is too deep for show, and it is incurable. As long as life, and as deep as breath. What worse insult than to be treated as an 'exception' to your class. Why? Money. Great indeed is Diana of the Ephesians. Truly the jingle of the guinea helps the hurt that honour feels. And such honour; money—the blanket that covers a vast assortment of bedfellows and mixed facts—certainly—even the terrible fact that I am—"

The curtains at the doorway trembled just then and parted. A maid appeared and announced: "Mr. Harold, Miss Liberta."

"Mr. Harold" had already entered the room. He was a young Jamaican of about twenty-eight, a shade darker than was Liberta. Though somewhat slight, he was well set up, and carried his erect figure well, with an air of ready manliness and gallant spirit that bespoke one who could hold his own. His clothes were noticeably well chosen and they fitted to perfection. On his face one read evidences of high intelligence and shrewdness, but these were rather in reserve, latent powers found when sought for, but masked by carelessness and an occasional air of something approaching weariness, oftener by a light, not ill-natured, air of mockery. This face you concluded belonged to a man who toyed with life, using idly, though perhaps this was in the meantime only, a strength and ability that could have taken him far and high.

Liberta and this young man greeted each other with that indefinable air of comradeship, that tells of a friendship, strong and intimate, but not tender.

A handful of small talk was offered on the altars of Convention, ending with Harold's remark about one of his sisters:

"She is haggling with Providence for one last dance before Lent." They isolated this remark by a moment of silence, and then Liberta asked with new interest in her tone:

"Have you finished it?"

"I have finished it," he replied.

"And sent it in?"

"And sent it in, Miss Liberta."

"And now," she said with sudden pleasure in her eyes, and something to pride in her voice.

"And now," he answered catching the word from her lips and beginning in the same full, eager tone, and then dropping ridiculously to bathos. "Now its slumbers are deep, full many a fathom down, at the bottom of the Governor's waste paper basket, or it travels on in slow marches, while the muffled drums of official memoranda beat funeral marches, to that remote pigeonhole, where the dust of departmental ages will cover it. The bourne from which no such adventurous traveller ever returns, dust to dust; dryness to dryness."

"I fancy," said Liberta, disregarding his humour, "that I know pretty well what you put into it."

"You do. It is largely yours, but in any case I have brought you the original, and with the permission of Your Royal Highness, I will read it to you."

"That permission," replied Liberta, with a smile of fun and pleasure, "you have, and with it our Royal thanks. Our, Royal self will take a comfortable chair and seek that shadow which chimes in with our complexion. And see that your chair is also 'comfy,' and that the light is good; I am pleased that you thought of this."

"And I," he returned gravely, "am rewarded by your pleasure. Thus something attempted, something done has earned a night's repose; that is what is left of a night after a man has been to Lodge, for I am bound for that haven when I leave you. My brothers expect every member to do his banquet speech, no matter what a bore it is to him, and to them. I will read you asleep, and then fold my sheets (of foolscap), like the Arab, and as silently steal away."

The document he opened was entitled; "THE UNFAIR TREATMENT OF JAMAICANS IN JAMAICA," and was addressed to the Governor.

"There are four pages," he resumed. "At the first you will yawn; at the second, nod; you will sleep at the third, and I will depart with the fourth unread. Here then I pitch my moving tones. To HIS EXCELLENCY—"

The maid, putting the curtain aside, made a second announcement:

"Captain Burns."

Without hesitation, Liberta signed that he was to be admitted; equally without hesitation, Harold began to pack away his document.

"You will stay," suggested Liberta. "Probably he won't belong. Stay him out."

"No? My Lodge expects me to bore it, and Burns does not. Besides I would tire him only a degree less than he would tire me. Absence makes the heart grow fonder, when it is a case of Burns. If I may, I will pass through your sitting room, and so avoid the man of war. A burnt child dreads the fire. I wish you patience."

"One needs it—with men," she answered, "Goodnight."

In the sitting room Harold searched swiftly with his eye, and finding the person he expected to see, accosted her lightly:

"Well; Ada, is that all right?"

"Yes I am quite decided now. I mean to tell her tonight."

"What a time you have been finding your mind, and making it up."

"Yes," she answered meekly enough, "I have kept you waiting."

"A regular slow coach," he continued, "in coming to a decision."

"Well, I had to think about it."

"And you actually succeeded in thinking," he quizzed.

"I think a great deal, let me tell you," she replied with a serious air which had its charm for this young man.

"Ah, well," he said, "I will see more of you now."

"Perhaps," she answered with some degree of sauciness, putting her book up to her face and looking at him over it with merry eyes.

"In any case," he responded nonchalantly, "it will be a livelier life for you; and better suited to that pretty face."

"But," she said with sudden gravity though it was gravity of a somewhat whimsical kind, "I may be doing wrong." She watched him a minute as if curious to hear what he had to say to that; but he only smiled very little. "There is my soul to think of," she ended.

"Think of the salary," he responded mockingly.

"Ah, no, you must not talk like that. I mean what I say."

"Ditto," he said tersely.

She lowered her book and attacked him as one with a grievance over which some thought had been wasted.

"You talk to me of my face, and my lips, and my figure and my eyes and my voice—but there is my soul, you never say a word about that. You must know that that is the most important part of me. I am afraid they have not taught you much about your soul—in the right way. You can lose it you know, and that is terrible."

"I fear," he acknowledged, "that they did not teach me much about my soul—in the right way. But what wrong is there in seeing you oftener? Do I look so bad?"

"No, no," she said, with a pretty and half shy laugh, "you are very nice to see. I like to see you. You are not bad."

"Good," was his reply. "Look at me at close quarters now."

He brought his face down to hers, then without further ado kissed her on the lips. "I won't hurt your soul, Beauty. Ta ta"; and, carelessly erect, he went on his way.

The girl in the sitting room was Ada Pearl Smith, one of the heroines of net battle with Aunt Henrietta. She was now a young woman of twenty-two or thereabouts, a small but extremely pleasant-looking person, with a round, pretty face, that was childish in its softness, while an interesting, unreasonable wistfulness came and went in her eyes, and suggested more of seriousness and thought than the little woman ever really had at her command. Serious and sad she was indeed at times for a brief space, but the shadow was that flung by passing circumstances, as on a June landscape the shadow is cast by an over–drifting cloud that speeds on and is forgotten in a minute. Ada was a being of pretty shallowness. She possessed little tricks of manner that, for a time at least, were all but irresistibly attractive. A man felt as much inclined to waste spare moments in trifling idly with this girl as a child feels inclined to play with a light-hearted, frisky kitten, with a quaint way of breaking into oddly solemn gambols. Ada's anxiety about her soul was her oddly incongruous gambol.

In the meantime, while Ada was *tete-a-tete* with Harold, Captain Burns had entered the drawing room and was entertaining Liberta, or being entertained by that young lady. The Captain was an English man of a type that hardly merits very close description. His head was poor-looking, with a forehead narrow and sloping. His chin was an insignificant chin, but his eyes were true and clear to look at and never flinched from an encounter. He was at all points well-groomed and was at home in a drawing room. In many things he was a better fellow than he looked, for if not a wise man, he was not a fool, and while in some respects a thoroughly honest man, in no respect was he a coward.

Liberta received him without anything to hint at the fact that her habitual indifference to his presence was just then varied by annoyance at his interrupting something in which she was really interested. She mentioned, with an apology for his absence, that her father was temporarily detained upstairs, he would probably be down in a few minutes; but she was not unkind enough to actually send up to disturb her sire where, in his study chair, he slumbered peacefully. Had she sent, she knew well that, under whatever tons of sleepiness his old head lay, he would have come down promptly; but though Liberta was well enough aware what these evening *tete-a-tetes* with the English Captain were likely one day to end in, and though she had a strong dislike to the approach of this crisis, she felt herself quite equal to the occasion of dealing with Captain Burns, or with any other man whatever, under any circumstances whatever, and she was not of the kind who conceive it to be their duty to guard the man's heart as well as their own from mistakes and injury. Liberta, therefore, did no more than mention her sire to show decently that he and she recognised his duties to his guests, and then hostess and visitor chatted on, lightly and easily, saying nothing worth remembering still less recording, but keeping the ball of small talk speeding to and fro, now gracefully and elegantly flung, and then exchanged with more rapidity and skill.

Liberta was thinking far afield, and she pursued her own mental way while she talked readily to her guest. She was used to this bifurcation of attention. Her inmost line of thought just now led through this country:

"Yes, I am a Jamaica brown girl. What a terrible thing for this poor man, who is making up his mind to ask me to marry him—to ask my money, I mean. Persuading himself first, and his people in England afterwards, that I am an exception to other Jamaica brown girls. Poor man; I fancy how it goes between him and his fond, but pauperized mother and sisters in England. He dare not spring such a surprize upon them too suddenly; and so he dare not marry his rich brown girl out of hand and take her home to the ancestral ruins of the Burns. So he has been sounding them, depend on it, as to how they would regard Liberta Passley as a daughter and sister. He hastens to smooth the first shock by assurance that she has any amount of money. Her father is one of the richest old fellows here, quite the uncrowned king of an entire parish. She will get all his money, for, most fortunately, he has not a chick or child besides her, and she is the apple of his eye, the brown appple of course." Here Liberta asked Captain Burns about a tennis tournament; while he replied, her busy mind pursued its silent course:

"Is she quite black?" asks Sister Number One.

"Is her hair very woolly, dear Herbert?" asks Number Two.

"Nonsense, Caroline," he answers, "her hair is not woolly at all, only a little wavy. Really very elegant, quite distinctive. She is not black, Eliza, how silly you are; and I can tell you she is as well educated as you are, and indeed a great deal better for she started with the natural advantage of having some brain. She plays divinely." He add splaintively. "We have to make some sacrifices of our pride in this world, and really Liberta is not half bad. I know, Mother, that you and the girls would have chosen a different sort of girl for me; but Liberta behaves quite like a lady, apart from her colour. You could not really tell the difference if you shut your eyes." "And am I expected" puts in Mamma "to shut my eyes when I meet her always. Her darling smiles and proceeds giving wit for wit. "She is the best imitation of the British family twig, done in mahogany, that you could get. The mahogany has gold mounting."

Captain Burns all this time was telling her a long story, about tennis, and to all appearances she was listening carefully, replying tersely when he made a point, and smiling; meantime she thought.

"And suppose I married him, what would the children be like? If we had any children," she shuddered at the thought, and he noticed it.

"A draught," she explained. "I will take another chair."

"Will you give me some music?" he asked.

"Very well; let us select."

"The children," she continued to herself, "would barely show colour; for after all I am a light brown girl." She glanced at the mirror on the other side of the room as if to recall just what her degree of brownness was. "Their hair would be hardly even wavy." She laughed at the thought and to explain this told a clever fib about a mistake a stupid legislator had made in talking to her at a King's House Ball about Wagner. It had just then tickled her memory. Then she sat down and playing divinely, deluged Burns with delicious melody, sped a perfumed sun-lighted stream of sound through the very soul of him, so that for a time he actually forgot all about debts and money and colour; and all about the player too. While upstairs, in his sleep, Old Peter dreamt that he was walking into Paradise and the choirs of cherubs were singing to welcome him and Liberta.

When the Captain left, Liberta went into the sitting room.

"Read to me Ada, will you?"

"What, Miss Liberta?"

"Choose," said laconic Miss Liberta, arranging a screen to beat back the light from her eyes, and taking her place on a lounge.

Ada selected a volume from a small book case, and after a minute or two, began Tracy Robinson's poem on The Palm. It was not in any individual or personal sense her own choice, for, in truth she cared little for any book and very little indeed for poetry, but she felt that it was this poem that would best suit Liberta then.

The reader's voice adapted itself naturally and effectively to the measured language, and, as she interpreted the theme it was pleasant to listen to her tones, for they fell like a well-fitting robe round the curves of the author's thoughts and emotions, though in Ada herself there was little appreciation of what she read.

The poem was one which she had read many a time to Liberta and she had learnt perfectly how to interpret it. She did so now instinctively and so to speak mechanically. She herself was thinking of something very different from "the Sea's Miserere"; something much smaller, but to Ada much more important.

It has fine verses, has Robinson's Song Of The Palm, and the sound of some of the surging lines swept through Liberta's soul with a thrill.

Ada read on and on.

> *"Wild in its nature, as it were a token*
> *Born of the sunshine and the stars and sea;*
> *Grand as a passion, felt but never spoken*
> *Lonely and proud and free.*
> *For when the Maker set its crown of beauty.*
> *And for its home ordained, the torrid ring,*
> *Assigning unto each its place and beauty,*
> *He made the Palm a king.*
> *So when in reverie I look and listen,*
> *Half dream-like floats within my passive mind,*
> *Why in the sun its branches gleam and glisten,*
> *And harp-wise beat the wind;*
> *Why when the sea waves heralding their tidings,*
> *Come roaring on the shore with crest of down,*
> *In grave acceptance of their sad confidings,*
> *It bows its stately crown;*
> *Why, in the death-like calms of night and morning,*
> *Its quivering spears of green are never still.*
> *But ever tremble as in solemn warning*
> *A human heart may thrill;*
> *And also why it stands in lonely places*
> *By the red desert and the sad seashore*
> *Or haunts the jungle, or the mountain graces*
> *Where eagles proudly soar;*
> *It is a sense of kingly isolation,*
> *Of royal beauty and enchanting grace,*
> *Proclaiming from the earliest creation*
> *The power and pride of race,*
> *That has almost imbued it with a spirit,*
> *And made it sentient although still a tree*

With dim perception that it might inherit
An immortality.
The lines of kingship thus so near converging.
It is not strange, Oh heart of mine, that I,
While stars were shining and old ocean surging
Should intercept a sigh.
It fell asighing when the faint wind dying,
Had kissed the tropic night a fond adieu—
The Starry Cross on her warm bosom lying,
Within the southern view.
And when the crescent moon the west descending,
Drew o'er her face the curtain of the sea,
In the wrapt silence, eager senses blending,
Lo came the sigh to me."

When Ada ended the poem, Liberta took the book, and turning the pages read again some of the lines that moved her spirit.

"The waves of ocean catch the miserere,
Far wasted seaward from the wintry main,
They roll it on o'er reaches vast and dreary
With infinite refrain.
The Sea-grape hears it and the lush Banana,
In the sweet indolence of their repose;
The Frangipanni, like the crowned Sultana,
The Passion Flower and Rose."

Then she turned back and back till she read the name "NOEL MAUD BRONVOLA." Liberta knew the name was there and read it idly without aim or motive; but an impulse came as she read, and in little things as in big, Liberta was given to acting on impulse.

"Ada," she said, "return this book to Miss Bronvola tomorrow. I have had it long enough."

When Liberta put the book down, Ada spoke.

"Miss Liberta."

"Well."

"I want to speak to you."

Liberta resumed her seat and, as this showed that she was prepared to listen, she made no further response.

"Please, Miss Liberta," began Ada awkwardly, her clumsy manner now and her ill-fitting tone contrasting strikingly with her recent elegant and well modulated reading. "I want to give you notice to leave."

"Very well," said Miss Liberta, "give it."

"I would like to thank you very much for all your kindness."

"Very well," said Liberta with graceful quickness, "thank me."

"I do, Miss Liberta very much indeed. You have been very kind to me and I will never forget you." Ada managed to say this with real feeling.

Liberta smiled and replied;

"There are kinder people in the world and you may meet them if you go far enough; and look near enough."

"I hope you won't think me ungrateful," continued poor Ada Smith."

"I won't," said Liberta. Her West Indian intuition told her the girl expected to encounter argument and persuasion and her West Indian vein of waywardness made her resolve to employ neither.

Ada's plan of campaign, so far as there had been a plan at all, presupposed opposition, meeting none, it became at once confused as well as amorphous. She thrust excuses and explanations in a disorderly pile before the silent Liberta.

"It is a good place here, Miss Liberta, and you are very good to me."

"But you wish to leave it," said Liberta, imparting as she so well could, a light touch of ridicule to the words.

This increased Ada's confusion.

"It is not that I want to leave you, Miss Liberta" she began, "but—" she could not think out the rest of that sentence and so stumbled back to the beginning of another, while Liberta watched and listened without a sign or word.

"I don't think I altogether suit—that is that the work altogether suits me—my constitution—I don't feel quite well,—you know, Miss Liberta, I suffer from indigestion—"

"I know that you think that you do," said Liberta with just enough emphasis on the 'think' to leave the listener in doubt as to whether there was any emphasis at all.

Then for a minute or two Ada Smith contiuued to drag up and deposit half-finished sentences, like a workman diliently bringing up planks for a structure the plan of which he has forgotten, so that every new bit of material only made confusion worse confounded. She was labouring under the difficulty of meeting the unexpected and of having much to conceal as well as something to reveal. When her assertions, maimed and marred, lay in a tumbled pile of confusion, like the debris of a fallen house, she was inspired to come nearer to truth and into coherency once more.

"I want a change, Miss Liberta," she said and became silent.

"You would like to go—when?" enquired Liberta without comment on the laborious sentence-making.

"I must give you the two weeks' notice, Miss Liberta; if it were not for that—"

"You have a place you can get?"

"Yes, m'm."

"Then you can go at once." Liberta spoke quietly and without stress of tone. She was not annoyed in the slightest degree, but to be decided and prompt was her habit.

Ada on the spur of the moment, genuinely concerned at the idea of inconveniencing her employer, burst out with:

"But how will you manage?"

"I can do without most people," said Liberta, quietly. "I will manage."

Ada felt now for her own self-importance thus wounded, far more acutely than a second before she had felt over the idea of inconveniencing Liberta; her mortification mingled with discouragement, and both clouded her face while tears of anger came into her eyes. We all like to think that we are at least next door to being indispensable.

Liberta who was far from unkind, soothed Ada's distress with the truth:

"You have done very well indeed, here, and I am satisfied with you, quite. But, if you wish to go, of course, go."

"Thank you, thank you, Miss Liberta," said pretty, emotional Ada, "I would like I have tried to please you. I would like to stay but M—" She paused just in time to prevent the entire truth passing her lips, and Liberta, wondering for a moment what it was that trembled behind that "M," said:

"Well?"

"I mean just as I have explained to you, Miss Liberta. That is why I want to go."

Then Liberta smiled, for as a matter of fact, Ada had not explained at all. "You can go tomorrow or next week, just as you like."

"I will wait, Miss Liberta," said Ada suddenly shrinking from a course she had herself planned out.

"Think the matter over," said Liberta rising to leave the room. Then as she saw that Ada was again on the verge of tears, the rain-cloud before the confidence, she applied the coldly prosaic to disperse the attack.

"Remember to take that book back to Miss Bronvola in the morning."

Liberta, herself as emotional as Ada, though in a different way, felt that peculiar dislike to a collision with the emotional that so often accompanies emotionalism.

Ada went to her room and had a good cry, why it would be hard to say. Then she fell asleep and had a most wonderful dream in which she was dancing with Harold while she saw her soul in the shape of a kitten that trotted across the room and then sat on a table to watch with much gravity the two dancers. Ada could not take her eyes away from the kitten and she noticed that sometimes this curious animal grew bigger and bigger still; then it shrank and dwindled till it became almost a speck. Ada was just thinking that at last it had vanished altogether, when with terrible rapidity it grew to a monstrous size. Then it sprang right at the dancers. Harold stepped aside with his mocking smile, and the savage kitten seized Ada with large sharp teeth and bore her away.

That dream travelled round and round in the silly, little head where it was born till morning dawned, by which time Ada was quite sure that it meant something very bad indeed. Something awful hung over her, that was evident. She was more irresolute now than ever, and vastly inclined to sit and shed tears. And then as she wandered about in this state of desolation and distress, full of the dream, the name of Miss Bronvola shone for her like a magic beacon, first of hope and then of assurance.

It rose on the horizon of her thoughts if anything as confused as Ada's mind-wanderings could be called thoughts at all it mounted, it swelled, it glowed, it positively streamed with brilliance on this dolorous mortal.

Noel, it may remembered, taught a Sunday School class. Each of the eight scholars in that class radiated from the centre, as the spokes of a wheel radiate from the hub of a wheel. And thus to points very divergent and to directions vastly different passed abroad the fame and powers of Miss Noel; for at the end of each spoke stood an enthused scholar who declared to all and sundry the wonders of her wonderful "teacher," her readiness to help all in trouble and her absolute ability to do the impossible. Naturally this in a world full as is this of grievances and worries, drew not a few to this invaluable personage. Thus it was that Noel's name and high repute were known to a great many odd people.

All that Ada had ever heard of this wonderful teacher from her pupils came now shooting up in her mind, each memory strong and vivid like a blade of green pushing its way up from a seed that had lain hidden for long, quite forgotten till the May rains fell. Ada fairly quivered with conviction that Noel was the being, the only being, able and willing, and as it was now very plain, specially appointed by heaven, to guide her steps aright in this most important matter. She set off, therefore, next morning to return the book Liberta had given her orders about with excitement fermenting in her mind. She trembled at the door and asked quiveringly if Miss Noel was at home. Had she happened to be out, sudden dread would have deluged this poor Ada. Finding Miss Noel at home impressed her on the other hand as another sure sign that heaven was taking her to a worthy adviser. The matter of the book was quickly disposed of, and Ada opened up her great business. She concentrated her thoughts on this one thing, with the result not of putting it before herself and her listener in the clearest and most balanced way, but of so putting it as to secure the decision desired. Many weak persons seek advice in this way. They fish not for truth, but for the opinion after their own desire, and relief from the sense of responsibility. They seek the position of being able to say with an appearance of truth; "I did it on your advice." They unconsciously deceive those whom they question by rooting out from their story everything that would lead to a conclusion other than that which they wish to reach.

"Miss Noel, I want to ask your help."

Noel nodded very slightly, and suppressed an inclination to ask a question, which as she soon saw, would have led in quite a wrong direction. It was by resisting such temptations that she made herself a ready help in time of trouble to the garrulously anxious, and was regarded as a model confidant. They interpreted her silent following of their chatter from the very first as evidence that she realized the story that they had to tell, its meaning and aim. Silence is like darkness, and soothes the aching heart with the same soft touch as darkness; but a sense of sympathy behind it may add to it this further of charm that it makes the darkness that transparent shadow that covers the earth when the sky is clear and crowded with stars. Such translucent darkness as dwellers in the Tropics know. Noel's silence at this stage had its charm for poor muddle-headed little Ada who talked away in her pudding-stone style, for many minutes, looking all the while into the serious lucent and sympathetic eyes before her. In that time she conveyed the outlines at least of her troubles to her listener.

Noel began to ask essential questions.

"Have you another place to go to?"

"Yes, replied Ada, with the mild reproachfulness of one who has told her story at great length but has left out a main feature without being conscious of the omission. The feeling is that not one's self but one's listener is to blame.

"Will you earn as much?"

"More," said Ada, pleased to be able to play one of her best cards.

"And what is the work?"

Ada's talk spread out just as a little stream spreads out and soaks and sops on a bit of grassy level.

All her words amounted to this, that she was offered the position of cashier in a store downtown. "Cashier" is a big term for very simple duties.

"It seems to me," said Noel after hearing all about it, "that the matter is very simple. You will have a little more work to do in the store, but it will be more lively and you will evidently like it better."

"And," put in Ada, remembering that she had not mentioned it before. "I suffer from indigestion." She felt quite sure that this bore in an important way on the matter, somewhere and somehow, and took Noel's slight smile as one of acquiescence in the enumeration of a vital point.

"Your change of work is a matter for yourself to decide," said Noel.

"But," said Ada, disappointed, not to say dismayed at seeing the burden of responsibility on her own shoulders once again, and that just as she thought that the load was safely settled elsewhere. "You don't think me ungrateful for leaving."

"Ungrateful," echoed Noel, surprised as she always instinctively was when she found merely conventional ideas being accepted so seriously. "Where can ingratitude come in? You agreed to do certain work and Miss Passley agreed to pay you certain sums, in return. If you left her without proper notice that would be dishonest, but if you have given her notice, go to the place that you like best."

"The other place would suit me best," continued Ada, returning to the subject with unneeded pertinacity.

"Then take the other place," said Noel.

"Thank you, Miss Noel," said Ada now she had heard the exact words she had held before her minds as a goal when she sought the interview. She could now always recall the fact that Noel had actually said. "Take the other place." So this matter was settled for Ada Pearl Smith as she wished it to be settled, and she was persuaded that it all rested on Miss Noel's advice.

But the mantle of mental satisfaction falling so smoothly and quietly over her mind, was suddenly disarranged. It came to her with a shock that all through this interview she had said nothing, absolutely nothing, of her soul, she, a girl who thought so much about her soul, had been guilty of this omission, and that when concern about that soul had given her such a dream and had positively been the compelling cause making her a refuge to seek advice.

Late as it was, Ada felt she must remedy her sad omission.

"And," she began as if what she said was in close connection with a former remark, which as we know it was not. "I am a girl that think a great deal about my soul Miss Noel. I have always done so." She had said this a great many times and to a great many different kinds of people and all of them, except Harold, had applauded her, even those who acknowledged that they did not themselves do much in that line. To her deep surprise this young lady said.

"Don't do that; it is unhealthy."

"Unhealthy," gasped Ada.

She associated the word exclusively with smallpox and measles or diseases of a similar kind, and the incongruity of its present use fairly bewildered her. "Unhealthy," she repeated as if the word must be a mistake.

Noel realized that it would be a difficult task to make the matter plain to Ada Smith, so much was shock surprize and even consternation visible on her face, indicating how far she was from the view which to the other seemed so natural and plain. She was conscious that she had not done anything to help on Ada's comprehension when she said:

"You run the risk of being carried away by wrong ideas."

Ada immediately thought of the kitten in her dream, how that carried her off.

"But," she said, "I thought it was good thing to think of your soul. You should think of it every moment of the day. It is only because we are wicked that we do not. We can't think too much of our souls."

"Do you think a great deal about your eyes; they are very pretty ones?"

Noel had a way of galvanizing her listeners into truthfulness, and though Ada felt that it would be more self-respecting to make no such admission, she was constrained to reply: "Yes, a great deal."

Noel, it must be confessed was slightly taken aback by the unqualified acknowledgement, nevertheless she resumed;

"But you feel that it is not good for you to think a great deal about your pretty eyes, do you not?"

"Oh, yes!" said Ada, glad to be back on safe ground; "it helps to make me vain, and it is very sinful to be vain." She had been told that over and over again and though it had no effect on her practice, she was scrupulously careful to make it her profession.

"Well," continued Noel, "the eyes and your soul are both parts of you. God who gave you the soul gave you the eyes, too. The same laws govern your life through all its parts. You feed another kind of vanity by thinking too much about your soul."

Ada was so much puzzled that she decided this could not really have the meaning it seemed to carry, but at any rate she comforted herself that she had obtained from Miss Noel what she wanted, she had shifted the burden of responsibility for an action to the shoulders of another. So at least she was convinced.

III

MRS. GYRTON AND THE AFFLICTIONS OF SOME OTHER MUDFISH—
THE FATHER WHO WAS RESURRECTED—THEORIES OF TAXES—THE
PRINCE OF WALES AND THE SECRET OF RAPHAEL WHITE—
GOVERNORS AND COLLECTORS—"COUGHING UP TAXES"—MARRIAGE
AND MONEY—MR. GRANT'S PROPOSAL AND HIS VIEWS ON A WIFE.

M rs. Gyrton sat on the steps of her house, with the gloom in her heart deeper even than the gloom which oncoming night was at that moment spreading round her. Time had been using her hardly. All had gone badly with her since the death of her little daughter. It is marvellous how the displacement of even an atom of life may affect the bigger existences with which it stood related. Mrs. Gyrton would have scouted the idea with some heat, the idea that her fortunes were dependent to any appreciable extent on the continued existence in this mundane sphere of her small daughter. Yet such was undoubtedly the case. Her fortunes, while Becka lived, might have been compared to a large rock that had slipped some distance down an incline, and then been brought to a stand by sticking against a much smaller rock, but yet one firmly enough embedded in the earth to stay further descent. Becka's death had removed the small but firm rock, and now the bigger rock was slipping, slowly but surely downward. Below the sad slope of poverty waited the still drearier flat of degradation and destitution. The loss of Becka made the woman feel suddenly lonely and forsaken, mainly it must be confessed because she had not now anyone who was bound as a matter of course to receive her orders, abuse and directions on all subjects, and at all times.

But besides this, finances had taken a distinctly downward turn. Mrs. Gyrton had lost some of her washing, because it was not delivered in time, there being no Becka to take it out, yet, even with the shortened list the day did not seem long enough to get through the residue. In the washing scheme, as a water-carrier, Becka had been of very great use indeed, there was not a doubt of that. Mrs. Gyrton tried the plan of adopting a girl to take Becka's place. It failed dismally. There was, it is true, no difficulty in getting a girl, there are many in Kingston, waifs and strays, so made by their own choice or by hard necessity. The child that Mrs. Gyrton selected offered her every proof of her parents' death, except the production of their dead bodies, but this did not prevent the damsel summoning a very much alive father when she thought the circumstances demanded a parent's support. From the first she got along badly with Mrs. Gyrton, for her tendency was to eat a great deal, and then to slumber long and deep. Work she did languorously or not at all. The thunder of the washer-woman's anger, which at first cowed her, ultimately broke idly against her bullet head and then in an evil hour, Mrs. Gyrton chastised this child, and that with great severity. It was immediately after this that the father who had been guaranteed dead, appeared on the scene. The torrent of blasphemy and abuse which then eddied through the Gyrton's yard was such as to win the unstinted admiration of the most renowned exponent of the ungentle art. Through all this tempest of indignation, the small creature who had evoked, it sat meekly down on a log in the yard and steadily displayed the dress that had been badly torn while Mrs. Gyrton held her wriggling form to apply the strokes of vengeance aright. She was also skilfully smeared and daubed with blood coaxed to flow from a scratch or two received from the washerwoman's nails. In the end, Mrs. Gyrton, driven from her last ditch, compromised by paying five shillings.

"Which," said the one-time deceased father, "you ought never to finish render thanks to you Master in heaven and to you sweet Saviour that you meet with a man as me today, for another man, a cruel man, would not only broke every bone in you, you ever count, or loss to count, in a you body, but would a put de law on you, and you would a eat dis Christmas Day dinner in a Queen's lock-up. For I needs not to tell you what white gentlemen law does a female dat massacree a poor little gall, such as dis; look how him clothes all tear up, look how the chile bleed; look how him poor little yeye all full up wid yeye water and sand, an' him mout kind of a look as if it rip open by de holler dat force and shove its way troo. You is a lucky woman, I tell you, to get off so well and so easy; and a' night time when you say you prayers, if you don't pray fe me, you is a most ungrateful female; and next time such a ting happen you will meet not a gentleman like me, who is a kind-hearted man, sake a which I nebber yet able to get rich, and you yourself see how I only tek five mac' and no more from you dis day; but next time you will encounter wid me brudder Thomas, a man dat will peel off de berry skin, and done wid dat, would 'a tek iron skewer, *wid a hook*, and feel in a' you flesh, try find you bone dem. Dis is a very fortunate and happy day for you. If it had been me brudder Thomas, by dis time you would a' been coughing up you back teet dem and sending you farmbly to pick up the hair him pull out a' you head. Him is a very different man to me, a meek and mild somebody. I hear dat when dem is dah try him a circuit court dem send special message from de Penitentiary to tell de judge if it can possibly done, to let him off and don' send him a' prison, causen dem actually fraid to hab de man in de prison. Such a man is me brudder Thomas, and it might a' been fe him chile you beat and murder up. A blessed and a fortunate day is dis fe you, and you must be thankful." This man had once had considerable vogue as a street preacher, and was warming up to the old tricks of style as he continued. "It is a vale of tears here below, and a mountain of tribulation, also a desert and a howling lion seeking whom he may devour, and a fiery furnace; and we must take comfort and go forward."

To all of which Mrs. Gyrton answered only: "You got de five shilling, me dear sah, I beg you take it and goes you way out a' me yard."

"Get up, gall," said the father, "and mek a curtesy to dis lady, for, me dear female, creature, I must tell you, dat I bring up ebbry one a' me pickney strict and particular to pay dem respect to the old somebody dem. And, look yah ma'm," he continued, affable now that the five shillings were safely in hand, "ef dis chile ebber meet you any ways and talk disrespectful to you, just come a' No. 23 Bamboo Grass Lane and call for me, and I will mek the little brute know who she dah fool wid; and it will really please you to see de way I walk round him wid me piece a wild coffee wood."

But, when, in face of this handsome offer, Mrs. Gyrton was a glum as ever, and as sullen, the good man was filled with a disgust that he did not conceal, and said with a jocular sneer:

"Well, old creature, don't kill yourself, fret and pine over five maccaroni."

That was unbearable, and the dying embers of Mrs. Gyrton's anger blazed up.

"What old creature I for you? And who you call old? You head stan like a' when dem take dem half dirty piece a' white cloth and stop up window pane. You better go tek looking-glass and see how you hair white, before you come call me old creature; and how you face rough worse dan dem cane-field when dem just finish dig cane-hole. You old till you very flesh wash out from under you yeye. It just left fe you to broke up and lose; and you nebber know. Come out a' me yard."

"Well," he flung back as he departed, "To see how dat poor woman lose him temper and pull down him jaw, which tremble as if him going cry, and all fe five so-so shillings. I shame fe see me colour stan' so. It is solid meanness and not a ting else. I hab a mind to chuck de little money in a' de yard." With that he put his hand into his pocket and rattled the coins. Then he went his way.

After that Mrs. Gyrton adopted no more children.

In those days Aunt Henrietta was creating a brisk tide in the local market by the rapidity with which she discharged Peter Passley's servants.

Mrs. Gyrton decided to abandon washing, for domestic service, and was installed as the Passley cook. It was not an arrangement that endured. It parted with the vehemence of a hempen rope torn asunder by the surging forward of a steamer from a pier. The record was a short and lurid one, a page in a chapter of violence. When Mrs. Gyrton resumed washing she found that some of her old patrons had fallen into other hands; so things went from bad to worse.

The idea depressed her soul, either that some very strong Obeahman was overshadowing her with his baleful eye, or that the Almighty himself had not her case properly before Him and so was making a horrible mistake in dealing with her. The Past stretched from her tonight in long review, and its events glared at her, ghastly and uncannily like white gravestones that shine through the dusk of early night, weirdly distinct. Becka, her daughter, had died, killed in the street by a car, without so much as a dream or a dog's howl by night to forewarn her mother; there was the washing, week by week growing less and less; there was the discharge from the Passley kitchen, which had left a chronic irritation born of uncertainty as to whether or not she had really given Miss Henrietta as good as she had brought to the cook in those tempestuous days. Then there was the bad luck that had attended her attempt to adopt a girl, and finally there were the taxes, knocking loudly and more loudly at her rickety door.

She flew to pious cries to heaven, "I trust to my sweet Saviour, to my blessed Jesus," she said again and again, but little was the real comfort that she drew from these well-meant repetitions. They were in fact less evidences of faith than props thrown out with a forlorn hope that they would support a trust that had begun to totter visibly. Fairly staggered by her growing misfortunes, she reminded herself ofttimes that Big Massa could do nothing that was wrong, but, like a lean and hungry dog creeping back to the kitchen, after being a dozen times kicked out, the doubt returned that Big Massa was forgetting that He was here dealing with a respectable married woman.

She sat on the dirty step in her untidy yard, and tears splashed down into her lap. Round her the deepening darkness thickened like inundating waters flowing heavily into the pockets of a marsh.

The single hen that remained to her had gone noisily to roost, and continued at intervals to make an outcry as if it felt timorous in its loneliness, and, like a man of fearful heart, was trying by a great hullabaloo to put new courage into its bosom. Outside a passing woman loudly invited purchasers to take the last of her mangoes "at a farden fe four." A dray was moving, creaking and straining. As it swayed and joggled down the roadway, the light from the lantern which swung beneath, gave it a grotesque appearance. It looked like a mishapen and oddly crawling glow-worm.

The wind was beginning to move down to the plains from the far off hills that rose an imposing line on the northern horizon; but as yet the sun-baked city, radiating heat after its day of suffering, could not feel the breath of coolness, the air was tainted by stale and heavy smells, shot through and through with the odour of fried fish or frizzling steaks, and it vibrated with the dull noise of distant tramcars rumbling along their iron lines. The sound of this was like a pathetic groaning from the town's tortured bosom.

The fact that her taxes were in arrears rose like a spectre in the gloom and shook a threatening hand before her. She had reason to fear the very worst. She saw the hand of the bailiff, like a great patch of evil black shadow, reaching into her home to seize her furniture. Though that was scanty, she took immense pride in the fact that she had kept till now all that with which she had started her married life, battered though some of it was.

Another spectre grinned maliciously into her face. A year previously, she had stood sorely in need of twenty shillings. One of those money-lenders who hide in the lower social depths like dangerous reptiles of prey lurking in muddy pools, had then drawn her to him. She obtained a loan of the twenty shillings and undertook, till it was repaid, to pay the lender one shilling weekly for its use. That was more than a year ago. She had failed to pay the interest for ten weeks altogether, and the total debt had been increased by that amount. So that after repaying more than twice the sum she had borrowed originally, she still owed that amount plus half as much again; and she saw the last prospect of getting quit of the debt vanishing from view. They would sell her house and her land; they would take her furniture and, worst of all, they might end by puting her into prison.

It was about the taxes that she fretted chiefly and against which she most angrily rebelled. The scheme which to educated folks explains, if it does not recommend, the collecting of taxes was entirely unappreciated in the circle of this woeful woman and her friends. To her and her kind the hand of the Collector came arbitrarily down, unreasonably as a bolt from the blue, that destroys and explains not. What became of the taxes? That was a much debated point, gradually forming a nucleus for remarkable stories. It was realised, and candidly admitted, that a man must do something for a living, and hence it was understood that the Governor and all his army of inspectors and collectors had devised this system of government to give themselves work to do and salaries to draw. Taxes were raised to provide the salaries.

No reasonable person grumbled at that, save in his unreasonable moods. Of course, as Mrs. Gyrton often said, "We all can see dat ebbry ting would go 'long just as good, Gubbernor or not; Collector or not. For after all said an' done, I nebber meet de man can tell me dat him see Day sit down a roadside dah wait fe Gubbernor or Mr. Anybody to tek candle go look fe it. I nebber see dat any ob dem got 'casion to climb top a hill so holler tell sun or moon dat him sleep too long, and it ripe time fe him get up and go 'bout him business. I nebber see dat, wid all them blustification, dem ebber mek moon come when it is dark night, which is just de time, when you come to tink 'bout it, dat we want moonlight. Who ebber see, 'causin Gubbernor dah come, Death stand one side to give him pass, him hat in a' him hand, waiting patient till Gubbernor and de rest seh dem is reddy to tek road and follow, and to trabbel. And, surely, if dem was all de use dem want to seh dem is, and was dat familiar wid Big Massa dat dem pretence to, Him would certain gib dem some latitude more than Him gib udder white people; but it is not so a piece; for, while it is true dat white people as white people does get Him faber, as Collector and all dat dem don't. Time come to dead, dem dead, dat is all about it. I see some berry bad ting happen to dem same Collector when dem wring poor people too much.

"Me Fader, when you stan up sometimes and hear de way dese Gubbernor and Collector and Minister does talk, well you will swear to you King dat a dem dah manage all dis land and all dis sky and all de moon and dem stars and de berry sun self, and dat God would know better dan to drop one a dem outside sake a de mix-up and pop-me-down dat would come in if Him lose eben *one* a' dem self. Just like when you see man hab servant who know him business too well and deh wid him too long, so dat de poor gentleman half and half fraid fe use him own horse, and at de same time fraid fe fire de servant out a' road, sake a' him don't know how to run de place widdout him. A so dem talk would a mek you tink dem backra stan' to Big Massa. But what an astonishment to see de way Him pitch dem way like old shoe when dem day come, and what I notice is ebbry deaf ting go 'long all de same.

"And road dem been yah since de beginning, and it will stop yah, Gubbernor or not; ground will grow breadkind and corn, Gubbernor or no; likewise ribber will run water, hen will lay egg, and horse will carry tail. But dem gentlemen must all get work to do, so dem mek employment for demselves, and I don't blame dem, for, if not, what de debbil dem would do; dem gots to feed demself and dem pickney same as we useful people. Dem white people is not usual to work dat is useful like black people."

This was all very fair-minded and just; but, behind it, peering eyes saw further mysteries and out of those mysteries like insects to the light crept the stories that accounted for increases in the severity with which the taxes were collected from year to year. It was told that the husband of the Queen was not dead at all, as people generally said he was; but that he was a very bad man and had been paid a large sum to go away and live by himself, letting it be announced that he was dead, and promising that while he got his money regularly he would not trouble the poor lady. Necessary to secure money to pay him well; cute on his part to every now and then demand an increase in the sum given to him; when he did this, all over the Empire went the mandate to take more money. Hence came rises in taxes, and increase of money due to the Collector.

But another authority rather slighted this story, and spoke instead of the dark doings of the Prince of Wales: "What, a young gentleman wicked asdat; as I hear. Spend money, spend money ebbry day like when gardener man tek flowers pot and water roses. Call me a liard if you like, but I hear say dat him gib away ebbry day dat him lib one tousand solid pound and dat no furder dan him door mout. All you gots to do as I understand the ting, is to be at de spot time come fe him to *discatter* de money; you can tek all you can grabbel up and carry go, only dem tell me dat it is not lowable for you to tek jackass to seh you will load it up; dat is against dem rule and you must careful to mind it. Talk 'bout spend money, I hear say it is against law for dis young man to spend less dan one pound at a time. De berry nail ina' him boots is pure and simple gold. As fe buggy, I is made to undertand dat him got more dan would cubber de whole a dis Kingston from one beginning to the next. And as fe headstrong and rude, him mudder self, Queen and all, don't fit fe say "A" to him. Whenebber dat man come to de trone, you gwine see someting. Today it is bad enough, but wait, only wait, you will see dat dere is ting hotter dan fire and hebby more dan lead."

In this glittering talk of gold and vice, and what not, the sagacious mind of old Ebenezer Raphael White fixed itself on one fact, namely, that daily the Prince "discattered," at his "door mout" "one tousand solid pounds." Could White but get to the Prince's door, then the role of giving would be exchanged for taking which if less blessed, is more pleasant to the ordinary sinful man. Once reach that door, and instead of the sorrow of paying taxes, or the trouble of telling lies to escape them, there would be the inexpressible joy of receiving gifts in gold. Ebenezer planted this thought deep in his mind, and cherished it there, as in his younger days he had cherished his plantations set far-away in remote mountain recesses, where the chances of their being visited by the praedial thief, or the proprietor of the land which he was using without rent, agitated his soul even while he was soothed by the moral certainty of the cultivation escaping the attention of the tax-collector. Round his secret he erected his silence like a fence. Old, experienced, wary, he waited, opening and opportunity to get away to England, to the region of the Prince's gifts.

"Once get me deh," he said musingly, "once get me deh, at dat said door mout when de discatterment is dah go on, and if I don't get nough to feed me till I dead, tek any piece a wood you like eben to piece a barrel stave self, or dat whity whity saltfish box kivver, and box off me head." But many things hampered White sorely. He was old and was getting older; his foot was heavy and sore, and the sore got no better as the years went by. He had very little money. He needed help, yet, from his companions, he felt it necessary to guard his scheme with dragon-like fierceness.

"I know dem," he cogitated, "I know dem nigger people. Dere is not a scale on dem outside I don't acquaint wid, same as if dem was fish and I did scrape dem; and dem head don't got place far enough back fe dem to crawl in and get out a' me sight. If I ebber say 'B' to one a' dem 'bout dis fe me business, dem will bruck dem neck to get dare fust, turning dem back, if you please, on dis dem own born country; and run go yonder, like hog run when dem smell ripe guava, else dem well ripe rotten mango. And which a dem gwine help me ober. Ebbery one only too jam glad to go tek me money and to see I can't go. Eben dat long side son a' me yeller sister, doh him know all I do fe him Mudder, eben to gib him recommend to me old employer as a berry good man to tek him pickney dem as day labour, eben him I know would only too glad to knock me down becausen me foot sore, and I is not a man of property and substance nowadays."

To the "Backra dem" he confided a little more. He even made a point to go down one day and see the Superintendent of the R.M.S., a jovial being who heard him through not only patiently but genially, and promised that when the time came he would save for Ebenezer a berth on one of the best steamers. The Superintendent even gave a shilling to help on the great scheme, and though the shilling was actually spent on buying tobacco, it always remained in Ebenezer's mind as a shilling in being, awaiting the application originally intended for it. He always spoke of it to himself as "dat shilling, which Superintend gie me; an' which I hab in a' me box." Ebenezer told his story to other white people, and they all seemed to think it very interesting and they all promised faithfully not to say one word to any black person on the subject.

But we wander far afield. Mrs. Gyrton and her neighbours were just then feeling the severity of the Tax Collector. To explain this, they referred to the well-known fact that the new Governor was about to be married.

"When a man is to marry," said White. "De one ting him needen to hab more dan anyting else is money, money *me son, money*. Lord, sah, de day you hear say female is gwine married to you, tek de longest stick you can get and get you forth and pick money where-ebber you can glimpse it. Get it, brudder, get it. Get it, get it; a me dah tell you; ef you no got money, no 'casion you bodder wid wife. It is as a mill-stone hanged round you neck and drowned in de uttermost part of de sea. Widouten money, matrimony is like when man start to cross dis harbour out yah widouten a boat; or when bird set out to fly widouten wing dem. Money is de stick to pick wife wid: and money is de basket to carry wife in 'a. Me dear sah, you know what woman is de day dem shut yon up wid him in a house, husband and wife. Him may seem feeble and ketty-ketty at a distance, and picky-picky, like a dem not too strong young chicken and so him scarcely can talk loud 'nough fe you to hear him; but when you married to him it is a different ting altogedder, oh yes, it is transcendentalism den. De way dat little ting can bawl and holler, it shake you ear's hole as when raskill boy shake a man guava tree. Get him money, sah; gib him money, sah, and if you don't got it, beg Big Master look after you close, close and put one particular angel for to be wid you when Himself gots business elsewheres; for you will need it, you will need it when dat woman raise pon you. De Gubbernor hab to sabe up ebbery maccaroni him can crook him fibe finger on fe him marriage. White people in particular do so, and I nor no intelligent and educated man, don't blame him; but it is becausen a' so Gubbernor want money bad, bad, mek dese Collector dem dah sabbidge fe taxes an likewise rage like de roaring Nubian Lion, and de glittering eye ob de vulture. Dem jus' left fe chaw off you foot and you two hand dem. Dem got nex to nutting left but to come when poor man is asleep and gnaw and bite off you nose level wid you face; and scrape out you eyebrow, just like ratta come and nibble you new boots, if you don't wrap dem up, and same as dem nasty little cockroach chaw, chaw on you finger top dem: or mind gravel and scrape off all you pretty picture dat you paste up on you House wall to *artify* de place and mek it look luxuriant.

"I like to see man married, more so all Gubbernor and Minister, and all dutiful Pastor and Master; for Sin no bwoy; a me tell you; and me and him is acquaint, me and Sin, all times quarrel and mek it up; all time bust out and sew it up again; a me tell you; Sin is no bwoy. But me master, de tax hard, sah; and you can see dat dem tell de Collector, 'mek no fun to tek it' by de way dem insist 'pon it, and insist 'pon it, and insist 'pon it, like a gimlet mekking hole in a board, and dem won't hear you gib reason or excuse. When a man gots to talk to you dat him don't want to hear anything, but all him want is to see you money, as dis Collector man is talking now, what you tink it mean? Why, me dear sah, it can't hide from an intelligent man, such as me. I want de tax, I want de tax, I want de tax, all him can say just like you hear dem sing sing de same ting ober and ober in some church; and den dat Collector jam you and blast you, and mek steep straight road fe you go a hell; meanwhile him dah push and push you deh. But I can well and see dat Collector fraid fe de Gubbernor, well as if I did stan' up and hear it. I know how de Gubbernor, say to him and dem udder Collector 'Jam and blarst you, sah; blarst and jam you eyes; and jigger you libber and libber you lights,' for a so dem biggest Backra is habituate to swear, so as to tangle up de debbil and confuse him in de account him keep in a' him big book against dem fe all de swear dem swear, and de cuss dem cuss and de bad ways dem go on wid pore naygur people, till de day come when Big Massa hold Grand Court so say: 'Debbil, what you got 'gainst dis man? dat dem did call Gubbernor, else Busha else Keeper,' as it may be. Den ole man Debbil catch up him spectacle quick, quick and seh, 'One minute, Big Massa, one minute, sah,' and him rum him finger down de book, like you see dem men do in a' store, when dem dah look up to tell you dat you owe' dem money dat you pay dem long ago; and bime-bime ole man Debbil say: 'Yes, you Honour, dis man did swear fe true, causen him coachman bring de buggy at ten 'stead nine or causen de butler smash up him bes' glass mug.' By which said time you see de Gubbernor widder up, and try all him know to catch Big Massa yeye, and smile sickly and shaky, as if him kind a dah seh, out a' de side of him mout, 'You know me, you know I is not a bwoy to do all dat,' when all de time ob course him well and did do it.

"But all dat is bime-by, now Gubbernor is big man: 'Jam and blarst you,' says he to de poor Collector, 'you is not getting in dose taxes proper; you is lazy, else you is a tief man; else you is an incapacity man; and if you tink seh I will fraid fe fire you out a' dutty, you keep on wid you foolishness, and you will see; you will soon smell dutty right under you nose when I kick you slap out a' street and don't look place fe you fall neider. You is massa fe you runner dem, and fe children' and I is massa fe you; so you wait; and before mango done fe ripen, and before Squire Morton finish fe find butcher man fool 'nough to buy off dem half dead old steer dat him done fatten up, after dem beat dem to leather and bone ina' him cattle cart, you will see someting dat dem udder one will turn to laugh after.' Lord, sah, if it is a time when you youself is finish fe pay you own share a dem damn taxes, it is pleasing ting to stand studdy and see dat Collector frighten fe de Gubbernor wus' dan female frighten fe duppy and cross cow. To see him squeeze dem tax payer by de neck back, till dem cough up de money, ak-kasham-ak-kasham, ebbery maccaroni a' de money; him can't hear nutting till you knock you money down before him. Granmudder dead; farder dead; house mash up, trade bad; sickness ketch you and all de family; cough dah hunt after you like dem bad dog dah bark after cow dem; doctor let down sounder in a' you chist and tell you, 'de condition is serious, me fren,' you sabe you mout-blowing. Collector not going hearie one deaf ting while you don't bring de money. Pay him de tax, dat is all and only what him want. De way de man fraid fe Gubbernor soak slap in a' him berry bone dem, me son, and gib him sort of an ague; becausen him seh: 'All berry well fe you men when I let you off you tax dem, you gone home and you wife and pickney dem sit down round you, talk pleasant and hab you little quarrel and udder enjoyment dem, or you gone sleep; or you dah nyam you dinner'; when dis brute ob a Gubbernor, like as a raging tiger, else like a big ole taffy goat, lub buck someboddy don't trouble him, got me dah cuss and buse me and blustificate me shameful to see; and dah tell me him gwine tun me out, and dat if him paint a bamboo self white and put it up it would look better dan me and do more work; and dat him dah going broke me to de debbil and all dem profanious and sepulcheral exclamations Gubbernor dem is habitual to use."

The circles upon which were shed the light of White's shrewdness and the radiance of Elias Broggins' sagacity touched but slightly on regions where toil those devoted but ill-paid servants of the State, the elementary school teachers of Jamaica. But some inter-communication there was.

A little daughter of Broggins, hearing the wonderful and veracious stories concerning the Queen, the Prince and the Governor, related them at school where they created some sensation, and in due time, through the medium of the scholars' anxiety to make their "composition" interesting, reached the Teacher. That worthy man, as he subsequently wrote to the Manager, "seized the opportunity to disabuse the mind of these mistaken people of their absurd notions"; and the children in due time carried his statements back to their homes. "Now," said White, "dis is what I all times saying. You see dis man, a man same as you and I, not a white man but a yeller skin man, and not too yeller eider; you might a seh him is black wid a few washouts dat sort a' bleach him out little bit. Now you see how dat man change side becausen him get place wid white people; you see how him tek up wid white people talk. We is a race, we black people, dat can nebber get on, and a dis mek so; by de time white man so much as hold up him han', black man pick up him book, split it wide open, slit up him mouth and begin sing and bawl, 'Amen, good Lord.' We is a wutless set a people. Young, young boy like a dis teacher, what him can know more dan you or me, eh me dear sah? But him must talk and talk as him hear white man mout go. Why dis bwoy wasn't yet begin to bruck eggshell to come out and see daylight when you and me was already tired fe eat corn. I don't belieb a wud a what him say. And I seh it is a shame dat dis man should bamboozle up dem poor pickney dem. What poor pickney in school can do but swallow wha dem teacher gib dem; it is same like young nightengale shut up in a' dem nest, all dem can do is to open dem big mout all day, and whatensoebber dem mudder put in, go down dem mout; causen if dem don't eat dat, dem don't get nutting dat is de way wid pickney and dem teacher. It is a matter dat de Gubberment should look into."

"Really, sah, really"; said Broggins, who agreed with the sentiment but, being engaged with his own thoughts, had not followed the oration in detail.

"All de Gubberment will look into is how to tek money as taxes," said Mrs. Gyrton, whom tax difficulties were at that moment hagriding. It was the struggle with this tax ogre which most depressed her mind and heart as she sat where we found her at the beginning of this chapter, on the steps of her door in the deepening darkness. A knock beat with sudden imperativeness on the gate of the yard. Someone stood in the street and struck loudly and sharply on the weather-beaten boards so that the rickety frame shook and even rattled. Loud as was the summons, Mrs. Gyrton made no response whatever, though she stayed her tears. It is the elemental impulse of the animal beneath the shock of fear or surprise, to seek concealment. That dates back to those simple days of woodland life when pretty everything new and surprising was also dangerous. Instinctively, as the knock on the gate sounded in her car, Mrs. Gyrton's thoughts clamoured that this had to do with overdue taxes and water rates, and that there stood without, behind that imperative rapping, some messenger of power, or as she had it, of oppression. "Miss Noel," she reflected, "might come as late as dis, but she wouldn't knock and bombard me gate like dat." She waited in silence, not imaginng that silence could protect her, but resolved in any case not to give help to a possible enemy.

The knock was not repeated. The visitor was one of Nature's logical minds. A knock like his must have been heard all over the yard and through the house. If it remained unanswered, either there was no one to answer it, or no one intended to do so. He pushed the gate open, and stepping into the yard, demanded: "Anyone at home?"

Mrs. Gyrton, peering through the gloom, distinguished the man by his figure, and answered, as in so often the case in Jamaica, by asking another question: "You want me, Mr. Grant?"

She offered no explanation or excnse for her silence and Grant asked for none. If this woman had remained silent when he knocked, he presumed she had her reasons for that course. Even if he had been curious about those reasons, as he was not, he knew that, if a woman wished to conceal her reason, she would do so, though she answered all your questions. Certainly Mrs. Gyrton had heard his knock, and certainly her silence had not prevented his finding her. These were essentials, and Grant, uneducated as he was, had some of that gift of centring his mind on essentials which, in a higher degree, went far to a make Napoleon the conqueror he was.

"Yes, I want to see you," he answered as he seated himself on a log, and, producing a wooden pipe, began to load it with tobacco. He was a short, stodgy fellow, bearing all over his face the footprints of a bad attack of smallpox. In some places the pockmarks showed dark than the dark surrounding skin. In others they were a shade lighter; the effect was not beautiful. A few black, curly hairs pushed out above his lips, which though thick were rather noticeably resolute. A very strong chin was also ornamented with a few straggling hairs. The man evidently allowed these to remain by intention, but there was no sign of his otherwise caring for them, for some were long and some were very short, some curled, some stuck out like bristles; they grew anyhow. One eyelid had a peculiar droop, and between the brows there was an irregular shape of very dark skin. This was a scar left where a bottle had once been broken full in his face. That face, considered by itself, suggested a man of somewhat advanced age and decaying physical power, but a glance at Grant's arms and trunk dispelled that delusion. Still in the prime of life, he was reputedly the strongest man in Kingston.

"Yes," he continued, "I come purpose to see you. I got a thing to tell you." He struck a match to light his pipe, guarded it from the wind, lighted the pipe and proceeded; "and I also got a thing to ask you. I know seh this house belongs to you. You don't pay rent for it."

"But I pay taxes," said Mrs. Gyrton dolorously, "Taxes and water rates. It is enough and more than enough." She paused a second and then said: "It is like two hamper, and one full wid iron and de udder wid led and we is de jackass stoop down between and mus' carry dem."

"Well," said Grant, "taxes is a hard thing. I don't contradict you, and it is like some a dem thing dat de furder you go wid them, it is the heavier dem get and not the lighter; like when you take up a load of sand, and as you travel wid it, rain fall and wet you properly. But better taxes lonely than taxes wid rent on top as well. The house belongs to you?"

"It belongs to Mr. Gyrton."

"Gyrton dead long time," replied Grant decisively, "else you would hear from him. You ever hear from him all these many years. You never hear from him not one time."

"No," assented Mrs. Gyrton. "I nebber hear from him not eben once. I nebber hear him whisper to me in a message by anyone come back here, let alone get jetter from him."

"Dead man can't write letter," commented the man, "any more than sun which set yesterday can come back and warm you today. De house is fe you."

"Till dem tek it from me fe taxes and water rates," moaned the woman.

"Well them don't take it yet," said Grant.

"Not yet," was the refrain.

"How much you owe? Taxes and all?"

Grant had chosen the time well for the proposal he was making. Under accumulating trouble. Mrs. Gyrton's mind, generally so quick to resent interference, resembled some muscular body which has for the time being lost the power of reaction. Prod it you might; it was as nerveless as a wet blanket. It was as dead to all intents and purposes as sodden leather. In fact, the outworks of temper having been thrown down, the ramparts of morality were revealed as a defence paltry indeed.

The woman now obediently detailed the position of her affairs.

"And ebbery day you live," said Grant directly and decidedly, "you will be worse off."

The woman, womanlike, unwilling to face disagreeable truth, darted passionately aside down the paths of vehement irrelevance.

"Why all dese Gubbernor and Collector must so jam craben for taxes. Duck pickney dem dont want water a piece more. Drunken man, it is de same him want rum. Why dem mus' so rage and raven and claw people fe money; hungry worse dan hungry dog; run wilder dan crazy ants. Dig in a' you head as woman wid fine teet comb search you out for lice. Gravel round you house like man dah get out sweet potato in a'you garden. Lord to see de big house dem all got, wid garden and coach-house and big dinner and all, and berry hose to water dem roses garden, and somting to cut de berry grass in a' dem yard, and man to clean dem boots and all. And to see what we poor ting got fe we part, so-so yard, so-so house and so-so bittle and little a' dat; and yet dem nebber 'top for one single year to come and rake and grab money from poor people.

My God, but you don't see it nuh? You big house must 'a hab wooden jalousie and you must 'a keep dem shut, for if it was glass windows you must see how dem use poor people down here."

"Well," said Grant, quite unmoved, "taxes was before you time and mine, and dey will be going when both you and me is dutty again. Don't bodder to fret. What I want to tell you, you must think over very careful, and if you tek it in the right way it will fetch you out of all these you troubles. I is man work me twenty shillings, thirty shillings and even to forty shillings a week but I don't have no house in this Kingston. Now I will come here an live wid you, if you agree. What you owe now I will pay it; you will have to bittle me and wash me clothes, and at the same time I will give you ten shilling certain every week. You can have you little washing and what else you can get to do, same as now. What you say?"

For some time Mrs. Gyrton made no reply whatever. Shamefacedly she at length muttered: "Mr. Grant, why we couldn't married an done. It would be same ting."

"No," said the, man bluntly, "it is a d—d different thing If I married you I take up the whole of the load and I tie it on me back wid rope and chain and not wid twine—twine you can break, but rope you can't break, nor can you cut chain. This way I tek up only what I want to carry and the day I tired I put it down same place."

"You needn't pay but ten shillings same as you say. But you know, Mr. Grant, I is a married woman, and from de beginning I always stand up for married and moralment. I is a woman gots church connection." In that last phrase she embodied the fact of a casual attendance at a church where her name stood on the membership roll with the supposition that she paid church dues, anchored to some unredeemed promise sunk deep in the years.

"All dat," replied Grant with no hesitancy, "is your business. You can tek what I say or leave it; I won't married. I want a strong woman like you, not a young or a foolish woman and not a woman wid a face going draw udder man to come here as ripe fruit draw wasp-wasp. I want such a woman to tend me clothes and my food and I will willing to do what you hear me say. But married I won't."

He looked round the yard. Here was room for a little garden. Some fowls and perhaps even a goat could find living room, and in such things Grant took a never-failing delight. He had been born in a far-away country district, and, though snatched thence by the intruding hand of Circumstance, he had travelled into distances remote from the quiet out-of-the-way mountain village, and through scenes very different from the still mornings there that fell with broad shadows and sparkling belts of light across the green leaves of the banana and the dew-diamonded leaves of the Cocoa, or the odorous evenings when the fireflies streaked the dark of the night-time's garments and the fragrance of the Sweet-wood passed like a refreshing hand over the hill-side; old tastes were still verdant in his heart. Men who knew him in capacities neither peaceful nor simple would have been surprized to find in *his* heart, this yearning affection; but there it was verdant and persistent. Old likings still lingered there like patches of grass, fresh and green, in the midst of a weary land. It was an unexpected oasis in the desert of a hard disposition.

He threw in a few more words now to remove any feeling the woman might have of being despised on individual grounds. He did not wish her self-love to be injured for he did not wish to have her, on that ground, set against his plan. His objection to a wife was a general principle and not a particular instance. It was to woman that he objected in that capacity not to a woman. Therefore after a short silence he continued:

"I did married once—to a pretty yaller-skin gal. My good woman it was de debbil. It was de very doorstep of hell. I tell you so. She did get tired and I did get tired, and then it was worse for we both get vexed. I almost get meself into serious trouble over that said girl at dat said time. You see this sort of crooked mark almost nighst and betwixt me eyes, like as if you take the corner of a hoe mouth and drive down deh? She do it; dat same girl do it. She lick me slap down wid a bottle. Blood blind me dat day or I would 'a swing fe it sure. I would a' kill her stiff dead but blood chock up me eye, and she get away. And you tink say I wasn't glad say I didn't lick her back. It wasn't good six monts after dat when God remember me and she dead; dead sweet and sudden as when you swing a sharp cutlass and chop right through a fat sugar cane."

"Oh she dead?" said Mrs. Gyrton. Her interest centred on the fact that there had once been a Mrs. Grant; since the continued existence of that personage would have made impossible the fulfilment of her own ambition; but Mrs. Grant was dead and—Any hope that she harboured was destroyed by Grant's next words:

"I will nebber married again, not while I know this hand from that, or night from day or rum from sweet kola. You can catch mongoose in a iron trap one time, if you set it skilful; but you must kill him den. If him get away no trap you can set will ever catch him again; and man married once and get out a' it wont married a second time, not while him got sense 'nough to full a salt-cellar."

"Well, ma'm," he continued "I make you my offer and you can consider it. I am going to Port Antonio dis two week coming. When I come back you can tell me. I gone now."

"Walk good, sah," responded Mrs. Gyrton mechanically.

IV

The Slaying and Eating of the Last Fowl—The Pouring
Forth of Debate—Into Theological Mazes—Prayer—The
Devil and the Carpenter—A Final Surprize.

On the wings of the wind to Mrs. Gyrton's friends flew news of
Grant's proposal. Manifestly this was a subject for discussion and
advice, and Rosabella, old White, Broggin and others were ready for
the day of debate and counsel. It was White, as usual, who amid the
unsubstantialities of opinion aimlessly wandering hither and thither,
and through the froth of mere talk, seized on hard fact and held it up in
a suggestion which was endorsed by all.

"You is hab now a serious thing to consider on, and to debate and
drasticate about, and de fust ting you should do is to mek good road to
tek you to weh you dah go. Watch white person; it is de first ting dem
do—to make good road. Now Mrs. Gyrton, you still hab one fowl left."
This was a definite, undeniable fact and there was none to contradict
him as he continued suavely:

"It would be best for we all to meet and talk 'bout dis business which
you now bring before us. Now I propose you invite us all to your yard, and
dis one fowl you got left, you can tek—and kill it and cook it"; he added
the last words in an incidental tone of voice as if taking the fowl was all
and killing and cooking it of no significance whatever. He continued:

"And I, for fe me part, will gib you a yam, if it is eben to piece of
one; and dem udder one will bring fe dem someting, if it is eben a red
pepper. It is pleasant so, and besides if you keep dat fowl much more
dem will likely steal it same as dem stealsome of de rest; and 'siden dat,
when you lib wid Mr. Grant you will not need dis one fowl. Him will
gib you many more. I tink dis is a good plan."

So thought they all, and Mrs. Gyrton quieted her scruples by the
argument that if she did "tek Mr. Grant" this one fowl would not be
missed. A day was therefore fixed for the slaying of the fowl, for meeting
and feasting at Mrs. Gyrton's yard and for the pouring forth of advice.

"First to eat," said White on that great day. "When de stomach is
full de brain is wise and den de tongue trabbil a right road. It is a ting
I all times notice; talk when you finish dinner; don't talk before you eat.
Watch white people; it is so dem do."

The majority favoured this view and therefore the feast preceded the debate. The latter was opened by Rosabella, Mrs. Gyrton's sister.

"Take," she said "de best chance you ebber yet hab since you come into de world a homely pickney, and dada say "it ugly no sin"; and de best chance you will ebber hab till de day come when dem put you in white clothes and tie up you jaw and clap saucer on eye to shut it down, and nail you up in a you coffin and left you ina' churchyard. Tek it and don't fool."

"But," objected Mrs. Gyrton, though she showed very little spirit, "I belong to church and you don't; you know dat, Rosabella. I use to pray and you don't"

"Pray," said Rosabella angrily, "and why I can't pray as good as you? And who de debbil tell you I don't pray? And I can't pray? I tell you dis, I will pray you blind if you want try."

"Still you is not a married woman," insisted Mrs. Gyrton, though it was a halfhearted protest. Her spirit was not what it had once been, or red battle would have closed round Rosabella's words.

"And what de debbil married do fe you?" asked Rosabella contemptuously.

"Well," said White, judicially anxious to recognise a fact, "it gib her dis house anyways; and it gib her dis fowl, de last fowl we just finish eat; and I want say, Miss Rose, it eat nice."

Rosabella's advance having thus received a rebuff, old Broggin took the floor. His bent was much more towards the general than to the particular and specific. The question immediately before them was whether or not a carpenter's wife, or widow, should live in concubinage; but this was too narrow a matter to confine Broggin's thoughts and speech. The word "pray" called him forth to wide regions, and his reflections swept like blundering bat wings to the verge of Time and Eternity.

"Now, 'bout praying, Mrs. Gyrton, don't you mek dem frighten you out a' praying; pray is a good ting; it is an amphibious habit. Miss Rosabella is a smart young lady, and him know a grea deal, and what him tink him know, but don't, would fill a barrel and a half; but dere is a ting you call too smart. You follow go a church, me dear female; you well and need all Minister and Church dem can do fe you."

"Don't frighten fe kneel down and pull prayer out a' you mout like dem poopa in de store in Kingston pull dem twine out a' little round box hang up over de counter in de shop. Kneel down, me daughter, kneel down low. Knock dutty wid you knee pan, and when de debbil come pass, like a roaring wind or a bellowing lion, wid him mout wide open and him white teet dah say, 'gie me, gie me someting to chaw,' him won't find you head to catch and carry way; him will tek dem mind stan' up tall and look boastful and proud, like Miss Rosie."

Rosabella did not make this *casus belli*. Indeed she did not feel offended at the charge of pride. In her opinion she had something to be proud of. Her pickneys were all "white." She merely made a remark to this effect, and Mr. Broggins, who had by no means exhausted his theme, continued with zest.

"Dem read in de Bible seh de debbil is a rolling lion, and trabbel round to see what him can catch; and what him catch him eat, bones and flesh and yeye-ball; but it can't mean lion, for lion you nebber see out here in Jamaica; but, as we all know, debbil is in Jamaica. It is wind dat roll here, and dat is what de Bible mean; you tek me word fe it, de wind roll and rumble all ober de tree tops and dat tree dat stan' up too high is a dead tree, for the wind will knock him down, sure.

"You kneel down me daughter, and, follow go a' church. You is full of lust and pomposity and pride; prayer will pull you down; like a when come middle a' mango season, and sake a' craben after mango and eat too much ob dem, boy get feber and headache and dem gib him a good wholesome piece a' blue pill, also a proper swallow a' castor oil; it clean him out; it pull him down; it mek him feel better. A' same so wid prayer."

This was all very well; but, in expressing his views thus freely on what the devil might be Broggin had crossed the track of another guest who was also given to theological ruminations. Mr. White felt it to be his duty to bring home to this audience the extreme difficulty of reaching a conclusion on a question concerning which his friend Broggins had spoken with such unhesitating temerity. Moreover, he had the memory of a personal grievance, a festering wound that required every now and then to be relieved by the discharge of words.

"It is a berry difficult ting," he now interjected, "to understand what dis debbil is, and how exactly him favour. I ask Minister all times 'bout it, but dem don't got dat acquaintance wid de ting which you would expect dem to hab. Dem isn't quite satisfactory. You would tink since it is fe dem business to fight dis same debbil, dem would know him, to deseribe him form and shape from de first hair in him crown-piece to the last corner ina' him foot bottom; but if you ask dem 'Debbil hab tail Minister?' else him got foot split like a goat, dem seem doubtful 'bout it. De most remarkable one I ebber meet tell me dat de debbil was *ina' me;* now, me daughter, look at you Poopa, look how me poor little body meagre and shrivel wid hard time, and sake a pay Buckra taxes, and strive to walk ina' de straight gate lead go a' hebben, like needle go troo camel's eye; I mean Camel go troo needle eye. What place I got inside me to make house fe big, big debbil. Someting big till him mek old time Elijah and David and Moses shake and frighten, and Massa Jesus himself tek forty solid day to bruck de brute down.

"More and sumebber, why him should look to lib wid me? Why him don't choose some a dem ripe rich old backra; rich till dem berry skin begin to turn yellow like gold; and wicked till dem hair self, stop fe grow, and drop off, as good as seh 'No, me son, me gone; dis place too hot fe me. It is going a Debbil oven and not a place else.' But I done wid dat Minister from dat day. I nebber go a him church; or if I does let me foot wander troo the door, I mek sure to tek me big copper and put ina' de plate to pay for it, so him can't say yea nor nay to me; I go and sit me down, and I pay for me seat. I don't under no obligation to him church. Him gib me him sermon, and I gib him me big copper; and me cut it off and finish. And if him ebber speak to me in de street, I am quite short and severe and don't hab any argumentation wid him. I hold de man insult me grievous, widdouten any cause.

"Not becausen you hab a little theological talk, a man is to tell you de debbil got house inside me. I did feel almost to tell him dat debbil lib inside him, and since he was man hab red hair and walk a quarter and a half lame, it did really look quite suspicious; but, sake of respect, I did not tell him so. But I notice dat since dat time one a' him pickney dead, and him wife most dead, which, if him tek it in the right way, should show him how him run risk to insult man like a me, whom Big Massa know is a honest, hard-working nigger, always hab respect for man in respectful position."

This exhausted what White had to say for the present on this intricate problem Mr. Broggins then, without any reference to what had transpired in the interim, resumed his remarks on prayer.

"Pray, me pickney?" he now said, "don't mek fun fe rub you knee pan dem on de ground, dig dem deep in, so you can get someting you can hold on to, like tree hold on to roots or ship to anchor. Pray, till you mek Big Massa dat tired fe hear you, and bex wid you mout walking round and round him and knock pon him ears, dis side and dat side, dat side and dis side, dat him seh, 'tek it, tek it, tek it, Oh Lord, tek all you want. I tired fe hear you mout, you is monotonous worse dan when ribber dah run down cascade.'

"Pray, me gal, pray; don't neglectful fe pray. And I tell you what, Mrs. Gyrton, I find it is a good ting fe pray time when de mudder one don't tink fe do it. When ebbery one dah pray to him same time, Big Massa got so much fe do mind listen dem and answer dem, and withal some of dem so fretful and cry-cry, and don't know well what dem want; and when him gib dem what dem cry for, before dem can proper get out a door, dem come back say, 'Lord, Lord, it is a mistake you mek. It is not dis I desires. It is dat udder ting dat dis man dah carry away. Stop him, good Lord stop him. Don't gie me cow when I want horse; and don't gie me umbrella causen I gots one. It is hat I want. Mek haste, Big Massa, mek haste, I well and want it.'

"Saking and 'casion of which whiny-whiny and cry-cry person, dere is dat confusion in heaven, dat it is chance if Big Massa hear what you say good and can attend to you all at once. But you pick and choose you times when most people don't tink to pray, den Big Massa can spare to listen to you, When I usen to follow praying heavy, being a young man and wanting all kind of tings, I did pray early in the morning before day clean, when the rest of them sleep; and I pray middle day, and I pray middle night, I did pray fe true."

"All well, fe talk," put in Rosabella surlily, "but what good you know pray ebber do you? Doh if it come to pray, I can pray meself, I don't say I can't and I don't say I don't."

"What good pray do?" said White in a state of righteous indignation verging on heat. "Don't you know all dem story 'bout 'Lijah and de ravens, and Jonah and de Whale, and Daniel in den of lions, and Joseph and him coat and him breddrens? You don't know all dat? Den you don't know nutting."

"And 'bout de new wine and de old bottles," said Mr. Broggins contributing what he could recall on the spur of the moment, "and Balaam and his jackass?"

"And de fiery serpent and de ten foolish virgins?" said Denton, following suit.

"Of course I know," said Rosabella resentfully, for few things-offend a Jamaican more than an imputation of ignorance of the Bible. "Of course we all know dem story; but dem is like fruit hang on top of a tall tree and you can't reach it. Tell me some story happen today yah, like fruit hang a low limb where you can pick it. Tell me, fe yourself what good prayer ebber do you?"

"I will tell yon," said White vehemently, and was on the point of blurting out what he expected to accomplish when at last he succeeded in getting to England and picking up money at the Prince of Wales' "door-mout." That was a matter of frequent prayer with him, and so real did his anticipated success seem to his fervent imagination that it stood before him as an actual and accomplished fact. Caution, however, laid her grip upon his impulse in time and he swiftly switched off into the following edifying narrative:

"When I was a sizable boy, when me hair did kind a' begin to hold back and hold back, and yet to grow, on me top-most lip, and me voice did squeeze up and open out peculiar, as in de prognostication of dat ephemeral of life, where I did lib, dem did hab prayer meeting ebbery Monday night punctual and I nebber miss go to it. Well, once I and anodder young fellow did walk troo Running River pen, and right at de place which I remember to dis day, where a big Cedar and five Cocoanut tree dah grow, we did tek two or tree cocoanut; not to say we did want dem, but sake a de way de cocoanut seem next door to talk and say, "pick we, pick we, you is fool if you pass we."

"Someone go tell lie 'pon we, and wid dat de Busha send Police after we. Now it was a Monday night when dem come fe we, and dem come trait a me house. Peter dem find, but me did deh a' prayer meeting, and, before dem could find out dat and come fe me, someone run and tell me 'bout it. I fire meself troo de door and tek road same time fe trabbil go a' me aunt a' Clarendon. In due time all did blow ober, for you know sake of a few cocoanut, Policeman don't carry malice too long. You ax me what pray ebber do fe me and I tell you dat story, which is a true story."

Rosabella felt it was full time to bring the discussion back to the matter immediately in hand. "Me dear creature," she said to her sister, "better do as 'cording as de man propose to you. A' *you* want him, a' no him want you. Man can get woman easy as kiss me hand, more so when him got money. Woman is like star-apple hang 'pon tree. It must stay deh till dem pick it. Man stan a ground pick what him want. It is woman when him get ageable, and is homely like you, and is poor, dat find man hard fe get. Now dis man him promise you ten 'mac' a week, and dat fe little more dan wash him clothes and boil him food. If you don't tek it you is a fool. You mek one mistake when you married to dat carpenter, don't mek any more now. Land crab down a Panama Isthmus eat you husband long time since, and pick him bone clean and white; same as dem eat all udder dead man buried dere. So what you got to frighten for?

"Besiden, even supposin' him don't dead, and him come back, what him can do you? White people got someting dem call bigannimy, purpose to interfere wid what don't concern dem, as is dem way, and trouble poor black people wid; but for dat you must really married again, while you husband is libe. Now you not going to married to dis man, you don't run a piece a risk, save and except when Gyrton come, if him do come, and I say him won't come, him will raise de debbil of a row, and will cuss and jam and blarst sickening to hear; but don't care what you do or what you don't do, Gyrton would mek a row when him come; so all will be same fashion. Tek de man; get you ten 'mac' a week and don't fool."

"You talk berry positive, Rosie, but you forget say I is a woman got church connection."

"Church," said Rosabella, "don't I go a church? Don't I sing hymn? Don't I can use prayer book and Bible? Does dem ebber turn me out a' church when I go dere, and yet don't all of dem know I got Backra for me sweetheart and got pickney one, twice, tree times, and nebber can and nebber will married? Church! Look yah, if a church dah trouble you, go a you Minister and ask him flat to tek up collection fe you ebbery mont.' Tell him if him will do so you will do what dem say and tell dis man Mr. Grant you can't lib wid him. You tink any minister will do dat for you?"

"I is married woman," said the Carpenter's wife almost plaintively. "Backra dem all know me, dat I set me face against sin. I can go a sacrament any time. Rosabella, you know you can't tek sacrament."

"Set you face against sin," said Rosabella contemptuously, ignoring the point about sacrament which she could not meet. "How much a week Backra will pay you to set you face against sin? When Backra want Black-man to mek Constable, don't him pay dem two-and tuppence a day? Him want black woman to clean out church, else wash clothes, or even say pick common jigger out a him foot wid needle, don't him pay dem, if it is little or much? But when it come to set you face against sin which a dem you see pay you wages. And dat is why I say dem is all an hypocrisy and sham."

Unhappy Mrs. Gyrton answered weakly or not at all. Rosabella pushed her advantagee.

"Ask dem out and out," she said. "Ask dem plain and simple to gib you ten mac, or even seven, or even five self, to pay you to set you face against sin as you call it, and see if you will get one big copper from any one of dem. Minister oh, class-leader oh, elder oh, or deacon."

"Rosabella," said Mrs. Gyrton after a pause, "you is a sensible woman. I did not tink on all dese tings."

It was the sign of surrender. The Carpenter's wife, or widow, had hauled down the flag of respectability.

Again night was falling, and again, amid the gathering darkness, Mrs. Gyrton sat on the step of her house. Tonight there was no fowl to disturb the stillness of the yard, but it was shaken by a steady, jarring sound as the woman turned the handle of a small rackety coffee mill that reposed in her lap. She had before her mind a change in life, which was to neutralize all her previous laborious respectability; yet it must be confessed that her thoughts were brighter than they had been for many a week. Mr. Grant was due within a day or two and the answer that she had ready for him would, she foresaw, lift a great burden from her shoulders. It would take her out of that dismal morass of debt which threatened to engulf all her possessions. True, she was about to place herself in a position from which she could never again address Rosabella effectively on marriage and respectability. Rosabella could in the future take advantage of the change and say to her things hard and bitter; but after all words could be forgotten; unpaid taxes stick to one like one's shadow. Miss Noel would certainly be vexed when she understood what had happened; but as Mrs. Gyrton said to herself "young lady like dat, what she know 'bout such tings. I will tell her I is tekking lodger same as white lady tek in lodger. Any fashion it will tek long enough time before she understand it." Moreover, in her heart, the woman could not believe that, whatever happened Noel Bronvola would ever "throw her away." So the answer was ready for Grant; and Mrs. Gyrton, sitting there in the rapidly deepening twilight, twisted the handle of her mill, and was fairly content with the future she saw rising for her beyond the coming night.

Someone stepped up the street and stopped at the gate. There, without knock or summons, he laid a hand on the latch, pushed the gate back and entered the yard. Looking up in anger, Mrs. Gyrton saw the newcomer had a right to do all this and more.

"My God," she exclaimed, dropping the mill as she sprang to her feet, and, she made an instinctive clutch as at some form, near her that could help. "My God," and she stared with wide open eyes. The Carpenter had returned to his own.

Apparently Gyrton took it as the most natural thing in the world that his wife should spend some time in exclamation, and while she was thus employed, he turned a mildly interested eye on the yard, to see perchance if some well remembered features remained.

His silence, gave Mrs. Gyrton a thrill of superstitious alarm. "It is a dead. Him come back from the grave," she muttered uneasily, shrinking away from the apparition. "It is his duppy," and an accusing conscience reminded her that she stood on the eve of handing over the Carpenter's house to Mr. Grant.

"It is warning," she murmured. "Him come to call me. It is a dead man. It is so they always come. Him got a message for me."

At that the Carpenter spoke gruffly "Don't talk chupidness; don't you see I am somebody same as you.' It gave him a weird feeling to be regarded as a spirit. "You ebber see duppy carry pipe?" he added. He produced the pipe, then tobacco, and began to fill the latter in rather an ostentatious manner; as if bent on proving to himself and his wife that he was ordinary flesh and blood,

"But all these years, you nebber come back," stammered Mrs. Gyrton.

"The world," said the carpenter easily and largely, is a big place; and it is like a down hill; "when you start to roll on it you may roll berry far."

"But Rosabella said Panama crab eat you and dat dem pick you bones white," persisted Mrs. Gyrton, who had been impressed by that picturesque statement and not at all by the fact that the assertion was based on no proof whatever.

"Rosabella is a damned fool," said Gyrton warmly. "How de debbil," with yearnings towards a logical demonstration, "how de debbil Panama crab could eat me, when it is not Panama I just come from; it is Mexico. Tell me dat now."

To this poser Mrs. Gyrton attempted no answer.

"Where is Becka," said the man by and bye.

"Car kill him in Orange Street dis some years gone," replied Becka's mother, and for the present that was the only memorial raised in their conversation to their little daughter.

Gyrton looked round the yard again and asked a few questions; then in his own style he told his wife as much of his history during the last few years as he thought she ought to know. She for her part, detailed her troubles past, present and future, with the Collectors of taxes and water rates. To her great pleasure the carpenter seemed very little put out at the prospect of wiping out these arrears that loomed above her so fatefully formidable. He signified that he had come back with some money in his pocket, and he said, "I hear say carpenter work is very good here now; I will soon make more money."

Mrs. Gyrton said that she had heard the contrary. But her husband took no notice of that remark.

"One ting," he said, "I must have is a partner. I want a strong man, wid a strong heart and a man wid a quick head and a stiff tongue; one a dem tongue dat don't move easy on its hinge. Not like fe you. Somebody dat will learn it quick as I did," he added almost musingly.

"You mean the carpenter business?" asked his wife. "Don't you better get a man know it already?"

"Carpenter business be damned," said her husband emphatically much to the bewilderment of his wife. She, however, received no encouragement to continue asking questions. The Carpenter gave her money to buy a good supper, while he went off to bring in his trunk.

Mrs. Gyrton found herself in the street in a condition of mind somewhat dazed. The rapid movements of events had produced in her a feeling akin to the dizziness caused in persons of weak or sluggish brain when they watch a too quickly revolving object. That sense of righteousness and respectability which she had so lately thrown down and regarded as forever dismissed, began slowly to return to ascend its old throne. She was a married woman; she was still a respectable female, who during long years of absence had lived as wife, or widow, should. She felt more and more a sort of redawning of virtuous heroism. As this moral glow flowed through her heart, she insensibly felt that it would assist the process of rehabilitation to gaze at something that was identified in her mind with her religious respectability. She thought of church, of Sunday School children, of the deceased Becka, once a Sunday School scholar, and then she thought of Noel, Becka's Sunday School teacher. A few minutes later Mrs. Gyrton stood in front of the church schoolhouse, alive just then with a meeting of a girls' Guild. Becka had often talked of this meeting. From the lighted schoolroom now a subdued sound of voiccs spread out into the night. The Guild murmured like a hive of bees.

Mrs. Gyrton looked in through one of the jalousies; a girl sitting near at hand caught sight of the ill-natured eyes and shrank back. The woman muttered a curse at the idea of anyone being afraid of her, just as, under other circumstances, she would have cursed because no one seemed afraid. Then the angry eyes sought up and down the room for Miss Noel, but in vain, Noel as it happened was temporarily absent from the hall, Still, having come to seek her somehow assisted Mrs. Gyrtoe to realize more fully that she had not after all lost her foot-hold on the rock of respectability, and she turned away now to buy supper, repossessed of her old time self-approbation and self-assurance.

About half an hour later the lighted schoolroom drew to it two other persons from the surrounding darkness. They also sought Noel. One was a tall black girl, who was marked out by an air of distinction for notice wherever she went. The other was a diminutive black girl, feature and figure made thin and sharp by poor food, by poisoned city air, by the continual friction with the acute though shallow wits of the city folk of her class. This child could make a bargain as well as her mother. It was a tough job to deceive her by any untruth, however well planned. She was mistress of ceremonies tonight, for she, and not her tall cousin knew Noel. The cousin was there to be shown this wonderful Sunday School teacher of Charlotte Wedmore, and she gave herself up passively to the direction of the said Charlotte as anyone of us will do when we are anxious to satisfy our curiosity.

Charlotte was in daily combat with the real and with matters of hard fact. Nevertheless there lurked in crannies of her being a good deal of imagination, mystification and fancy. Mrs. Gyrton had walked straight to the window and looked in through the jalousies, without hesitancy. She had blasted the eye that she met with a scowl, had searched the room round and round and then, without further delay or manoeuvre, had walked away. Charlotte could have come to the window in the same direct fashion; but her manner of approach was vastly different. She halted her cousin some distance away; then manoeuvred elaborately to reach the window, as if she knew that deadly danger waited her in that vicinity. Low she stooped, carefully and silently she crept from point to point, always going where the shadow lay deepest. Arrived at the house, she pressed close to its walls, as close as she could possibly go, and moving along thus stealthily she at length found herself under the window. She paused now and listened intently for a full minute. Then very gradually she stood erect and looked into the room; at once stooping again she sank to the very ground, for she saw, or pretended she saw, someone watching the window.

Charlotte tried again, and once again she ducked her head incontinently. Her big cousin watching from the other side of the road must be impressed with the danger of this mission. When, for the third time the little girl looked into the room it was evident that previous rapid appearances and disappearances had at last attracted attention, for now a girl near the window whispered loudly:

"Charlotte, I bet you I report you."

Charlotte's reply was a terrible grimace ending with a red tongue thrust just as far as it would go between her white teeth. However the encounter did not develop, for at that moment every child in the room stood up to sing the doxology. The Guild was about to close its meeting.

Charlotte faded from the window and rejoined her cousin.

"Miss Noel," she said, "will soon come out, but me mustn't go nighst the window for she tell me all times never to come to the window, unless I could come to Guild."

Noel issued from the door, preceded and surrounded by a troop of girls.

"Watch me," said Charlotte. "Lend me your basket; you will see how she will speak to me. I tell you she respect me much."

Charlotte crossed the street to Noel. She was acting the part of a dutiful little girl returning home with purchases for her mother, carried in a somewhat heavy basket. The inference was plain; duty had kept her from the Guild.

As she foretold, Noel spoke to her at once, and Charlotte beckoned vigorously to her cousin, but the tall girl rather shrank back than came forward, Charlotte returned presently, after watching Noel enter a car. The young woman who had given herself up to the guidance of the little busy-body so long as she wished to satisfy her curiosity, now resumed her natural place of command.

"So that is Miss Noel," she said. "Give me my basket, and let us go home."

"Why you did not come when I call you? I would a make her speak to you."

There was no reply, and Charlotte continued emphatically:

"One ting you take and lock ina' you head, Delia, where you know how to find it. If ebber you got trouble, she is the young lady to help you. She is wringing down wet up wid kindness; and she is like a umbrella when trouble dah rain pon you."

"Perhaps," said the other quietly, "but I don't beg anyone to help me, even when I am in trouble. The world is there for me as well as anyone else."

"So you say now," said Charlotte shrewdly, "but trouble don't ketch you yet. Wait till it come out a bush on you."

"I can remember her without wanting her help," was the reply.

Meantime Mrs. Gyrton, supported by that sense of temptation overcome, which we have noticed as gradually suffusing her soul, and laden with materials for supper, were retracing her steps to the yard. There chased through her mind as she came in sight of the well-known gate, a grateful reflection that Grant's visit was not due till a day later. Tremendous would have been the row had Gyrton returned to find Grant as good as in-installed in his shoes. Now the latter would hear in good time of the new arrival, and he was not the man to thrust his head into the lion's mouth for no sound reason.

But the surprises of that memorable day were not yet exhausted. At her gate, Mrs. Gyrton became conscious that two persons were conversing in the yard behind. She listened. One voice belonged to Grant.

The woman opened the gate fairly dazed with surprise.

Still more surprising was it to find both men chatting amicably. Grant bade her good evening in the most ordinary manner, and soon after her husband announced that he proposed to take Mr. Grant as a partner in his carpenter's business. Now Grant had not hitherto been known to fame as a carpenter, so this arrangement was a further surprise for Mrs. Gyrton. She, however, was wise enough to be silent, and the next thing her husband told her was that Grant would come to board with them.

The fact was that Gyrton had returned to his native island extensively equipped for business much more remunerative, and somewhat more obtrusive and less monotonous, than carpentry. He had felt that he would need a companion, and the stronger minded Grant who, by the merest chance, had come to see Mrs. Gyrton twenty-four hours earlier than was at first planned, had speedily possessed himself of the other's will, and guided it safely to confidence in himself and to the proposal of partnership which so astonished Mrs. Gyrton.

In the following weeks remarkable changes were made in the Gyrton premises, and when these were concluded, anyone who had known that unkempt place before would have glowed with pleasure. The carpenter's bench, fitted with a tidy grindstone for sharpening tools, a prominent and capacious tool-chest and wooden "dogs" for holding in position the boards that were being sawn, a plentiful supply of shavings and sawdust all proclaimed that the carpenter was no drone; and indeed not a few remarked what a change for the better there was in Gyrton as far as work went.

He was more prosperous even than he was industrious; a visitor too with a previous knowledge of the place, would have experienced a sort of feeling of mystification. The kitchen certainly seemed smaller, and yet, otherwise, it looked exactly as it had always done. A brick wall closed either end with the same old, black, dirty look. Not a pin was there to choose between one wall and the other, yet somehow the walls seemed closer together.

Now, one of these walls was only a sham affair; though a sham so cleverly constructed as to almost certainly escape detection unless the observer had some reason for examining the place very minutely; and except when the skilfully fitted door through it stood open, or with the key in the lock. Behind that partition was a small room which was said to contain carpenters' tools; but the implements found there would have lain strangely in the hands of most carpenters. This was the background of the picture. In the foreground that Gyrton presented to the world, wrought the industrious Carpenter and his strong assistant Mr. Grant. In the background behind that clever sham wall, work was done by lamp-light which it was essential should not be exposed to the light of day. The photographer has his dark room, as we know, but the business in which Grant and Gyrton were partners was not photography.

V

Between the jaws of the Meffalas—Fidelia, the Coromantee—The smiting of John Meffala on the mouth—The Sot at Midnight—The Order of the supple-jack—The tragic work-seeker—Through wine to truth—A misinterpreted meeting.

The retail establishment of Meffala and Co. lay against Haven Street, Kingston, like a wide-mouthed sea monster to whose extended jaws the sweeping currents bring with them small fish and animalculae, the creature's food. The Manager, clerks, and accountants were the filaments of the yawning mouth, through which the purchasers were strained, Meffala's retaining their coin, and casting their persons and purses into the street.

On a certain forenoon the jaws, otherwise the doors, were open and the filaments, otherwise the Manager, clerks and accountants, were all at work. Sales were being effected at the various counters, but business was not brisk, and as Meffala Senior, paced the length of the shop floor he timed his steps to thoughts of reducing expenses. He could discharge one or more of the clerks. This salary could be pruned; that could lose a leg; this an arm. Times were dull; there were few demands for clerks and accountants, and these of his would stand a lot ere they cut the painter. It did not follow that any clerk would actually be discharged, or even that any salary would be at once reduced, for Meffala was much given to pursuing a similar line of thougut. It was pleasant to him to reflect that all these men and women stood at his mercy, and it interested him to calculate how much he might save by getting rid of one or two of them. It pleased him also to note how his gaze sent quaking apprehension through these men and women; how they would grow pale when he brought up the subject of dismissal. To see this one and that one dragged forward by his word like a criminal being indicted for some shameful offence; to watch the tense anxiety, the clumsily hidden fear, while he held up dismissal as possible; and the pitiable gratitude when he announced acquittal. It amused Meffala; it made him think better of himself, for it gave him the sense of power.

As the clerks took money from the customers they put it and memorandum of their sales into little tin cars which ras on wires overhead.

The wires converged above a raised platform. There, behind a railing, sat the Cashier. She opened each pan as it arrived, counted the money, and sent the car back, empty or with the required change. Then she "tilled" the cash, and filed the memorandums to be handed on later to the book clerk. It was the Cashier's business to see that the money tallied throughout the day with the memorandums. Meffala's Cashier was our little friend, Ada Smith. Just now Ada was moderately busy because although there were few buyers, they all happened to want change.

Among the buyers there was a black girl plainly but neatly dressed in brown linen and wearing a sailor bat. Her height marked her out to attract attention wherever she stood, whether by herself or in a crowd, and her face held that attention. It contradicted the opinion that every black face has the same broad features, the flattened nose, the low forehead, the thick lips.

This girl, in whose veins there ran no drop of European blood, had a forehead high and broad. The nose was well modelled; the lips, full but not thick, were firm and pleasant to contemplate. The chin suggested a character decided and resolute, a disposition hewn out in lines of strength. Here, one thought instinctively, is a strong nature, native principle and strong native intelligence, a bedrock of enduring character.

Standing near her, was a woman of a very different kind. The little of good that she had inherited from the ages had been devastated and desolated by the years. Her aspect bespoke a heart in which the milk of human kindness had long since curdled. The black, blunt features were coarsened. The eyes, a sullen light, glared like a mist-blurred sun, looking out over a country which a hurricane had torn and bruised. Here, in fact, was an existence that continued because Nature implants the desire to live so deeply in human beings that it remains after happiness has fallen above it into irretrievable ruin. Rage looked out here like a chained and savage mastiff.

These are the people who live on, not because life is dear or pleasant; but because they see beyond a greater darkness and possibly a more terrible burden. They endure the intolerable because they have no proof that they are right in thinking that it is the worse thing possible. They are like a man on a path above a precipice who goes on because he can neither turn back nor stand still. Mrs. Gyrton's happiness had not increased since we saw her last.

She had now handed over a two-shilling piece and was waiting for the chadge. As she stood there, her eye rested on the girl beside her with that air of hostile contempt at times observable in women of this class and temperament towards other black women who show superiority in dress and deportment. While Mrs. Gyrton waited, the tall girl had finished her purchase of a pair of boots which she had chosen with much care and right in the teeth of the counter clerk's advice.

There entered the store another woonman on whom we should bestow some attention, since we will meet her again in this story. This was an English girl of some four and twenty. Her pale face wore a look of refinement and her extreme fairness contrasted with the dark blue uniform which marked her as ranking in the Salvation Army. It was a thin face; but it bore no line suggestive of pain or privation, though of both these she had had her share. Nor had sorrow passed her over unvisited. She went forward through the years, following a great idea which, to her, appeared like a mighty pillar of fire moving and burning as it led the way across life's desert and through life's night to a distant dawn and a far-away day of perfected peace. Her face, lifted to the sky, was flushed by the rays that streamed from that guide of flame. Hers were not beautiful features, and yet they won in that irradiation a mysterious transfiguration; just as at night the gush of light from a passing lantern will change, strangely and beautifully, the look of the dust-draggled roadside which by daylight seems so commonplace.

The Army lassie was no buyer in this warehouse of Vanity Fair; what to her were the gay dresses and smart ribbons here displayed. She was present to say a word to a girl behind the counter, and with that word to leave a bunch of violets which someone had allowed her to pick that morning. She knew a little of the girl's story and was trying to help her along a steep path.

Now Meffala, Senior, had a weakness for the little lassie, with her pale face, neat uniform and cheery manner. He came across the floor and said:

"Well, Captain, not tired of the Army yet?"

"Praise God, no," said the girl smiling. She was a Major, not a Captain, but Meffala called every Army officer Captain, and thought there was a subtle joke in doing so.

"Ah well," he said, "when you are too tired to go on with the Army any more, you come to me and you shall have a decent place here. It will be easier than the Army and perhaps we will find you a husband, eh."

"When I am too tired to go on," said the girl, "I will go home."

"Ah," said Meffala with an odd touch of respect, "to England?"

"To heaven," said the Major, "heaven is my home—and yours," she added.

Meffala hung out a rather sickly smile, and looked round at his store. It would have seemed strange certainly to turn a corner in the heavenly city and to come upon the well-known large and brazen sign-board of the Meffalas. Clearly his gold would have been out of environment amid the celestial gold that is clear as crystal. Meffala felt this as he returned a lame "Thank you," to the Major's hearty "God bless you."

The Cashier, looking out between the bars of her railed-in space just as that "God bless you" was uttered, had the voice and face stamped deep into her memory. She had seen the Major before without noting her in any particular manner; but this afternoon her memory was in some way more open to the impression that is indelible. For one thing, the Major's last words to Meffala seemed odd and out of place. Meffala was the very last person among Ada's acquaintance to whom she would have said "God bless you." She detested the man, and really would have thought no better of heaven for wasting its blessings on him. At the same time, however, she feared her employer and this fear made her very respectful outwardly, so that Meffala had a good opinion of his Cashier.

As Meffala turned back into the store, he passed close beside the tall black girl, but on her he did not bestow a second glance. What was a black girl to such as Meffala, Senior? Besides this particular girl he saw almost daily.

Fidelia went out into the street, and Meffala came striding back, reviewing his counters. He paused to fling a few harsh words at a clerk who, he suspected had overheard the Major say that heaven was their home. He thought he detected on that clerk's face the eddy of a sunken smile, and he wished to impress the fact there and then, that, however Meffala, Senior, stood as regarded the heavenly country, in that store he would remain master.

"No wonder," he said, "business rots here, when you stand gaping like, like—a clucking hen, Smellie. To your work, sir, while you are here," he repeated that. "God knows how long that will be; but I have my suspicions."

There met that afternoon and parted unknown to each other, personally, or all but unknown, a number of people destined as it transpired in after days to affect one another's lives to a considerable extent.

Ada remembered the day because in the evening a bad two shilling piece was found in the till. It was not the first time that this had happened and Meffala said now that on the next occasion the Cashier would have the pleasure of refunding the amount to the business. That drove the matter home into Miss Ada's mind, and though, in telling Harold of the affair, she pecked at Meffala in the fashion of a spiteful sparrow, she began from that day to keep a vigilant eye on all coins that passed through her hands.

As to Harold, when she grew eloquent on the unfairness, unreason and injustice displayed by Meffala, he said mockingly. "The only just way to manage women is to be unjust to them; and as for reason, it is quite out of the question in dealing with your sex. You are never just, only fair. Angels fly they do not tread the paths of reason." He knew that Meffala who had business reasons for keeping in his good books, would not dismiss his present Cashier, but, within that limit, it was in Harold's opinion not at all a bad thing for the young lady to be made to feel that she was at her employer's mercy. When, however, Ada fretted, in his good-natured way he told her Meffala would not discharge her, though he might fine her. To cure her doleful dumps completely he took her for a long evening drive into the country, listening with amusement to her prattle about the store aud its occupants, and to her feminine invective against Meffala. Thus began Ada's dragonlike watch for bad coin in the house of Meffala.

In the afternoon of that day, Fidelia Stanton sat in the large, rather ostentatiously furnished but well-kept, home of the Meffalas, where she was employed to sew. In black humanity a European eye is apt to find nothing more than a monotony of colour. It is an unobservant eye in such matters, when all is said. But even to such an eye this girl broke the level of monotony.

She was tall and erect, with a well-shaped and well-proportioned body, that in motion suggested strength rather than gracefulness; strength and resolution. The unadulterated blood of her tribe ran in her veins and she was a Coromantee, daughter, that is, of the bravest of all the tribes that were brought to our shores during the 18th eentury, from the West Coast of Africa. They came as slaves; but the Coromantees, brave, enduring, haughty and resolute, made bad bondsmen. Men whom nature had made free in soul, their fellow men found it no easy task to fetter. Through their brief periods of quiet submission they worked wonderfully well, inspired by their pride of race to show their powers; but they sprang into rebellion as surely as the rays of the midday sun, passed through the burning glass, kindle fire; and those rebellions in which the Coramantees led were always the best planned, the best directed and the most desperate. On the field where the Coromantee was beaten, he died weapon in hand, scorning surrender. And as he asked no quarter where he failed, so he gave no mercy where ho succeeded. The duel with him was to the death.

When the great Easter rebellion of 1760 failed, Tacky and his Coromantees shut themselves in a cave and slaughtered each the other, rather than surrender to the hated conqueror.

The white man came to see ultimately that it did not pay to have these fierce free men as slaves, and in Jamaica their further importation was prohibited by Law.

Fidelia Stanton was a full-blooded Coromantee though she knew nothing of the history of her tribe. None had ever told her of the valiant deeds of her grandfathers and of their sires; but the pure tribal blood flowing in her veins was a conducting chain along which thrilled mighty but invisible forces that connected her in moments of emergency with that race and that past in Africa to which she belonged. In that tribal past lay buried sudden and bloody raids on enemies, hate of whom was as old as the Coromantee name, and as the tribal faith; desperate fighting in the blackness of night rent and gashed by the fierce, red fire of the torch thrust into the thatched roof of the temple or the hut; the struggle of men who knew not fear and feared not death to beat the enemy from their village homes, while the tumult of battle echoing through forests old as the creation and the glare flung out from the maelstrom of heroism and destruction, lighted up the dark foliage overhead and marked out the white boles of forest giants, as if it sought and showed there the skeleton of the land.

To Fidelia that blood, pure as it ran in her veins, gave instincts of irresistible strength and gave to her, also, an assurance that was entirely without uncertainty. This helped her in great crises, but, perhaps, it made her appear in the prosaic surroundings of everyday life a little tragic. She had that indefinable air of distinction which is such an offence to the many incapable of analysing its origin, and who first distrust and then hate what they do not understand.

Long ago, when her great grandfather had stepped on shore from the slave ship at Port Royal, the Planters, who were there to find the best of the newly arrived slaves were all of them struck by the man's appearance. Slave he might be and was by man's mandate, but by Nature he was less a slave than any man there, white or black. He was a Chief by birth, a King.

It had happened by grace of circumstande, that this man, and his sons after him, had found women of their own proud race to bear them children in the land of bondage; and so their blood had poured through the veins of three generations, unadulterated by tribal or racial intermixture, bearing in its pure current inspirations and vital thrillings born far, far away from the scenes amid which the blue Caribbean smiles bright besides Jamaica's wooded mountains. Fidelia Stanton, a girl who in her time had to go down on her knees and clean the floor with cocoanut brush, rag, and tub of dirty orange water, that she might earn the wherewithal to stay her hunger, was as proud a being in her way as that ancestor of hers had been, who answered the summons to surrender after a day's battle and defeat by driving his dagger with one strong, deep thrust through his jugular vein, and so spilling his life.

It is the conventional idea that the black men brought to the West Indies as slaves came from a life wholly savage and barbarous; through which there ran not a single vein of coherent organisation; a life unredeemed by a single spark of nobility and unsustained by aught of organised government, law or order. The truth, however, is that in some cases these men and women came from tribes which maintained a system and code of unwritten law that embodied, for the tribe at least, more thoroughly and efficiently than Christianity has yet succeeded in doing for the whole race in the West Indies, a great number of those moral obligations that are elemental and are vital to the well-being of a people. There are tribes at home in Africa, there are still such tribes, which amid all the appearance of mere barbarous existence, have so well learnt the lesson of purity, and loyalty, that to be branded among them thief, adulterer, traitor, meant, and still means, irretrievable disgrace, and in some cases even death. Happy would the mentors of West Indian morals be, if they could say that such offences meant generally in the West Indies even social ostracism. To this day tribes of the Upper Creek River, where the backwash of European advance has not corrupted the simple but vital virtues, take rigid precautions to preserve their girls' chastity. In some cases so rigid is the tribal conception of this virtue that a girl is held to be unchaste if a man, other than her nearest blood relations, has even touched her person.

Neat, clean, grave-looking Fidelia Stanton, with blood in her veins drawn from a source such as we have indicated, sat in the work-room of Mr. Meffala's house, sewing. The room was seldom invaded by the male members of the household; but this afternoon it happened that John Meffala wanted to see his mother and came to seek her.

"Fidelia," he enquired "Where is your mistress?"

"I don't know, Master John, I think she is out downtown."

"When will she be back?"

"I don't know, sir."

On this the young man did not depart, but coming further into the room, took a step or two about it, till he was in a position to watch, unobserved, the face and figure of the girl. It was not the first time he had watched her with an evilly significant interest and appreciation. He was a big, burly fellow, this eldest born of the Meffalas, with a face not unpleasant, though it had unpleasant features. The lips were sensual, the eye, when it watched a woman, too bold; the nose was a trifle too broad. But he was young, hale and fresh-coloured. The beginnings of evil that lurked in his face like thieves well hidden in a leafy garden, were not readily seen. It needed, not only several enquiring looks, but also some experience to discover the secrets hidden behind the rather full-moon appearance of Mr. John Meffala. The thieves were there, but the garden leafage was heavy and the depredators for the present hid well. John was not in his father's business, he was an employe of Peter Passley, and one may say here was a good employe one who did his work carefully and systematically. He was trusted and he well deserved the trust. He did not live with his father and mother but kept bachelor's quarters in another part of the town, finding this, for various reasons, more convenient for all concerned.

Fidelia, intent on her sewing and on her own thoughts of her mother far away in the country, was barely conscious that John Meffala had not left the room. So a few minutes sped by.

"What parish do you come from, Fidelia?"

"St. Ann, Mr. John."

"Ah, I know St. Ann a little. Do you like Kingston?"

"I like it well enough; but it is hard to live here. I cannot earn very much money."

"Do you know you are a very superior girl? I never saw a black girl who pleased me better. Are you educated?"

"I went to school and I learnt what I could. I am not educated."

"You are much above this sort of work, anyhow."

"I don't think so," said Fidelia simply.

"What does my mother pay you?"

"Four shillings a week and she feeds me, in part sir."

"D—d little," said John. "Just like the Mater," he added. She spends as much as that on scent in a day, I bet. She pays her as a servant and gets dressmaking work out of her." As Fidelia made no reply to his remark in that form, he gave it an interrogative flavour.

"That is very little?"

"There are others who would take less."

"Is my mother kind to you?"

"She is not unkind, Sir."

"Well, I hope you will stay here." He crossed the room and for a minute or so stared through the open window. Then he returned and resumed the conversation. For here was a spark he thought he would blow into a flame.

"Wouldn't you like to get more money?"

"Yes, very much, Sir. I need it at home."

"Oh, you have a home; and a mother?" he added at a venture.

"Yes, she is not strong and can't earn much."

"Where is your father?"

"Dead."

"You don't sleep here do you?

"No, Mr. John."

"And where is your home?"

"In St. Ann," replied the girl shortly.

"But you don't go to St. Ann every night?" he said with a laugh.

She did not answer.

"Come," said John. "Don't be shy. Where do you live when you are not in this house, or in St. Ann?"

"In Kingston," was the brief reply.

Virginal instinct suddenly sprang forth in Fidelia's consciousness crying "to arms"; she saw at length behind these questions the outline of a sinister motive.

"But where in Kingston?"

"Excuse me, I don't see why you should know."

"Oh," he said in a tone more careless than he had hitherto employed, and lighting a cigarette as he spoke, "I can easily find out from one of the other servants. It is small odds whether you tell me or not."

"But why should yon want to know?"

The girl flung the words at him bluntly almost harshly. Her inner sense was more informed of danger every minute by the instinct which tells the wild animal when its enemy is approaching, and which still at times comes armed and insistent to the aid of humanity also. It was her duty to remain in that room sewing; it was out of her power to send John Meffala away; but now a certain fierce resentment against him began to rise in her heart; all the fiercer because she had at first misunderstood the drift of his questions, and did not yet realise just why she should fear him; only within her heart the inner voice cried loudly and more loudly: "Beware."

"Why," said John Meffala, smiling, "why do I ask these questions? Because I take an interest in you."

The girl met this with absolute silence; but her blood began to boil as with heat begotten deep in her very soul. So little, however, did the man appreciate the situation, that he thought her silence was to tempt him on. He proceeded:

"Yes, I like you better than any black girl I ever saw; do you see, my dear?"

"Don't speak to me like that," she burst out with a touch of wild energy; then as the established habit of restraint and respect for a social superior reasserted itself, she ended lamely: "I don't like it."

John laughed, still quite blind to her real feeling. He looked her over appreciatively, marking the strength and soundness of limb, and the even play of muscle as her bosom rose and fell. Her eyes remained fixed on the work in her hands.

"Don't you want money? Well; I will see that you get plenty of it, and plenty of fun. You will go to dances with the best of them and have all you want to wear." He came across to her.

"I don't understand you," said the girl angrily, "and you have no right at all to talk to me like this."

"Oh, yes, you understand me," he responded coolly, thrusting his hands into his trousers pockets. "You are not a fool. All you girls understand. I will be a good friend to you."

Even amidst the suspicion closing round her, black as darkness, and in the midst of her deepening resentment at an oncoming insult, which was now all but foreseen, that fine word "friend" flashed like a jewel on a dung-hill, and held her for a moment.

She did long for a friend; she who, excepting her mother, had no friend in all the wide world with its crowded multitudes, though she possessed qualities that would have grappled a friend to her heart with links of steel; her truthfulness, her loyalty, her faithfulness, these would have made her a notable friend.

The soothing wrought by the word was momentary only; but it barred the return reply to his remark and again her silence misled him; and this time the result was fatal. He was so near the brink of mistake that he cast himself finally over the edge.

"It is quite easy to understand," he said; and then he stripped his meaning naked before her. He had felt a certain amount of restraint and shown some small degree of refinement while he felt his way to this point; but, once launched on his open declaration of passion; he was on familiar ground. His natural coarseness came fairly out of cover. His desire and purpose, nude and unashamed, thrust themselves full on her sight.

He was stooping slightly towards her; he whispered. He was very near to her and he came still nearer, put out his hand and touched her bosom. All her strength and all the intensity of her being sprang to arms about her insulted virginity. Fidelia felt as if a hand, dirty and filthy, brutal as the kick of a mule's hoof, had been suddenly thrust right into the most sacred recesses of her life. For a moment the source of thought and action within her was paralyzed.

Then the inner rage burst through the habitual repose of manner into outward violence. Her fresh, unblemished, unwasted youth, and health made her pretty nearly as strong as the man himself. In the instant of his touch on her breast she was erect before him. Then came the second of poise; and then she struck him with a full, fierce blow, straight on the lips whence had come the insult. With the force of the blow, his teeth shook in his head, one was knocked back, lose into his mouth, and against the ragged stump the lips and tongue were cruelly cut. The cigarette fell to the ground, crushed and blood-smeared, and glowed there for a minute ere its tiny spark of fire failed. John stumbled back with a curse.

Just in time to see the furious blow delivered, Mrs. Meffala entered the room. For a full half minute she could neither speak nor move, so much did the scene daze her. Then her words leapt to battle:

"You abominable black wretch. You miserable black brute, what do you mean?"

Fidelia had not a word to give her in reply; she barely saw the white woman was there; she barely heard that she spoke. Her own glare was driven home towards John Meffala like a keen, short, straight spear smitten into a foe.

"Speak," shouted Mrs. Meffala in shrill peacock rage. "You shall and must speak."

"He insulted me," cried the girl not looking towards the woman, but with her glances beating against the man before her. She was almost choking with a rage she was struggling to control, for the moment that the equipoise of her anger was upset she felt in its full force how wild was the passion roused within her.

She was terrified herself, not at what she had done, but at what she found it in her heart to do further, and at the desire which she felt that her enemy should again approach her and give her an opportunity to close with him in a life and death struggle. She had shrunk from insult and aggression a minute ago; now she longed, she hungered, to have him affront and insult her again. She yearned for an excuse to close with him. She clenched her fists hard, and stretched the muscles of her arm like one holding back an enraged beast.

Dimly she realized then, clearly she saw it afterwards, that her desire to close with the man meant the desire to slay or to be slain. The insult was mortal. Life on the one side or the other was the true forfeit. Red, warm blood must be the toll; she lusted to exact that forfeit or to pay down her life, did her strength fail, and so, choked with her own blood, to be done with existence there and then. It was one of those minutes when life shuts in on us, and we have no horizon. One action, one figure, fills our view. We ask only to fall on and end there. Fidelia held murder back with her straining muscles and tense nerves.

John Meffala, under the sharp pain of the blow, had made a movement towards her, uttering an oath; but this was the unconscious reaction to severe and unexpected physical suffering.

He checked himself directly and on his mother's outburst interposed for, though he had his faults, he was still a manly enough fellow at heart. The thieves hidden in the garden had by no means pillaged it all as yet.

"Mother," he called as forcibly as he could with a mouth full of bloody saliva and a broken tooth, "leave her alone. It is not her fault; it is mine. I insulted her."

"But how?" cried Mrs. Meffala in her loud excited tone. "I would like to have been here." Anger threw the natural coarseness and vulgarity of her nature to the surface as a volcanic eruption in a swamp throws up the mud. "Insult a servant! You could not; not if you took her broad, nigger nose and rubbed it over your boots. Brutes, beasts, insult them! How could you!"

It must not be thought that Mrs. Meffala's ordinary manner of referring to her black fellow-beings was in this style. On the contrary, she rather prided herself on getting on well with them; for though she despised them all, not as individuals merely but as a body of beings, she hid that fact under well assumed good nature and ostentatious kindness. The objects of her contempt and the beneficiaries of her good nature, with the impassive philosophy of their race safe hid under smiles, knew that she despised them; but were quite satisfied that she should pretend not to.

There were moments of friction, but the indignation expressed then by the black objects of Mrs. Meffala's wrath was largely manufactured from motives of policy; as a fact they were indifferent to her contempt. The world was large enough for Mrs. Meffala and for themselves; and, as for themselves, with Providence, and the British Government, on their side, they were content to tread all roadways and meet all foemen.

"Better leave it so," said John, getting the tooth out and looking round for water. "Better ask no questions. I said something to her I should not."

"But for a black girl like that to strike you—and here in our own house and under my own eyes. Good God! What is this country coming to! I wish the British Government that set all these wretches free could stand here today, in this room, and see this picture. I would like to have them here to see for themselves," and the irate lady made a gesture as if she would have ranged in a row there all the British Ministers, dead or alive, who were in any way responsible for the events of 1838, and pointing to each asked them to note Fidelia and repent. "If this did not convince them nothing would. It is abominable. What are these black devils coming to next, I wonder. How could you insult her. What was it? You tell me then, girl, or I will have the Police in at once and march you off to gaol."

"It is not a thing for me to tell you," answered Fidelia, her frame erect, well-nigh rigid; "and if there is a law to punish me for doing what I did to your son, it is not God's law."

"Canting wretch," replied Mrs. Meffala. "Who are you to name God to me? But," she sneered, "it would not be a nigger not to talk religion, and that when you have done a wicked, abominable action. John, will *you* tell me? I demand that you shall tell me."

"Look here, Mother," replied John petulantly, "you shut up. I said what I should not have said. I took her for another sort of a girl. Don't bother me any more about it."

He was beginning to feel that he was being made ridiculous, as a man always does feel under a woman's championship of him in his presence.

"You mean—" began his mother, then stopped, for at last she saw what he did mean. "Even so," she cried after a pause, "it was an honour for such as you—though, of course, it was very wrong," she stammered realizing just what she was saying, or implying. "It was very wrong, indeed, but for such as you to dare to strike my son—you black—thing."

"I am a woman," said the girl with passion. "I am not different to you or your daughter. I am flesh and blood, too. Is not my blood red like yours? Is not my flesh tender too? I am a woman, I tell you, like you, like your daughter. What is shame for you is shame for me. If a man had spoken so to your daughter or to you, my God, would you not strike him? I—" she closed her white, strong teeth firmly.

Wild words danced on the tip of the raging passion that she was controlling as foam, shown by the glare of the lightning, gleams on the waves when a storm runs high. Again her muscles strained and quivered, her nerves tingled and the throbbing of her heart beat like an iron gauntleted hand flung against a locked door. Her physical form seemed magnified by the indignation to which it responded, and she was so commanding and so threatening that, angry as was Mrs. Meffala, she shrank away, overawed. But that was for a second only. Then she burst out:

"How dare you? What insolence to put yourself on a level with me and the young ladies—you dirty, black nigger. You have been laying traps for my son and plotting to bring this on—it is all pretence now, I am sure of that, you hypocrite. Perhaps, he would not give you money, or not enough money."

"You lie," said Fidelia, too furious to impose any check on her words. "You lie; I did nothing. I would die rather than be such a thing as you think. Because I am black, do you think I must be like that?—My God," she said in a tone suddenly shaken with a pathetic sorrow, "what a world this is. Yes, I am black, but my God you know me; you see my heart that there is not this filth in it."

"Mother," interjected John Meffala angrily, "don't make a fool of yourself, leave the girl alone. What she says is the truth. It was my

THOMAS MACDERMOT

fault alone. As to the pretence, you should have had her hand on your mouth as I did, then you would have known whether or not it was pretence, whether it was only sham indignation. It battered into me like a beam of wood I can tell you. This mouth of mine is real enough, and nothing will give me back my tooth. Leave off ragging her, I took her for another sort of a girl."

"So did I," said Mrs. Meffala grimly with a difference of meaning. "You can never tell, she looked quite decent, and she could really sew well. At any rate, she cannot remain here, not a day longer, not an hour (not for all the sewing in the world)." Disgusted by all this talk by excited women, her son at this stage walked out of the room, with what sounded like an bath. He proceeded upstairs to bathe his face, and meantime in the workroom his mother continued:

"You go at once, you worthless wretch. Here is your money to the end of this week. It is all you can get, and I give you no further notice, and if you have anything to say I will tell everyone that you tried to entrap my son; you ought to be glad I don't send for the Police. Prosecute me if you like. Get all you have in this house and go. I regard you as I would a leper, a snake, a—a zebra." Her natural history falling at this point, she pulled the money from her purse and flung the coins on the floor.

Fidelia looked at her for a second, then at the money. Her look gave Mrs. Meffala a rather chilly feeling, remembering as she did that she was alone with the girl. But Fidelia did nothing more now than pick up the coins slowly, and one by one; going to the table she composedly gathered her scissors, needle, thread and work-bag.

Mrs. Meffala, reassured, hurled angry remarks at her, but the girl said nothing further. Having put her things together, she took her hat, and left the room and the house without again glancing at her maddened employer. She walked out of the Meffala house in proud silence, but it would have pleased Mrs. Meffala to know just how discouraged the girl felt that night when she looked into the future.

None knew better than did Fidelia herself how uncertain was her chance of getting another place as good as the one from which she had been driven. She remembered her bitter experience when she first came to Kingston. She shuddered to recall the months when she was forced to do casual jobs, very badly paid, in house-cleaning, nursing, and washing. Compared with that, the position at the Meffalas had been comfort.

There she had been able to send money to her mother weekly, and to save a few shillings towards the time to which she looked forward when it would be possible to bring that mother to live in Kingston. There were now in the bank two pounds to her credit; But unless another place was obtained quickly the small hoard would melt like snow in the desert, for Fidelia was resolved while she could, to continue the weekly remittance to her mother; first because she knew it was needed at home; and second because she would not let her mother know that she was not getting along as well as she had been. Her letters told little of her real sufferings and privations. Days of hunger and mortification, shabby clothes, torn boots, hats rusty with age, and nights haunted by fear of absolute starvation were smoothed over as "Some difficulties" when she mentioned these matters at all to her mother.

Till a few years before, Fidelia had lived in a village in St. Ann where her mother owned a small house and a piece of land. The mother made a scanty livelihood by sewing and by writing letters for the villagers; by helping the village shopkeeper with his accounts and by teaching the elements of education to a few of the most ambitious, who for one reason and another, would not attend the day school.

The daughter, after her school days were over, was received at a neighbouring Great House, where she learnt domestic service. When her training was complete, she found that the chance of ever earning more than a casual shilling or two was slender. The mother was now in failing health, and her income dwindled with her strength. Fidelia turned her face towards Kingston, with the country girl's simple hope of finding there abounding good fortune.

Fact tore her hope to rags. For weeks she obtained nothing but odd jobs, rough work badly paid. She would have gone under and starved possibly, but for the fact that with an Aunt she found sleeping room and in the morning a slice of bread and a little sugar and water. On this she could depend, but there were days when she ate nothing besides that slice of bread. It was all that could be spared by a poor woman struggling to bring up five children by her wash-tub and higgler's bowl.

For Fidelia the task of feeding herself, of keeping moderately decent clothes on her back and boots on her feet, and of putting by something each week to send to her mother often verged from the difficult to the impossible. On some weeks the remittance to her mother amounted to a few pence only, sent in postage stamps. There were weeks when nothing at all was sent, but those were weeks when Fidelia earned only the right to food, or not even that. She never earned money but some of it, however small, found its way to the village of Mountain Piece.

After these initial experiences of toil degrading in its uncertainty, Fidelia reached a haven of rest. One night at the Cross Roads Station, she noticed that she was observed by a man of somewhat advanced age. Presently he asked: "May I enquire if you are wanting work?"

"I want it very badly, gentleman."

"Then we meet happily. I want to engage a servant." He was in weak health and had need of a decent, reliable woman to cook and to attend to the house. He offered Fidelia her food and five shillings a week. Tears of gladness filled her eyes as she agreed to begin work next day. Her letter to her mother that week ran over with joy. For the first time during many weeks she had enough to eat and was able to send to her far-away mother three shillings at one time.

There was much work to do at her new post, for on many days her employer required almost minute attention. A sorry, battered body, in truth, was his, haunted by the ghosts of troops of byegone illnesses and diseases. Some familiar of Death seemed to have passed over that pale skin, seeking a resting place for his master, and to have set the mark of his lord's signet ring on this wretched being. The trembling hand proclaimed it, the bleary eyes, the loose skin and uncertain gait spoke of it. In this world his course was all but run, nor did he seem one who would find much ground for satisfaction with himself beyond the grave. Vices of the flesh crowded in his mind as coarse, rank weeds stamp each other down in a swamp. When he drank, the foul impurity, an inky pool in his wicked old heart, oozed from his lips in vile and abominable language. The girl soon realized how contemptible he was; but he paid her wages regularly, she was well clothed and well housed. It was, too, only when he drank that he became foul-mouthed. Otherwise his language was chosen with much care, and was even refined; but drink opened in that heart a sluice-gate of moral filth.

In the dead hour between twelve and one, on a night some weeks later, Fidelia was roused from sleep. Some one was fumbling at the handle of the door. The latch held a second, and the girl, springing across the floor, turned the key in the lock.

The drink-sodden voice of her employer demanded admission. Fidelia stood beside her bed and made no reply. The demand was repeated again and again. Oaths and words reeking with the gutter mud of lust were pelted at her. Then the man flung himself against the door and tried with all his frail strength to force the lock in. The girl barricaded the entrance with a chest of drawers. Presently her assailant withdrew, cursing.

Next morning he remembered that his real attitude towards the girl had been revealed, and he tore the rest of the screen to tatters. "Do what better girls than you have done," was the gist of his argument. "I feed you well; you are well housed and well paid. If you want a little present now and then, ask me. It is for you to decide whether you are fool enough to throw all this away. I tell you that there are women a thousand times better than you who have been only too glad to live on my money in their time."

So strong, so healthy, so clean-minded did she stand beside the miserable creature who tried to tempt her, that what he said failed even to move her anger. It was not by such as he that she could be insulted. She simply went to her room, gathered the few garments that hung on the wall, packed them in the small and battered tin case that had once been her mother's. Then she put on her straw hat, and went downstairs to her employer.

"Give me an answer," he called at sight of her.

"I am leaving at once," she replied. "That is my answer."

"Oh, that is your answer," he sneered. "*Damn* you; that is how you treat me after my kindness to you. Just like a nigger. Why, curse you; it was nearly starvation for you when I found you at Cross Roads."

"Never mind that," she said without anger, "I was glad enough to get the work and I have done it well. Give me my money for this half week. That is what you owe me."

"Money," shouted the man. "May your black soul be sunk in the deepest pit if you get any money out of me now. I have not told you to go."

"You must pay me my money," she answered quietly enough.

"I tell you what I will do," he cried. "I will prosecute you for leaving your work without due notice to me. The law is on my side."

"The law," she said, "no law can be on your side—you are worse than a hog in the gutter. You know why I have to leave you, you dirty beast."

"And whose word will they take in court," he sneered in reply. "Mine or yours? You tell that story and I will tell another. Go on, I tell you; go on."

Fidelia was one of those beings in whom the elemental instincts are very strong. Whether or not the law condoned the injury which this man had attempted to do her, whether or not it was possible to mislead the law, the right and wrong of the matter stood clear before her eye, and by that and that alone she would act at all costs. She had worked half a week and was resolved to have her money. She looked round the room. In one corner lay a supple-jack and in the lock of the door stood the key. Fidelia picked up the supple-jack and crossing to the door locked it.

"Now," she said, "I want my money, and if you don't give it to me I will thrash you till you do. If it is wrong they can punish me for it afterwards. But I will make you pay me my money before I go out of this room. And you will never live long enough to forget the beating. If you like to tell why I beat you I don't care." She drove him back from the window into the corner and cried "Now."

"You shall go to prison for this," snarled the man.

"Afterwards, perhaps," she replied "I am not afraid but—now."

"Take care," he cried. "Take care, curse you."

"Will you pay?" she demanded relentlessly.

Then suddenly he stooped and ran at her, reaching handgrips; but she was at least three times as strong as this human wreck, and she hung him back all along the ground, laughing as she did so. She stood over him and laid the supple-jack smartly across his legs once, twice, thrice. As he winced and tried to crawl away like an injured reptile, he presented a pitiable sight. After the third of those cutting blows he gave in.

He flung down the money. "Take it and get out of my house, you she-devil. I will send for the Police." But that he did not do.

This was one of the episodes of Fidelia's search for work, and it was with a sinking heart that she hied her out from the Meffala's to sail those dreary seas that she remembered so well. She belonged to a class which in Jamaica rarely if ever reads the papers, but a week or so, after leaving the Meffala's, she heard through a friend at her aunt's of a vacant place. She applied at once and was soon taking part in the following dialogue:

"Who did you work for before?"

"Mrs. Meffala."

"For how long?"

"Nearly a year, lady."

"Let me see the character she gave you."

"She gave me none."

"Why not?"

"I did not think of asking her; I forgot."

"Forgot!"

"I left suddenly, lady."

"How was that?"

"I offended her."

"But how? I must know all I can about you."

"I struck her son in the face."

"Struck him! Struck her son in the face?" The lady in her excitement and surprize sprang to her feet. She was more than surprise. She was alarmed. "This," she thought on the sudden, "is a lunatic." Reassured by the girl's calmness, she continued: "No wonder you left suddenly and you are looking for another place and here." She stared at the girl as one may look at a curious insect of a rare, stinging kind.

Then other thoughts came into her mind. She moved in the Meffala circle and had not failed to hear of Master John's proclivities. She was curious for details.

"Nothing can excuse you," she said safe-guarding the following question, "but tell me how it happened. I suppose you were very angry?"

"I was very angry," replied the girl; "but I have been more angry without striking anyone. I struck him because he insulted me as a woman."

"Insulted you—as a woman—but how?"

"As a woman, lady. He said something to me that it was a shame for him to say to any woman."

"Ah," said Mrs. Nuget beginning to understand, "but you should not have struck him. If I took you, you might imagine that you were insulted and strike someone here. You evidently have a very bad temper and cannot control it. I am afraid I cannot take you." The girl looked so tragic, however, that she added, to soften the blow: "I am sure you see yourself that you were very wrong and are sorry now, only of course it is too late. You must let it be a warning to you."

"Lady," Fidelia answered, "I was right; I was not wrong, and I am not sorry."

"That is very sad. Did you strike him more than once?"

"If I had," replied Fidelia, "I would have killed him."

"You had better go," said the lady.

"Goodmorning, Ma'm," said Fidelia and departed. It was not in her yet to beg for work as a favour. But when she had for week after week tried vainly for a situation, new feelings crept into her heart. Sometimes it was alarm that she found there; sometimes it was despair. At other times her heart thrilled with bitterness and rebellion.

One of the most heartbreaking of her disappointments took place in this wise. She was taken on for a day or two to fill the place of a sick servant. The servant continued sick for several weeks and Fidelia remained in her place. The mistress of this house was of a type very different from Mrs. Meffala. She was not only kind-hearted but she really tried in her daily life to live by the religion of fairplay, justice and truth. Her household had the peace of firm, humane and almost affectionate governance.

The sick servant died after a month's illness and it became a question of replacing her. Fidelia had done so well as her substitute that it seemed the most natural thing to give her the place. Mrs. Grafton was greatly prepossessed by her manifest intelligence, her fine-looking face and specially by the faithfulness with which she had worked. But Mrs. Grafton considered it her duty to discover more about the girl ere admitting her permanently into the house; so she sat down to ask some questions. It occurred to her then that she had seen this girl before.

"Fidelia, I am sure I have seen you before you came here."

"And I have seen you before, ma'm."

"Where was it?"

"At Mrs. Meffala's house."

"Ah, now I remember. I came into the room where you were sewing one day. Mrs. Meffala wanted me to see a particular kind of cloth."

"Yes, ma'm." Fidelia volunteered nothing further and after a moment Mrs. Grafton asked:

"Why did you leave?"

"She discharged me, lady."

"Why?"

"I struck her son on the mouth."

"But she has no little children?"

"Her son is not a little child, ma'm; he is a man. I struck him on the mouth and broke one of his teeth."

"What!" said Mrs. Grafton, literally jumping with surprize. Then she saw a possible explanation.

"You did it accidentally, I suppose."

"No, lady, I did it on purpose."

"But, how! What! I never heard of such a thing; and you seem such a decent girl. Why did you?"

"He insulted me."

"But how?"

"He insulted me as a woman, ma'm."

"But—" she paused and the significance of the phrase came home to her, for a simple expression will convey a whole situation of this sort to a mind which has retained the sensitiveness of purity, while to one more impure, nothing but words raw with reality will do. Mrs. Grafton had none of the coarse curiosity for details that had led some other employers to seek for full details. She sympathized with the girl; none the less she was deeply shocked at the picture painted by the direct words.

"What a dreadful thing for you to do," she said at length.

"And what he did, lady?"

"Oh, don't misunderstand me; that was wrong, very wrong. It was abominable." But the prejudices of her upbringing led her to a conclusion and she could not refrain from expressing it. It is characteristically feminine to think that under such circumstances the woman must be to blame.

"Surely," she said, "you must have encouraged him to take liberties with you. You may have been inexperienced and done it unintentionally."

"I did not," said Fidelia in deep tones.

"There must have been something," persisted Mrs. Grafton, "to lead him to think that you would not resent it."

"There was my colour, lady," replied Fidelia going straight to the tragic centre of many facts. "I am a black girl, and he thought that all black girls are alike."

Mrs. Grafton had not moral courage enough to face the idea that the girl had not been at all to blame; it would have necessitated a reconstruction of many parts of her world of thought. She followed still on the heels of her prejudices.

"Are you sure that you did not encourage him in any way?"

"Lady," answered Fidelia, and there was a deepening in her tone that told of rising temper. "I have told you already. Ask him. He is a bad man; but he will tell you the truth about this. He told his mother the truth."

Mrs. Grafton mused. Reason and justice crossed swords with her prejudices. The result was nominally a drawn battle, but really a victory for prejudice.

"Well, you see, it is only fair that I should hear from Mrs. Meffala before doing anything. Is it not?"

"As you say it, lady."

"And I will let you know if I want you. We are going out of town for a few weeks so that there will be a break in any case." The matter ended there.

Thus day by day passed, weeks lengthened into months, and still Fidelia's fortunes floated on a bleak ocean of disappointed hopes, like a ship earnestly seeking, and even approaching, the harbour entrance, but only then to be driven out and away, to wander once again before fierce winds, over dark waters. on the open sea. She obtained temporary jobs, but as soon as it came to permanent employment, the absence of a written character, or the narration of the smiting of John. Meffala on the mouth decided the matter against her. And still, whenever asked therefor, Fidelia repeated the story of that smiting with absolute truthfulness She slurred nothing over; she extenuated nothing; first, because she was by nature truthful as she was chaste; and, second, because her self-respect and pride were bound up with that incident. She was convinced that she had been right and wholly right. She would yield not an iota on that point to anyone's opinion, come what might.

Monday after Monday she took her place in the army of girls and women who on that day go from house to house in Kingston with the monotonous enquiry:

"Want anybody to work?" She was thrown on from one job to another, with gaps of non-employment yawning between; her body was ill-fed; her, mind grew embittered and demoralised.

It was during this period that the lady whom she was just then serving gave her a message to a washerwoman, and, after the manner of certain employers, suggested the errand could be done on her way home. She did not stop to hear that the washerwoman lived at one end of the town and her servant at the other.

At the time when Fidelia was receiving this direction, the Gyrton household was having a rather exciting experience. Gyrton himself was out. Grant, after a hard night's work at the business that was more profitable than carpentering, was asleep. To Mrs. Gyrton had been entrusted the task of cleaning the secret room beside the kitchen.

Without further ceremony than a hand on the gate latch and a shoulder shove, there staggered into the yard a white man, old, thin and unwholesome-looking. At this moment he was very drunk. Strong liquor affected him in different ways at different times. At one time it made him sullen and despondent, so that he had been known after a heavy debauch to attempt suicide. At another time it filled him with unresting inquisitiveness which sent him poking his nose into the most out-of-the-day corners, and tacking his crazy course along the most extraordinary thoroughfares. If he found liquor anywhere he drank it on sight, even if it contained preserved spiders. If he found no liquor, he satisfied himself with peeping and prying into everything that he could get under his eyes.

On one of his voyages of discovery he had now pushed his way into the Gyrton's yard.

"A blooming carpenter's bench," he muttered, after taking a lengthy and solemn survey of his surroundings; "aud a pipe to give us water; and a ugly pigeon coop" Next he focussed his inventory—"A nigger yard— and here is the nigger," he continued as Mrs. Gyrton, all unconscious of his presence came to rinse her dirty house cloth under the water pipe. She glared at the drunkard, and he, in what he intended to be jocular and endearing tones, invited, her with obscene embellishments of speech, to come to his arms.

A drunkard in his cups has some of the liberty allowed to the imbecile, and Mrs. Gyrton said nothing worse than that this man was more beastly than a white pig; with that she took her cloth to the pipe. She had hardly noticed the man move, when she was startled to hear his voice in the kitchen; ere she could reach him, he had entered the secret chamber, the door of which stood open.

"My God!" was all the woman could exclaim, and she flew into the house, driving Grant's slumbers like chaff before the wind.

"Lord, Mr. Grant," she shrieked in his ear, "someone is in the yard."

"All right," said Grant calmly. "Nothing to see in the yard but carpenter's tools."

"My God, but him gone in de room by de kitchen."

"What!" cried the man in a voice that made Mrs. Gyrton, frightened as she was already, turn cold with fear. "Hell. Who is it? And who opened the door to let him in?"

The woman was too dazed to answer at once.

"Open you beak and speak, woman—" He bludgeoned her with threats. At last she exclaimed:

"It is an old white man and him drunk."

Grant ran into the yard.

"Well," he said, "if he has gone out already, our chance isn't worth a curse. If he is still in the room, it is a little better."

The man was still in the room.

"Perhaps," said Grant to himself in comfort, "he is too drunk to understand, and it is dark in there and all." He hitched up his trousers, a trick he had learnt at sea, tightened his belt a hole or so, and, selecting a tough piece of guava wood from the carpenter's bench, passed into the kitchen.

Grant slipped through the door in the sham wall, closed it and grappled at once with the man against whom he stumbled.

"You drunken beast," he hissed, "what the debbil you doing in here? in my carpenter shop?"

"Drunk?" hiccoughed the Sot, "Drunk? Praps so and then praps not, but not too drunk to see that this a rum sort of carpenter's shop, old man. Seen this kind of thing before; not in Jamaica, oh no, in parts nearer hell. Oh much nearer—you can stay there and fling your slipper clean in—right into hell, seen it in Limon and Panama. I know, I know. I will talk, too, I will talk. Tongue is an unruly member. you know. Scripture says so. That is fact. Very unruly. And money is the root of it, no I mean the root of all evil, same thing though, old man."

Grant held him firmly, but made no reply. He could see the man very indistinctly. The other, who had been longer in the darkness, had a much clearer view of his opponent. He did not quite like the grip on his arm and still less the eyes looking into his. He was very drunk, it is true, but he could see through his drunkenness the looming shape of a big danger.

That danger was for a minute or two greater even than he suspected. A rather ugly assault, perhaps a broken arm was what he thought of; but the black man who peered at him in silence was thinking of death, and was rapidly discussing with himself what chance there was of killing this enemy and of so disposing of the body as to escape detection; whether the situation was so desperate as to leave room for nothing but revenge which he felt a strong inclination to wreak on the meddlesome fool who had come blundering into his plans. Should he kill him, make a dash for life, and take his chances.

On these thoughts he wasted time for a minute only. It was not in him in his cooler moments to murder a man when there was no object to be gained by so doing; and to successfully conceal the murder was a task that was too dangerous to attempt, unless he knew more than he did about the circumstances under which this man had lived.

"Well," he said. "We will talk business, but let me tell you plain from the first, I got here what pay me well and what please me well; and if you want a bite I will give it to you; but if you try to tek it all, or to give me up to these police, dat day I think you going do it I will kill you. So help me God, I will. I have killed men before this as, well as pig. I kill both kinds."

"Let us talk business," said the Sot. "Why should I tell the police—damn them. What are they to me? What I want is a little money—a little money to buy a few drinks. I have a little money; but it don't last," he continued as if announcing an extraordinary discovery. "And I was robbed this week; a b—y girl in the house cleaned me out. Sucked two pounds five shillings and a quattie as if you had sucked an orange. Let us bargain; I will not be hard on you—a little money every quarter—keep it regular and I will be all right. Oh, I am not a bad sort, only I must have a little money. Give me a little money."

Why indeed should such a being help the Police, or any force representing law, order and decency? To get a little money to buy drink, he would have taken the white, innocent soul of a child and burnt it to cinders over the fire of vice; he would have taken the honour of his sister, his wife, his daughter, and sold it to the first libertine who would pay; for to this being truth, honour, loyalty and good faith, had become mere names, the mention of which did not even make him think of the realities themselves. A little money to buy drink; that was in fact, all that he asked of life now and all that he got. Everything else lay buried in the dead years.

When the Sot came out into the yard, Grant remained in the secret room. The disturber of his peace made a few rambling remarks to Mrs. Gyrton, then stumbled to the pipe to wash his face. Before doing this he extracted from his pistol-pocket a white-handled revolver. He laid this on the carpenter's bench and forgot it there. Mrs. Gyrton drew Grant's attention to it.

"Leave it same place," said that logical man. "He may come back for it or he may forget it clean; in which case it will come to me." If the man did not return it would support the hope that he was too drunk to remember. Grant remained in the yard to keep watch with a lurking fear that the Sot would go straight to the Police.

There did come a knock at the gate when it was dark and the gas lamps had been lighted. However, it was neither the Police nor the drunkard, but merely Fidelia Stanton to deliver her employer's message. Grant went to call Mrs. Gyrton and as he did so the girl's eye rested on the revolver. Somehow its curved white handle impressed itself on her memory as something she had seen before. Mrs. Gyrton when she had dismissed Fidelia, noted that the revolver was gone; but she did not venture on questioning Mr. Grant.

Just outside the Gyrton gate Fidelia met Noel Bronvola face to face. She stopped short, staring at the white girl as if entranced; she had been thinking of Noel persistently, recurring to her little cousin's idea that in time of trouble here was a ready helper. The thought had become a sort of focus for her hopes, the single spot of enduring light in a darkening field. The girl by constantly brooding over her situation, and also in consequence of the poorness of her food was in a highly nervous state. In fact she stood in the outer courts of hysteria.

Once or twice she had made her way to the very steps of Noel's house; but it was difficult for Fidelia to ask help or to give her confidence to anyone, and she had on each occasion turned away at the last moment, overcome by the idea that she would be received with indifference, or with pity worse to her than indifference. Essentially independent and proud, she would prefer to starve rather than take a false step or ask a favour and to be met with a rebuff. By her own courage, resolution and endurance to make her way through the world without seeking the patronage or assistance of anyone; that was her ideal of life. She drew back in open rebellion at the idea that the poor must be suitors in humble guise at the door of the rich. The approaches to the heart of this girl, poor as she was, were guarded by a hundred feelings of reserve and restraint, planted there by nature. She turned back from Noel's door because she felt it would be wronging herself to ask help.

This abrupt, dramatic, unexpected meeting outside Mrs. Gyrton's yard found her in a different frame of mind; and, as she gazed into the other's face and deep into her eyes, she stood ready to drop every barrier that shut in the pain and trouble of her heart, and to conduct the other mind, like an angel of deliverance, through and through the dungeons of her own being, full as these were of starved hopes and ominous with the shadow of fear.

Her attitude was unconsciously one of high tragedy. Noel appeared as a messenger might have seemed who had been sent to her by a great and divine power, sent with the direct and express purpose of receiving her confidence and rendering her aid in her hour of bitter need. Had Noel spoken words such as angels used when of old they visited men on earth; had she told in thrilling language that the Creator-Father had seen this girl's desperate plight and sent her His message of comfort thus, Fidelia would have found it all in harmony with what she read into that sudden meeting.

Noel, on her side, had been on her way to see Mrs. Gyrton whom she occasionally looked up in memory of her dead Sunday School Scholar, Becka. She saw this tall, striking-looking black girl pause before her in the street and she asked quietly:

"Did you want me? Can I help you?"

Kind words, and most natural; but Fidelia's mind was set just then to respond to more tragic vibrations of feeling. The words were to her a repulse. She had not been sought out by this beautiful and kindly face. Their meeting was merely one of chance; she was addressed as any other person would have been addressed. It was death to her opportunity.

If she had been mistaken in interpreting the reason of their meeting, then, she argued, she might be equally mistaken in thinking that Noel was interested in her. There was probably in the white girl's heart no more than the ordinary politeness and easy kindness that to Fidelia just then would have been as useless as dew-drops to one dying of thirst after a long journey across a desert. Up flew the barriers that guarded this heart as stoutly against pity as against scorn. To Noel she answered tersely: "No, lady," and stood aside. But the change in her face was so marked that Noel spoke again:

"Are you quite sure that I cannot help you?"

"I am sure, lady," and Fidelia went her way with a curious feeling that if she stopped to think the circle of darkness would close in on her completely. She strode rapidly along, hardly seeing whither she went. A string of cars filled with children returning from a fete passing in front of her forced her to stand still. As she stood waiting, a hateful and well-remembered voice smote on her ear.

"Fidelia," it was her old employer. The next moment he was at her side, reeking with liquor.

"You black harlot," he said leering nastily and stretching a hand across her breast.

Fidelia half closed her fist and, swinging it wide, fetched him a buffet that knocked him off his shaking legs. A detective laid a prompt hand on the girl, but an English Inspector had heard and seen.

"No," he said. "Let her be. Fair play is a jewel, even in the Tropics. That girl is no harlot. He troubled her and, by George, she bowled him clean out. Took his centre stump in fine style."

The man on the ground screamed out oaths and demands for the girl's arrest.

"Come," said the Inspector, giving him a hand up, "if we arrest her we must take you too. You are drunk and incapable if we come to look closely into the matter."

"Drunk," said the sorry human specimen trying to wipe away some of the street mud that stuck to his face, "drunk I may be, but by the holy Moses, incapable I am not. I can shoot; my revolver—" but revolver where he sought it in his pistol-pocket there was none.

"Well, well," said the Inspector good-naturedly, "here is a bus. Get into it and I will send you home. You are quite capable, I know, of giving me more than a sixpence worth of trouble. Here, Rogers, see they take him safe."

A few days after this the current of events was again disturbed at the Gyrton's yard by the reappearance of the Sot. He had got to the weather side of his debauch but remained in his sober senses in some respects a much bigger fool mentally than he was in his cups. He had forgotten everything about his revolver except that it was lost, but he dimly recalled the fact that he had chanced on a nest of mystery and profit, during his last bibulous wanderings. Staggering far, he had dived deep into the lanes of Kingston, and to retrace his steps in his sober moments with anything like exactness was a task quite beyond his powers. It was as much by chance as anything else that he found himself in front of the Gyrton's gate, possessed by a dim consciousness that he had seen its curious latch recently.

Gyrton, Mrs. Gyrton and Grant were all at home. The woman was at once placed in the back-ground, as the Sot had seen a good deal of her on the former visit. Grant, who had met the intruder only in the shadow of the inner room, reasoned that his face must have made a very slight impression on the man's memory. As it happened, however, the Sot retained a much more distinct remembrance of the man than of the woman, because for a few minutes his attention had been so painfully focussed while Grant seemed about to strike him down.

It would have been wiser for masterful Mr. Grant to have left the visitor in the hands of his weaker partner, whom the Sot had not previously seen at all; but this man had the fault that cleaves to strong minds, that of doing too much himself. He thus really helped the Sot to reconstruct the former scene and events.

He made a second mistake by handling his enemy harshly and abruptly, with the idea of dismissing him quickly. That being, under this rough treatment found his hitherto dim memories standing out in greater distinctness, just a scar on the face, which under ordinary circumstances is hardly noticeable, marks itself out in angry red when the brain behind is roused by passion. As Grant plied the luckless drunkard with words of opprobrium and abuse, he helped to deepen, instead of to erase what had been at first rather faint memories.

"Drunk or not, I remember some things, my man. You dare take me into that kitchen and I will convince you."

"No," cried Gyrton, springing up. But Grant had at last realised his mistake. He waved Gyrton aside and assented.

The Sot entered confidently; but gradually his look changed to one of bewilderment. The sham wall was so good, when the door was closed and properly concealed, that it baffled him completely. At length he drew quietly back as if accepting defeat, and Grant felt that wisdom was justified of her children.

But next day the Sot was back, and this time he was drunk. He walked straight to the sham wall and shook the door. Drink had lighted up his memories. Grant saw that he must keep his part of the bargain.

As he came to know the Sot better he realized that the danger was far less than he at first thought. It was the simple truth that in this wretched being there was nothing left but the desire to drink; and as long as he got a little money every now and then to aid him in his debauches he was content. He never threatened, or, hinted at disclosure; and the remnant of an old sense of honour showed itself in the fact that he never from the day on which he bargained to receive so much asked for more. His money went faster now than it once did, because he was less able to guard it against the human beasts of prey that surrounded and robbed him mercilessly the moment that his drunkenness made him a safe victim.

Grant found that so long as his pittance was paid regularly he gave not the slightest trouble, and the sum thus absorbed was after all a very small tax on the industry that was being conducted so prosperously at the Gyrton's.

Later on, and at a period that does not belong to our immediate story but to the tale of "The Dead Man Who Lived," a new fear crept into Grant's heart. The Sot might have the very best intentions, but it was clear that his brain was going to pieces. Lock after lock smashed;

restraint kept a loose and ever looser hold on tongue and limb; inch by inch the inmost chambers of being were forced wide and left open to the hoof of the world. The man approached the condition when though even sober he could no longer command what he said or did. He was like a vessel with many holes which it was impossible to prevent leaking. In this state, without intending it, he might reveal their common secret. Perhaps, Grant thought as time went on, he had already revealed the secret in broken hints, only fortunately not to any who could grasp the significance of what he said. But any day he might speak of it to some one who could understand, and would act.

Pic-nicking on the Mountain-tops—And on the Plain—
Dragons of the Past—In the Tropical Moonlight—The
Reader and her Audience of one—Miss Vera and her Story.

VI

For most days of the year, the rich depths of air above Kingston, the smiling blue waters that stretch away from the city-front, southward, and the pleasant spaces of pasture and hill-land, of grove, field, valley and defile, that close round it, northward, are all merely so many prison bars to the immense majority of its 70,000 citizens. Pent up behind those bars, in street, warehouse, hall and residence, they are guarded where they toil by the sentinels, Care and Circumstance. A public holiday withdraws the sentinels, unbars the iron shutters, flings wide the formidable doors. Then it is like the discovery of a new country for the town folk to stream into the outer spaces where the green trees whisper back the wind's love messages; where blue seas as they, bound are touched with white foam; and where the mountain air is light and cool as a gentle hand laid on a fevered brow.

It was a holiday; and Kingston awoke in the morning coolness, under dawn-pink skies, happily conscious that the next twenty-four hours were for pleasure. The early hours smiled with the promise of one of those bright, windy, loitering, cloudless days that show nature in the Tropics in her most alluring, most captivating attitude.

It was June; the May rains had been laggart, and straggling showers still sparkled as they flew over the countryside. But the fear that shower or cloud-gloom would mar this holiday passed with sunrise. The sky was an open ocean of blue and the clouds that did appear floated, light, beautiful, snow-white, far away, sprays and fragments of foam drifting from mystic lines of breakers fleecing themselves in unseen regions, where ivory-limbed gods bathe under cascades of radiance, and fairies throng the plains of light.

The great Liguanea plain, bearing in its sands records of the events that emerge first from the night of Time in the Island's history, lay that day in full leaf. Buried in its brown earth, are the relics and reminders of the Arrowak, when he clustered his villages on this level, or, from the overlooking Long Mountain, watched the sky-line fearfully for the onset of the dreaded Carib. Here the Spanish Don and the Portuguese Jew reared pleasant halls long before the thunder of British guns disturbed their dreams.

Over all the Past, the Present flowed with its day of light and song and blossom, like a perfumed and fire-sprayed tide glancing over hard, grey rocks.

The rains had revived the heart of the plain country. The hills that stand about Liguanea, through their flower-set, bee-haunted valleys, glowed with loveliness. On the heavily-laden Mango the ripening fruit was being touched by the earliest tinge of red and yellow. Baby pears with glistening green necks and swelling bases were hidden in the mother foliage. Akees, crimson and yellow, with their glossy black seeds, handsomely ostentatious, hung in clusters amid strong green leaves. Such colour, as theirs no leaves could effectively hide.

Tempted by passing zephyrs, the silky down from the great Ceibas flew wide and far. Like flaunting standards borne in the procession of Emperors, the great Poincianas spread their crimson blossoms in great patches against the green of their exquisitely fine leafage.

On such holidays the Law, entering the City, comes to first-class establishments such as Meffala's and closes their doors unconditionally against buying and selling. Their army of jaded workers is released from duty. In these stores no employer, however mighty his sense of his own power, dared to detain, without his or her consent the humblest of his employes.

More license was given on this day to the smaller shops to continue their service of Mammon. They remained open through the morning hours; but as the day grew old they too closed.

The Government Offices did no work. The Post Office itself, that nerve ganglion of the modern City, was open for two hours only, instead of for all the weary nine. No printing office did a stroke of work, except by grace of its employes. The markets shut their gates after ten. Every gang of labourers struck work. The very bread-carts had an air of hurry and preoccupation, as if bread delivery were only an incidental fact to be got out of the way as rapidly as might be, so as to make room for the day's main event, which was pleasure.

Even the domestic servants, that chain of service which has no end, had the tension of labour relaxed. Those who did not get leave as a free gift, obtained permission to find a substitute for that day, while they themselves sallied forth to picnic, excursion or dance.

To Fidelia, still the wandering, diligent and, for the most part, unrequited seeker after work, this day brought the welcome opportunity to fill the place of a holiday-making cook. It was her holiday to work, just as it was the cook's holiday to rest.

Liberta Passley gathered her friends and enemies to entertain them in one of the unique picnics for which her name was famous, and which justified Harold's description of her "as the Lady who has given picnics a new meaning."

Some of the hills that close their ranks round Liguanea, stand in rugged woodland, through which dash streams which in their upper courses are as little known as they are the reverse when once they reach the lowland. It was Liberta's picnic idea on this occasion to close with one of these streams just where it sallied out into acquaintanceship with man and his water-wheels and water-pots, and to trace the current back through wood and tangle, up gully and glen, beside palm-decked cliff, by rock and root, through shadow and shine, to its source far above the plain.

The hours of morning were still cool and fresh with dew and the song of birds, when Liberta's company gathered at a rendezvous near where the stream left the shelter of its mother mountain. Here the picnic began with a morning meal; steaming coffee, crisp bread, fresh butter, fruit of many kinds, from the yellow banana to the ruddy mango, milk taken from the cow at dawn that day, eggs not twenty-four hours old. If Liberta had no lack of ideas in planning her picnics, she had also ample means at her disposal for carrying them through. Peter Passley placed penns, buggies, horses, money, men and boys at her word of command without stint of stay. A small army of uniformed boys and girls swarmed to wait and carry for the guests.

Late coffee or early breakfast over, for it deserved either term, the party set forward in twos and threes, or as single units, to make a brave attempt to follow to its source the brawling mountain brook that rushed plainward with such joyous clamour. Each picnicker aimed to reach the goal first, and to gain the right to wear the tiny silver medal that was Liberta's token of victory. But, first or last, all were to gather on the hill-top for luncheon, for a siesta, and then, while the afternoon grew shadowy, for some hours of song and music, tale-telling and witty improvisation.

Rough, wood-beset and steep, as this hill was where it faced the plain, it was approachable with comparative ease on its northern side.

The summit, too, was clear and grass-grown. The point of honour, however, was to climb the difficult south side, leaving the supplies of food, rugs, awnings and musical instruments to travel by the less glorious road on the north.

Liberta and her guests plunged merrily into the tangle of vines, bushes, trees and rocks, to win the summit by hard climbing. Many there were ill-trained for such adventure, but there was a retinue of neatly clad and handy youngsters armed with sharp cutlasses and skilled in bush-craft. When a party was in difficulties, one of its number whistled and almost at once a boy was at hand to point out and clear the way. Thus the feeble children of the town had the credit of mountaineering with a minimum of its fatigue.

Liberta had, without being particularly conscious of it, the gift of attracting men to her side, and now as always was well attended. In Noel, on the other hand, there dwelt that which, if not exactly repellent, tended decidedly to spread round this beautiful girl an isolating power. Rambles with her father had made her an adept at climbing and at puzzling her way through intricate woodland ways. The young man, a City bred youth, who set out now to accompany her, as an escort, soon found himself a victim to difficulties which failed entirely to stay Noel. At length he covered failure by turning aside to secure an orchid, and was merciless left behind. Noel mounted alone.

After half an hour's brisk effort she stood on the top of a jutting cliff, and rested for a few minutes. Doves were cooing in the woods; the shrill, plaintive cry of the Hopping Dick sounded near her, and there was the murmur of rushing water. The voices of the climbers rose from various parts of the woodland below, and, satisfied that she was winning easily, she resumed the ascent in a more leisurely fashion.

At length she bathed her face in the bubbling spring-head, where the water thrilled with the whispers and secrets earth's inmost recesses. A minute later she emerged from the last outpost of the wood, and stood on the hill-top clearing. Large stone boulders, mottled with grey and black lichens, were strewn on the green sward. Noel stood beside one these and gazed silently away at the scene below. She had removed her hat a stood bare-headed, her dark, luxuriant hair, rumpled and rebellious, framing her glowing face. Far away, as she looked, there was the sea, its deep, fresh blue, flecked with white foam and fading softly and vaguely into the sky-line; like thought passing into emotion. The land showed first its strip of white, gleaming sand, and then a dark green belt where the Mangroves throttled the tides in their network of roots. The noble harbour of Kingston lay full in view from end to end, with Port Royal fastened like a brooch to the very tip of the long arm of land that circles and shelters it from deep sea rages.

> *Like the lifted hand the fighter*
> *Curves to stay the threatened blow,*
> *See the far-stretched Palisadoes*
> *Check the inrushing ocean's flow.*

Before her, on the hitherward side of the harbour, lay Kingston itself. After that came the dusty, white roads leading inland; green pastures; white and grey-coloured residences with here and there a red roof, nestling amid trees or looking out from the slopes and the clefts of wooded hills.

In the woods that crowded to her feet the Dogwood had shed its pink and white blossoms and stood now crowded with the yellowish green masses of its curiously winged seeds.

The cloudless sky was blue, but with a blueness paler than the ocean. The sun shone brilliantly. A wind came, pleasantly borne over field and hill, and stirring gently, in the woods about her

The air had tender vibrations, as of a garment of delicate fabric through which the slightest of fairy movements are being sped. The wealth of light indiscriminately scattered suggested the gifts of some Lord of the Earth who gave with magnificence because he is mighty and kind, and entirely without regard to the merit of those who receive his benefits.

The voices of the outdistanced party sounded faint and far below. Near at hand, with a splash and musical murmur, the stream rushed out from beneath a huge rocs only a few yards within the woodland. The water slipped melodiously across the green grass and straightway plunged into a cascade, filling the air with the sound of its leap. Noel smiled, for she loved to succeed.

"A good first," she said aloud.

"A first-class second only, if I may correct you," replied a man's voice. "I am the good first."

She turned and found him standing near at hand. He had risen from behind a boulder which had concealed his presence. She saw now a man of about twenty-nine clad in khaki and wearing a Panama hat rather negligently. The dominating fact about his face was the concentration of resolution and intelligence. Purpose ruled there, and it struck the observer that here was purpose not only strong and definite, but purpose which slept so to speak under arms, ready at a moment's notice to be flung here or there on exact and vital work. Behind that face was a brain ever ready for battle.

The eyebrows were a trifle heavy, for such intelligence. The eyes were so darkly brown that deep excitement made them appear black. They had a noticeable trick of not shifting for a moment after focussing the object in which the man was just then interested. They watched without even a wink. The nose was slightly too big to be in just proportion to the rest of the features. The chin was strong, almost to harshness; but the lips, rebelling occasionally against a look of severity habitual to their disposition gave unexpected evidences of tenderness and mirthfulness. The greatest surprize came with the man's hair. The sum total of these features made one look for black or very brown hair. Instead it was almost golden, of a shade very rarely seen on a man's head.

In one instant Noel thought that his face was wholly unknown to her; in the next she seemed to remember it dimly.

He showed well-bred anxiety to obviate embarrassment on her part.

"You will, I hope, pardon my introducing Howard Lawley to you. At this height we may perhaps look down on the conventions. He is like yourself one of Miss Passley's picnickers."

"I am Noel Bronvola," she replied readily. "Being Mr. Lawley, you are our new Colonial Secretary," She remembered the name better than the face.

"Guilty," he returned, "but the Colonial Secretary in his unofficial moments." In Jamaica, where Colonial Secretaries are men of much importance, even to others, they are not often seen arrayed in khaki and lurking under Panama hats at mountain picnics.

Noel wondered whether he ever became unofficial enough to lay aside that tense readiness and watchfulness. His face was like a camp that a single bugle call would fling at once into order of battle.

"I was late for the muster below"; he saw fit to continue explanation.

"Last there and first here; you must be a good climber."

"I climb well," he said lightly, "or I would not be Colonial Secretary at thirty; but in this case I knew the way up by the north side of this hill, and I rode."

"Since we are confessing," she responded, "I know this hill too, and the way up through this wood. It was not quite a fair race with the folk below." She thought then, for the first time since losing sight of him, of the young man who had gone to obtain orchids for her.

Lawley expected some sign of embarrassment, at least some trace of constraint at an encounter so unique. She looked merely a girl, and she was very beautiful. He was himself mildly amused at the respect shown to the Colonial Secretary of the Island, but he was quite aware of its existence, and it was to be presumed that the fact of his being that functionary, and of the introduction to him being so very much out of the common, would not be without its effect on the girl's composure.

He could not suspect that she shared his view of such matters, half easy-going, half cynical. He had already learnt enough of local Society to be aware that an encounter of this sort between this beautiful child and a bachelor Colonial Secretary, without previous introduction and where, if neither broke away by some extraordinary method, the tete-tete must last for half an hour at least, would be more than enough to start a fusillade of lively gossip.

Noel reseated herself on a boulder and he flung himself on the grass, suddenly interested to see how this meeting would develop. She looked away across the plain; and he studied her face, his angle of view allowing him to do that undetected. He expected to find there at least sign of the art by which embarrassment is held at bay; some proof of the recognition of the fact that his presence had made a change; some evidence that she could not enjoy her view exactly as she had intended doing when she thought she was quite alone. He waited for some artfully artless suggestion that she must go back to meet the rest of the party. But she made no remark whatever. He had decided that the initiative lay with her, but by and by, to smooth her way he remarked:

"Miss Passley and her friends are still some way down."

"Judging by their voices, half an hour below," she answered. She accepted his sudden appearance and their unconventional meeting with the same repose and calm with which she accepted the landscape before her. She had inherited her father's gift of putting embarrassment off her own shoulders, leaving it to others to assume it if they saw no way of escape.

Presently, as she paid no further attention to him, Lawley also resumed his study of the plains.

His eye wandered from sea to land and from plain to mountains, but it rested at length on the City—a patch of gray and red roofing, of white walls and dark warehouses, a tower or two, and a steeple that won some distinctiveness by its height; there a fringe of masts, here white roads, teries that poured the country's life into the town's eager heart. Next his eye swept round the City and beyond, going from sky to plain, from plain to sky and then back and out across the sea.

In that view, as is always the case where height and distance are present, all that man had made looked insignificant and small. It was noticeable; not at all impressive. What were impressive were the mighty arch of sky, like an ocean of deity full just then of glorious sunshine the distant sweep of deep blue sea; the curve of wood-dim mountains, bending round to right and left of the fertile fields, green and still, held within their embrace, dominated by their eminence.

By and by he offered his field glasses to the girl. She fixed them on a black object crawling slowly across a far away pasture beside the white ruins of old masonwork. It was a buggy. It stopped, turned and was lost to sight behind the trees.

Lawley began to be conscious that although so little had been said, perhaps because of that, his opinion of this girl had undergone a change. If he had been surprised at her composure, he was more so at the unaffected absorption that she showed in the view before her. Evidently, for the time being, he counted no more than the grey rock boulders round her. It surprized him to be drawn more and more out of the mood in which he generally met the world. Except when he answered the call to battle, that mood was only half serious, a careful avoidance of statements that might provoke thought. Just now, however, he found that he was going deeper and deeper into those feelings and musings that were intimately his own; into the life that he had trained himself to live in concealment, as it were, giving the world only its results and never unveiling its processes. At length he spoke out of this change.

"What do you see there? below the surface?"

Noel looked again over the scene, thoughtfully and slowly, and replied: "The spirit of Life sleeps; and in her slumber she smiles."

"And behold," he responded, his tone dropping sarcasm, into the words as when some strong tincture is dropped into water, and, after clouding its transparency for an instant, dies into its clearness, "Behold everything is very good."

"All is well," she answered with a calm that prevented the words being a contradiction or a challenge.

"You know Kingston?" he said presently, "The hovels in the West End as well as the drawingrooms; bare-ribbed starvation as well as the skipping simper to sweet music. I see you know. But does it ever strike you how idiotic it all is? How unreasonable? How stupid? It is actually irrational. If you saw a house on fire, a well beside it, and a bucket there, would you not draw water and attack the fire? You would bring well, bucket, water and fire together; it would be your first thought. But there is hunger, here are empty lands; these hills flow with streams of water; there in Kingston are the hands that could make these lands grow food enough to feed the population of three such cities. Nature means the one for the other, and the others for the one, and the end is rational and sensible. She would drive hunger from the land and abolish poverty and want. What separates the man who needs food from the land which means food; a prejudice worshipped as law."

Suddenly he checked his opening confidence. Was he misjudging this girl's fibre? He had no mind to lay bare the pulse of his thought to a fool. All is not thought that is silence, and often times nothing is so deceptive as attentiveness.

She turned her eyes on him and he read there thought, interest and comprehension. Reason shone at the lattice of those windows into the mind. Reassured, he resumed:

"Shall I tell you what I see there?"

She inclined her head gravely.

"The smiling, sun-kissed plain is the Present. It is beautiful; it is happy—peaceful, joyful—what you will—Look at the long hill line on this side and on that; see, they are like lengths of great dragons, asleep, but alive. The dragons wake and devour the plain. The Past falls on the Present and picks the very bones clean."

Her eyes turned from him to the plain. They rested on the old mason work below as he continued. The white stones shone out amid the green, and a tiny spot of reddish brown strayed on the grass. That was a horse grazing as it moved.

"The Past sits down and devours its meal beside the great ocean of oblivion. See, down there it is the sea. In the end it washes down and engulfs Past and Present, the Dragons and their prey; the beast that eats and the skeleton whose bones it has picked."

"And yet—" she began, then she checked herself and looked away again to the distant sea.

"I see the same truth in another figure," he resumed. "A great giant is this Past, and mighty, and he has flung himself down here. This hill where we stand is the sleeper's head, and those long, circling ranges are his arms, flung carelessly out. The Present is a happy child, with its light and music and beauty—to be crushed in those arms when the sleeper wakens—poor child."

"Poor giant, also," said Noel, "since the sea of oblivion is his fate, too, I suppose."

"But the child's agony comes first. The Present dies first. The Past has lived long and wrought his desire. The Present has only planned and purposed, and realized its helplessness and hopelessness. There never has been a day that was not the slave of yesterday, since the first day went by."

Noel turned to him and then paused on the brink of speech, as if uncertain that her thought was sufficient.

He did not break the silence which followed. A consciousness that seldom was clearly revealed even to himself rose to the surface of his mind. He realized that the Past had left him in a certain attitude of mind towards women—the attitude of appreciation mingled with distrust. The appreciation he could vary; the distrust he could not. It was part of his very self, a thread of his being. Memory after memory passed, all flashing the same light to remind him of this. Suddenly now it dawned on him that there must be somewhere in the past, an explanation of this attitude. What was that explanation—the secret of the dominance of the byegone? He was not curious and he bestowed on the matter now no more than a thought; but he put this aside as one among other problems into which he must look when occasion served.

The first group of the climbers broke through the wood into the sunshine of the open, and Liberta challenged at once.

"A deserter."

"A deserter from the rear to the front. I submit that Generals treat these with a soft touch. Temper Justice with forgiveness."

"Generals have been court-martialled and shot before this for winning battles without orders. But, if this is the front, where is the enemy? Have you been attacking Miss Bronvola? Or has she been attacking you? And who is victor?"

"Shall we say honours even."

"At anyrate, the unfortunate cavalier who attempted to escort her, was left lamenting. We overtook him on the hillside, tangled with vines, with, I believe, his heart on his sleeve, if not in his mouth, and, certainly, an orchid in his hand. Well we will leave the court-martial till later; but don't think it is forgotten. Mr. Howard Lawley, will you obey orders now?"

"Your orders," he assented. "I must do something to mitigate sentence."

"To bribe justice. You doubtless are aware how these things are done officially, better than most of us."

"But Miss Bronvola? I consider she is quite as guilty as I. What is she to do?"

"They also serve who only stand and wait," replied Liberta, and led him away.

Noel's out-distanced escort appeared with his orchids. She took the brown and gold flowers with a manifest pleasure that was reflected in his face till she said: "I am to see a sick friend this afternoon, she will be delighted with these."

The young man would have been better pleased to have been left to imagine thaf the flowers remained with herself. She, for her part, was unconscious of inflicting a wound. No sympathy reached out from her heart towards him, seeking intimacy or union, as had once begun to be the case. All possibility of that was so dead, that she hardly remembered now a day some years before, when this young man had stood with her on a Kingston street, and a child had died before them, while his hand on her arm restrained her from the danger she sought to dare, from the sacrifice of her all that she yearned to make. He saved her life possibly, but he struck their mutual sympathy dead.

On his side it was otherwise. A hope, a yearning, a fatal impulse to love her, a desire to be loved by her, was ever and anon reaching out from his heart and then withering, like the tender tip of a vine seeking new support and striking against hard metal. They met almost daily, and yet spiritually they would never meet again. When he was most reasonable he saw that clearly; but he was often less than reasonable.

On the hill-top, luncheon over and the siesta finished, Liberta's party woke to new life. A harp, some flutes and violins and a guitar gave the music. Songs echoed away through the woodland; there was glad talk. The tellers of tales, of short stories, thrilling narratives of adventure in the days of buccaneer and pirate, of the quaint stories of

A'nnancy, took the field. The sun was low in the west ere the company began to descend to the lowlands.

The day's enjoyment ended amid other scenes. Peter Passley owned a magnificently kept property on the plains. There the water from the hills was collected in a large artificial lake. Into this ran the clear, crystal streams, thrilling still with their rush from the fern-haunted ravines, that scored the mountain side above; and from the lake's other end the water escaped, running seaward. Thus the lake was ever fresh and sweet. Round its calm expanse stood gracefully drooping trees, and fairy-like fern shelters. Boats floated near at hand to bear guests among the water lilies or to the rocky islet in the centre where there was an aquarium. By night the scene was lit with electricity when such light was needed. Tonight, however, there was brilliant moonlight, and the guests as they boated, promenaded, or rested on the garden seats and listened to the softened Band music that crept like a bewitchment through the light and shadow, had the radiance round them that is matchless in its beauty and mystery.

"You," said Lawley to Liberta as their boat glided on the quiet water, while the music seemed to fall round them like a shower of perfume, "You are a magician. You have taught me what a holiday should be."

"If it has not been too strenuous," she replied. "In our country the holiday secret for men like you is, rest. I hope you have rested." she added significantly.

"Ah," he returned, "you are my best friend; you know what I need most."

"And get least of."

"You must let me remind you," she continued in the low, soft, soothing tone that sounded almost like a caress, "that here in this climate you need to be cautious. Energy, yes; but sheathe it. Rest is not a luxury; it is a necessity. Every hour is a robber; every day is a bandit."

"By the way," he said presently, "I have discovered a rather curious thing about myself—quite accidentally."

"What," she smiled, "that you have a heart—or perhaps that you have lost it? I have always called you 'Achilles,' you know, from the first day I met you in England, because you are invulnerable: but even Achilles had his weak spot."

"My heart," he smiled, "is in safe-keeping"—She looked full at him, rather suddenly. "It is guarded by my head," he concluded. "But this discovery of mine is that my father was a West Indian by birth. He had a property here in Jamaica and he actually worked here for some years. Then he sold the property and went in for banking in England."

"All this you discovered at one time," she said quizzically.

"Yes, it was all new to me, when I chanced on it last week. The fact is, I know very little about our family history. Strange that my father who was hardly ever without me at his side, told me so little of his own life or of my people Besides my aunt, who is coming out to keep house for me next month and whom you saw once in England, I know no one of our blood."

"Expect a surprise," she said.

"Well?"

"I knew that your father came from Jamaica—I will tell you something further—you yourself were born out here. No wonder, however, you don't remember that, for you were taken to England when you were only three months old."

"I said rightly that you were Queen of Magic; but I fancy there must be a number of persons who know more about my father than do I. I at least know practically nothing of his story before I came on the scene. I know that he was one of the ablest and noblest men who ever lived. The relationship between us was curious in its way. He kept me so near him in the present of his life; but I never remember his referring even once to the past."

Noel was not present at the last part of Liberta's picnic. She had parted company with the holiday-makers to spend the rest of the day elsewhere.

Across the face of the plain of Liguanea, there slants the ruin of an ancient aqueduct, and by this, those who know the neighbourhood well, can secure a short cut into Percival Road. The mortar-lined gutter is still for the most part sound and clean. It is pleasantly hung on both sides with ferns and is broad enough for two to walk abreast. When exactly this aqueduct was built, I cannot tell. This Liguanea Plain was under cane cultivation, they say, while Diego Columbus still survived to carry on his struggle with the grasping Spanish Court for a due share of his father's honours.

This aqueduct at any rate was built long before the price of sugar had sunk from £30 to £10; it was probably constructed by a master who owned five hundred or six hundred slaves, and it was constructed by men who were not shaken by the modern irresistible impulse to hurry on to completion. These men wrought into their work their ideals of permanence and endurance. It was not the restless hand of doubt that handled the trowel here; no vibrations of uncertainty were cast into this mortar. This was not labour on which the fatal touch of negation had fallen. They built; and their work has remained, strong even in its ruins; resisting the flood of rapid change that tropical nature and the passing toils of man have poured around it.

Canes have long since failed from these plains. Their purple feathers no longer greet the dawn of Christmas as they once did for mile upon mile of these levels. The last vestiges of row and trench and broad interval have been smoothed away. Spaces once open and free have grown crowded with woodland; been cleared for grass growing; billowed for years under the wind-swaying flood of light green Guinea Grass; and then again grown shaggy with bush and tree. The fortunes of owner have waxed here and waned; prosperity has come, smiling; and dark-browed ruin has trampled by; times have changed and systems been over-thrown; where the slave worked, the free man has taken up his burden; descendants of those who were the slaves of the man at whose word the aqueduct was built, have come to wealth, while his posterity have descended to poverty, and still time has not been able to annihilate the aqueduct.

Here and there it has been broken, probably by earthquake, and so it can no longer serve its purpose, but its skeleton is there. The Wild Fig has planted itself on its sides and, casting its terrible roots into its heart, clasped and clawed at its mortar and stones, rending the solid structure cruelly; vines and shrubs, grasses, ferns, lichens and mosses, have made it their foot-hold, but the skeleton remains stout still; its finely built curves, its rock-firm mason work, arch after arch, it still spans the pasture-land, practically as sound and strong as when it was built. It defies the attacks of tropical nature, swarming to the assault with all her luxuriance of vegetation.

Noel was making the old water-channel a short-cut to Percival Road, for there were few of these by-paths and nooks that she had not long ago traversed with her father. The evening coolness was beginning to steal over the face of the country; the lengthening shadows stretched lazily out on the grass; the sunshine seemed only the more beautiful as it lost the fiercer heat and glare of the noon. The wind lingered in a loitering mood. Soft clouds were moving slowly westward, as if called by some mysterious summons to be bathed there in the splendid dyes of sunset.

On the east, trees crowding well-nigh up to the aqueduct, all but shut out the landscape; here and there came openings. Before one of these Noel paused to gaze at the well-known scene; the swelling level of bahama grass, tree-studded and lengthened out towards far-away hills. Cows were grazing or lay at their ease chewing the cud. Nearer at hand her eye lighted on a picture no less pretty than the rest of the quiet evening landscape.

Two persons, a man and a woman, both young, had, on this bright holiday, chosen to make each other their only company, and so had driven out together to this out-of-the-way nook of the common where interruption could hardly intrude. Their buggy stood under the deep shade of a Mango. The horse, with harness tucked up, cropped the grass hard by. The two picnickers were down on the clean, sweet, green sward beneath a large Guango. She sat on the trunk of a fallen tree, reading aloud. She had bared her head to the balmy coolness and her pink blouse, in contrast with her black skirt, lent a solitary bit of bright colour to the scene, Stretched at her feet, and dressed in flannels, the young man listened to her reading. A pretty sight, truly, two young persons caring so much for each other as to wish to be alone, sufficient the one for the other.

But Noel watched the scene with the feeling with which one sees a child put a pebble into a thin wine glass and stir it round, trying to dissolve the fragment. The impossible is so apparent to the onlooker; the shattering of the glass so certain. The girl was Ada Smith; her companion was Harold. Future disaster stared through the quiet and beauty of the scene like an adder's head thrust out from a green bank.

Harold would probably have met the accuser with a denial of the statement that he was making love to Ada. "She reads—I listen— where does Cupid come in?" One could imagine him answering. He really was not stopping to think.

The reader paused. Some word or phrase needed explanation, or so Ada pretended. Harold rose and, going across, leant over her shoulder looking at the book. He answered her question, but he did not resume his former position. Instead he stood toying with her hair: She recommenced reading, but did not continue very long to attend to the printed page. Bye and bye she turned her soft, childish eyes to his face, looking up. His hand fell caressingly on her cheek and eyebrows. She held up her lips and he bent over and kissed her. He did it gracefully, tenderly even, and yet clearly he was not much stirred;

THOMAS MACDERMOT

that was evident, for directly after he flung both arms out and up in a mighty yawn and stretch, Then he looked at his watch, threw himself once again on the grass and bade her go on with her reading. Ada meekly obeyed.

Noel was stirred by the humorous side of the situation as she stood looking down on the two sinners whom her severe gaze transfixed, quite unknown to them, but whom she could not reach. Her impulse, always towards the most direct course, was to go right into their presence, throwing on them any awkwardness or embarrassment that attended the encounter. She was a young woman who fully realized where the moral advantage lay in a situation, and who was well able to use what fortune placed in her hands.

But, however fervent her will, she could not on the present occasion jump down fifteen feet of abrupt masonwork; nor could she glide through the air like some avenging goddess of old. To reach the delinquents, she must go to the end of the aqueduct and return, probably to find the sinners gone. She smiled as she pictured the scene should she make her presence known where she stood; she could see Harold with quiet sarcasm bowing before her, fifteen feet below, and pleading elaborately like a prisoner at the bar, or pretending that he could not hear her remarks.

She went on her way and in due time arrived in Percival Road; but she had postponed action, not abandoned it. She recalled Ada's visit to seek her advice. She liked Harold; besides, now as ever, she responded to the impulse to aid others which was as deep-rooted as her very life.

Myrtle Cottage, Percival Road, was a small house which Time had very noticeably frayed and shaken, but there was about it and the surrounding yard scrupulous neatness and cleanliness.

The little garden in front was kept in the most careful order. The beds were marked out, some with conch shells, a bit time-worn now, and others with black bottles sunk upside down in the earth. The flowers themselves were cheerful-looking, but not rare. Here were sunflowers, Martinique roses, verbenas, a few geraniums and some chrysanthemums. The slender income of the cottage folk was augmented by the sale of cut flowers, as a notice on the gate proclaimed to passers by.

At Noel's knock, the door was opened by a little spectacled lady in brown linen dress, protected in front by a blue apron. Her face was marked with lines of mental pain and anxiety, but the features were delicate-looking and refined. The gray hair was somewhat primly arranged, and the plain dress looked stiff.

"My dear," said Miss Elsie, "how good of you to give us a bit of your holiday. I saw you pass this morning in a waggonette of gay young folks, some as pretty as yourself and some only as young. Let me take your hat, for surely now you are here you mean to give us at least an hour; that is right. Always get rid of a hat when you can, especially when you have such a head of hair under it. Now we will go in and see Vera for a few minutes, then you must come and give me some of your company in the pantry and I will show you the last lot of preserves. I am making some more now. I have been at it all day. After that you can sit with Vera as long as you like. Poor Vera, she has had a lot of pain lately."

"Will she like my orchids? I brought them for her."

"Beautiful, she will just love them. Where did you get them, my dear?"

"A young man gave them to me at the picnic."

"And I will be bound, he would have liked to have given himself in the bunch. I will go surety there is a heart somewhere in the flowers." Speeches of this kind were a part of Miss Elsie's very self, Noel accepted them as such, and answered smiling:

"Well, he did not offer himself, you know, and I have not found any heart here. Miss Vera must search carefully, I hope it did not drop out on the way."

"Ah, well, my dear," responded Miss Elsie, with mild severity, "the day will come when you will not talk like that about the right man and the right heart."

"Till he comes and brings the heart, we will give the orchids to Miss Vera."

Miss Vera lay on the spotlessly white sheets in her neatly kept room, as like Miss Elsie, her sister, as a plump and juicy orange can be like one shrunken and withered by time.

You traced in each little woman outlines of the same model; the same eyes, the same hair with its tendency to crinkle and reveal "colour." It was on both heads ruthlessly disciplined for this offence by combing and brushing, as it had been disciplined for all the years since girlhood, when these twin sisters had heard their mother lament that it was her hard lot to bear children who insisted on taking the "bad hair" of her husband's family, instead of the superior article that she held up to their view. Her daughters entered then into a lifelong battle with that rebellious and shameless hair, trying gallantly to force their pretty curls into tame imitation of the prosaic straight hair that proclaims the pure-blooded white.

A curious ambition as some may think; but great is the prejudice of the Ages, and these two little women who would have bitterly resented being discriminated against, because they were coloured, as inferior to the whitest of the white, showed a disparaging discrimination without stint or pause towards any who were more deeply coloured than themselves. Their never-ending struggle with this hair of theirs was a mute acknowledgement that in their heart of hearts they also surrendered to the tyrant, Prejudice.

Miss Vera was to all appearance Miss Elsie made plump and healthy-looking. She was not exposed to the "harrassments," to use her own term, that beset her sister. In fact, the latter was the break-water behind which the other life lay sheltered. It was the break-water that showed the effects of the long continued battering by the surging seas of trouble. But Miss Vera had this to endure which her sister had not; she was bed-ridden. She could not walk a step; she could not even stand without help.

Her disease had come on her gradually, and doctors were powerless before its slow and certain advance.

"It always happens in our family," Miss Elsie explained to Noel. "It happened to my Aunt Lucy just when she was thirty, and my mother told me it began with her mother at forty, after she had about brought up her family. Vera woke one morning and she could not stand. The doctor came and after a few days she was quite better. We had almost forgotten; but a month after the same thing happened again. It stayed longer and came back quicker. Then it did not go away at all. The doctor can do nothing; no one can. It is in the family; in the blood; it will go on forever, while there are any of us left. It will come back and back while the blood runs. Thank God, there are none from Vera and me. For, my dear, we never married as you know; there were those who asked me, I can tell you, though I am not one to boast of these things. I seemed to have something whispering in my heart from the very first, that Vera would be taken as you see her now. I did not actually make up my mind that I would never marry, you see, my dear; but while I was hesitating and thinking he got tired of waiting and married some one else. Well, it was just as well.

"But though we have no one to come after us, there is my brother Charles with five children. He is strong and healthy, never been sick for a week in all his life, and the children are little dears. But one of the girls is bound to go like Vera, my dear. It is only a matter of time. It is in the family, and they are all that are left now for it to choose from. I tell you a strange thing, it is always the girls that it takes, never the men. So one of Charles' little girls it must be, and when they come here to see me, I find myself wondering which it will be, and I have the curious feeling that something near by is watching the three little things with bright, greedy eyes, deciding which it will seize.

"Vera, as long as she lives, can only get worse. Poor dear; may God reward her on the other side."

Noel gave Miss Vera the orchids and Miss Elsie told her they had come from a young man. On this both little women had their joke at Noel's expense; and in that surrounding it lost all suspicion of vulgarity or offensiveness.

Noel went then to the pantry, tasted Miss Elsie's new guava jelly, and watched her make other preserves. On the sale of those preserves depended the main part of the income of the home.

"Oh, my dear," said Miss Elsie. We have had such a misfortune today. This morning a gentleman who was driving along this road with a lady stopped when he saw our newly lettered sign "Preserves Sold Here." The one you did for us, my dear; I said it would give us good luck and business."

"And it has not?" put in Noel.

"Listen, I am telling you. He sent in a boy and bought four shillings worth; but I am sure now that both of the two shilling pieces are bad. Look at them."

"I am afraid you are right," said Noel. "That is bad coin."

"It is such a loss," wailed Miss Elsie. "Such a terrible loss to poor people like us. If the Police can't find out the men who are making this bad money then the least the Government can do is to make it up to us poor people who get it given to us for good money. It is a shame."

Miss Elsie was an inveterate gossip, and they had talked long and widely ere Noel returned to Miss Vera, to conversation and reading there. Noel sketched for the invalid, making a series of comic cartoons to illustrate the humorous side of the picnic.

Then she flooded the little room with song. The last notes rose amid the falling darkness and after that was over there was silence for quite a time. At length Miss Vera said with a sob: "Sing it again, Noel."

Noel sang:—

I must enter where 'tis darkness
In the unknown land;
Friend Divine, Thy hand shall lead me;
True Thy pledge shall stand.
Master, when the shades of darkness
Deepen over sea and land,
And the light of Life is passing,
Reach to me Thy hand.
Deeper still shall be the darkness,
For the long, long night is here,
Life is ending, death receives me;
Saviour, be Thou near.

"My dear," said Miss Vera, "I want you to promise me something."

"What it is?" The girl bent over her.

There was silence again and the darkness was deeper ere the answer came.

"Promise me when they know that I am going, if they have time to let you know, that you will come to me. I would like to see your face then, my dear. It is so young and so sweet and pure and lovely, I would like to see it, just before I go into the dark, I would like to have it to remember in the darkness if I have to wait long there. I would like to hear your voice at the last—to hear you sing what you sang just now."

"It is a promise," said Noel bringing her presence down to the very lips of the sick woman.

"Sing to me again, now, while it is dark and quiet."

Noel sat on the bed beside her and sang quietly, holding the sick woman's hand till her grasp unclasped itself and Miss Vera slept peacefully.

VII

The Letter addressed by a Lady—Harold Entertains
Ada—The Beauty and Her Beast—"I do Love You"—Two
Interpretations—When One Receives and Gives a Shock.

On the very top of the pile of letters on Harold's Office desk lay a
square envelope addressed in a lady's handwriting. The paper was
finely webbed and breathed that delicate fragrance that makes the very
receipt of such communications a bit of romance.

That this letter lay thus prominently displayed was due partly to the
curiosity of the Office Boy This young being, who knew many things for
which he asked no credit, had duly noted that here was the handwriting of
none of the ladies who corresponded regularly with Harold. After studying
it diligently, he gave up the problem as a bad job, and left the letter in a
prominent position that his employer might be plagued by it at once.

Harold, strolling into his Office on the day after the picnic, saw
this letter at once; and he too was curious as to the sender. But Harold
was a perverse being; because he was curious, was precisely his reason
for not opening the letter. Instead, he put it aside till all the rest of
his correspondence had been dealt with, and until he had done all the
business that he felt moved to get through that day.

Harold was the son of a man, who, handicapped it must be
acknowledged by a very small weight of principle, had made money
keenly and largely. He had done very little else, except bring up a family
of two girls and one boy. He passed on to the boy a great deal of his
money, some of his ability and a very little of his keenness.

In business, as in some other things, Harold remained to a great
extent an unknown factor. Most of those who met him as a friend or
acquaintance declared with no hesitation that he was neglectful and
incapable in business. Neglectful he was; the fact was patent. That he
was incapable, also, was more problematical.

His father had bequeathed to him, along with the business, an
invaluable Chief Clerk, and to him Harold turned over the Office.
Harold might come down for a month regularly, day by day, or he might
stay away for the month and come regularly for a week. Only one thing
was certain about his movements, so the Chief Clerk grumbled, and
that was their uncertainty.

But the Chief Clerk did not agree that his employer was a fool. He knew that business affairs of great importance seldom found Harold out of touch with the essential particulars. A crisis called him to his post at once, just as a storm called a captain on deck, and crisis or no crisis, when he was on the spot he both saw and foresaw well.

The first time Harold crossed the Chief Clerk with an order to drop a speculation, that worthy remonstrated warmly. The point in question involved the buying of a run of land known as Tremeaven. Now the Government had informally committed itself to running the new railway through that land, and the investment seemed a sure thing. But Harold said:

"Land there will dip abruptly at this time next year and will not rise again after going over the precipice. Drop it, my dear C.C."

So it turned out.

The explanation was that the new Railway was not after all to pass through Tremeaven. How Harold knew that twelve months in advance of the business world, he never took the trouble to explain.

But he was not to be reckoned on. He would come to the Office and work the whole staff tired and cross, staying on himself till nine or ten at night, and continue this for a week. Then the tune would change altogether, and he would not be seen at the Office for many weeks, or if he did appear, it was merely for an hour or so.

Systematic ambition had no place in this young man's character. He had more money than he needed. There was no master feeling in his life. He loved many persons lightly, airily, pleasantly, but no one person deeply or thrillingly. His outlook on life was for the most part that of a kind-hearted, able, but slightly cynical loiterer. How small life really is he saw, and how worthless are its trinkets and gew-gaws; but he saw no pearl of great price amid it all.

Really penetrated by good and honest principle, he laboured hard to conceal this fact. The foundations of his character were sound, another fact that he toiled to hide; but on that foundation he busied himself with erecting and demolishing elegant sheds, rather than an enduring temple. It is not an unheard of thing that foundations thus tampered with should be at length invaded by the rot and damp of deterioration.

"I am casual," Harold said at times of himself; and the quaint idiom was really an excellent description.

As to business, he once put it thus to Liberta: "I have a Chief Clerk, of whose knowledge all that I can ever scrape together on this side of the grave will only be a moderate percentage. He could no more be dishonest than a tree could grow upside down. Supposing we don't make any more money, but just hold our ground, we have more than we could spend, even if I gave my sisters their head. Why then should I worry to do badly what the Chief Clerk cannot help doing well?"

"I can't tell you," was Liberta's answer, "if you can't tell yourself."

Today when he had done all the business he considered proper, Harold opened the mysterious letter and read:

> Will you come to see me this evening at 6 P.M.; or let me
> know where and when I can see you tomorrow.
>
> NOEL BRONVOLA

"And what may this mean?" cogitated Harold. His conclusion was: "It must be a bazaar and she wants to bleed me at close quarters; still I will go." The invitation mildly stimulated his vanity.

Harold had reached his house that afternoon ere he remembered that Ada had an invitation to take tea with him at five. She arrived promptly. It was her first visit to his house and she crept in through the imposing entrance, timorous and ill at ease. Harold received her with a charm of easy courtesy that at once made her happy.

They had tea in the garden on the lawn of green, close-cut Bahama grass. Above them trees whispered. Round them flowers shone like rich jewels; great roses displayed their deep pink bosoms; there was the starry jasmine; here were masses of white and yellow chrysanthemums. In the evening hour the mignonette breathed its perfume abroad; against the green hedge showed the red and salmon hibiscus. Now was the hour, too, when the evening shadow softened the glare that had lain all day like an invading force over the city. Amid these surroundings they talked the prettiest nonsense and he fed her with sweet-meats.

They rose at last and went into the house to see the pictures in the great drawing room of which he had told her. Harold looked at his watch surreptitiously. Six was approaching

"By the way," he said, "Beauty, what about a drive next Wednesday?"

To his surprize she hesitated.

"Well, is that an unlucky day?"

"No."

"Then am I an unwelcome companion?"

She looked up suddenly and said: "I am afraid."

"Of what?"

"I don't know."

"Afraid of me, Beauty?" His tone softened; he was touched by an unexpected answer evidently so sincere.

A faltering look at him now was all her reply.

"Well, what is the trouble?"

They both regained their natural tone.

"You don't mean to marry me?"

"No," he said without any hesitation, "I do not mean to marry you. I don't mean to marry anyone at present. Whatever put the idea into your head?"

"Then I am afraid of you."

"In that case, give me up. Snuff me out, Beauty. Bow your cavalier to the door. Dismiss your Beast."

"I know someone else who will marry me."

"He *says* so."

"Yes," she said failing completely to interpret what was meant by the emphasis.

"Are you going to tell me who he is?"

"Mr. Meffala's son," she replied, looking at him sideways.

"John Meffala?" he said sharply and in a new tone. Then he looked hard at her, thrust both hands into his trousers pockets and walked to the window. There he stood looking out, smoking.

When he turned he had relapsed into his usual ease of manner. He half sat, half stood against the window-sill and fixed his eyes on her face once more. She bore the scrutiny with ill-grace.

"Look here, Ada"; she noted the "Ada" instead of the half endearing 'Beauty.' "If you are afraid of me, give it up. I don't see any real harm in what we are doing; going for drives, chatting some sense and more nonsense; now and again a kiss and a dinner together; or the frequent and chilly ice-cream; but if you want to stop it, say so. It is in your hands entirely. Don't go on if you are afraid. Has the soul been giving you trouble?" he added whimsically. "What is it; a touch of spiritual rheumatism?"

She took no notice of his little jibe, but said tremulously: "You—you won't miss me?"

"Bless me," he replied his heart touched by her plaintive tone, "of course I will miss you, Beauty. Would I miss the Evening Star if it fell plump into the sea and we could not fish it out? Or the moonlight, if it faded gradually into white-wash? I will miss you very much—for a time," he added. He had a freakish but irressistible turn for exact truthfulness the moment that his conscience was stirred.

"Only for a time?" she said piteously, drooping under his last words, just as she had revived under the first part of what he said.

"I don't tell lies, Beauty." He felt savage at having to say things that she found so cruel; but his wayward virtue was now aroused, and, once put on his guard, he avoided a lie like a precipice. Then, seeing she was taking his words to heart, he continued playfully;

"Of course, you want me to say that I will never forget you—never, never, and forever; nothing shall our love divide, etcetera. Try and stretch that little brain of yours to the meaning of 'never;' why it is a continent of years, Beauty, with several oceans thrown in. How could I vow to travel all through it and not to change? Ah me," he went on pensively "nine years ago I would have said all that and more, and meant it. I would have thought I was truthful; but you learn how long 'Never' is as you grow older, Beauty, like me. If I promised never to forget you, it would only be putting a sugar plum into your mouth to melt behind those little pearl teeth of yours. A sugar plum with a lie in the middle of the sugar."

"You can do without me?"

"True," he responded tersely.

"I should never have left Miss Liberta," she cried woefully. "My soul is in a danger; I feel it now; I see it all."

"I told you to do just what you liked, that alone; remember," he made answer with a shade of irritation.

"Yes," then not bothering further about the point, "you do not love me." It was almost a wail.

"Oh, yes, I do," he said his heart melting towards her, and with the smile that made his such a winning presence. "I do love you." And that was true, for he loved all beautiful and graceful things, and he loved pretty, empty-headed, little Ada as he loved a shady nook made rich with the mauve flowers of the Wild Petunia, where they touch with colour the dew-tipped green of fern and grass. He loved her as he loved the golden sunset, or sight of one of our woodland crowded mountain defiles with the austere blue of distant peaks crossed by the gleaming whiteness of the hill-born mists, while the pure, cold breath of the mountain wind fans the cheek and renerves the brain.

It was the first time he had ever said in so many words to Ada "I love you"; though, as a matter of fact, he would never have denied it, had he been challenged. He loved her in the sense we have indicated. In that love there was no doubt latent vice; but as yet it had not taken to itself the body of passion. It was a pity, however, that he had not explained to Ada just what he meant when he said 'I do love you.' Beauty gave the words a very different meaning from that which he attached to them and this fault affected after events: Indeed, from those words so lightly spoken were to ensue results of very grave significance in the story of several lives.

There was silence for a minute or two. Harold was wondering if it would occur to Ada to go now. Ada was resting in the sense of delight that followed that confession of love, which she took in tragic earnestness. Harold looked at his watch:

"Beauty, I am desolated; but I must leave you. I have business at six, and Time won't stand still even for pretty little girls. As your soul has rheumatism, we will drop that drive on Wednesday. Night air is not good for rheumatism."

"What it is you must go to at six?"

"Ah, I see it is curiosity and not rheumatism after all."

"Is it important?"

"Very."

"You must go?"

"I must go."

"All right," she said doubtfully and dolefully.

"Make yourself at home here as long, as you like, and if you want a servant, press that bell button. It is pleasant in the garden and you will find a piano yonder. Ta-ta."

He had reached the door when a soft touch fell on his shoulder.

"Come on Wednesday," said Ada. "I am not afraid."

"We will see how the soul is," he smiled, "and you may change before that."

"I change!" she replied. "It is men who can change, not women. Come. I cannot do without you." All this brimmed out from Ada's over-charged heart. Her eyes were filled with tears and her eye-lids quivered.

Harold wiped away the tears, and left her. She stood watching him. Then he turned back.

"Beauty," he said in a constrained voice, "I give you a bit of advice; have as little as you can to do with John Meffala." It was evident that he hated to say it. He wondered at himself for doing anything so distasteful, but there was something that impelled him with the strength of the irresistible. Unconsciously he was paying toll to an accusing conscience. Was it not he who had brought Ada into the Meffala orbit?

"It is not true," sighed Ada.

"What is not true?"

"That he said he would marry me."

"So," said Harold in his ordinary tone, "it was a fib, was it? No wonder that soul has rheumatism—hut when do you see the gentleman and talk to him?"

He tended towards severity again.

"Hardly ever," she confessed. "He see me at the Store and looks at me a lot, but I have only spoken to him *once*."

"Yes—and said then?"

"Goodmorning, Mr. Meffala."

"Well, well, well," he said, "your soul seems to digest fibs pretty freely."

But mention of her soul gave Beauty a relapse into the doleful dumps.

After he had left her, she went up to the drawing room and for some time stood timidly surveying the pictures and the furniture. An open door led into an adjoining apartment and through this she presently strayed.

A jacket carelessly tossed to a chair had only partially reached its goal, and as it hung there, half on and half off the chair, a letter had fallen from the pocket. The letter addressed to Harold in a woman's handwriting, drew Ada like a magnet. She snatched it up and read its contents. It was Noel's letter to Harold.

"My God," said Ada tragically, "he has left me for her." She read all sort of terrible truths into the brief, commonplace note. "She has stolen him from me."

There lay huddled in the big drawing room a miserably disconsolate Beauty, bitterly weeping. It was an hour or two later that she crept out of the house into the darkness. As she descended the steps into the street a bus passed and its passenger looked at her. He was John Meffala. She was too distracted to notice him, and he for his part merely changed his cigar from one side of his mouth to the other, and muttered an exclamation of surprize.

Ada made her way to Noel's house and took up a furtive watch there to see how long it would be ere Harold left. As a matter of fact Harold had completed his business and departed long before the girl reached the house.

VIII

Just about the time when Ada was reading Noel's note, Harold was being ushered into the Bronvolas' house. He found Noel at the piano and stood entranced. His finest self, artistic and eclectic, expanded and luxuriated in the shower of beautiful sound. He was mute and motionless till she paused, then, as she rose, he said, smiling:—

"I beg you feed me still with that same nectar."

She reseated herself without demur, and a great storm of music went up from a martial march. When it was over, she closed the instrument decisively and said:

"We will go into the study. I do not wish to be disturbed, not even by mother,"

"Upon my word," said Harold to himself, "what a girl! Is she going to propose to me!" He still had the music in his mind, and for a minute or two they talked of that. Then Noel said:

"I did not ask you here to talk about music."

"I am at your service, and your mercy, what ever it is." And here, he thought, beginneth the Church Bazaar.

"You are making love to Ada Smith."

She planted the next blow at once, with the same directness.

"You do not mean to marry her."

There was a second of silence, a poise; then she added.

"You are acting dishonourably, and you know it."

It was seldom that Harold lost his self-command. He did so now. For a minute he felt completely dazed. Not a word trickled into his mind by way of a reply.

The confusion that showed in his face was painful to see. Without uttering a syllable he sprang to his feet and crossing to the window stood looking out. He was struggling to reconquer himself; to recover his mental balance and sangfroid; but for a time the effort was in vain. Surprise at being thus challenged by this young and beautiful girl; shame at having let an affair begun with no thought of evil take on this sinister aspect, met in a furious rush, and produced such a mental eddy as to uufit him for either thought or speech.

Noel, for her part, waited in silence.

At length Harold turned, and his first words showed his innate politeness.

"Pardon my abruptness; I was very much surprised."

"I will tell you," she said now, "just what I have seen," and she did so.

Still he was silent, no longer because he could frame no words, but because he could see everything that he shaped mercilessly destroyed by a girl prepared to attack him as Noel had just done. Everything that suggested itself seemed jejune or clumsy, and he detested being either clumsy or ineffective. He felt the unmanliness of leaving her to continue, but he was helpless.

The silence became a torture chamber to Harold ere Noel broke it.

"Do you then mean to marry Ada Smith?"

"Miss Bronvola," he cried involuntarily, then paused like a man who saw no road open before him. His gaze held her, and she gave him glance for glance with a perfectly composed serenity. He knew that he appeared an awkward fool, and writhed in the knowledge. Surprise still thumped the brain centres of control with demoralizing violence.

He thought of one thing to say, but it seemed petulant; of another but that seemed rude; of a third which seemed colourless; a fourth sounded smug. Something else that he thought of implied more penitence that he felt, and his quaint fidelity to truthfulness was now astir. The fact was, that he was deprived for the time being of the ability to judge the value of his thoughts, and that to a man of his temperament was a severe punishment.

Noel, for her part, convinced that the burden of speech lay now with him, did not speak till the silence had again grown painful to Harold. Then she asked another question:

"How long has this been going on?"

She looked still straight into his eyes, and he found it difficult to recall his gaze and prevent its passing into space beyond her. It needed a decided effort to meet her eye. This last question, however, helped him; for it was undoubtedly a mistep. He answered:

"That is a question, you will excuse my saying it, you must not ask me—that I cannot answer," he added with characteristic courtesy, "supposing you press it. I must refuse to answer."

She had made a mistake and her face showed that she accepted the check in good part; that he had risen, not fallen, in her estimation.

This much of more of good resulted from the passage. Harold began to realize that the way to understand this girl was to accept her as something unique, and apart; as a living force, with the surprizes of life thrilling in her words and deeds, fresh, true, elemental, in a way like a mountain stream, a strong wind, a full, tide-tossed sea. She must be studied for what she actually was, and so met and understood. The foot-rule of the Conventions must be laid aside.

Again her silence threw the burden of speech on him, and this time he lifted it.

"Will you tell me why you come into this matter? Why should you?"

"Why should I not?" she questioned without hesitation, and forced him back into silence, behind which many inner voices clamoured. He expressed none of that crowd of thoughts. If there was an advantage in finding her unconventional, he felt now the corresponding disadvantage in dealing with one not afraid of creating her own precedents. He saw that she would put aside one thing and another which would have served to stay and confuse other girls of her age.

If he said: "You are young for such a talk as this?" she might reply: "Youth is strong; it is the time for action. Difficulty should not daunt it, nor yet danger."

If his word was: "People may misunderstand your motive and probably will"; hers would be: "That does not change the motive." If he descended to the banality of asking: "Is it proper?" he expected the response from the steadily severe, yet beautiful, face: "It is proper to do right."

"Is it right?" he might insist. He imagined her reply: "Right is the crystal stream deep in the heart's well; what hand can draw from it but one's own?"

The more he thought of his possible comments and of her replies, the more he saw the latter as rare and distinctive, and his own as commonplace and trite. He stumbled at length into the poor sentence.

"There are reasons, I think, for you to keep out of this."

"I help where I can; this girl needs help."

"Miss Bronvola," said Harold, suddenly reaching the determination to be himself unconventional, and ceasing to shrink from putting the matter in any way that might wound her sensitiveness of feeling, "I ask you to think of this without prejudice, reasonably and naturally. What harm have I done that girl? What harm can it do to give her some pleasure, to take her for a drive now and then, to talk to her, to give her a pretty present or two? Hers is an isolated kind of a life. She is poor yet fairly educated. Her people are clowns, washerwomen and street nomads. She can never marry except below her standard of taste and feeling, and that would be chaining a bird to a stone."

Noel's reply was simply:—

"This is the beginning—of what?"

Conscience, reaching over for the words, and flinging them like a scourge smote Harold cruelly.

The situation was not the simple picture he had painted. No such thing. He had been trifling with passion in himself; and as he watched the fine face of the girl before him, and her splendidly moulded form, he realized that there stirred within his nature something that was like the savage head of a venomous reptile thrust through a mask of flowers. An appetite was waking which not only craved but demanded more. He had no doubt but that he could still control it; but that the effort to do so was needed, annoyed and mortified him.

And then Ada; he had reason to know that her feelings were straining her power of control dangerously. They had reached out and intertwined with his; he had tempted them so to do To tear them apart would be to rend, to bruise, to rob. It was no simple task. Memory handed to him, fresh, stamped and distinct, every detail of that evening's interview.

Unaccustomed to be scourged by conscience, the discomfort made him impatient, and like a desperate animal his impatience rushed forward. He would pass through all half-way houses to the ugly conclusion of the whole matter. He was too fine a gentleman to say it in so many words, but he was practically resolved to make the truth enter her mind now in its unadorned ugliness. "You are young, pure, beautiful and modest; but you have chosen to act to me so that these considerations should no longer avail you; they shall not. You have pushed aside the curtains of the Conventions. Good, we will look together on what is revealed. It is not a pretty sight; but since you demand the real, the actual, very fact, let us have them, with all the mud sticking to their boots. Grant the extreme consequence, and that this girl becomes the mother of my children, my paramour, whom I will care for but never marry. I ask you what would really be so bad in her position. She being what she is, and I being the man I am?" He thought his way through all this and then actually said:

"But supposing," he was speaking deliberately and watching her boldly and mercilessly, "the end should come as you think; if one takes it without prejudice and without convention, how can it be shown to be such a bad thing for a girl of her class and fortunes. It would give her a friend, someone to care for her. It would give her comfort and ease. Her life would be really as decent as any one's, putting aside a convention? You have spoken frankly, so have I; I ask you to use your reason not prejudice. Do not bow down to what the world says merely because the world says it."

Noel looked at him with direct frankness.

"Now, think of her as your sister; and accept the same argument from another man. Or apply what you have said of her to me. Tell me if it satisfies you."

Again his confusion became painful, he rose and began, without noticing his own action, to pace restlessly to and fro. The unexpected had unbalanced him. His was not a base mind, but he had yielded to a base impulse, and fruitlessly. He had meant to push her to confusion; to make her realize that it was not for a girl to discuss subjects of the sort with a young man—That she might start bravely enough but dared not continue to the end. He had meant to show her her place; and the tables were now completely turned. She sat calm and composed, the only signs of excitement in her were spots of faintly glowing red on her cheeks. It was he that was ashamed, confused, nervous and unready, hardly daring to meet her eye.

Suddenly as his restless glance fell on her face, like a sharp blade cutting keen and swift, it was borne in on him, through all his confusion and mortification that she was the most beautiful girl he had ever seen. It came with a force that could never be forgotten, making an impression never to be removed. Curious, that he had never thought of it before, though he had seen this girl so often. How could he have missed such beauty? or failed to see how peerless it was? He wondered dully. Now her loveliness seemed brilliant as the sun; a blind beggar must realize it, were his blindness three-fold.

An impulse entered his mind and grew rapidly to strength in the midst of the chaos there. It was the insane inclination to kneel before her and cry:

"You are more beautiful than ever woman was before, or than woman ever can be again. Love me; and together we will make worlds; call forth life and death. Destroy and recreate Time. Defy the millions of men and women who crowd the earth. Love me, Noel."

He stood rigidly still, afraid to move at all, lest he should come to this madness.

By and by Reason swayed him again. He came back to his seat and began quietly:

"I will acknowledge indiscretion; and ask you to acquit me of worse, and yet, if it were proper and right for me to tell you the story, or if I could even appear to try to excuse myself, you might see that through it all I have never passed a fixed line."

"The point that matters is that she loves you now."

"Yes."

"You created that love in her."

"Yes."

"Then you are responsible."

"Miss Bronvola, will you tell me just what you want?"

"Your promise," she replied unhesitantly, "to leave this girl alone."

"Believe me," he said, "I will play the game fairly, I persuade her to nothing. I told her only this evening that I would not marry her. I told her to stop at once, if she thought our friendship wrong."

"It is not a game," answered Noel, "and you cannot be fair if you continue it all. All the strength is on your side. All the weakness with her. You see far; she does not see at all."

"You are right," he said at length, "You have my promise."

He reached the street with a sense of mental comfort to which he had been a stranger for the last hour or so. He had hardly taken a step, however, when his emotional nature rebounded. A suspicion leapt into his mind, fully armed and raging. It mastered the mob of his feelings in a second. At once he turned and reentered the Bronvolas' house.

Noel was arranging flowers at a window, glowing red and pink carnations and white chrysanthemums.

"Excuse me," he said bluntly, "you had spoken of this matter to Ada Smith before you spoke to me just now, and you," he added to himself, "put her up to asking me to marry her." He was certain she had; and that he had detected her conpiracy to humiliate him.

She placed her hands behind her back, like a child facing a stern taskmaster, and smiled deliciously.

"Are you really in earnest? Must I plead to that indictment? A prosecutor should believe in his case—he, at least. Shall I plead?"

"No," he said, suspicion leaping into the outer void, even more swiftly than it had come into his mind. "I was a dolt. Forget I ever asked you."

"Or shall I hang it up in my memory that you were not in earnest?"

She smiled, and her beauty and grace swam before him like a single great star in an evening sky of pink grey. Never, he thought, had earth seen a face as beautiful as that. Not in her thousand million daughters was there one whom a man could more desire, or better worship. His brain felt the exhilaration of intoxication. As he passed for the second time into the street, he even said aloud: "Am I sane? Am I really Harold? What has happened? What has touched my brain? What follows?"

And memory answered with the picture of Noel's face, as he had just left it, glowing with life and beauty, a human jewel, gleaming richly beside the superb flowers. Once again he saw her smile, place her hands behind her back, and, looking up at him with the touch of childishness, which was in such piquant contrast with her severity of a few minutes before, ask:

"Shall I plead? Does the prosecutor believe the charge?"

The new feeling in Harold's heart struck, sure, swift and strong to the very centre of his being and captured the citadel there; but it was rather with the rush of a band bent on a foray, than with the measured advance of an army carrying out conquest. It was love, certainly, but love cast into a medium that had been deteriorated by the insiduous saturation of passion.

He was chained down to the sensuous. Her beauty made his memory drunken, and it could do nothing but paint him pictures of a skin without blemish; of red lips curved like Cupid's bow; of dark hair overshadowing eyes which melted from severity to the look of kind comradeship he had won from them at the very last. Her finely proportioned figure, her pulsing bosom, on these his imagination feasted and his blood was on fire to be master of this splendid being.

He had been conquered, as after events were to show, by her personality, by the woman she was in the inmost hall of being, in the soul behind all these courts of physical beauty; but in his present mood it was that beauty that dominated him. He was the slave in the procession of her loveliness. In his veins, like fire, went the desire to possess her, to crush her to his heart and to hold her there against all comers.

As regarded Ada, his decision was terse, simple, direct. He would end once and for all that trifling. His eyes were opened now. He was being entangled; she was being injured. It should all end that night in his mind, and in hers the morrow should see it perish, to be as if it never had been.

Such was his resolution. A scene he detested, and as a formal announcement to Ada might precipitate a scene, he would next day leave the island for a season. Where he went to mattered very little; the thing was to get away at once, and to be no longer where there was the possibility of straying daily to trifle with the pretty chit. He would take an outward-bound steamer tomorrow and by a note of two lines Ada should know that he was off. In two months her fancies about him would have withered; and he would see to it that there was no renewal of these dangerous fooleries. Dangerous, was a word that he interjected as he recalled Ada's appearance during one part of their last interview. He really meant the girl no harm in the world. A fancy he might have for her; he had a fancy, he admitted it now; of passion he had none.

Here then was a programme very simple, compact and definite; Harold could not be truthfully said to feel any difficulty about dropping poor Ada thus suddenly by the way. Yet he felt strangely upset, and excited; strangely sad, even, at the idea of this abrupt departure. Somehow the balance of his mental and moral nature which he thought a few steps in the cool night air, and a little thought, would restore, was not to be so easily recovered. He went down one street and along another, and in a short time had each detail of his departure ready for action; still he felt no more composed. At length he called a bus and jumped into it.

"Anywhere out of Kingston? On a quiet road," was all he troubled himself to say.

"What sort a backra dis now," grumbled the driver.

They were soon on a road which the silent hills watched over. Once the driver asked if this suited.

Harold did not even hear the question Engaged in retracking every detail and each event of the evening's second interview, his will was for the present none of his. Noel's every look, every gesture, each word of hers he recalled again and again, as if, chained to a post in the centre, he was condemned to travel round it at an equal distance all the time.

At length he ordered the man to go back to the town. While that worthy was resolving to raise a row about the sum due him, or which he would claim, Harold threw down so much money, that the bus disappeared as rapidly as the horse could take it, its owner dreading to be recalled and told it was in a mistake. "Dat's de kind of backra for me," he said emphatically when at last at a safe distdnce he moderated his pace, and re-counted the coin.

Meantime Harold plunged into the preliminaries of his trip abroad. Late as it was he rang up his Chief Clerk on the telephone and desired his presence at once. It was 1 A.M. before they parted.

At a little before twelve on the same night Howard Lawley, riding slowly home from an evening party, drew rein at sound of hysterical moaning. The sound came from a young woman who lay huddled and all disconsolate at the root of a Mango tree.

Ada was by this time in such a state of hysteria and weariness that she could give no coherent account of herself. Two sentences recurred on her lips: "He is mine; he said he loved me," and "She has taken him away from me; stolen him."

Lawley felt neither desire nor special ability to administer comfort or help to a young woman in such straits, but he intended to get her back to her home, and, therefore, the first thing he needed to know was, where that home was to be found.

"You are mistaken," he said brusquely. "No one has taken away your lover. You are lying."

The words and his manner acted like magic. Ada stopped moaning and sat up at once. "Oh," she said, "I am a liar, am I?—And what are you?"

"Oh, I?" he answered, "I daresay I come in somewhere under the same banner, but at present it is you we are talking about. I say you lie. You have lost no lover."

"That is all you know about it. Her letter to him is here at this very moment, in my bosom. Written and signed, telling him to come to her."

"Nonsense, what you have in you is hysteria. Perhaps though, you have been drinking a little. One wine glass would upset a brain like yours I should say. Come, get up and go home."

She held a letter up. "There is her name; Noel Bronvola, the beautiful white girl, with the long hair. A stealer of lovers she is; of my lover, Harold."

"Bah," said Lawley harshly, for the present at least hardly conscious that he had noted the names used, so disgusted was he with the position, and with having the details thrust on him in this way. "Listen, girl, do you know me? I am the Colonial Secretary?"

But Ada was of the class that knows nothing of Colonial Secretaries. "Who is he?" she asked wonderingly.

Lawley smiled in the midst of his vexation. "You have heard of the Inspector of Police?"

"Yes."

"The Colonial Secretary is above the Inspector; I am the Secretary. You know the Police?"

She nodded.

"Well they will have you directly, if you stay here. Do you know it is near midnight?"

"What," she cried in alarm, "is it so late?"

He looked at his watch.

"It is midnight."

At that moment there came up from the City the sound of the public clocks striking the hour, while all the smaller timepieces hastened in a thousand and one houses, large or small, to hurry after their bigger brothers with their toll of noise.

"Where do you live?"

She told him; it was buried in the City's further extremity.

"What folly?" he muttered irritably. Ada whimpered; fear was beginning to lay hold of her.

"Here," he said, "stay where you are, and I will send a bus up from the Corner Roads. Give no trouble now, or you may suffer for it. A pretty place and plight for a decent girl to be found in. Sit quite still till the bus comes."

But on the contrary she scrambled to her feet and began to follow him.

We take our inmost and most sincere convictions and beliefs for better or worse; and Lawley's opinions and beliefs left him no choice but to render aid to humanity when he saw it suffering, and could help. We all have intuitions of duty that we disregard only at mortal peril to that moral self-respect without which we cannot live as souls. Ready though we may be to trample over what others think for us, frequently as we disregard the voice of our own conscience in its less imperative moods, there is that in us which, when it speaks, we obey, feeling that to do less would be to tear ragged a wound in our humanity.

We speak of irreligious men, but, as a fact, every man has a religion which he obeys. It is that sum total which remains behind everything, giving the impulse to life, exacting obedience, a power, which is no more successfully resisted than the central power in the steam engine is resisted while the engine works at all. As Lawley had learnt life, it was his deepest sense of duty to aid distressed fellow beings. Sometimes, as now, he obeyed the inner voice with a chafing sense that convictions impose a hards lavery on a man. Still he obeyed.

Ada, instead of sitting down and waiting as she was told to do, was pressing up to his side. As he paused, uncertain how to compel obedience, a woman's figure stood out in the road across which there lay now bands of brilliant moonlight and the dark shadows falling eastward from the trees that stood in the flood of light pouring from the moonrise.

"What is the matter, Gentleman?"

Lawley glanced appreciatively at the tall, erect figure and the intelligent face, and answered tersely:

"Here is a fool at large; and it is midnight."

"You want to get her home?"

"Yes."

"Shall I see to it?"

"If you will."

"Yes, gentleman."

"You know me?"

"You are Mr. Lawley. I was butlering at the house you were at this evening."

"Well, I assure you that I am much obliged to you. I will send a bus from the Corner Roads. Pay expenses out of this."

"And the change, where shall I send it?" she enquired holding up the half-sovereign.

"I would wish you to get something."

"I am not doing it for pay, gentleman."

Next day at the Colonial Secretary's Office, Lawley received a packet of change addressed in round unformed writing. On a slip of paper along with it was written:

I took her home, gentleman.

IX

A Duel: Harold vs. Noel—Love, Creator and Creature—
Responsibilities—What Percival Road Held in the
Starlight—The Cross Roads' Pause in Life—What
Noel Remembered: and What She Forgot—Calling
a Beautiful Body to the Bar of Judgment.

Harold could hardly be said to have waked up next morning; he had slept very little, if at all. The new day changed his resolve. That afternoon, at about the time when the steamer which was to have taken him on his travels was leaving her berth, he strolled into the Office, and told the Chief Clerk casually that the excursion was off.

That evening he received a letter from Ada. It was long and confused. Some of it he read, then, irritably, he threw it aside. Next day there was another letter. "Dear Beauty," he wrote, without reading a line of it, "You won't see me just now. Be happy and good. Doctor your soul. HAROLD." Then he bundled Ada out of his mind.

It was Noel that he could not forget. Fret and chafe as he might at his slavery to that evening interview he never wandered far from it. Still there stood before him the picture of her upright, glowing figure, standing at the window and turning to him with a smile almost mischievous. After a time he despised himself for this servitude of emotion. He rated himself for his folly, but he could not shake off the infatuation. Strung to high tension, he could get no relief, no slackening of the strain. Vainly he paused to take stock of the situation, and to ask himself if it could be his old easy-going self, who was thus hand-cuffed wrist to wrist with this excited and unbalanced mind. He had treated Love and Passion with careless gaiety; now, like living creatures with strangely awakened powers of magnetically binding all that touched them to their tentacles, they closed on him with an unrelenting embrace. Harold was for main intents and purposes another being.

The question recurred: "How was it, that after knowing Noel all these years, he should thus suddenly and completely fall before her?" It seemed a sort of witchcraft. In view of what had already happened, he grew afraid of himself, uncertain, since this strange-thing had come out of the unknown, what else there might be in his path of which he had not dreamt his personality capable.

Time might have been his physician had he at once left the island, but, as it was, weeks passed and still Harold, though appearing much the same to the outside world, was shut up within his own consciousness, to companionship with the new strange being that had been created within him.

Letters came fluttering to him from Ada. They were hardly looked at. Sometimes he was told in the house that a girl had been there asking for him. "Ada, perhaps"; he said to himself and dismissed the matter.

His own house seldom saw him. Restlessness gave him her hand and away he danced with her, as he roved about to join shooting and fishing parties and to seize on whatever promised to distract his thoughts. He was feverish, and in a state of subdued anger.

Weeks of this new experience had passed over Harold's head, when one night Noel stepped out into the darkness from Miss Elsie's house on Percival Road.

At the garden gate Miss Elsie herself remonstrated with mild forcefulness against the risk that beautiful young ladies ran in travelling about at night by themselves. Noel turned the remonstrances on the shield of laughter.

Dark it was at first, truly, but one's eye soon got used to that. As for danger, it was late in the day, or the night, to try to daunt her with that, she, the veteran of so many night walks. Tropical Nature had made the day to be looked at; the night, with its cool, shadow and clear star-shine, to be used. So she bade a cheery goodnight.

Noel had gone but a little distance when a man's figure rose from the bank beside the road and came towards her.

"Good evening, Miss Bronvola."

The voice told her nothing. It was strained and strange beyond recognition; but presently in the starlight she discerned who addressed her. She held out her hand to Harold.

"And what brings you here? Is this out-of-the-way road a favourite of yours?"

"I have not been here twice in my life. I am going your way now; may I accompany you?"

"Certainly," she said cordially, "and what a relief it would have been to the little lady I have just left had she known so trusty an escort was near. She is shuddering now, I fancy, as she thinks of me alone with the night and its ogres."

They walked on together between an avenue of trees. The dark mass of foliage was outlined against the clear sky where the large stars shone brilliantly.

Harold was deeply preoccupied. To a casual remark he made no reply. Noel repeated the question with which she had greeted his appearance:

"What brought you here tonight."

"You," he answered abruptly. "I followed you when you came; and waited under that tree while you were in the cottage."

"You wish to see me, specially?"

"Yes."

There was a pause.

"Miss Bronvola, if a person creates a thing, a thing that will not die, is not the creator bound to give it some care and attention?"

"That seems reasonable."

"I am glad you think so."

"Have I then a personal interest in the matter?"

"Yes."

"As the creature?"

"No, as the creator."

"And the creature?"

He touched his breast. "It is here. It was nowhere in my being before that evening. You looked into my eyes; it was in my life, after you spoke to me that night. It was full-grown at once. What magic have you to change a man as I am changed? Till I hardly know myself; till at times I hate, I despise myself. And yet I am powerless. I cannot change back to the old self which was at peace. The spirit here has passed through death and the tomb and can no more come back to the flesh. The past is there like the corpse of my life. It is dead, cold, a mass of clay; I am not there in that past. I am not that. It is a shell, a frame-work. Here is a new man."

"And I have done this?"

"You? Yes. You have destroyed and recreated. You spoke to me and changed me; you looked at me and made this new being. I cannot hide it now. It is useless to try to destroy it. Believe me, I have tried. It is by no good will of mine that I have changed like this, in five short weeks. I am a different man altogether. I cannot rest; I cannot pause. I am a slave; a fanatic; a devotee. There is a life inside my life beyond my power. I am a slave."

"Well," she said, and he saw her earnest eyes fixed steadily on him, "what would you have me do?"

"As I sat waiting for you here in the darkness, do you know how I made it heaven for myself? I kept repeating again and again to myself, 'Noel, Noel.' It was as if each time that I said that name I loosed bursts of music, sweeter, rarer, stranger in their melody than earth ever heard. It fell from somewhere in the sky, above these dark tree-shapes, down from the stars, falling, falling, like scented mists. It rose and again it fluttered through the night, that beautiful music. It burst and showered melody like a peal of bells dying far away in perfect harmony."

Instinctively they stood still, as if now the body resigned every function and movement that could be laid aside, so that, undistracted, save by the functions without which life must cease; the heart throb, the tide in the vein and artery, the coming and going of the breath; the senses might crowd about the meeting place of two souls. The passion of the moment seemed to hold the attention of Night herself. Suddenly the stillness seemed more profound, as if the darkness listened and watched. The noise of the insects in the grass sank and sounded far away and faint, as if hushed by some one's gesture. The man's breathing was audible, indrawn with painful intensity, in that profound silence as if lightly rippling the waves of the air ocean.

Each of these two felt, though in different ways, that Life was pausing on the ancient and solemn highway of Time, and that after this pause, in the going on that would follow, each soul would bear with it a difference from the influence of that hour never again to be erased.

Harold had come in despair, not in hope; but it ran through him now like the thrill of fire that there was hope. The beautiful face, radiant in the starlight with a subdued, mystic illumination, seemed dearer and nearer than it had ever been before. Her eyes poured spiritual balm on his heart.

"Noel," he cried. "I bring you the love you created. It is happiness, or misery, as you decide." He had spoken in deep, intense tones, through which had crept some of the glow of exultation, but his hope sank at the end and he halted with the words: "You are responsible."

"Yes, I am responsible," she answered simply.

"And what have you to say to me?" An icy chill followed the wave of flame that seemed but a moment before to be sweeping through every vein of his being.

"What is your question?" she asked calmly.

"My God," he cried to himself, "she is stone; she is ice. Love for me? It is hopeless; such beings never love."

"Ah, what is the good," he said aloud. "It is useless; useless"; and he pressed his hand to his eyes, unconscious of what he did. The violence of his emotion shook him.

"Come," said her quiet voice, and her hand rested softly on his arm; "Sit down here on the bank beside me and say what I can do."

Her touch and her words calmed him. He sat down beside her as if in a dream.

"What is the question to me? What am I to do?" she repeated.

He sprang to his feet again, trembling. It came home to him that the strength was with her, the weakness with him; but it failed to renerve his manhood.

His agitation was the reflex of her calm. Had she been moved and unbalanced, it would have been possible for him to regain mastery of himself and the situation. As it was, her complete serenity drove him well-nigh to madness.

"I love you," he burst out hardly knowing where his words sped. Then suddenly he flung himself on his knees before her where she sat on the grassy bank, and, seizing her hands, looked up at her face. It showed under the shadow of her hair, white and still in the starlight. He smote in the interruption with passionate words "Do you love me? That is the question for you, Noel. Will you marry me?" That is the question—the only question. It carries life or it strikes at me with death." Then he paused and resumed more at the normal.

"Forgive me, I am completely unmanned. I am not myself. Love has been burning in my veins all these weeks, night and day, and it has destroyed everything but itself. Nothing else matters now. The flame burns life to dust. The flame burns the flame. Love me. That is the question for you, Love me; marry me."

She made no attempt to withdraw her hands, nor did she hesitate to meet his eye. Her answer was in quiet, vibrant tones. "I never could marry you."

"You hate me."

"Oh, no."

"You do not love me—it is hate."

"I like you."

"In time you would love me."

"No."

"In time after years."

"I am sure not."

"You are so young."

"I am sure of myself—quite sure."

He dropped her hand almost roughly and rose to his feet.

"You love someone else," he cried impulsively. The stress on the accentuation of the words showing pain, explained the impertinence to her but did not excuse it. She remained silent.

"You do," he repeated. "You love some one else. Some one has mastered your heart."

She smote him with a glance that made him feel his degradation.

"That you have no right to know, do not answer your question at all, since you demand an answer. Did I feel I should answer, I would do so—I would say yes or no, whichever were true. I would not be afraid."

He was silent for a few seconds, then he said in more natural tones:

"You are right. I am a fool and that question was an impertinence. Forgive me."

"I will answer your question to show you that I do. There is no one I love as you mean it in asking like that."

"No one?" he said, in quite a new tone; then suddenly as if he saw the solution of a problem on which he had been pondering in despair, as if he saw a light where there had been hitherto impenetrable darkness, he burst out in strong, positive, joyful accents:

"You do love me; you must, you must. You shall; and you do. You do not know it fully yet, but it is there in your heart. Love creates love. I understand it at last. You created love in me because you first loved. God understands world-making; he makes love, and love creates love, and then the creature as turns to the creator. I love you; it is God's gift and you will love me."

She was silent, perplexed by the perversity of events, and he misinterpreted her silence. He began to tell her, in low soft tones, of his love; of how in a moment it had entered his heart and filled it; of how her face was unforgettable through every minute of time, memory of her voice unescapable. "It was memory of you that called me out of a world where love is a name, a fancy, a casual ornament, to a world where love is life. You must love me; you do, you do. You are too young to know yet in full, but love is in that heart. You could not create love like mine unless you loved. It is impossible."

Still she was silent. He watched her with a feeling of triumphant assurance filling his heart as with a white light. Passion was bounding to the summits of existence in a thrilling rush. Like the rosy light of morning, sweeping up over a commonplace landscape with a transfiguring illumination, the confidence that at last the problem was solved spread through his mind.

Everything else in the world seemed lost to view. Existence closed in, presenting to him a single face, a single figure. The conviction was almost sublime that Noel was worth the world to him, that all without and within himself was well lost to win her. That here he found the great, the priceless pearl of life, for which a man will sell all that he has gladly, if he may but gain the treasure.

She fed his madness by a simple, and almost unconscious, gesture. It was her habit to remove her hat as she walked in the balmy coolness of the tropical night. She did so now. The clear starlight illumined her superb beauty. Shadowed by the abundance of her dark hair, it glowed with a touch of rareness, even of mystery.

Suddenly Harold encircled her with his arm and drew her to him with a force that was well nigh violence, till her bosom was crushed against his and the heartbeat of the one life echoed in and vibrated with the heart-beat of the other, the while he kissed her again and again, his kisses falling fast and warm on her chin, her cheeks, her lips.

For a second, the second of complete and entire surprize, she lay passive in his embrace, and his joy rose to rapture. It surged through and through him as a certainty that she yielded, that all his agony of doubt and fear and despair was past forever; that love had answered love in that beautiful heart.

More swiftly than ever was the flash of the lightning, time rolled back, leaving the girl's figure central still, but it moved in the foreground of long distances of years that lay glorified like sunlighted landscapes. He had penetrated to the inmost meaning of existence. The pearl of price, won from the water of the very fount of life, lay gleaming in his hand. He had conquered; and his blood was as flame through his veins; his brain exulted as with strong wine: his thoughts were as the thoughts of a god.

Then sudden hideous ruin fell on all this beauty and triumph.

Through the form that he crushed to him with such devouring force, there crept an involuntary shudder, deep, convulsive, repellent. It delivered her far more effectively than struggle or outcry could have

THOMAS MACDERMOT

done, for it struck to the man's heart a paralyzing dread he knew not clearly of what. Was it that he feared to see Death appear like a ghastly spectre and snatch this splendid life from his arms. Was the tremor, the mortal chill and convulsion of a spirit leaving its earthly tenement; the vibration trembling through the flesh as the cord of life snapped suddenly. His passion shrank into miserable smallness before his own eyes. He opened that mad embrace and left her to stand free. She was erect, alive, strong.

Sudden Death was not the terror. What then? Who was the guest that entered into the very citadel of life in this girl, and caused the horror that showed itself outwardly in that deadly shudder. Perhaps it was the collision between the crystal pure soul and the passion-soiled mood of one whose selfishness was for the time being akin to madness.

He drew back and stood in silent stupefaction. Noel leaned for a minute against a tree trunk, then she picked up her hat, and, without a word, set off again towards the car-line. Her pace was no whit accelerated. Almost mechanically Harold accompanied her.

"Speak to me," he said at length in a tone so demoralized that he would have been surprised to hear it was his own, could he have listened to it from outside. "I am a cad, a beast, a scoundrel."

Then he cried with more spirit: "You don't know how beautiful you are. You don't dream how beautiful your face is."

"You are contemptible," she said with an inflection of bitterness and anger that threatened self-restraint dangerously.

"My God," he groaned.

They were nearly at the crossing before he spoke again: His tone was quiet and profoundly dejected:

"Shall I leave you?"

"Why?" she answered, and he noticed how remarkably her voice had changed its tone, recovering its calm and peace.

"I thought you might wish me to," he stammered.

"Do you think I am afraid of you?" she asked calmly but not unkindly. The fury of his passionate kisses had made the blood flame in her cheeks; the colour sank reluctantly; with its slow recession she regained control of herself.

They stood waiting now for the down car. A buggy passed, and Harold saw that it contained Lawley.

From the car, rushing on its down grade lines, the night outside the narrow limits lit by the eléctric bulbs seemed dark as the pit. One after the other, each electric centre of brilliance balanced itself on the rim of the dark in front, rose slowly, and then rushed faster and faster towards the car, till it passed from view over its roof, So it seemed as one looked out ahead.

"Did you think that that could bring us nearer?" said Noel in a low, clear tone.

"My God," said Harold, "I am a fool."

"Are you not more than a fool, or less?" She looked at him with a gush of doubt flooding her eyes, that doubt terrible to any man who is more honest than dishonest. "Will you boast of this to your friends?" she asked coldly.

"Boast," he responded. "I feel more like cutting my own throat to get out of the whole wretched tangle of life once and for all. I am a fool—and worse."

"And death?" she said, "do you think that is not a tangle too, out there in the dark?"

When they alighted from the car and stood together, Harold said nervously:—

"Am I to leave you here?"

"Do you wish to?"

"It is not that," he replied in some confusion, "I thought you might object to my company. I am a beast."

"I am not afraid of you," said Noel, and her tone now was almost kindly.

"But you despise me. You think me contemptible. I am a scoundrel—a beastly cad. I feel it."

She looked at him with a calmness that was almost reflective; then, without the slightest emphasis to suggest the extraordinary, she said quietly but distinctly:

"You are my friend."

In the sudden relief and joy coming to him from those surprising words, he could have fallen at her feet. It was some seconds ere he could trust himself to respond, then he simply said:

"Thank you"; but he burst out bitterly by and by: "I deserve the whip; you can never forget what I did."

"I will remember," she answered, "that you were ashamed of it." Perhaps the phrase like one she had employed at their memorable interview weeks previously, slipped in naturally; perhaps she employed it now on purpose, with the subtle intention of marking that he stood again with her just where they had parted on that day; that all that had happened in the interim had been annihilated.

When they seperated now he ventured only to raise his hat. It was she who held out her hand frankly and naturally. As he grasped it he knew that he could not make this beautiful creature his, his alone. He could seize her, crush her to his heart; he could not master or annex her life. But, if he would, he could be man and play a man's part; a man and not a beast; a gentleman and no cad. She was his friend, looking past that in him which was poor and base and mean and vile, to that in him which embodied the noble and the enduring.

At Noel's home nothing passed between mother and daughter but question and answer as to Miss Vera. Later on when they sat on the verandah, and her mother asked for music, the girl hesitated.

"I am not calm enough tonight, Mamma. It would have trouble in the heart of it." After a pause she added, "Shall I play in spite of that?"

"Yes; if you will."

"Come in and sit beside me. I will turn the light low; it will be soft for your eyes." She looked calm and composed enough, but a faint colour lingered still in her cheek. The mother's eye did not fail to note this, but she asked no question. Her love did not demand tribute in the spoken word as under some system of feudal lordship.

Noel took her seat at the piano and began to play from memory. At first it was a slow movement, a quiet filing forward of deep notes like the pouring onward in pent columns of an army great in number but silent, save for its tread.

Then on the sudden the music changed. It spread out like an armed line that deploys and catches as it moves the sparkle of sun-beams smiting on gleaming steel. Broad plains billowed into the distance, and the shadow of woodlands was a dark rim on a far horizon. Winds passed fresh and free.

Without sign of changing emotion on the musician's fine face, there came another change in the music. The heart lay a pool, clear but deep, and it stirred with a swirl of dark waters.

On and on went the music repeating itself, and at each repetition making the picture of the troubled pool more distinct. The listener came again and again to that pool, with its depth, its stir, its darkness. There seemed no stopping for Noel, as she sat grave and composed to all appearance, her fingers sweeping the key-board with trained rapidity; but at length she stopped suddenly.

"Is the trouble drowned?" asked her mother.

"Ah, you saw the pool, I always do"; but she did not answer further.

They returned to the verandah and Noel asked a question, a curious question for one so little moved by self-consciousness. "Mamma, am I very beautiful?"

The mother took the young face between her hands and looked at it, as if bent on studying it anew and carefully, ere she replied. She looked deep into the frank eyes, pushed back the overhanging hair that hung intrusively over the shapely forehead. Almost solemnly she kissed the broad brow and answered. "Yes, Noel, you are very beautiful."

The deep, clear eyes met her own as free from many trace of vanity as the star-space above the house was at that moment free from cloud or mist. It was not vanity that had prompted this question apparently vain. The mother divined that for some reason the girl desired information as to how she appeared in the eyes of others. Stroking the dark hair, she said:

"You are the most beautiful girl, Noel, that I have ever seen." The trouble haunting the eyes into which the mother looked, did not leave them. It deepened.

Noel looked away and presently said:

"Is it a dangerous thing—beauty?"

"To oneself or to others?"

No answer was forthcoming. Noel could not make her thought definite enough to respond. The mother understood her silence, and her mind sped ahead to meet the younger spirit at another turn of the long road of thinking.

"Mother," said Noel at length, "I am thinking of the earth. There are the pastures and the hills and the sea and the sky, there is so much beauty, and it all seems so good, so peace-giving. It helps to joy and life and strength. It does no harm. Why should a woman's beauty bring danger?"

"Ah, why indeed," said the mother, and attempted no further answer; for at such questions, Life turns to Age and Experience a face as inscrutable as that which she directs towards Youth and Emotion. It is only in our folly and conceit that we conclude that we know, because we have lived.

"Should one wish not to have beauty?"

"But if you have beauty already, how make room for the wish?"

"You mean one should not give it room?"

"Naturally; a wish is out of place when it is useless."

Suddenly Noel smiled. "Mamma," she said with a touch of merriment, "Don't fancy I have that wish; I have not; I am only thinking."

The smile added to the beauty of the face as a band of sunshine suddenly showing adds to the loveliness of an austere landscape. The mother noted that the colour in the girl's cheek was now failing to persist.

"And what is the next thought, about beauty, Noel?—About women's beauty?"

Instead of fostering self-consciousness the conversation was relieving Noel of it, by checking the dominance that something still unknown in detail to the mother was imposing on the daughter's mind

"This is the thought. Would it be right to destroy your beauty for the danger's sake."

An imperative pulse of alarm beat in the mother's heart, and she looked searchingly at the girl. Such an idea, pushed from a certain angle on a mind such as Noel's might conquer it for acts of exalted fanaticism. But the look that she met was reassuring. The idea was receiving intellectual entertainment only, not emotional.

"Was there not a saint who destroyed her beauty?"

"Saintship did not always mean sanity."

"It is quite possible, though," was Noel's answer, "to have a saintship that lies outside the accepted circle of sanity, enclosing it and making it a part of itself."

Before going to her room, Noel searched the book-shelves for a volume which told the old world tale of a saint who for the sake of the kingdom of heaven had destroyed her exquisite beauty by branding her face with a searing iron.

Robed at last in her long white night dress, her dark hair loosened and falling free and full, far down towards her knees, Noel stood before the large mirror and regarded the face and figure reflected there with a grave and careful scrutiny. There was something of reproachfulness, something even of sadness. She looked with painful and minute attention at another self, as it were, and that not with complete approval. It was as if she had called this beautiful body of hers to the bar of her judgment to be tried; and this with no inclination to show mercy.

X

Human Fingerposts Up and Down—The Sinner by the
Wayside—"God's Best Dog" smells Sin—Into the
Silence—After Church With Meffala and Ada—
A Minute in Oblivion.

"We are bound for the land of the pure and the holy,
The home of the blessed, the kingdom of love;
Ye wanderers from God on the broad road of folly,
Oh, say, will you go to the Eden above?"

The tambourines rattled and rang, forming a lively level, and amid
this, like a bluff hill shoved up, blunt and massive, in the centre
of a plain, came the deep loudness of the notes from a drum, beaten
somewhat too heavily.

It was chiefly on the treble notes of women's voices that the hymn
rose. Of the many men in the crowd, but few sang, and the detachment
of Salvationists which was responsible for the meeting were all women,
except the boy who bore the flag and who could not sing, the cornet
player, and a Captain who was so hoarse from continual speaking, that
he could now speak only in a whisper. The hymn was the finale of the
Sunday evening's "open-air," which was a preparation for the march to
the special service at the Town Hall.

The singers formed a centre to a crowd of gaily dressed women and
men in their Sunday best, who, after the manner of City folk, were
abroad on Sunday afternoon to take the air and to display their finery.
Incidentally they attended service.

On its fringes, this crowd was engaged for the most part in chatting
and in observations of its own. It paid littleif any attention to the
singers. Many even had their backs turned to the flag and the group
round it. There was more attentiveness among the inner circles of the
audience.

In the great world of Nature, under whose mighty arch of sky
singers and audience were an insignificant cluster of dots, it was an
hour of rare and mystic beauty, the brief season when the softness
of the fading daylight meets and mingles with the tenderness of the
moonlight—the hour when the spiritual seems no longer to be a thing

to be thought of painfully and laboriously, to be realized but dimly and vaguely, after infinite endeavour, but a presence that one does not seek or invite, but which flows in at the open doors and wide-flung windows of the soul.

The larger stars were beginning to shine in a sky touched yet by sunset colours. Snow-white bergs of cloud drifted slowly up from the west, moved by a current of air which had its own course in those lofty regions, in a direction quite different from the gentle sigh of the rising land breeze, that shook the fine foliage of the Poinciana, played lightly over the clusters of its crimson bloom, and stirred the leaves of the Palms to make them glint and gleam in the moon's rays.

"Will you go? Will you go?"

Very near them in the quiet hour seemed the entrance to a life other than that of earth and of the things seen and visible.

It was as if a great sea of invisible waters was flooding with, a full tide, through that hour; as if in some mysterious way even sound was seized and woven into the silence; the pealing of the church bells calling to evening worship; the occasional jar and crash as a vehicle sped by along the stony street, these sounds seemed no more an interruption of earth's brooding mood of stillness than ripples and the splash of raindrops on the great bosom of a broad river interrupt its slow, onward flow.

A tide of Church-goers swept along the street, some travelling in buggies or busses, but most of them on foot.

The Officer in charge of the Salvationists, darting a look over the crowd, saw a gentleman on horse-back draw rein. His eyes fixed itself on the Army Flag with the quiet attentiveness of one who studies the phenomena put before him.

"God bless you," said the Officer to a soldier; "that gentleman on horse-back will give us something; and the collection is only four shillings and seven-pence half-penny."

The next minute the tambourine was close under Lawley's eye and the soldier said brightly:

"God bless you, sir, will you give something?"

Lawley dropped a shilling into the tambourine, noting casually as he did so, how the newly minted coin shone in the moonlight. Again he fixed his eye on the Flag, and apparently listened to the hymn. In reality he was thinking that it was curious how people whose belief was so narrow, and, to his mind, so illogical and crude, could be so comprehensively useful; and he speculated when the impulse would run itself dry in the deserts of Time, as so many similar impulses have done in the past.

"God bless you, sir," said the soldier reappearing, "don't you think this shilling is bad?"

"So it is," acknowledged Lawley, and he gave her another. The bad coin he put carefully away in a breast pocket, resolving to take an early opportunity of waking up the Inspector-General and his Police. This little incident was a reminder that there were quite a number of complaints filed in the Colonial Secretary's Office about the bad coin in circulation. The hymn ended, the Officer began to give out notices and Lawley, his interest in the scene exhausted, went on his way.

Half an hour later, beside a neighbouring street, a young woman sat disconsolately on a step. She was accompanied by a child, little more than a baby. The woman was gaudily arrayed in flashy jewellery of the most aggressive type. She wore a pink blouse, a black skirt and a straw hat, heavily trimmed with enormous coloured flowers, set off in hard green leaves.

The child stood obediently enough at the mother's side, but it was beginning to whimper. The Mother was worn out by the task of getting the small creature along, partly by carrying it and partly by dragging it. Pain as well as weariness showed in her face. Tears stood in her eyes. Her small stock of endurance was exhausted. She sat there a bundle of human discouragement, wrapped in pink and black cloth.

Her class was obvious. She was one of the empty-headed unfortunates who enter light-heartedly on the paths of vice. She was still very near the beginning of her journey. The banks were not yet stripped of flowers, but she had already found the thorns. The child was of course illegitimate. The Mother was half proud, half ashamed of the fact. With these mixed feelings she had sallied out that morning on an excursion by train.

After providing for the finery she desired, and purchasing her ticket, she had only a few shillings left over. The purse containing these had been taken from her by a boy from whom she attempted to buy oranges. One shilling escaped, and this she tried to employ in buying something to eat and drink on board the train. But still misfortune dogged her steps, for the shilling was a bad coin, and the bar-maid, who happened to be of rigid morals, in returning it made some stinging comments and declined also to supply even a drink of water without money. Hungry and parched with thirst, she completed the list of disasters by slipping and straining one foot when she alighted at Kingston.

Without a penny to pay for a car drive, she was making her way home on foot, when, endurance failing, she sank by the way-side and crouched there.

All the details of her bankrupt holiday might not be patent to the stream of passers-by, but it was clear at a glance that she was a sinner and was in trouble.

"Ah, sin burn her now; she feel it," said one of a pair of respectable matrons.

"Yes," responded the other, "she is getting the wages; she is getting the wages." They passed on.

"Mother, look at that poor woman, she is sick," said a child.

"She is a bad woman," was the reply, and they passed on.

A young man, escorting some ladies, looked, recognized the face, wondered whose was the child, and passed on.

"That woman is suffering," said a young lady to her sister.

"We can't stop now; the bell has almost finished ringing. Come on, we will be late for Church. She must have friends some where."

Ebenezer Raphael White was on his way to church when his eye lighted on the girl at the side of the street. He detached himself from the church-going tide at once. He wore his Sunday black coat, aged but still presentable, especially when placed, as it now was, in contrast with his snowy-white trousers. He was Sunday-hatted, also, and while, in the one hand, he bore a conspicuously large Bible and a hymn-book whose edges were stained an aggressive red, in the other he carried a walking stick.

Slowly and impressively did Raphael approach the object of his attention.

"Sin."

He pronounced the one word as he came to a standstill.

"Sin."

He sniffed the air and said again "Sin." Then selecting a step near at hand he seated himself there, brought his stick to the front, placed one hand upon it and then the other hand upon that. Upon top of all, he rested his chin. So he sat, gazing steadily for a minute or two at the sorry pair before him. His books had been carefully placed beside him, a white handkerchief being spread to prevent them from being soiled by contact with the stone step.

"Sin," exclaimed Raphael again. There was another pause then he said:

"Who for de pickney, Missis?"

No answer.

"Ha," said Raphael, "you shut your mouth now but it will open wide enough day a judgment. It will open wide 'nough—to bawl.

"Sin, I smell it at once. Dog which follow in a woodland place where mongoose and wild hog pass, and know all 'bout it by de so-so smell, doh him nebber see hog or mongoose; dat is one; and me is anudder. Where sin hide in a bush me is Big Massa best dog to scent it out."

"Who de pickney for, Missis?"

"Can't answer, noh. Good. I is de dog to head you up for Big Massa to throw rope wid running noose and catch you, same as Cattlemen swing dem rope and cast young cow while dog bark 'bow wow' and stop dem. I is de dog fe Sin, Bow wow, wow. Lord you servant is here, you best dog is right here; and him smell Sin.

"Lord, lick him. Lick sin. Tek up your biggest stick and lick hard; and here is me, you servant Raphael, you Penn dog, to run and bark and bite and head off de sinner dem, so deh can't run away none 'stall and mus' stan up and tek you chastisement.

"Same as dog run and bark at cow nose hole and stop him and tun him and penn him up till cattleman fire rope 'cross him head and him catch. Same so is I, Lord. Same so is you. You is the head cattleman, and I is de dog, and de sinner is de cow, Dis sinner is de cow. Lick, good Lord, lick him. Fire de rope wid de running noose and catch him tight. Now choke him round de troat, choke him."

"Who de pickaniny is for, Missis? Lock up you mout, eh? Wait, one day dem will force it open, same as dem tek handle of spoon and dislocate a child teet when him shut it up tight a bacausen him won't swallow physic. De child want favour Marse John. Dat is a wild young gentleman now? first cousin to the devil couldn't be worse."

The bells stopped; then, faintly heard from the churches round the Parade came the sound of music and singing. Only a straggling church-goer or two were left on the street as Howard Lawley, riding down the street, turned his eye on the woman and thinking here was an accident drew rein.

"Are you sick?"

"I believe so," was the despondent reply.

The story of the day's adventures rambled from her lips.

"You are hungry and thirsty," he summarized, "and your feet is sore. My good man, can you get her a drink of water?"

White regarded the speaker attentively for a minute. Then he said:

"When parson take him little bowl and sprinkle over me, to give me name, it was not 'My Good Man' him call me. It was Raphael Ebenezer White, and de world sake a respect call me Mrs."

With that Raphael got upon his legs and stalked solemnly away, saying as he did so. "Pity man like you don't got manners It was your business to say 'Goodmorning' or 'Good Evening' to me before you ask me 'bout water. Not 'causen I is black you must'nt show you manners out side you pocket. Fe my part I gone a church now." And he went.

The Passley carriage came down the street at this moment and Liberta caught sight first of Lawley, and then of the picture that held his attention. She solved the difficulty by taking the woman and child into the carriage with the promise to see them home.

Half an hour later the inhabitants of a certain mean street in Kingston, with no reputation worth losing, were agreeably fluttered by the arrival of a large carriage. Out of it stepped the Sinner and her child.

At the same time they had a vision of a lady who leaned from the carriage and said:

"Goodbye, I hope you will soon be all right again. Get something to eat and drink right off."

"Now dat's a lady," said one of the Sinner's neighbours, also a sinner, "and dat's true Christian."

"If you ask me," said another neighbour, "I say dat white people dese days is beginning to get confused and tie up in de work of sin and salvation; looks to me as if dem begin to buck and miss de way lead go a heaven. If you going to treat sinner kind and good as decent somebody, dribe them ina' buggy and all, tell me dis, why sinner should want to lebe sin.' What dem should do if dem wants to drive sin out of de country is to put nail and tacks through shingle, and spread these where sinner gots to walk and so pitch them back ina' heaven."

"A no, lie," admitted her neighbour. "Ebbery subject gots front-stairs and back-stairs into it, same as house, and yours is back-stairs here.

As Liberta drove back, still with some vague idea of going to church, late as it was, the sound of lively music and somewhat vociferous singing drew her attention to the Town Hall.

"Salvation Army, Miss 'Berta," said her coachman explanatively.

"I would like to see what these people do," said Liberta.

"Dem don't go on same fashion as fe we church, you know Miss," said Robert remonstrant.

"You pull up in Duke Street and wait there."

Inside the hall, Liberta saw one of those crowds that suggest to the eye a pond or lake on which the winds, blowing from different points, have produced confusion and clashing of waves. All is roughened, interblent, unequal.

The brilliant Zouave uniform of a few West Indian soldiers attracted the eye at once. They were touches of colour-flame amid the drab of neutral tints. There were other soldiers in brown khaki, and one or two policemen in blue serge faced with red. Here and there was to be seen a woman dressed in the quiet, unobtrusiveness of a more educated mind; but the women generally were arrayed in cheap material of the most glaring colour and wore hats, much over-trimmed and presenting a gladiatorial combat of conflicting hues. Shallowness of purse and poverty of taste were at one and the same time suggested.

Intermingling with the rest of the audience, without let or hindrance, were the Women of the Street, sordid as they rose from those lower depths of shame which they inhabited, repulsive in their dirty gowns and torn blouses, the very dregs left in the cup of vice when all the beauty and sweetness have been quaffed. The street boys, too, were dirty, ragged and unkempt, but because youth has its own magic power, not so repulsive, even in all that dirt and vice, as their elders. On a bench by themselves lounged five or six tipsy white sailors who had strolled in from the darkness and monotony of the streets where the liquor shops were closed during the hours of evening worship, and who cast into the boiling stir of noise occasional loud guffaws, and hoarsely hummed tune snatches.

No one here seemed put out or offended whoever happened to be one's next neighbour.

All this mixture of humanity before her, appeared to Liberta to be thrown together there without plan or idea. There were no underlying threads of system. It was chaos, slightly modified, that was all, and for a few minutes, standing by the entrance she saw nothing which she could use to interpret the scene. Then her eye rested on the platform. There was the clue she sought,

On the right side were the female officers and on the other the male. In the middle sat a woman, the leader highest in rank. For the most part the officers were Europeans and their pale faces showed in effective contrast with the dark uniform almost black, relieved with crimson ribbons and seams. The conrast was made still more effective by the few black faces that mingled with the others.

The calm, sweet, grave features of the women drew Liberta with the power of a strange attractiveness and inspired her with confidence. The odd, incongruous, restless mass of humanity heaving with in that hall was not without a controlling centre, a power that was capable and intelligent and that could command the situation in its own way and by its own methods. On the platform, she found the explanation of the scene. There was the centre, where what seemed so disjointed and so incongruous gathered meaning and coherency.

Liberta no longer hesitated. She went forward and took the empty chair.

On the platform a man began to relate his experience.

"I," he said speaking in a loud unmodulated tone of voice, as of one who had said what he was now about to say many times, "I got salvation as I stooped down to tie my boot. I said 'God damn my soul' as I stooped. Just then a Salvation Army Officer was passing and said, 'No, not God damn you, but God bless you; and don't you get up till you have found salvation. Judgment is at hand.' I tried to get up and could not. I knelt down with him; praise the Lord I surrendered right there. He gave me the victory."

"Amen, Hallelujah, Praise the Lord. Victory." Exclamations burst out from scores of voices, man's bass mingling with the treble of women and children. A thicket of sound was suddenly raised and tangled itself, dense and close, right across the hall. It came as by magic and seemed in permanent possession.

To Liberta's trained ear it seemed very disorderly, a bursting up of the primal lawlessness and desire for confusion that lurks in man's heart. But she kept her eye on the platform with the inner sense that ere she left that hall she would find there the nobler meaning of spirit behind all this outcry.

The man of experiences had paused a second to take breath ere continuing. In that moment of pause an officer sprang to his feet close behind the first speaker and struck up:

> *"The Lion of Judah will break every chain*
> *And give us the victory again and again."*

The chorus, repeated once, twice, three times, filled the room and the man of experience subsided; he had had his innings.

Shrilly and suddenly, a whistle was blown. The singing stopped like a horse thrown back on its haunches by the curb.

Another man rose and related his experience, and this was again followed by a thicket of shouts and exclamations. Then four voices raised in prayer, were all struggling like tigers in a jungle for predominance. Two voices died by the way and the battle continued between a deep bass and a male voice of shriller power. It was weight against edge. By and by, the bass, pouring his words, like a stream in full volume, triumphed and survived.

Instinctively at the idea of prayer, Liberta had fallen on her knees, but her soul recoiled from the noise and labour of this loud voice. Its uncouth pronunciation bruised and lacerated her offended ear. She retained her kneeling position but she ceased to abstract her thoughts, and she let her glance wander round her. Near by they rested on women devoutly following the prayer, word by word. The sight was a rebuke and Liberta made another attempt to fix her attention on what was the petition which was being carried to the gates of heaven on the wings of such a storm of sound. It was in vain.

Again a chorus came thundering through the hall:

> *"What can wash away my sins?*
> *Nothing but the blood of Jesus."*

Once more the whistle blew, shrill, imperious; and silence came like a drop curtain.

"The Major will pray."

The Major stood up, her pale, refined face under its stiff dark, bonnet showing like a blade of wrought steel in a handle of ebony. She lifted her hand, and stood perfectly still, until among those noisy hundreds there was utter silence. Not a whisper, not a movement broke the stillness. Then she said:

"Let us go into God's presence." She paused. "Let us leave this room and go before the Eternal. Let every head be bowed and each eye be closed while we adore Him." Liberta had instinctively resumed her attitude of devout prayer and now throughout the hall there was a movement and stir as the audience generally knelt or leant forward.

When there was complete stillness again, a woman's quiet voice was heard, distinct and clear to the last syllable.

"Give us, Oh Lord and Father, silence—the silence of the heart. Make still our noisy affections, stay the restless moods, calm the quivering longing—in the perfect silence, Father. In that silence let us rest, let it brood over us as the shadow at noonday dwells on the tired land. Let Thy silence rest over these tired hearts of ours. These troubled hearts that ache, that pain, that so much confuse and mislead us. Our hearts stand confused amid so many voices of the world; voices of the street, of the loud market place. Still our tremors; receive Thou into Thine ear our whispered fears and hopes; let not our voices be heard calling to the callous, unfeeling world. Keep us in Thy silence."

The large room, filled with people, was as still as so much space crowded with human beings could be. So still that a woman's stifled sob was heard through its length and breadth with an almost painful distinctness. There was audible the rustle of garments as a deeply moved woman or girl here and there buried her face away from the view of her fellows. A man said "So be it," deeply and solemnly.

"Empty our hearts Oh Father; and into this silent room come Thou, Oh Christ, Lord, Master, Friend, Redeemer, God." The prayer was ended.

Silence closed over the last words then there rose a hymn, not sung with the loud emphasis of those which preceded it, but in pleading subtones.

"Jesus, lover of my soul,
Let me to Thy bosom fly;
While the nearer waters roll,
While the tempest still is high,
Hide me, Oh my Saviour, hide,
Till the storm of life be past,
Safe into the haven guide,
Oh, receive my soul at last."

Again silence, like the lapping water of a sea, closed over the words; and again from the silence rose a hymn; but now it was sung in louder and more confident tones.

"There is a fountain filled with blood,
Drawn from Emanuel's veins,
And sinners plunged beneath that flood,
Lose all their guilty stains."

When Liberta raised her head most of the officers had left the platform. They were here and there among the audience, speaking individually to persons there.

As Liberta had listened to the Major, she had changed from the mere attitude of prayer to the very spirit of appeal and yearning after the strength and counsel of the Almighty and Unseen that is really prayer.

Many an officer passed her by now, noting her costly dress and her graceful figure, so much in contrast with those around her. One stupid woman said to her bluntly: "Sister, are you saved?" Liberta smiled but said nothing, and the officer passed on, looking uncomfortably round her to see if her failure was being noticed.

But presently Liberta was conscious that someone sat softly down beside her.

"I am so glad to see you here," said the Major. "I hope it has helped you."

"Your prayer did."

"Bless God; your face was the last thing I noticed as I shut my eyes. You reminded me so much of my only sister, so graceful and so finely dressed. My heart went out to you; I have not seen that dear girl for six years."

"Is she not in the Army?"

"She lives at home with Father and Mother."

"And you," asked Liberta, "did they wish you to join the Army?"

"No. Oh, no. They tried their hardest to prevent it. But His voice was stronger." She looked into Liberta's eyes. "I have never regretted it."

"You were well-to-do!"

"I am richer now."

"And happy?"

"Now; not then."

"I am most unhappy," said Liberta, yielding to a sudden impulse.

"Do you know I never found happiness till I gave on searching for it."

"That is a new idea to me," said Liberta musingly.

"I stood still and was quiet, and it closed in round me. God bless you; I see a dear woman over there whom I must go to. I hope you will come again."

Liberta had become intensely interested in all that was happening in the hall. It was novel and piquant to her present mood. She stayed till the meeting ended. As she was about to step into her carriage, she caught the words "Poor Major; I wonder what she will do tonight. The last car has gone and she lives so far." "I suppose?" reflected Liberta, "she can't afford a bus." She turned to the Salvationist who had spoken and said:

"Will you ask the Major if she would like me to drive her home?"

John Meffala stood talking to Ada in a somewhat lonely road in one of the smaller suburbs of Kingston. He had brought her there after meeting her by appointment at a church door, now he urged her to answer a question which had been put some time before.

"Well?"

"Well what?" she replied petulantly.

"Are you going to have a snug time?"

"She turned from him angrily.

"Harold is playing with you: that you must know. A bat with one eye could see it, in daylight even."

"I don't know anything of the kind," she answered sharply. "You don't suppose I believe you, do you?"

"But it is true all the same, he answered placidly. Has he written to you since he left the Island?"

She was stubbornly silent.

"If he had," he smiled, "you would tell me at once."

"He *has* written me," she burst out.

"Once?"

"Many times."

"That is—a—lie—" Meffala answered lazily. "He has uot written you once."

"He has" she insisted.

"Bah," he said, "that sort of lie would be of no use in business. Women's lies are blank cartridge; they kill nothing. I have heard Harold say that," he added with the dull man's uncertainty as to the value of a *mot*. "Harold has not written you, and he cares no more for you than he does for a dozen other girls."

"That is not your business," she cried angrily.

"You are my business just now.

"I hate you."

"You do, eh? Why?"

"Why do you not leave me alone?"

"Ask me something easier; or ask heaven why it made you to obey me."

"The devil is more likely to have to do with you."

"Perhaps," he said with imperturbable good-nature. "Then ask him. The point is that you must obey me; you can't help it. The world is not large enough for you to escape me. Better give in first as last. I will treat you better now than later."

"Leave me alone; leave me alone. I am working for my bread and butter. Why can't a poor girl be left to go her own way. You want me to lose my soul."

"Such as you are born to go on the sand banks, if sand banks you call them. You are bound to fall into the hands of some man."

"Well," he persisted after a long pause. "Are we to be friends?"

"I hate you. I detest you. Your very name is like a blow in my face."

"And how does my face strike you?" he returned, not at all irritated, and looking at her mercilessly.

"Your face," she replied, looking towards him for a second and then snatching her eyes away, as if tearing them from a whirlpool of danger, "I think of poison and the devil when I see you."

"Look at me, and say that again, if you dare," he said in a provokingly careless tone.

For an instant she seemed about to do so. Her eyes moved in his direction; then with an effort she looked carefully and decidedly away from him and said passionately:

"Can't you leave me alone. I am only a poor, miserable girl. There are lots like me. Can't you leave me alone."

"Worse luck, no. You are so confoundedly pretty."

"Why don't you go away?"

"I am waiting for your answer."

"I pray I may never see your face again."

"And yet you meet me tonight, for instance."

"To tell you once and for all that I am done with you."

"As you have told me before—three times."

"This time I mean it."

"So you said—three times before."

A less brutal man would have pitied her. She was well-nigh weeping now.

"Why don't you go away?" she began again.

"Because I am waiting for your answer."

"No, then, no, no, no. I have said so before; I want to have nothing to do with you. I wish you were dead; do you hear."

"And yet," he sneered easily, "you arranged to meet me tonight after service, too. Funny."

"You know why."

"Why? Not because you wanted to, of course. Oh, no, not that."

"To tell you once and for all, I hate, I detest, you. To tell you not to speak to me again, not to send me flowers or letters. To stop it. If you send me letters, I will burn them. If you send flowers I will trample them on the streets. Do you understand?"

"Since this is the third time you have told me all that, finally, I ought to," he replied.

"I tell you now; and I take God to bear me witness. Stop it."

"Very well," he said "but there is one thing that I can't stop."

"What?"

"Loving you," he returned with a laugh.

At that moment the light from the lantern of a passing carriage fell across the two. Ada looked up, caught sight of Liberta, and, imagining that she was seen also, shrank back. Liberta, however, had noticed nothing. The Major's eye was quicker. It mastered the bit of human drama framed here in the darkness—the girl's troubled face with its look of something like fear, but the man's face was turned away from the carriage. He was not recognised. The light flashed past and Ada spoke once more to John Meffala:

"Go. You have heard I hate you. I hate. I don't want you at all. I never will. Go."

"Goodbye," was the answer. "I am going." and he sauntered away, but, a man who knew something of the heart of women, he nevertheless lurked still, waiting for his prey.

"What next?" said Meffala to himself. "Is it too late for a game of billiards?" He looked at his watch. It was one minute to eleven. He drew out a cigarette; lighted it and flung away the match.

MEFFALA FOUND HIMSELF SITTING UP in the road, and the next second was wondering what could have happened. He struggled back to full cognition of his whereabouts like a man reclimbing a rock from which he has suddenly plunged into deep water. Thus suddenly had the man fallen into complete, though passing, oblivion.

A dim recollection came presently of the last thing felt and registered by consciousness; the abrupt sense that something, sudden, swift, irresistible had pressed him earthward with a weight that was overwhelming. So might one imagine comes the sudden end when, with a swinging stroke, the head of an unsuspecting man is shorn sheer off at one blow, when the bright, sharp steel cuts, blood and bone, nerve and muscle, all, but as cleanly, as swiftly, as if it clove no more than the air apart.

Meffala scrambled to his feet and looked round for an explanation. Not a living being was in sight. Carefully he felt for his purse, his watch, his pocketbook. Then he looked at his ring. It was no robbery then.

Next he sought over his person for trace of a blow. There was no bruise, no pain or smart anywhere.

By slow degrees he mastered and accepted the idea that this astonishing experience came from within himself.

He drove into the mystery, determined to make his way to some solution of it. He went feeling along the sides of Time and Space for some clue. How long had this all taken to happen? He drew out his watch. The hand was just leaving eleven. Incredulous he held the watch to his ear. It ticked steadily, and at that moment a laggard clock entombed in a house on the other side of the street began to strike the hour. One minute covered it all. The well recollected lighting of the cigarette; the drop into the abyss of oblivion; the return to cogitation.

Again he groped among the tangible things that his hand and eye knew. A spark of fire still lingered in the newly lighted cigarette. The watch told truth then; it was a minute, not an hour.

What did this thing mean? He leapt forward to the resolve to see a doctor—when? now, at once. The lateness of the hour impressed him, and his resolve slackened. He walked without let or stay, as well as he had ever known himself to be. The commonplace reasserted itself. Was there any mystery after all? The first deeply stamped idea began to fade away.

What had happened? Possibly he had slipped without being aware of it. He was not hurt; not in any way. He had no pain. But how did the mind work. It might be the brain. He tested it by several processes. First on a business proposition.

That was all right. Then he recalled the events of the preceding evening. All right. The machine toiled true to command.

The suggestion of a slip and the sudden fall, rooted itself in his mind. He was not at all imaginative. The ordinary was to him not the probable, only, but also pretty nearly the only open solution of events. At any rate, instead of going to knock up a doctor now, and getting laughed at for his fears, he would wait the morrow and see how he felt them.

Next morning he had clean forgotten all about it, but he recalled the accident in the afternoon when discussing the business point he had used to test his brain.

Now, in the broad daylight of the everyday and ordinary, how absurd seemed his idea of doctoring being needed.

"A pretty yarn to go knocking a doctor with up at eleven at night."

WHEN BACHELORS ARE MERRY—HIGH JINKS, MUSICAL AND
OTHERWISE—SOMETHING THAT "STANK OF LAWLEY"—GEORGE
ANNOUNCES AN INTERRUPTION, AND A LADY—WHAT HAROLD
EXPECTED ON ONE SIDE OF A DOOR—AND WHAT HE FOUND
ON THE OTHER SIDE.

Harold entertained a choice dozen of his friends, in the house where
Ada, huddled on a sofa, had once wept long and bitterly over
Noel's letter. That scene lay buried months deep in the past. Harold was
but newly back from a trip to South America, a certain maddening heart
disturbance of which he and but one other knew anything, curbed and
mastered. Once again he was his old self, held well in hand, airily kind-
hearted, light-heartedly good-natured, and as of yore a loiterer still. True,
a certain crisis a half year or so ago had cast its seed into his life.

Noel Bronvola was enshrined in that recess of his heart which one
woman, and no other, ever reaches; but he no longer expected that
she would love him in return. She trusted him and he meant that she
should have reason to trust him to the end. He had persuaded himself
that he was content with this.

He had been to see Noel, and had also strolled into Meffala's and
shaken hands with Ada as if it had not been a day since they met, except
that he brought her back from his travels a bracelet of coral obtained
from Venezuelan Indians.

Ada seemed perfectly well and quite happy. Harold's eye could not
detect a single tendril of the affection that had been so luxuriant only a
few months before.

He himself was merely pleasantly interested at sight of the pretty
child-face where trouble had left not a single footprint. Ada shone
under his eye, as a flower glows responsive to its sun. Their mutual
relationship was now on a happy footing and, said Harold, a safe one.

Pretty, empty-headed Ada. Had there ever been danger for her in
that relationship?

"Oh, Love Oh fire once he drew
With one long kiss my whole soul through
My lips, as sunshine drinketh dew."

Harold mentally completed the quotation between puffs of his cigar and smiled to think of the abyss of difference which opened between love like that and Ada's; between the deep glowing fire burning in such kisses and those which from his lips to hers fell soft as a spray of rain on a rose leaf. "As much of passion there," he thought, "as of wine in moonlight. Her sleekness is finished to the last pin's head. Noel Bronvola need not have been so mightily alarmed for my kitten."

It was evidence of the good fibre of his make-up that he felt nothing like pique at Ada's having learnt to do without him so easily.

Tonight dinner was over, and, there being no ladies to protest, Harold had brought his friends into the drawing room to smoke. Here, amid easy chairs and comfortable lounges, they wooed and won a leisurely enjoyment. They smoked heavily, but, they drank very little wine, for this was not a drinking set.

Through the crowding talk a remark shot up that brought the pause which follows a successful claim on general attention. "By the way, Harold, do you know the news from Peter Passley's dovecote?"

"If it is younger than two months—no. My letters and papers kept following me from port to port, always arriving there, I believe, the day after I left. What is the news?"

"Liberta Passley is engaged to Burns."

"All things are possible," began Harold.

"And most things improbable," interjected one of the listeners, like a mischievous boy who interferes with the smooth working of a machine by inserting a pebble into the wheels.

"No reflection on your veracity," Harold continued addressing the first speaker; "But I don't believe this."

"The fellow is at *liberty* to believe what he likes or can," said Smelton.

"Where hurts in your headpiece, Smelton?" said the man next him, with exaggerated concern. "You must be in pain when you afflict us with such a pun."

"I tell you who does believe in the forthcoming marriage though, Harold; that is old Josiah Naphthali. He is giving Burns money at only eight percent. That old and wary vulture must have his glittering eye on Peter's coin at short range, you bet, or much of loans from him Burns would see."

"Still even Naphthali can let the wish father the thought."

"I wonder what old Passley would cut up to."

"Anything above £400,000 and below £600,000," said Harold carelessly. "But Liberta won't marry Burns. All things are possible; but some are not."

"Burns is certainly a fool," someone threw in.

"All here agreed on that, I fancy," replied Harold. "But I say, to turn to fairer fields, has Mrs. Tempus and her little pack of sisters pulled down anything yet?"

"They gave Masters a long stern chase, but he got away after all. Lost a few tail feathers though, Masters, did'nt you?"

"Speak with more caution and respect of your superiors," responded the person addressed. "Tempus and I are still the best of friends."

"So near and yet so far," gibed his neighbour.

"Oh they may pull him down yet," said Harold, "they are a persevering brood; but, tell me, what has the Governor been doing?"

"Drawing £5,000 a year, damn him," said Masters savagely.

"And not giving poor Masters a job," chaffed Smelton.

"Who did he stick in as R.M. at Westover then?"

"A confounded noodle," snapped Masters.

"Named?"

"Fitz-Roy de Vincent, and dragging degrees after him as a slave drags his chains. He knows so much law that he has no room left for common sense."

"Well," said the Mocker, "that is a variation on our poor dear Masters, who has loads of common sense, according to himself; but, as his friends and clients know too well, no room for law."

"You be damned," was Masters' reply.

"Little doubt about that," grunted fat Smelton.

"Well," said Harold languidly, "I don't want to go to extremes, and I don't stretch it to say I would like to be tried by Masters—bad enough to be defended by you, old man (Masters was Harold's lawyer) but in my opinion, it is time we Jamaicans backed our man every time for public posts. Why should this fellow, Fitz Looloo Roozle Noozle, hoof it over poor old Masters. We all know the real reason he got the job. He could not butter his toast with his merit. It is 'pull' with the Colonial Office. Probably his dad has a thirty-second cousin in the Cabinet; or a spinster aunt gave the Secretary for the Colonies a green parrot from Jamaica which led him to learn for the first time where the island was, and he was therefore so grateful that on demand he handed over the R.M. ship."

"Swopped an owl of Law for a parrot, eh."

The subject was warmly taken up. Presently the stories told to illustrate Colonial Office iniquity strayed sufficiently far from the truth to gather picturesqueness. Smelton narrated:

"That new man over the Department of Sanitation, how did he get shoved in? A doctor certainly, with the usual learned stuffing of L.R.C.S., etc., etc.; but small physic or surgery took him into harbour of his fair desire. He might have been the ablest man going, had not fortune favoured him. Was in a jam with the Secretary of State's second cousin's third son's piccaniny, and blacked his boots one morning when his nigger was too sick to take on the job. Further, wiped his eyeglasses for him daily, and once lent him a rubber collar; also in a crisis blew the dear infant's nose and cleaned his teeth, that is, his false teeth."

"Little seeds of gratitude
For his blackened boots,
Watered by reminders,
See the golden fruits;

Now he draws his lucre,
Sanitation's chief,
Happy in Jamaica,
To Jamaica's grief."

"Rotten weak line, the last," sneered Masters.

"Sorrow has blighted your taste, dear boy," responded the proud author.

"And it never was much to boast of, Masters," was another stone hurled at him.

Masters answered not to the last insult; but, strolling to the piano, threw the cover back and sat down to play. He improvised music and words and sang:

"There's a corpulent fellow named Smelton,
He fancies himself quite a bit;
And he worries his friends and acquaintance
With rotten and versified wit.

The best of his friends they are sorry
For him, when he opens his mouth,
'Tis the grave-yard of victuals and liquor,
Where knowledge has perished in drought.

The viper named Envy is gnawing
His fat heart as he gazes on me,
We're sick of his un-ending jawing;
And that is the end of my glee.

"Now," said a third poet, without hesitation, rising, striking an attitude and declaiming in mock heroics:

"Let M.L.C.'s and M.P.B.'s
Fight, as they always do;
And let the Parsons growl and scratch,
For 'tis their nature to;
But, Fatty Smelton, do not let
Your angry passions rise,
Those chubby hands were never made
To blacken Master's eyes."

"Oh, hang it, Harold, I did not know that this was a prayer meeting," broke in Alten, the scornful.

"He is such a pagan," grumbled Smelton, "that he takes poetry for prayer."

"It is the *whine* in both that misleads me," lisped Alten.

"To say nothing of the wine in your head," suggested a friend.

"But I say, Harold, do you know that the Old Man printed that letter you sent him about Jamaicans being ill-treated, and printed his answer to it?"

"No, I did not."

"But surely he sent you the answer and told you he proposed to turn the newspapers on to the job?"

"Probably. I noticed a bulky envelope marked O.H.M.S. waiting among those travelled letters, but I have not opened many of the batch yet."

"Well, the Governor played the devil with you, old man," put in Masters cheerfully, "and it should be a warning to all of you fellows not to go writing letters to Governors without taking your lawyers' advice."

"And paying for it," suggested Alten.

"Much Governor in that letter to Harold," objected Smelton. "It stank of Lawley from beginning to end. Do you remember what you put into your letter, Harold?"

"Not I," said Harold imperturbably.

"Well the only thing in it that was more untrue than the alleged facts were the alleged figures; that is, according to Lawley and the Governor."

"Trained liars who ought to know how to size up lies," commented Harold "I remember now a lady thought highly of that letter. I should have suspected it was rotten."

"It was the facts and figures, old man. The arguments were all right and the phrasing was consumedly clever. You got home several times and drew the old Governor's most treasured heart's blood. But what did that beast Lawley do? Why pull out every single fact that was wrong and each figure that was astray; it was like taking out the nails. Then he calmly assumed to the gaping multitude that, having shown these facts were wrong and your figures worse, it followed that he would be a lunatic to waste time over your arguments and conclusions. You were butchered to make a Colonial Secretary's holiday."

"And what did the people say of me, Sarson?" said Harold to the sub-editor of the Kingston "Rambler."

"The profane summed it up that the Governor had played h—l with you."

"And the saints?"

"That you chose a good text and then wrecked it by your sermon."

"Well, let it *lie* at that," echoed Masters with slow and evil emphasis.

"Harold," said Alten, "are you going to race your mare, Ella, in August?"

"If Two-bits is not too drunk to ride her," was the nonchalant answer.

"Then I have something to beat her."

The conversation, sinking again from general interest, lurked and eddied among little groups. The room was filled with talk and laughter, above the main level of which, nothing rose into distinctness.

Masters remained at the piano and continued to shed tinkling accompaniments and occasionally a snatch of song, comic or sentimental, on the audience. At length he dashed off into some lively dance music, waltz, polka, hornpipe, and when it reached the hornpipe, a gay youngster stood up and began to step it. General and genial uproar wrapped his effort round and criticism smote him thick and fast.

In the midst of this Harold's factotum, George, appeared at the door seeking his master with a merry eye and only half hiding a smile.

Harold did not see him for some time, George regarded with much apprehension the prospect of navigating the floor where two other dancers were now attempting the horn-pipe. Smelton after bantering George unmercifully and trying his best to egg him on to risk entering the room, stood up and shouted in stentorian tones:

"Silence."

Then he continued, "Marse Harold, George dah look fe you, sah."

"Well, you scamp?" called Harold across the lull this announcement produced.

"Please, Marse Harold, some one come to you, sah."

"Then let him go away again."

"I tell him, sah."

"Say I am busy."

"I tell him so already, sah."

"Tell him to go to hell," advised Masters, "and say your master is coming close behind him."

"Attended by his lawyer," added Smelton.

"An old acquaintance," finished Alten. George grinned and waited.

"Well, George," said Harold, "why did you not tell the fool I was out. Say I am in the country, and won't be back till tomorrow."

"I did say so, Marse Harold," replied George and his look reproached his master for not giving him credit for some sense.

"Was that before you told him he was busy upstairs?" enquired Alten with curiosity.

"Before, Sah, of course. I tell him dat him gone a country yesterday in him single seat buggy and don't expect back till next Tuesday. I even tell him he would send me letter on Monday to say certain if him was coming. And seeing him wouldn't believe me, I tell him dat him was upstairs and busy; sake a de noise you gentlemens did dah make him wouldn't believe 'bout de country."

"Well," said Smelton, "go back, George, and tell him that your master has suddenly gone mad and that the noise is caused by his devoted friends, who, at great risk to their own valuable lives, are trying to soothe and control the maniac with bad poetry and piano music, hoping to restrain him from smashing the furniture. Did you tell him all that, George?"

"No sah, I did not tink of it."

"Well," chimed in another wit, "if he will not swallow that, George, tell him that your master is just dead of the smallpox which he contracted in South America, and that he better cut and run for fear of infection and stop fooling here."

"Too much noise for him to believe dat, sah," said George sagaciously.

Harold, lounging in a chair and talking to Alten about racing, was by this time taking only a casual interest in George and his dilemma. One thing was certain, and that was that Harold was not going downstairs for any man alive, not the Chief Clerk himself, and it was George's trouble to get rid of the inopportune visitor. Such was Harold's view of it.

"Tell the man, George," he called now, "what you like, but get rid of him. I will see him tomorrow."

"But it is not no man, sah."

"What!" shrieked Masters, and he banged notes of melodious exclamation from the piano.

"A boy!" said Harold, "and you come bothering me; George, I am ashamed of you. Drop him through the window; or give him to the cook to make lamb cutlets; or pitch him to your picaninies to cut up with the cocoanuts for the fowls."

"But it is not no boy, Marse Harold."

"Oh! Ho!" cried the room generally.

"Den, Marse George," said Masters dramatically—"it—is—a—"

"Him is a lady, sah," answered George.

"What!" shouted Masters, and the whole room burst into hilarious laughter at Harold's expense. But that worthy took it calmly still. When the laughter had spent itself, he began with mock seriousness:

"Gentlemen."

"And ladies," interjected Smelton.

"The lady downstairs, you mean," corrected Alten.

"You are aware," resumed Harold, stopping occasionally to puff his cigar, "that my many and eminent virtues; my sterling ('and coiny', put in Masters) character, and my great charm of manner have endeared me to a large number of staid and elderly ladies in this community ('and to no young ones, of course,' threw in Smelton). I have no doubt that one of these, whom I may have omitted to visit, on my return, is now below to pay her respects to me—or it may perchance be my washer-woman—or an applicant as cook—your profane and ribald laughter is out of place, gentlemen."

"Yes," cried Masters, "poor, dear, innocent Harold. It is probably his Sunday School teacher come to hear him recite, 'Once there was a Little Bee,' or to instil a timely text, like 'Go to the ant thou sluggard,' and find that industrious insect in your friend and guide, Masters. George, de lady well and old, don't she?"

"Lord, sah," responded George, grinning, "she jest ketch to dat part of life when you done fe call him pickney and yet don't ketch proper to call him young lady. Like when filly stop fe run after him mooma and don't break in yet, you know, sah."

"Ha, ha," said Masters above the general laughter, "see what it is to have a first-class lawyer and cross-examiner on the job."

"And, I suppose, George," he resumed, "she ugly like sin, don't she?"

"Him is lubly, sah," said George impressively, "lubly as a lillie bud just come out a' dew water and begin to open in de sun. Him is a beautiful jewel, sah."

"This man," drawled Harold, "should have been a poet. What similes and what imagination."

"And don't she black as you boots?" pursued Masters.

"White as milk, sah," responded George, who was warming to the work and beginning to give his imagination loose rein. "White as you shirt front, sah. Same as cloud in a sky when August day is hot and bright."

At this answer a subtle change passed over Harold's face. A sudden, disturbing conviction shot through his mind, rose.

"Well," he said, "you have told enough lies, George, I will come down. Show the lady into the sitting room downstairs. You fellows excuse me a minute. I must go down."

"To give out the washing," explained Smelton.

"No," corrected Alten, "to engage the new cook."

"Or to receive the chaste salute on the brow and cheek of Dorcas, the local and withered Secretary of the fund for making fat children thin by feeding them on the Society's soup."

"No, no, no," sang out Sarson. "It is the Sunday School teacher and he is going to recite:

'Little drops of water
(Not to say of wine)
Make us mighty merry
When the blinkies shine.'"

Harold heard them out while he lit a new cigar with matches borrowed from Smelton, then he left the room.

"That mad Bronvola girl," he muttered to himself, for he was convinced that Noel and no one else was his visitor. "She has got some new notion about me and Ada into her head, and has come to go for me." His dislike of anything approaching "a scene" was as deep-rooted as his love, and he saw the awkwardness of the present situation. At the same time he felt his wonder big within him as to what could have brought Noel there.

He swiftly reviewed his actions since his return.

Noel, by her determined indictment of him, on the former occasion, had asserted a supremacy over his mind in this matter, that he was never to be able to throw off. He pleaded now at the bar of what he imagined might be her accusation, and memory swept the last week with a shaft of white light. But there was nothing of which he could accuse himself. He did think for a minute of the bracelet given to Ada, but he was so void of any sense of wrong-doing that he pitched the notion head long from his mind. He felt sure, too, that Noel was too strong-minded to come to him like this on a small matter. An emergency alone could have brought her.

A thought cut him with an edge he had felt there before. Had Ada gone off? and did Noel suspect him in the matter? But he had seen Ada just the day before, and she showed to his eye as quiet and contented as a meadow pond sleeping amid tall grasses and starry Spanish Needles.

When a man loves a woman deeply and truly, convinced as he may be by reason that she does not love him and never will, he is subject forever to spasms of wild expectation that shoulder Reason roughly aside. Harold was now suddenly captured by this madness.

Wild, vague, beautiful ideas swept on to the stage of his mind and passed before him in a delirious dance. In some wonderful way, Noel's coming meant that she had found the secret of love; of loving him; and if that was so, what did they oddness of the visit matter, what mattered anything but the single, central transforming truth. In a minute his life would be transmuted; the world and the years for him transfigured.

With that as his last and final thought, he opened the door of the sitting room. The cigar, so ostentatiously lighted upstairs, he had put safely on one side. He stepped forward now softly, and as with reverence for the unknown that lay at his feet, like one who places his tread for the first time on the sward of a magic land. In the few steps that had brought him from the midst of the noise and laughter upstairs, he had been changed almost into another being.

Love makes the ground over which it comes holy; and already to Harold the familiar sitting room was strangely glorified.

To his first glance, the room seemed quite empty. Then there was a movement behind a Japanese screen.

Ada stood face to face with him.

XII

In Which Everything Depends On Noel—When One Decides By Refusing To Decide—The Way Harold Did It—The Way Noel Did It.

The shock of surprise with which Harold saw Ada there, was painfully deepened by the manner of her appearance. Here was a face that proclaimed crisis; features that stared with tragic intensity of emotional abandonment. Here was suddenly a new Ada, a being different entirely from Ada of old; this present picture and that but a day or two old in his memory of the Ada to whom he had handed the bracelet collided in sharp contrast.

Her look met his in a way that told she had travelled far beyond the milestones of appeal; here was complete, absolute, unreserved surrender; surrender that asked no terms. This took him aback; but it also sent a thrill through his veins. A sparkle of fierce joy crackled in his brain. Through his heart, a thrust sped, half of pain, half of pleasure.

He had been drinking a little wine, not enough to affect him at all ordinarily; but when the mind is suddenly strung to high, tension by surprise, the slightest stimulus tells dangerously. For a second the impulse was all but irresistible to open his arms and to take her to him with passion. All trembled on the brink of that second, as on the front of a precipice. A very little thing saved them both.

The conviction so strong a moment since that it was Noel who waited behind that door, was still powerful enough to make him ask if she was not here also, along with Ada. The glance that he diverted served a double service, for, while it assured him that here was no Noel, it also, bifurcating his attention for an instant, broke the fascination that had all but closed its snare on his senses. Memory forced her way back to her place. He remembered his promise to Noel. But, it was not the promise of itself that had saved him and this Harold realized. It was the diversion of interest that expecting to see Noel had caused. He was all the more on his guard for the rest of the interview, because a ray of light had searched his possible weakness. If Harold broke a promise he wished to do so in the poise of cool intent, not in the blinded moments of passion. He hated to feel that he no longer controlled his steed.

Beauty came straight to him, her arms outstretched. With an easy grace, and as naturally as if he had expected the visit, he took her hands, then, disregarding the look that called for a caress as with words, he led her to a lounge chair.

"So you have come to see me, Beauty? Sit here and be comfortable." That was all he said. He remained standing.

Beauty's eyes were brimming with a depth of emotion that wrought towards tragic issues.

He crossed the room and pushed a half-opened window higher. She followed him, near and noiseless as a shadow. When he turned it was to find her arms flung round him, softly and appealingly.

His will was strong and tenacious when he called it fairly into play; he had taken a true and enduring resolve to stand firmly by his pledge to Noel and to his purer self; but he was young, gay-hearted and a great lover of beauty and of women. It was not in his nature to resist this charming caress. The danger was that such things meant less to him than to those who gave.

He took Ada to his arms quite naturally, but now it was without that thrill of passion that had threatened to master him a minute before. Her head rested against his breast and nestled there, and when presently she lifted her face, inviting his lips, he kissed her sweetly and fully. Then he stroked the black hair slowly and watched the childish face with eyes filled with tenderness and feeling.

"Come back and sit down," he said by-and-by, "and I will sit by you."

"Now," he said in quiet tones, "what brings you here? It is late for a visit."

"I want you," replied the girl, in those bare, simple words, and in tones so vibrant with passion that they drove a tremor of storm through and through him. His veins heaved and quivered as the waters leap when the wind smites a hard blow suddenly.

Harold had said once: "Beauty's soul is nowhere more than two months deep. Give her that time and she will clean forget the man she loves; to forget me, a week will do." She had had already half a year and it was thus that she came to him now.

"I cannot live without you," she whispered in a tone very low indeed, but lifted above all indistinctness.

That drove deep to his inmost being as the message of rich wine speeds to the brain. He seized and crushed an impulse that surged forward within and threatened to draw him towards her. He was silent, for he felt the danger behind that struggle of emotion and conscience.

His silence drove her to excuses and pleading.

"I have almost died wanting you. You said you loved me. In was in this house here I have never forgotten it. I know the very spot."

The memory to which she appealed in her own behalf, that dear memory, was traitor to her cause; for her words recalled vividly to his mind not only the event upstairs but also the after interview with Noel. This reduced, his passion to the level of a horse trying to defy bit and bridle.

"Alas, Beauty," he said, "you are as pretty as you are silly." But she did not hear him.

"I have left them all." Her look never moved from his face. It searched there, hungry and anxious. "I have come to you for ever. I don't care; I don't care." She sprang swiftly up and flung her arms round his neck, as a child might, and her eyes showed the veiled look denoting utter abandonment of will.

"Kiss me," she murmured, "Kiss me. You love me. I don't care for anything else. I don't care if you marry me or not."

She turned her face from him and hid it on his bosom.

"You can kill me if you like."

He caressed her in silence. Again he had reached a moment of abrupt peril to his resolution and he saw the abyss below; but he threw his impulse to continue caressing and kissing her back on itself, disentangled her embrace, and said simply:

"You should not have come here, Beauty. Especially at night."

"But you care for me?" she cried. Nothing else mattered. That was her life; her all. While she clutched that she held her treasure. If she lost that, her pearl was gone and where was the value of the empty casket of days and years.

"You care for me?"

"A good deal," he said at once and decisively.

"And you want me?"

"I want to do you nothing but good."

"Then let me stay with you. If you don't, Oh, I know I am lost. There is a danger—a great danger to me. Don't push me to it—I am lost if you send me away."

"Yes, there is danger, Beauty. There is danger here."

"You won't tell me to go?"

"I can't tell you to stay."

"But you won't tell me to go?" Fear rustled through her tone like a swift deadly animal pushing a headlong way through parting foliage.

"No," he replied; then: "God forbid" for to be stern or harsh or repellent to her, seemed to him nothing short of a crime.

"I want to be with you. I don't care for anything else, or for anybody else. They may tell me it is wrong. I don't care. What is the good of being right if your heart is breaking with unhappiness."

From his silence the shadow of alarm fell over her.

"You won't turn me out?" she cried, "You won't send me away?"

"If you leave this house tonight, Beauty, you will go of your own free will. I will not turn you out." He committed himself to that involuntarily, answering the mood that forbade him to hurt her feelings in the slightest degree, if he could possibly avoid it. The next minute his promise turned back to him and he realized how serious was this thing to which his word was pledged.

"And if you don't turn me out," she said positively, "I won't go." There were tears in her eyes, but she smiled through them; a charming face.

"Now, Beauty," he said after a minute or two, "You must stay here by yourself for the present. I have guests upstairs. I must get rid of them."

"I will stay here till you come back," she answered quietly.

He closed the door and ran upstairs.

Smelton greeted him: "Has the washerwoman made her report?"

"I am sorry, you fellows," Harold said, "but I must ask you to go now, right off. I have just had news of an important kind and I must deal with a serious matter at once. You, will be good enough to take my word for it. I have to do this."

"Damned cool," said Masters; then he caught Harold's eye and rose to his feet. The others followed his example.

"Remember," shouted Smelton from the steps, "that you owe us the rest of the evening." Then they trooped out and gossiped for a minute ere dispersing.

"What's up do you think, Masters?"

"Have'nt an idea, but when Harold has that look I always do what he asks me, and I advise to always do the same. Tata. Perhaps it is one of his sisters in debt and the bailiffs are in." He pitched the first lie that occurred to him at the questioner, and went off with Smelton.

"A woman in the matter, you bet," said cynical Alten gloomily. "They keep the world's trouble department."

Somewhat dismayed as he regarded the full bearing of the concession he had made to Ada, not to send her away against her will, Harold had reached a sudden resolution. Failing his promise to Noel, he would have settled this crisis in his own way, by taking the line of least resistance. Noel was responsible for his promise; and therefore he would go to Noel. If she saw the way to persuade Ada to leave of her own will and purpose, well and good. If she could not, then a man after all could not hold back a mountain. Harold surrendered to circumstances, that was all. If Ada stuck to her resolve to stay, no promise to a third person, no consideration whatever would induce Harold to send her away. He had at length reached his final position in this matter.

In this mood, he set out for Noel, resolved to let her try to solve the problem if she could; secretly convinced that she could not; convinced that there was no solution.

Noel had chosen to enter this corner of life's mazedom boldly. Let her act now if she saw how. Let her learn that life is not the simple thing, of straight lines and right angles, she seemed to think it was.

His terse, clear description gave Noel the situation in a dozen words.

"You have come to me with some definite idea? You propose something?"

"I? Nothing. It is in your hands; I thought you should know; I have told you. That was all I came for."

She rose at once without hesitation to accompany him.

In the street he asked if she would drive; she preferred to walk. He made some further remark, and she said: "Pardon my asking you not to talk; I have to think what to do."

"She is here," Harold said at the door of the Sitting Room. He went upstairs and sat in the Drawing Room, smoking.

In the Sitting Room, Ada sprang to her feet at the sound of the opening door; and came forward. Then the joy faded and for a second she stared as if fascinated.

"You here," she said slowly to Noel. "What! You have married him already—and are living here? You have come to turn me out; but I won't go. I tell you that." She stamped her foot in her excitement. "They have always taught me to obey and respect white people, but I won't go, whatever you say, I don't care if he has married you or not. He loved me before he knew you. I am sure of that. I don't care if you are his wife; I won't go. He promised me."

"All this is wrong," replied Noel very quietly. "I do not live here; I have come to see you."

"Me? that is a lie; a lie, I tell you, though your skin is so white and your face is so beautiful. It is a disgrace for a white girl like you to tell lies."

"Come," said Noel, "sit down here and let me speak."

"He said I was not to be put out," panted Ada. "That no one should put me out; and now you come."

"Not to put you out. Going away from here will be quite left to you. You must decide that; you alone."

Weak persons can often bear up well against opposition. To push against it forms in itself a support. Withdraw that prop; clearly leave responsibility and decision to them; they sway and tremble into confusion and dismay.

"You have come to force me to leave," repeated Ada.

"So little of force will there be, that if you tell me to leave you now, I will go back at once."

"Then leave me; leave me; go."

Without a word, Noel rose, and left the room. She was but a step outside when the door behind her opened; Ada's voice called softly:

"Come back."

Noel reentered the room and met a malicious look.

"Now I will show you that I know that all you white people are the same. I know how deceitful you are. You lie without teiling lies with the mouth."

"Well," said Noel, "please begin," and she sat down.

Ada drew from her pocket an open envelope.

"Do you see that?"

"Yes, it is a letter from me."

"Asking him to come to you."

"Well?"

"On the very evening that he asked me to come here."

"Well?"

"Trying to steal his love from me—you thief."

"No."

"But I say yes, yes, a thousand times yes; and now you are angry because I have come to him and you come here to turn me out. He was with me that very evening I tell you; and he left me to go to you." She was out of her seat now and moving restlessly about.

"Your letter stole him away. A thief, that is what you are—you fine, pretty, white lady. Oh, I told that gentleman who found me that night all about it. I forget his name, but he was above the Police. I told him you stole my lover."

"Now listen to me, Ada?" said Noel, firmly and severely. "Sit down here. Look at me. Look into my eyes. Now tell me, do you believe my word?"

"Yes," said Ada reluctantly yielding to the mastery of the eye and voice that commanded her.

"Now, I will tell you about that letter. Do you remember that holiday when you were together at the Aqueduct?"

"Yes. ah, I was happy then." The vista of that happy day drew her away from the immediate object.

"Well I saw you, and I wrote him because I knew you were in danger. He came to see me about that. Do you understand me?"

"Yes; you are not going to marry him then!"

"I? No."

"Why are you smiling?"

"Because you are so mistaken. I do not love him at all; and he knows it."

"He loves me," Ada cried triumphantly. "He told me so, that very evening in this house. He loves me. He said it."

"And for that reason he does not want you to make a mistake now—a fatal mistake, and be unhappy when it is too late. You know that he can't marry you."

"Ah, it does not matter," she replied. "I give up everything I am and have. I will not go away, and he said that I should not be forced to go."

"No, you will not be forced to go."

"You go; you are wasting your time."

"If you go it will be by your own decision; if you stay it will be by your own will. The responsibility is on you and on you only."

"I will stay," replied Ada rapidly; but she shook already under the idea of responsibility. She looked at the girl before her, yearning to see some sign that there was mercy for her, something to free her from this load. Then her longings burst out, calling for Harold to decide for her.

"Remember," said Noel, "that it will be for life. You cannot go back after tonight."

"I have come to stay."

"The step is irrevocable. You can't go back."

"Why?"

"Because you can't go back from today into yesterday."

"Oh, yes. I understand you. I understand. It can't be helped now. It is fate now."

"It can be helped still. You can help it. The matter is not decided yet. You can turn back now and no harm is done. You have to decide now."

Ada hid her face in her hands.

"It is very late now."

"I won't go away from him."

"Very well," said Noel, "but don't you feel it is wrong? Tell me that before I leave you."

"No, no, no," said Ada passionately. "I will be happy. What is it worth to be good if I am unhappy as I have been this whole half year. Do you think a person can feed on glass beads instead of bread? It is not wrong, I don't feel it is wrong, not with him. Your words are only words; they used to frighten me, but not now. They only strike on my ear, that is all, but I don't feel them here," and she touched her breast. "I feel here that I am his. I have come to him. I will stay. I will stay."

"Now listen to me," said Noel quietly. "Was there not a time before, when you saw that to do this would be wrong? The very thing that you cannot feel is wrong now?"

"Yes, but that is all past, far, far away, long past. I have almost forgotten it—but not quite—not quite."

"But then you saw it quite clearly."

"Yes."

"And it was truth that you saw then. You were high enough up to see."

"Oh why do you bring it all back to me now? It is all dim now, far away I can't see it any more."

"You were high enough up to see far, and the air was clear. You were like a person on a hill and saw the country before you. Now you are in a valley, and love is making the air dim round you. But remember that you saw truth then, and it remains there though you have lost sight of it. It is there as the country is there, though you lose sight of it by coming down from the hill, or when a fog surrounds you. In the end this will be misery. You will be bringing it on yourself."

"Ah," cried Ada, swayed by new emotions and affected by the firm, clear tones and gravely menacing words; "but I love him, I love him."

"You have seen the truth and it waits there for you; you cannot destroy it because you forgot it. You have seen it there and it is there still like the rock behind the fog. Remember that now, when you cannot see it, any more for a time. It will not change. It will be there waiting for you further on in the years, when you stumble through the fog on it."

"But I can't feel now that it is wrong. He would not tell me to go, he said so."

"Did he tell you to stay?"

"No," she answered and her heart grew cold as she realized that. She was left alone to decide. She began to see her situation now. She stood in the middle, in loneliness, and both side drew away to watch her. Harold, who would not say 'stay'; and Noel who said 'Go,' but both agreeing that the decision lay with Ada and with Ada alone.

"No," repealed Noel, "he would not say stay. And now decide. It is getting late and I must leave you. You must decide. You alone."

Ada was weeping. Presently she pushed out her hand to Noel and whispered coaxingly:

"You decide. You decide for me; but have mercy. I love him. I belong to him."

"No," fell from Noel's lips, clearly and almost coldly. "I will not decide. It is your responsibility, yours alone. Will you stay and meet the truth later on, where it stands and waits for you?"

In the pause Ada shook and shivered. Her sobs grew more convulsive.

Again Noel's strong, full voice sounded in absolute distinctness, rendered all the more distinct in the silence that was slowly settling down upon that hour of midnight. Outside the noise of the street was ebbing and failing. Inside the only sound was the voice of Noel, grave and unfaltering, the ticking of a clock marking the passing seconds, as with significant emphasis, and the sobs of Ada.

"Will you go away from here, now, at once? Decide."

At length, as if coming forward from the very depths of her soul, Ada's words arrived:

"I will go—but where can I go—not to my own people again never, and I have no one else."

She sprang at this and hugged it, as if it would shut her from the course which she had but that moment chosen.

"You will come with me—to my home," was Noel's answer, and rising, she went straight out.

Ada followed in her steps.

XIII

The Yielding Of Weakness—Ada in Noel's Room—Phantoms and Realities Today on The Hills—Tomorrow on the Plains.

The strong will approaches the point of surrender, slowly, reluctantly, with stubborn resistance. Once arrived at that point, it performs a completed act.

To a weak will, on the other hand, the act performed at the place of surrender is only one of a series of actions, and reactions, which may or may not be progressive; which are not infrequently, on the whole, retrogressive.

A position is given up; then it is reoccupied; again it is abandoned and again repossessed. There is another retreat; another return; and so on through an indefinite number of advances and recessions.

Ada yielded, as we have seen, not before the force of Noel's arguments, and not under any sense of penitence or shame, but mainly because Noel threw on her the responsibility of action. Ada cowered away the moment she realized that the weight of something important and irrevocable was left wholly on her shoulders. She was utterly unable to endure such a load. She had really been saved by her weakness on the present occasion.

Hardly, however, had they reached the street when she was casting about for some excuse to dart aside from her conceded purpose and to refuse absolutely to go further with Noel—in fact, for an explanation or reason that would excuse an immediate return to Harold.

The physical weariness which she now began to feel mastering her senses, gave her a suggestion. She was weakened and unstrung in the hour of reaction. She felt bold enough, it is true, to turn back and to fly for refuge to Harold's side; strong enough to renew, with greater force and more insistence, her demand to him to take her and to make her his forever; but she was utterly unfit to walk a dozen steps, if those steps led away from Harold.

She felt exposing herself to the gaze of even the few passers by who at that late hour were to be met with, as if she were passing naked in their midst. In that her hour of exalted sensitiveness, it seemed that each and every eye turned on her must read what she had tried to do, and failed to consummate; the surrender she had attempted but had come short of.

She shrank under the lighted windows looking down on them as if they were eyes that watched, hungry for her shame. The street lamps gave the bold stare of the indifferent.

She waited but for Noel to suggest walking along these streets to hold herself struck free from the chain of her resolve; justified to turn abruptly off. Without word or cry she would flee again to Harold, and he should know that she would never again leave him. At that distance, short as it was, the final decision to remain with him despite everything, the decision which had seemed too weighty for her mind a minute or two before, seemed the easiest thing imaginable.

Noel called a bus, and Ada, even while she was trying to adjust herself to the unexpected and to discover a new grievance behind which she could stand to resist further advance, stepped quietly into the vehicle and was driven away through the gaslit shadows.

Her thoughts flew now ahead of her, and centred round the manner in which she would be received at the home of this white girl. Treated as a friend and equal, she knew she could not be; but Love and Passion, burning and thrilling through her blood and brain, had lifted her to that exalted sense of being which knows not the idea of inferiority. It was the hour for her when, however, dimly and vaguely it may be seen, the secret of the equality of all human life is before us. It is revealed to us from the heaven of our origins.

With a spice of savage joy Ada seized on the fact that at a point which she foresaw they must approach, there was bound to be irreconcileable grievance. There she would break from the restraining hand of the girl whom she hated more and more every minute that passed.

Silent and motionless but filled with bitter rebellion against her helper, she sat beside Noel as the bus rattled along over the stony streets. She pictured the arrival at the house; a degrading reference of herself to a place in the servant's room. She would be put to sleep with the house-woman or perhaps the butler.

On that insult, she was resolved to hold no parley. "I am no servant," she would cry. "I am not a bit below you, white as you are and rich. Once, yes, but not now. Bad, wicked, vile, I may be, say it all. I do not care. I smile at you. But I am no servant; no inferior to be treated kindly and condescendingly. He has loved me and I am on a level with you and Miss Liberta."

With that she would plunge again into the street, and through its shadow and gaslight, make her way at all costs back to Harold. She would cry to him: "You must take me; for life elsewhere cuts like a jagged rock bruising my naked flesh. Everything shames me, where you are not; and nothing can touch me where you are."

The Bronvola household was in bed and the house was without sound or stir. Noel led the way upstairs to her own room. Here Ada was placed in an easychair and soon her eyes were being gently bathed with delicately perfumed water.

An emotional reaction moved the girl. Tears welled up in her eyes; once or twice she captured Noel's hand and stroked it gratefully. It was wonderful to be thus treated. Ada was familiar with rooms as dainty and elegant, but only as an inferior, present there to perform the work for which she was paid.

Here she could detect in Noel no sign of an attitude of a superior towards an inferior. Suddenly and for the first time, a sense of shame came home to Ada's soul, as she thought of where she had been found and how.

She began to weep and it was a little while before Noel's soothing had any effect on her. At length she found calm.

But by and by suspicion crept back, and with it came the impulse to reverse the decision that had led her away from Harold.

Noel had left the room to see her mother. Ada's surmise was that she had gone to arrange for a separate room for her, among the servants. In any case, whether among the servants or not, she was to be alone. She was no fit being to associate with such as Noel. She was too filthy; she was too low.

Ah, she might have known it; she scourged herself with the thought; girls like her were no roommates for such as Noel. Least of all when they had been found as she had been by this proud, white girl, whose goodness and purity were as spotless as the white sheets on her bed. One thing was certain; Ada would not sleep with servants. As she felt that night, it would have been an unendurable insult. It would have been an outrage on what she felt was the most exalted thing that had yet touched her life. She would not sleep with servants, and she could not sleep by herself. She was too much afraid.

A terrible dread of solitude came over her, so that even there where she sat she grew chill with fear and trembled. She stole across to the dressing table where the lamp was burning, and turned the flame higher; then she looked nervously at the door and at the windows, ere slipping back to her chair. Her heart throbbed with the dread she knew not of what horrible unknown.

Nowhere do more weird and grisly spectres rise, than in the mind where emotion moves, devoid of knowledge.

Noel was away for some little time, and a complete transcript of the terrors and apprehensions that tortured Ada during her absence, would have been a remarkable record.

She had heard somewhere, vaguely, confusedly, of bad women falling into the hands of the Police, and of the Law, to meet there with punishment. What if, in following that impulse which had been so irresistible to throw herself at Harold's feet, she had offended beyond pardon against that great and unknown power which they called the Law, and about which such as Ada knew hardly more than the name.

Noel perhaps had gone even now to summon a policeman. Anything was possible to her in her ignorance, and every thought admitted as possible flamed straightway into the probable and the certain, just as a smouldering object introduced into oxygen bursts into flame and is consumed in a minute.

She went to the door, opened it very quietly and listened. Somewhere in the heart of the silence a clock ticked distinctly. There was no other sound.

She ventured a few steps along the landing; drew back in fear, and resumed her seat, She hid her face and her frame shook with sobs.

Then came another mood, and the words of bitter, scathing denunciation grew heavy on her lips. They would trap her; they had trapped her; she was taken like a bird in a snare; but her tongue was free, they could not bind that, they could not fetter her mind; and she would say to this false white girl such truths as would never leave her memory while blood ran under that pale skin, or the light of day crept in through her eyeballs. The words of truth should be branded deep as with a searing iron. "Liar," she heard herself crying, "You do love him; you trapped me here to insult and destroy me. I went to him because I loved him. What harm is that? Why bring your Policeman here? I cannot escape, but neither will you; with your cold heart and hard, beautiful eyes, that have no pity for a poor girl's heart. God will punish you, and all your false race who cannot feel, who cannot pity, I understand now why they distrust white people."

Then as she hid her face and wept, a hand rested quietly on her shoulder. She sprang up and faced Noel; this was no Policeman.

"It is time to go to bed."

"Yes."

"You will not mind sharing this room with me tonight?"

"This room," said Ada dully, looking round the dainty fittings. "But it is your own!"

"Yes."

"Then where will you sleep?"

"Here with you, if you don't mind it."

Ada buried her face in her hands once again, and such a storm of weeping followed that Noel at last wondered if it would not be wise to call her mother. Her reliance on her own resources was shaken for the minute before this inexplicable tempest. For self-reliance such as hers the greatest danger is excessive emotion to which it does not hold the clue.

But at length the storm subsided, and Ada reached out for Noel's hand.

"I am not even fit to kiss your hand; but I must"; and she kissed it again and again.

Noel lifted the childish form in strong arms from where it lay huddled at her feet and kissed the girl on the lips.

Youth has its own poignant sufferings that are sharper than age can ever know; but it has, too, its own compensations; after all this fury of emotion, Ada fell asleep, despite her desire to remain awake and think of her sorrows, and she slept soundly.

Next morning she awoke with the feelings that we may imagine in one who has gone to sleep on a mountain and wakes to find herself on the plains. The keen, clear, stimulating air of the altitude has been exchanged for the dull, flat, relaxing surroundings of the lowland and the energies of life, drop to a correspondingly lessened pace.

Ada shrank now, from the doings of the preceding day. The exaltation that had lifted her to a sense of equality, had subsided. Yesterday night she had resented with her whole being the idea that anything should be offered to her which was less than Noel's due. She could not see that any woman was her superior. This morning she felt awkward and out of place in this dainty room. She was no fit bed-fellow for its occupant.

Noel still slept, lying on her back, one arm curved over her head and her hair, pouring a dark flood round her fine and peaceful features and contrasting with the spotless whiteness of the bed clothes.

Through the window, came a gentle wind, blowing the light curtains about with the lightest of touches. The morning's fragrance, and the morning's sounds entered there. In the large garden lying just below, the carnations were sacrificing their most delicate odours to the new day.

Ada crept out of bed and began to dress noiselessly.

"Ada."

"Yes, Miss Noel." All the abnormal exaltation of the preceding night, had ebbed and the title of respect came naturally to her lips.

"What are you doing?"

"Getting up, Miss Noel."

"But it must be very early still. Come back to bed."

Ada remonstrated feebly: "I will have to go to my Aunt's before I go to the Store—to tell them where I have been."

"You don't look fit to go anywhere," said Noel, sleepily. "At anyrate, come and lie down now. I will send a message to your Aunt, and I will let the Store people know, if you can't go."

Ada came back to bed. Her head throbbed with pain. She felt chilly and feverish by turns. She dozed and dreamt that Harold and Noel were shaking hands and squeezing her between their palms.

XIV

Tells The Beginning of a Soul Hunt—The Trail Of a Woman's
Soul—Noel Follows It—The Last Step On Life's Staircase—
Liberia Tries to Pick The Meffala Lock—How Cariton
Unconsciously Did Something Important—The Major Sees
Behind the White Sepulchre of Decency.

Ada Pearl Smith had disappeared.

Meffala entered his store one morning to find the Cashier's place empty. He remembered her former dereliction of duty, as if it had been only yesterday, instead of nearly a year ago, and with the mainspring of anger wound tight in his head, he waited for her reappearance next day as a crabbed spider may be supposed to lie in wait for a fly. He shaped the exact taunts with which he would put her on the rack; the threats with which he would make her tremble; but next day brought no Ada. Then he sent to Noel to enquire if anything was known of the girl there.

Noel knew nothing of her.

Ada's own people said she had left them on Wednesday; that was all they knew of it. At least that was all that they acknowledged knowing.

Meffala accepted defeat. "She has gone to the devil," he said, "and I am only sorry I did not get the chance before she went to give her a piece of my mind for being away from the Store twice without leave."

He arranged to employ a new Cashier.

The arrow of conviction entered Noel's mind. Ada had gone again to Harold, and he had declined, as he had half indicated he would decline, to play the unheroic part he had filled on the previous occasion.

She would not let herself doubt him outright; but she could not trust him entirely. He had appeared to waver. She recalled his words: "It is kismet; but for my promise to you, that is how I would have taken it. As I promised, I come to you to see if there is any way out that you see. I am no hero, you see."

Harold had for some time passed out of Noel's view. She did not know that he had gone wandering again, and had, during his travels in Central America, contracted a dangerous fever. He had lain seriously ill for some weeks. Now the fever was past; there was no longer headache or pain of any sort to torment him; the crisis was over; but there he lay, unable to make any decided rally. His mind was clear but weak; his body lay inert, exhausted. There was no progress towards recovery, beyond that implied in the negative that he did not suffer.

Noel's name was stabbed into the silence of the sick room by a stupid servant. Harold's mother, a small, mournful looking woman, rose, with low-toned but voluble reproof. An intense affection for her son had never enabled her to understand his disposition. It was as impossible for these two to commune together as for a plant to confide in an animal. He cared for her, but could not like her.

The name "Bronvola" roused Harold.

"Ask her to come in," he muttered.

"Here!" remonstrated his mother.

Harold frowned.

"You are not well enough."

"Bring her."

"But—"

Harold frowned again, and his mother obeyed.

Noel was in the room ere she had noted whither she was being conducted. The shock of finding Harold as he lay there, came suddenly and with pain.

"Ah," he said smiling whimsically, "I have bumped down to the last step on the stairway of life. I won't go over finally, and I can't go up again—ridiculous."

Noel's eyes filled with tears, born of both sympathy and shame. Shame for the half-fledged doubt which half an hour ago, she had not destroyed at once.

"You did not know."

She shook her head; her voice was not to be trusted.

"I am all right," he said with a pathetic attempt to speak crisply, though the syllables drawled away into weakness. So easily was he exhausted.

The words came like worn-out soldiers limping along after a regiment.

"Don't talk," was the obvious thing to say, and the futile. She saw that he meant to talk, so far as he was able, and she waited in silence, using no vain words.

"I am very tired," he resumed, painfully and laboriously, "and—I—will—die—" the weight of another sentence was too great a burden.

"You need rest," said Noel.

"Life," he answered with his faint smile.

She realized that their converse must rest in a word or two, significantly intense. His strength could support no more—barely that.

"You—want—" he began, then stopped because he could not go on. "Ada Smith."

He looked the question: "Disappeared?"

"Yesterday?" she nodded.

"Me?" he whispered.

She caught his meaning and replied almost hurriedly. It was one of her rare moments of confusion.

"You might know—where—some—clue." Then as his glance lit up for her his group of anxieties in the fore-ground of his consciousness, she continued

"I remember your promise."

"I—" he began.

She stayed his endeavour to speak by touching his hand lightly.

"You must not tell me. I know you have kept your word. I knew you would. I trusted you." She was stung a little by the knowledge that she had suspected him. This memory of her doubt she crushed now as one crushes a scorpion carefully and thoroughly under foot.

"Good," he breathed. His eyes closed and his face rested in calmness and content. It reaches perhaps more deeply into our nature than does anything else to find we are trusted by one we trust and admire.

That restfulness appealed strongly to Noel to let him be at peace; but, strong as was the appeal, she was resolute to follow the trail of her sister woman. A clue lay here and she was determined to take it up. She held herself now with the tenseness of purpose of one who treads, pursuing another where the narrow way skirts deep and dangerous precipices, where, as the Scripture put it, "the steps lay hold on hell." Her imperative resolve forced her on, treading down the comfort of this weakened being.

"Can you help me?" she said in low, clear tones.

He opened his eyes with the surprize that steals into one on whom the restraint of good manners rests, but who has been too preoccupied with another matter to be able wholly to suppress signs of that pre-occupation. He had been concerned with her trust in him. He was not thinking of Ada. His look said plainly now:

"What are you speaking about?"

"Ada Smith," she answered, intent on the significant brevity.

He looked at her to give memory and will a place to rally on; for their powers were far spent and widely flung apart. To Noel's face they drew now, as scattered troops, fighting hard in the masses which they have charged and been engulfed by, turn and struggle towards an officer where he, standing stirrup high, flashes a lifted sword and shouts "Rally."

In due time the wearied, weakened mind had crept back from the shadow of vague consciousness, the borderland of Death, into which it was departing as a figure fades into the evening gloom. It had returned now to the point of memory indicated by her words.

"John Meffala"; the whisper was barely audible. It was the utmost that his mind could lift into speech. But she watched intently and waited after his eyes closed because she saw that he had a wish to say more. There were words in reserve.

He muttered, and, stooping over him, she caught the words:

"Not good sport."

Then she realized that the movement in his mind was man's deep instinct against betraying to a woman another man's "hunting secrets."

The realization was a pain to her heart, cruel as the edge of naked steel. It was one of these black moments when we come out upon something abysmal and primitive amid our veneer of civilization. The chill that the words brought to Noel was lessened, perhaps, by the fact that he had broken through so much to trust her; nevertheless, it was a black moment, when she realized how strong and complete are the bonds between the men who hunt against the women whom they hunt.

It is only in his worst moments, and to the basest of women; or in his noblest moments, and to the best of women, that a man breaks through the rule of the field, that aboriginal instinct so horrible to logical morality and so strong.

Suddenly she saw the nobility in Harold. He had put into her hands that which he knew would shame him to himself and among his fellows, were it ever known. He trusted her. She appreciated what it cost him to tell so much; his trust, his sincerity towards his promise, his inclination towards purity. She stooped down and whispered, close to his ear, so that he might hear the words well:

"Goodbye."

He opened his eyes, sought her face, till his glance rested and was met fully and frankly by hers. He smiled.

A fount of admiration welled up within her for his calmness and composure at the line, a hand-breadth beyond which lay death, the shadow to which he drew with such deadly steadiness. A woman, when all is said and done, admires nothing as much as she admires courage; and here was courage, disciplined and trained.

Tears sprang to Noel's eyes, and obeying an instinct which for the minute removed all self-consciousness, she bent over and kissed him on the brow.

The gathering clouds of unconsciousness rolled back for a minute and his mind was clear. He loved her, but with his characteristic discernment, he realized that she could never love him as he coveted her love. But her kiss was a pledge of the sureness of her trust in him, the clearness of her insight into his spirit's best deptht. A man's passing soul could have no better shriving.

Noel stole softly from the room. Below an open door revealed a picture that cut its way into her memory. Harold's mother crouched against a chair, a look of desolation on her face, her tears literally splashing on the floor.

The thin, shrunken form, the signs of hopeless grief, they held Noel for a second, but they could not stay her purpose, for once again her whole being was nerving itself under the impulse to aid Ada. Till that was done, her powers were not her own. So she felt.

She knocked softly on the open door as she passed, to show that she was leaving. The weeping woman rose inertly, crept out to the stairway, up the stairs, and into the sick room. Then she sprang across to Harold's bedside. He lay grey and ghastly. The interview with Noel had been too much for his strength.

Noel left Harold's house with swift, determined steps; but she had gone a very little distance when she realized that she had not yet answered the question: "What am I to do next?"

She had no answer ready; she held a clue but how it could be followed up she did not see. She only guessed who John Meffala was. Of his whereabouts, his personality, she knew nothing.

Then she thought of Liberta as an ally.

Liberta was at home, and as Noel told the story, the graceful languor that as a rule veiled the inner intense being of Peter Passley's daughter, fell away. Her mind seized eagerly and quickly on the incidents as Noel related them, and she answered at once and decidedly:

"Leave it to me, now. I will act."

Noel, turning back on her tracks, found that burnt deep into her memory, hung a picture of a sick man's death-haunted face and the drooping, hopeless figure of a woman whom Age and Sorrow were pressing hard.

Liberta suspected that Ada's people were not as innocent, or as ignorant, as they pretended to be. She therefore interviewed them at once and obtained this bit of additional information. Ada had left the city by train on Wednesday, travvelling by herself. They did not know what her destination was.

The Junior Staff at Peter Passley's Office remembered that day as marked by an event without precedent in their history.

Like a jewelled hilt to the blade of her resolve, Liberta glittered, flashing and sparkling, amid the dust and dullness of the office. Never before had she been seen within its walls. She often drove down to the door, and picked up her father; but she had never before been known to come upstairs.

Now, her coming swept a wall in the memory of the Juniors clear of all it bore; and there, in the blank space, painted for them in colours vivid for many a day, a lifesized portrait of her captivating self.

The office was by no means an inviting place. Peter had the fancy to keep it as it had stood when he first took it over. He desired it to be the same place in which he had succeeded.

"Not what is outside the office walls; but what is inside my head makes money," he said. "Those who I want to see will come here, if I send for them; and those who want to see me can please themselves."

Liberta was right in the midst of the Juniors, who, like a grove of supple and wind-bowed trees were just then all bending over their ledgers.

Fancy looking up in a dusty office from a ledger, to see Liberta within hand-reach of one, glowing like a dark ruby. That was what her question lifted them to.

"Yes, Madam," said young Smithson, snatching at the politeness for which in his own circles he was renowned. "Shall I announce you?"

"No, but will you take me to him," smiled Liberta.

"Madam," returned Smithson with a bow that Jones Secundus never forgot, "be pleased to follow me."

"The Old Man's face," Smithson related afterwards, "looked like a sunrise when he saw who it was; and she simply floated round and filled the room. By George! what a girl. Not an angle in her! As graceful as a clump of bamboos."

"As rich as they make them," added Jones Secundus.

"Dad," said Liberta "I have come to ask you a favour."

"So I thought," he chuckled. "How much?" and he took up his cheque book.

"Not money," she said. "Something you are to do, and ask no questions."

"Anything you ask, Liberta," he answered with his trust, blind and complete. "And never the feather of a question, my girl. It is all yours, my Sweetheart. It is your own."

"John Meffala is employed by you. I want you to send him away."

His righteous old soul, accustomed all his life to keeping to the highway of fairness to all men, rebelled, even though the unfairness was from her.

"What! Dismiss him? He does his work first-class, Sweetheart."

"No, No, Dad," she came and stood over him to rub his hair endearingly. "Not to dismiss him, only to send him away for a time. Send him on a trip."

"I would have done the other," he said stoutly, as if trying to convince himself as well as her; "if you had really wished it, Sweetheart; but I am glad you did not ask that. It seemed unfair. When shall I send him?"

"Today, now. It can't be too soon, Dad."

"And where?"

"Anywhere out of the Island. You can make him do business for you abroad. You have lots of business abroad, but it must be now, Dad."

Peter thought a little.

"No steamer from here today, Sweetheart, but we'll manage it. I will send him to Port Antonio to catch one there." He pulled down a ledger and examined it.

"You don't know him?" asked Peter suddenly.

"I think I have seen his face, Dad."

"Ah," he muttered to himself, "I said he was a good man here. Nothing about outside, mind you. Steer wide of him outside, Sweetheart."

Liberta smiled. If there existed anywhere on the planet a girl able to take care of herself, it was Peter's only daughter.

John Meffala's eye was one to note whatever of the female world of humanity came in its way, and he was by no means unconscious of the presence of Liberta, as Peter gave him his final directions; but the thought never crossed his mind that the elegant girl was keeping a keen watch on his face, and noting his every word for a particular purpose.

"I can do the Port Antonio train nicely, if I can get home now, sir, to pack a portmanteau."

"That's right," said Peter, "and mind you look close into Stephen's accounts at the Port Cabellos agency; and smell his breath, Meffala, smell his breath. He swears he does not drink now; but let me hear what his breath says."

Liberta left the Office, blessing her father with words; and cursing her fate with her heart.

If Meffala left without disclosing the secret of Ada's whereabouts, that was like knocking the head off of a gimlet buried deep in wood. How was the gimlet to be got out then?

Liberta's mind teemed with a dozen wild schemes for effecting her purpose. As she sat in the carriage, her mind was invaded by plan after plan. She was strung to things dramatic, melodramatic, to desperate schemes and subtle plotting. In her excited condition, anything that promised success seemed justifiable. But she kept returning to the necessary consideration of what was possible and practicable. After all it was the nineteenth century, the period of the prosaic and matter of fact, of Police Courts and newspaper. You cannot assassinate a man without getting into trouble; you cannot even steal a letter or waylay and rifle a mail bag, whatever your excuse, without running the serious risk of being detected and sent to prison

Liberta argued that Meffala must either write or telegraph to Ada. Probably since spare time was so short, he would telegraph. Could she bribe his messenger and get hold of that telegram on its way to the office? Could she have an agent at the Telegraph Office who would by hook or by crook obtain the information she sought?

Then all her elaborate scheming was wrecked by a new idea. Meffala might not send the telegram till he was on his way to Port Antonio. It might be despatched from one of the stations en route.

The carriage rolled on its aimless way, obeying the command: "Drive me anywhere till I tell you to stop. I want to think." Such orders were not wholly unknown to the experience of Robert, the Passley coachman.

But Liberta's thinking seemed to take her more and more into a tangled wood. She was ready to act decisively and resolutely, but was in the position of an army whose General cannot decide on its tactics.

Presently, gazing straight ahead, she gradually had Robert's round head piece at which in that attitude she looked persistently, borne in on her consciousness, and she began to wonder if there could be anything in it to help her. She recalled certain veins of native sagacity not at all to be despised which she had quarried from that same head on former occasions, with distinct profit to her plottings. Besides, whether practical or not Robert's remarks were sure to be worth listening to.

"Robert."

"Yes, Miss 'Berta."

"I want your advice."

"It is like cornmeal in a pudding pan, Miss 'Berta and you have the spoon. Take all you want."

"Supposing you knew a man was sending a telegram, and you wanted to know very much what was in the telegram, what would you do?"

"If me was you, Missie?"

"Yes, if you were I."

"You write down telegram, don't it, Miss Liberta, write it on a piece of paper, same as letters?"

"Yes."

"Den you can do it two ways. You can call de messenger one side, knock off him head and tek the paper."

"And the head, Robert, and the rest of the Messenger, what would you do with them?"

"Well, Missie, dat does certainly stan' in de way," Robert admitted, "more so wid all dese police and 'tective dat is round the place nowadays." He spoke as an inventor may speak who has put forth a machine that can and will do its work, but which is out of court on the insignificant point that the cost of operating it would ruin an empire. "Dat way couldn't 'scape notice," he admitted; "but dere is another way."

"Yes."

"Put ten shilling in you pocket and meet de messenger. You say 'Morning'; him say 'Morning.' You say 'Times' maugre.' Him say 'I just finish fe count hij rib.' You say 'I know where ten shilling is ripe fe pick.' Him say; 'Only show me.' Den you introduce de business. Den you say 'you dry?' and him will say 'Worse dan when drought is down at St. Elizabeth Savanna.' Have a drink,' is what you to say. 'Gots a messidge fe telegraph Office fe delibber fust,' is fe him side a de story. Den you must say? 'Drink will dry up by the time you come back.' 'Well,' says he, 'don't keep me too long. De man send me wid dis telegram and tell me must quick go and come, got a two-inch long patience and a two-foot long temper; also him got more cuss cuss words ina' him head dan when you see bees dem dah swarm.

"Den you introduce you business. Him will talk 'bout Backra law, and how it punish man fool wid telegram. You is to say 'Cho man, Big Massa gib Backra brains to mek law and gib Black man brains to find out to bruck it and poor Backra nebber know.' 'True,' him will say, 'a no lie.' Den you got him."

This edifying discourse, did not, as the reader will have perceived, give the Liberta any new idea. Her eye travelled past Robert's head, and then presently it fell upon Mrs. Cariton who was descending the street seated in her buggy. Liberta had no taste for Caritonisms just then, and averted her face; but the Cariton buggy being driven right across the track of the Passley chariot, and its inmate unceasingly fluttering a small lace handkerchief, and launching flight after flight of exclamations at Liberta, that young lady had at length to recognise that she was out-manœuvred and to surrender.

"Dearest Liberta," was the Cariton message of great joy, "I have something of the greatest importance to tell you; it is quite a providence that we met."

"I know you would stop me for nothing short of importance, as you understand it, Cariton."

"I have a most beautiful pattern of Ecclesiastical embroidery to show you. I would have it here now, but I think it is mislaid."

"How very like you Cariton, to tell me of it before you have found it."

"But I am not at all sure it is lost."

"How still more like you, Cariton, to tell me I shall have it after it is found; before it is lost."

With that, Liberia cast the flutterer forth to flutter on her way, speeding her with the sweetest of graceful gestures, a kiss blown soft as flying thistle-down.

"Let the fool flutter further," was her unspoken farewell; and yet it was to the fool that she owed it that Opportunity found an open door through which to squeeze to her rescue in her hour of dilemma. Had Mrs. Cariton not fluttered across her way and delayed the advance of the Passley carriage for three or four minutes, while the important story of the embroidery pattern was told, it would not have been there when the Major came along the street.

Years before, Edith Merton had exchanged vows with a fellow soldier that they would both pray for each other at one P.M. daily. Wherever that hour fonnd the Major her prayer was sent up to heaven. At times the opportunity served for no more than a swift, silent appeal to her

God; a beam of stillness across the world's harsh noises; an islet of rest, large enough for the dove of thought to alight on, as it completed so much of its voyage across the surging sea of labour and endeavour. But when it was possible, Major Edith Merton liked to kneel in her own little bare room and there say the prayer for her friend.

She was trying to reach that room now in time for this purpose, when the fine Passley carriage drew up by her side, and Liberta's voice accosted her:

"Come, Major. Jump in. I want you."

"God bless you," was the bright response. "Yours in the service always, and at once; and my legs are tired I must say."

Liberta told the story rapidly, and the crucial point lay bare. "He alone has the address and he leaves within the hour. How are we to find out where he has put the girl?"

The Major mused. There was more to think about than Liberta saw. The story made the Major sad for more reasons than one. Liberta thought only of the girl; The Major was thinking of the man too.

She had suddenly opened a door that led her straight into a painful revelation. John Meffala had always been good to the Army, a ready subscriber, a cheery acquaintance, interested in hearing her tell of the work of failures and successes; her hopes, fears and ambitions for this and for that of her "cases." Many a time had he used his influence to secure work for men and boys in whom she took an interest.

The Major had that simplicity so often found in workers like herself. She had unconsciously set Meffala high in her esteem because he was "good to the Army." Had taken it for granted that he lived cleanly, honestly, as she imagined a man should, and would live, who was "good to the Army," although she knew he had not "taken religion." Here, suddenly exposed to her eyes, was the rottenness and stink of dead men's bones behind the whited sepulchre of decency.

The Major had a child's heart, tender despite her long campaigns against sin, and among all sorts of sinners; sanguine, still, despite numberless disappointments with man and woman and many a black vision of despair.

Such hearts as hers never grow callous, just as they never grow old. The pain, the sorrow, the poverty of the world make them suffer till the last; but they have their recompense; for to them the good God has given the gift of undying hopefulness. Winter may wither expectation into despair; but the spring-time comes again with life and bud. Faith fills such hearts as the atmosphere fills the spaces above the green pastures, the high hills and the quiet valleys. It is an unconscious presence.

The Major had a battle now with her tears. She fought it out while she seemed to think. At length she answered Liberta:

"I will find out."

"Now, at once?"

The Major saluted.

XV

Tells How The Major Handled Meffala, Junior— And Continues a Hunt—With Digressions.

W hat can I do for you, Major?" asked John Meffala, cheerily. "Is it a subscription? You have just come in time. I am off in about forty minutes for Port Antonio, and then for America. Or is it about that boy you asked me to help. I got him a place and he seems a likely enough kid."

Her irresponsiveness dammed his flow of words.

"I want you," she said with almost startling distinctness, "to tell me where Ada Smith is."

The blow was so to speak between his eyes. For a second he was dazed. The thing was so wholly unexpected. He flushed under her unfaltering gaze, fiercely, guiltily.

"Is that your business?" he said harshly and brusquely.

"Yes," answered the woman watching him with clear, brave eyes "that is my business."

The faces made a striking contrast. In his, the blood surged under the tanned skin; the angry eyes glared and expanded. Deep breathings made his nostrils tremble.

She had the pallor of her exceeding fairness, her air of purity and peace. There was nothing about her face that suggested anger or confusion.

"It is *my* business," he muttered surlily.

"It is *my* business also," she replied.

There was much wholesome manliness in him and shame tinged his consciousness at having used her roughly.

"Who sent you about this?" He questioned, not through curiosity but because the query came handy.

"God."

He could not sneer at the Sacred Name as she gave it, though that is what he would have done generally. He led hot anger down a bye-way.

"You are out soul-hunting, to save Ada Smith from my fangs?"

"To save you both from the Devil," said the Major gravely.

"Major," he said suddenly in a new voice, "You think me a very wicked man?"

There was a pause.

"Where is Ada Smith?"

"I may as well tell you first as last. Here is her present address." He scribbled it on a piece of paper and handed it over.

"She is quite safe," he added. "You are in time to save the lamb from the wolf. No harm has come to her." He spoke sneeringly, "and I am off this evening."

"That's good," was her reply. She credited him with more than the Recording Angel placed to his account just then.

"No thanks to me," he said almost roughly. He felt a fierce desire that she should think well of him, but, under her eye he responded entirely to the impulse to tell the truth wherever it led him. "I have not had time to go near her. That is what has saved her from me. And now I am off on the hop."

"There," he continued for the Major remained silent. "You have unmasked a scoundrel. Are you satisfied and are you done with me now, forever?"

"God bless you."

He took that to be an evasion of his question, and answered savagely:

"Yes—you leave me to Him. You—you—wash your hands of me— that is the woman's way—the saint's way, too."

The Major's eyes filled slowly with tears; but a smile sparkled through them.

"I would be a poor soldier if I did anything of the sort. It would be running away; deserting in the face of the enemy. We are going to be at the Devil over this. It is not our business to wash our hands of anybody."

"Not even of me," he said. "Bad as I am."

"You have been very kind to the Army, and you have given me a lot of money." She spoke in the simple sincerity of her heart. To give to the Army, in her simple view, was to give to God; and he who would give to God must have some good in him.

In his bitterness of spirit, he misread her meaning.

"Yes, you are afraid to offend me, or I will not give any more. You value me for that," and he added, flinging the words at her, "You are right. I won't give you and your Army any more; not a shilling."

Poor Major; she could not help a chill feeling of discouragement, like a wandering gust of icy wind blowing through an open window. She thought of her slender list of subscribers, divided into the few she marked as "Certain to give" and others who gave sometimes. Meffala was a strong tower among the few. Then she thought of the many things she had to finance. Besides, his roughness and injustice lacerated her soul. She had not anticipated a blow like that from him.

Begging for the Cause was her heaviest cross. But she faced about now as readily as well drilled soldiers shape their lines to beat off a new and sudden attack.

There rose in her heart the simple, intense prayer: "God, give me the Victory." Her steady eyes met the scowl that covered the man's consciousness that he had spoken like a cad, and that, to this woman, above all others.

"My dear man," said the Major, "God bless you. I don't want your money, if you don't want to give it. I want all the money you can give me for the work. I need it. I tell you. That is part of the fight; to take the money away from the Devil and to use it for God. Ah, I remember hearing the General say once, 'Plunder Hell of its money,' but I don't want your money if keeping it is more to you than giving it. I want to see you good and happy and I am believing for you."

"What!" he enquired, unfamiliar with the phrase.

"I am believing for you," she repeated, "that you will get the victory. That the Blood will be applied."

He was further puzzled.

"Why," she continued, "do you not try to be good? Why don't you wish to try?" The next moment she was on her knees, praying briefly and earnestly:

"Oh, God, help this dear man to try to be good. Help him to try, and give him the victory, for the sake of Jesus Christ, our Lord and Redeemer. Save him, Father and God. Amen."

It was her gift to do this naturally.

She rose, and bade him "Goodbye" with her hearty "God bless you." He followed to the door.

"Major, I spoke like a cad; like a low down cad too. You are welcome to the money; all I can give you."

"I believe it," she replied. "But you shall carry a little cross, too. I won't ask you for money for the Army again till you send in some of your own free will; and now I have opened fire on you I will fight hard. I mean to win your soul from the Devil. Think it over; I am believing for you—that you will get salvation. God bless you; He will give you the victory."

"Jehosaphat," said Meffala as he looked at his watch after seeing the

Major disappear, "I believe I am going to miss that Port Antonio train, and what will Old Passley say then? Damn the women."

Next day, while Meffala was speeding northward on the outward-bound steamer, with his thoughts turning persistently to the Major, she, seated at the bare but neat table in her room, was having dinner with her Lieutenant.

Several letters lay beside the Major's plate, for she had just returned to Kingston. She opened them as she eat, so as to save time. There were no minutes to lose in the Major's day. There was a registered letter and it contained £2 2s in a cheque signed "John Meffala."

"Victory," cried the Major. "Hallelujah."

"Amen," responded the little Lieutenant brightly as she sat opposite, eating dry toast and sipping cocoa. Discipline forbade her enquiring for details; but she saw the cheque and well she knew that money was needed. She read the joy in the Major's face.

"But," murmured the Major, reexamining the cheque, "I am believing for his soul."

"Amen," said the Lieutenant.

The Major eat her toast and drank her cocoa, thinking of John Meffala. She had a daydream of capturing his soul for heaven.

"Why can't he be good? He is so kind to the Army and to me."

But in thus peeping in at the Major's dinner table, we have flown a little ahead of certain events that transpired on the afternoon of the preceding day.

XVI

In Which we Leave the Soul Hunters—And Study the Soul
At Close Quarters—Under Coralilla Bowers—A Crisis,
via A Bad Coin Plays an Important Part—Ada's Theological
Convictions—Cold Water In a Glass and Elsewhere—An
Attempted Deal in Gold Bangles—Peeping In at the
Cottage Window—And after.

Ada Smith sat alone in the room of a pretty cottage in Pimento Town. From the window she looked forth on a pleasant view. A green yard, with yellow gravel walks and ardent touches of colour where the flower-beds shone in the afternoon sunshine; rolling pasture-lands swept away, till in the distance blue mountains rose into misty softness.

The cottage walls, right up to the sill of the window, were heavy with the blossoms of the pink and white Coralilla. Round these, bees murmured melodiously. Humming-birds shot from cluster to cluster of the flowers, like jewels, drawn with a flash through the sunlight.

On a Lignum Vitæ right opposite, the heavy foliage, stiff, strong and handsome, was set with mauve flowers of a most delicate shade and with bright yellow seeds that, opening, disclosed a touch of vivid red within the pod,

A Poinciana, hard by, was hung with huge seed-pods more than a foot long. Some were green; others were as dry and hard as wood. On the topmost branch of this tree, sat a nightingale singing untiringly to the westering sun, and trying over a number of imitative notes with zeal and persistence.

A little to the right, a garden walk led between gay rose bushes to the gate. The gateway itself was buried in Stephanotis and Honey-suckle.

Beauty drew its folds over the scene, peaceful and soothing. But Ada was not at peace; far from it. She sat at the window in a state of nervous unrest that was steadily culminating. Her heart fluttered behind that pink and white Coralilla like the heart of a bird behind prison bars.

She had yielded at length to John Meffala's importunities, partly resigning herself to the strange fascination that he exerted when actually with her, and partly in desperation at Harold's absence and silence. There was in her heart a pitiable hope that Harold would be punished if she showed him "she did not care."

THOMAS MACDERMOT

Quite on the sudden, and when Meffala had least expected it, she had yielded and had agreed to come with him to Pimento Town for a week-end. She had been to Harold's on the day before and had been told that he could not be seen.

The same stupid servant who had taken Noel's name with a straight stab into the sick room, had dismissed Ada without saying a word of her master's illness. Ada's interpretation was that Harold had declined to see her, and did not wish to have her pestering him at the house.

The little Cottage at Pimento Town was charming. Its inmates deferentially addressed her as "Mrs. Meffala," and were most attentive. Ada had money to spend and a strange place to see. For the first day she was happy; but as night closed in and she realized at closer quarters that Meffala would be coming to her next day, something like terror attacked her heart.

The hours swept before her like a steep incline down which she was slipping bit by bit, without chance of staying her descent. Meffala's eyes pressed on her like cruel sword points in the darkness, checking every movement save that which was slowly and certainly drawing her to her doom. His desire, like a hand, reached out and forced her nearer and nearer. His was a deadly strength.

She slept and dreamed that she was sinking in deep water. Noel appeared on the bank of the stream and looked down. She shook her head and walked slowly away. Ada heard someone say, "Too late."

She dreamed again and this time it was Harold who came. He was smoking and he watched her sink.

She had another dream from which she awoke screaming. As she lay, chill and still, awake in the darkness, she heard a stir begin in the rooms near. Voices questioned; a beam of light moved towards the door. Some one knocked quietly; then again and louder. Ada answered, saying it was a nightmare.

After that she lay wide awake, and fearful till daylight stole in from the rosy east, laden with the perfume yielded up by fields of dewy Bahama grass, by the flowers of the Sage, and the Vervain, and from the opening buds of the blue Covolvuli where they stretched their lengths amid the rolling spaces of the Guinea Grass.

With the coming of the sunshine, Ada's spirits revived to a small extent; but still fear dogged her pathway. She saw its face in every moment of reflection; in each pause for contemplation, it stole to her side.

She must escape. The idea grew definite and then strong. She could return to Kingston by that afternoon's train. It would pass the train by which Meffala was coming to Pimento Town. She would shrink back into the farthest recess of the carriage; little would he dream that in one of the carriages passing under his eye, the Girl he was coming so confidently to seize as his prey was escaping him.

She could imagine, as she thought of it, the sense of relief which would be hers when, once safely past, her train was moving inevitably away in one direction and his was fading from view in another. It was like thinking of the powers of Nature coming to her aid; something that, powerful as this man might be and sinister, could not be bent an atom in his favour.

Meffala would be very angry; yes. But she would be free. She would be beyond him. To picture his rage at a safe distance rather pleased her, exactly as a child who has run away from a tiger may turn when the monster is safely caged and watch its passion with laughter. Out of Meffala's immediate presence she only hated him; he had no power over her.

She stepped noiselessly to the door of her room and listened. A vague murmur of voices, told her the people of the house were well out of the way. The passage to the front door conld be made without witnesses. She put on her hat and stole forth on tip-toe.

The door was reached. She sped along the garden walk and projected herself into the street. Then she sped forward at a pace so rapid that presently she became conscious that her hurry was attracting attention. She turned off at the first cross street and moderated her rate of progress.

It never occurred to her that she might have left the house in the most ordinary way. An easy excuse to the lady of the Cottage; a pretext that she went shopping would have relieved her of any further interrogation. Once out, she could have slipped away to the Station. It was not in her at such a juncture to adopt the simplest and most natural course. Nor could she have trusted her face not to betray her real purpose had she seen the woman at all on the subject.

At the Station the time-table told her that she must wait for almost an hour. Her eye hardly left the clock. She watched the dial-face with an irrational dread that the hour that would separate the coming of Meffala to that room and her own departure from it would not be a sufficiently substantial barrier; though she knew certainly that he could not come till she had left, (that was as certain as day and night) yet the fact that he would be there, in that very same room, on that very day, made her shrink and cower.

The Clerk pushed up the little window of his office and began to sell tickets. She hastened to present herself; securing her ticket seemed to make her safer. It was one step in advance at any rate.

Face to face with the Clerk and with his "Yes, Madam?" interrogative and respectful in her ears, she searched her pockets in vain for her purse. It lay at that moment on a table in the Cottage. She had omitted to bring her handbag and the purse was in the bag.

"You might have time to get it, if you took a bus at once," suggested the Clerk, touched by the sight of Beauty in distress. From that well-meant advice she shrank as from a sudden jet of poison spurted at her. She dared no more return to the Cottage than a prisoner dares return to the Penitentiary walls from which he has fled. Besides the train might meanwhile pass through and take away her only chance of escaping that day.

Again she searched her pocket. Sunk in the folds of a handkerchief she found a two-shilling piece. There was a stray threepence at the bottom of another pocket. She could just get through with this, leaving a penny or two.

Alas for the catastrophes that certain persons working away on their own business in the deep, black heart of Kingston, thinking not of fugitive ladies, precipitated in one direction and another.

Like gases forming in the depths and rising in bubbles to burst on the surface, came the efforts of the diligent coiners from the very bottom of the black pool, to float and die in the daylight, at other people's expense.

Miss Elsie had drooped with shame at having to ask her butcher to allow a part of her bill to him to stand unpaid, because she had received several bad coins for her Preserves. We have seen the misfortune a bad shilling brought on The Sinner. Now it was the turn of Ada to be taken in the snare.

"I have got just enough," she smiled to the Clerk.

"I am very sorry," he replied pushing her coin back, "this is bad money. We have had special cautions against these coins lately. There seems to be a lot of it knocking round."

"Are you sure it is bad?"

"Sure, Madam?"

The would-be purchaser of a ticket next in the queue gave Ada a gentle push of reminder. She was still in the Waiting Room aimlessly looking, when the train grumbled and rumbled upon its way to Kingston.

Ada rose then and started down the road back to the town with every appearance of one bound for a definite goal, walking as purposefully as any of her fellow pedestrians. In reality she had no idea of where she was off to.

The cottage with its pink and white Coralilla was more than ever an impossible harbour. Besides the bad florin and the attenuated threepenny piece, worn thin by continued travellings through collection plates, she had no money. A painful thirst racked her; she needed food, too, but this, for the time being, she could not realize. Thirst held the first mortgage on her body. She longed for water till her tongue felt heavy and dry as sun-baked leather; till the roof of her mouth was hard and dead.

At length she mustered up courage to ask for a glass of water from a neat looking black woman who sat in front of a minute shop, selling fruit. Ada offered a penny for the drink.

The woman responded with a look of hostility and disgust. Nevertheless, she produced a glass filled with water.

Ada drained it to the last drop, and, handing it back with a sincere "Thank you," tendered the threepenny bit.

"But what make you Mulatto specially you white-wash ones stan' so?" asked the woman.

"What," stammered Ada; "It is all I have; but take it all if the penny is not enough."

"And what you tek me for?" demanded the woman with anger, and yet with a touch of good nature in her tone. "You tink a poor black woman would sell you a simple glass of water, God's own water? If I did, what you tink God Almighty would say to me? To sell water is left to white people and some a you brown people."

"No offence," Ada hastened to say.

"And no harm done," responded the woman; "but you will know better next time. You are heartily welcome. I never sell water yet and I not going begin dis blessed day."

Within Ada's heart a force strove to turn her steps towards the Station, the very spot which she must now avoid if she was to escape Meffala, because it was just there and only there, that she was sure he must be at some period of that day.

She resisted as she herself would have said with all her might, but her resistance did not destroy the suggestion. Instead of passing into silence, it reiterated itself like one voice rising high above all those round it. Its words were heard at decreasing intervals, and presently it had silenced all else. The picture of the Station fascinated her; the impulse to return to it tugged unceasingly at her will.

"It is the Devil," she said once or twice, and walked faster in the opposite way.

But in the end she turned; she hardly knew when she did it or how; but in due time she was again standing before the Station, in its empty yard.

The clock told that the train from Kingston was not due for fifteen minutes. A feeble whisper within spoke of a last opportunity. It was not yet too late to escape Meffala; he could not stand in that yard till the train arrived, and the train would not come for a quarter of an hour yet. She had but to turn at once and resolutely leave the place. She feared the man; she disliked, she even detested him. She longed earnestly to slip from the net which was closing on her; but she was the slave to the idea that she was fascinated by him, that he had over her a strange and resistless power; she was helpless because she believed she was helpless.

She was rooted to that spot where he was so soon to be; so she persuaded herself not because she wished to be persuaded, but because she could not resist the impression left by a long fostered notion. Here he would come, and here by his malign power he commanded her presence. She must attend. When she shook off the feeling sufficiently to think of going away at once, ten minutes of the time of waiting had passed by. Let her go out on that long white road now, so full in sight of each train that rushed into the Station, Meffala must see her as his train brought him in.

She had sprung up, but she reseated herself.

It was her fate. She was the slave of that repetition. She must wait here, the only spot in the world just then that she was sure she wished to escape from. It was her fate. That was her prison house, her tomb perhaps. Within its magic walls resolve was chained.

Five minutes, she presently thought, was a long time. There was no train yet; not a sound of one. Then it struck her that the yard was singularly still; none of those premonitory thrills that bespeak the arriving steam monster were to be traced. No buses had gathered; there was not a boy to be seen; the officials were as quiescent as wasps are in the twilight. Her eyes travelled to the clock. The train was five minutes overdue.

Ada ventured to question the friendly clerk.

The train would be over one hour late at least. All Pimento Town at all interested in the matter had heard of it already.

Little did the clerk realize with what a radiance of light and significance the ordinary fact, thus told in the most matter-of-fact voice, leapt into the mind of the lady before him.

It was not simply that Meffala was delayed; though to Ada the postponement of a danger was well-nigh as precious as its annihilation; a narrow ledge of delay was to her foreshortened gaze as wide as the spacious plains of absolute deliverance.

It was not only that she could now leave the Station with abundance of time to escape. The fact of that block on the line that hour's delay of a train so laden with fate for her glowed in her sky like a huge globe in which shone the inmost truth that Providence had not forsaken her. The Almighty was still on her side. Here was an act of God, if ever there was one, and there could be no meaning to it unless it was for her benefit.

The black woman's reference to the name of the Almighty had challenged the religious side of Ada's moods. When she had returned to the Station, drawn, as she insisted, by irresistible power, she saw in this, proof that a displeased Heaven had abandoned her to the tender mercies of the Devil.

But now her faith rebounded to the topmost heights. God was delivering her by delaying Meffala's train. And the light from that great fact, streaming back over the past, shewed her that it was by no diabolical power that she had been compelled to return to the Station. The Almighty had brought her there that she might realize how he could and would deliver her from her enemy. She thought of Israel crowding on the seashore, while a tumbling sea overwhelmed Pharoah and his host. So much for Ada's theology.

For a minute she stood at the door of the Station, that her soul might be well satisfied with the new prospect; then, choosing the road which seemed to lead most directly and decisively away from the Station, she set off briskly and almost joyously.

Her thoughts ran and skipped before her on the shining uplands of assurance. She felt brave enough for the time being, to picture herself confronting and daring Meffala himself. She marshalled a troop of thoughts dashing enough to send him to the right about face; and then the thought flitted through her mind that the Creator desired her, in return for the intervention which she had just recognized, to adopt the heroic role of waiting Meffala's arrival and addressing him somewhat like this.

"Leave me forever; my soul warns me. I have seen the danger; go; and never come to ask me any question again. Never write me; never speak to me again." A sudden little gust of chilly memory, slow-moving from some dead glacier, blew across this heroic altitude. She remembered how often she had said the same thing to Meffala; and the number of times he had returned to her.

Ada decided that she had better not climb to such heroic peaks of action. Her duty lay on the safer lowlands.

She quickened her steps as she reached this conclusion, and, outraged by the additional exertion cast upon it by a mind which with which it had been for some hours on querulous terms, an ill-treated body began to put in reminders of its grievances. Ada was very hungry, very empty; she was also very tired, saturated with weariness.

The long shadows across the road; the noise of Black-birds bathing and drinking in a neighbouring pool; the distant halloos of cattlemen to the stock they were herding told her that night was at hand.

She had no lodging secured. Worse still she had no money beyond the three-penny bit to offer for lodging. Could she starve till next day? The body rebelled clamorously, and threatened if she did she should faint for it. But Ada was prepared to allow that she could and would starve; after all one can starve for a time at least without the world being any the wiser. Ada would have felt the world's knowing more than the starving.

But where was she to sleep? One cannot sleep in the road and leave the world, to say nothing of the world's wife, none the wiser. She had hardly ever heard even the name of Pimento Town before Meffala had sent her there. She was enisled in a sea of strargeness.

Her eye rested on the golden bangles which adorned her wrists. She wore a watch also; both articles were gifts from Harold. Here was light in the darkness; here was the clue leading to deliverance. What was simpler than to select a house where she would pledge her ornaments for a night's lodging, and for enough money to take her back to Kingston next day. Once in Kingston she meant to go straight to Noel Bronvola and to leave everything to that strong-minded young lady. The latter part of the programme was characteristic of Ada Pearl Smith.

As to returning to her own people, that she was now incapable of doing. Had she actually thrown in her lot with Meffala, and secured the material advantage, her sense of shame would have been balanced by a certain pride of her own, in the knowledge that her relatives admired her for making such a conquest. But to return to them now was impossible.

That she had drawn back from what she had felt to be wrong was to her of no sustaining force whatever. She had little room for self-respect. She only reflected that in returning in this way her people would never believe that she had withdrawn voluntarily. They would be certain either that Meffala had backed out in the end, or that he had thrown her off like an old boot. He was tired of her charms already; in that way they would dispose of the matter and of her.

Ada examined her watch. More than half an hour had passed. Would the train come this time, or would it be further delayed? She quivered mentally, drawing back as she found that she was again drawing pictures of the Station and of the train running in with its harsh out-cry; of Meffala slipping from his first-class carriage and coming through the Waiting Room to get a bus.

This was a return to dangerous ground, from which she had but recently been delivered. It was a sin to think thus.

She must and would do something definite in another direction. Selecting a likely-looking house, she enquired for a night's lodging.

Yes she could have it.

And the charge?

"Two shillings; with coffee, two and six."

Ada, at this point realizad that her proposed deal in jewellery was not as easily made as it had appeared it could be not five minutes before.

She stammered out a statement in which a lost purse and catching in train were illogically coupled. The first impression of her keen-eyed auditor was that the girl was begging for a night's lodging and trying to hide the fact by a plausible story. This was indicated by her look and only half hidden by her words.

Ada, explaining volubly, introduced her gold bracelets. But one suspicion hatches a brood of chicks with marvellous rapidity.

These bracelets, the woman reflected, might not be gold; or they might be stolen goods. So much for Prudence and Self-interest; this woman was engaged in wresting her living from a world that she had never found too ready to yield it to her. Now came the turn of Morality. The nestful of suspicions queried: What was this girl, so young and pretty, doing in such a position. The lodging housekeeper declined to give her lodging but offered her good advice.

"Get back to your people, at once, my girl; and be more careful."

If God, said Ada to herself, stopped the train why not make the lodging house keeper take her in. She walked away from the house with exaggerated slowness till she had gone some distance. Thus she challenged Providence to remove her doubts by securing her lodging here at once; let heaven show its power and benevolence by softening the heart of this cruel woman.

Ada began to reflect on what she might have done in deed and thought since she left the Station which could be accounted sinful.

It was clear she must have offended a Deity Who would not now help her in a little matter like this of getting a night's lodging, when He had only a few hours before done so much for her by stopping Meffala's train on its way to the Station. That was how Ada had recorded the event.

Except that her feet followed the road, she was hardly conscious now of anything outside of her mind. In that simple way it transpired that, reaching cross-roads she, all unconsciously, took that road which curving to the left was destined to bring her back to the Station.

By and bye she looked up. The Station. Cold fear seemed to stream out from its grey walls and to smite her. Who but the Devil could have done this thing? Who else could have brought her to this place from which she was fleeing.

The net result of her religious training, whatever its aim, was to leave her with the conviction that the Devil, though less powerful than the Deity, was a great deal more enterprising. Here was clear proof of his enterprise. He had captured and led her to her doom even while her thoughts were knocking doubtfully, and fearfully timid, at the doors which shut in the will of the Almighty.

That she was still a free agent never occurred to her, and was a suggestion which she would have dismissed as outrageous, had it been thrust on her attention.

The first and distant indications of the approaching train were echoing through the wooded defile that brought the line from the mountain country out into the lowland.

It was Fate and she was Fate's prisoner.

For the third time that day she passed into the Waiting Room sinking down on a bench in the deepest shadow that the feeble light of a single lamp scarcely invaded. She resigned both Hope and Resolve.

In rushed the train, snorting and shriek-like a beast that seeks its prey. Did it not bring Meffala nearer to his prey?

Ada knew that he was there, amid the intermingling cries and greetings that poured over the platform like an invading flood which wrecked and bore away the preceding silence. She dared not look out; but she could see him in fancy standing a minute as he alighted from his carriage; looking round for a boy to take his bag and then—Some one opened the door. It was a man; he pushed the door wide and searched the room with his glance.

Ada with her back to the door waited, shrinking from his greeting, as her bare flesh would have shrunk from the sting of a lash.

Then she was conscious that he had withdrawn. Perhaps, she thought, he had failed to recognize her figure.

The train sped away, travelling slowly into the night and emitting shrieks from its whistle as one accustomed only to the daylight, and feeling the need of groping a careful way in this unfamiliar shadow. The noise on the platform ebbed. The crowd dispersed. Still Ada remained undetected.

She stepped into the yard. Not a vehicle was in sight. The Porter was beginning to shut up the windows. There was hardly a soul to be seen in the yard, or on the long road leading to it. Ada emerged beneath the light of the young moon, a thing as tremulous and uncertain as herself. She looked up at the wide sky and scarcely dared believe that she was actually free, that she had once more escaped. God, she felt, was there after all, in that great height, among the far-away stars. The wind round her was His solemn but comforting whisper. The waves of emotion lifted her to the heavens; then they descended till in the trough of the great waters she saw only the billows. Her mood declined, controlled, though she knew it not, by her physical depression after the day's long fast. She was free, indeed, escaped like a bird from the snare of Meffala, but she was loosed under high heaven to flutter forth like a tiny bird; and the world was dark.

Where, in God's name, was she to go now? She must rest; she must eat. Besides the Station, there was one other spot in the town that she knew. That was the one spot which she must shun. It was precisely the spot that attracted her with deadly power.

It was only while she wondered what Meffala was doing at the Cottage that the arm of excitement was strong enough to hold up her fatigue and weariness. That touched her being with the sting and impulse of a stimulant. If she wrenched her thought from that point, she felt in an instant that she would only drop by the wayside and faint.

It was wonderful in a way, the moment she dwelt on the Cottage and on Meffala, that moment she feit an electric shock rush through her being. All the world besides seemed vague, pointless, futile, a vast emptiness; a prairie of monotony, upon the face of which there was not a feature to mark out any one point from the rest of the grey, unvaried sameness.

The Cottage was the fatal centre. To that her whole being was drawn; on that each wave of her spirit rushed and fell.

As with magnetic force, her feet were drawn to the spot. She was drawn towards the Cottage, and without consciousness of what she was doing she had gone several steps in its direction ere any definite plan entered her head.

Then she saw herself stealing as far as the gate; or perhaps she would look in through the lighted window. She must see what was happening in that cottage now, since Meffala had arrived. There he sat, probably, like a bloated spider waiting for the fly to return to the fatal web. She imagined him pouncing on her; she panted at the thought; shuddered; shrank away; but the next minute she was assuring herself. "I will not be seen."

Again she pressed forward.

The road was all but empty; she crept to its shadowed side and moved along there.

When her hand was extended to touch the garden gate, she saw the front door ahead of her open. Panic swoopod on her like a bat with ink-dark wings. She turned and fled, not waiting to see who would come out. She knew it was Meffala.

A little distance she ran, then she paused, for her strength was far spent. Shelter, a covert, a hiding place; her eye searched road and roadside in despair. Again she broke into a run, her eye fixed on a clump of dark bushes ahead.

For this she made with all the poor speed she could muster. It would be enough to hide her, if she crushed herself together within its shadow. Hurrying steps sounded behind. How lightly Meffala could run when he chose. Such a big man, and yet his foot-fall was like a woman's, as it came after her down the road.

That was Ada's last thought as she sank amid the bushes and fainted.

When Ada reopened her eyes they looked straight into a face which at first she mistook for those of an angel's. "But," she muttered, "angels don't wear black."

"Nor bonnets either," said the Major, "and I fancy they are fatter then I am. Is it all right now?"

"All right? My God, no," cried Ada suddenly. "He is coming after me, running down the road. Come further into the shadow. Whisper. He will hear you."

The Major made a gesture; but the girl stared, her eyes wide with alarm.

"Hush," she listened intently. "I don't hear his footsteps any more. He came out, I saw him."

"I came out," said the Major.

"But he followed."

"He is on his way to America."

"But he came by the train that was delayed."

"No, I did. There was a telegram for you from him at the Cottage. That would have told you. He has been suddenly sent to America on business. He was in Port Antonio this evening and will be at sea tonight, or tomorrow."

A stillness fell on them which by and by, made the Major fear that the girl had again fainted. Then came a storm of sobs; and at length words dragged themselves forth.

"You came to save me."

"We have all been trying to help you; Miss Liberta, Miss Bronvola and I. But it is God that saves. Think that He is here with us."

"I am horribly wicked," said Ada. "I knew it was wicked to come. I knew it. I went before to Harold—one night. Miss Bronvola knows; she came to take me back. I was ashamed for a little, in her room after it, when she kissed me and had me in her own bed, and I told myself I was wrong and wicked, and bad. But I felt deeper down even at the time I was not. Not for going to him. He is my own. I feel it. I know it. Something inside me tells me so. I know it. It was not a sin to go to him. I can't explain how I know; but I know that. Oh, I know the Bible may say no, and we ought to mind the Bible, and the Minister and the good people like you; and I do, I do. I try to. But something in me, like a spring under a stone, like a voice very far away, something, deep in me, tells me I was not wrong then, to go to him; though I will never go to him again. But it was sin to come to this man. Oh, it was horrible wickedness. I am vile—vile. Don't touch me." She shrank away.

"It never came to me clear till last night, and then I dreamt I was walking on a road and it was very narrow and rough. It was strange, too, for though it was dark, light came through to show me the way, but not showing anything else. I went on and on; then I stopped. I was at the edge of a precipice, a deep hole full of blackness. I looked over and saw a great churning up and down there. There were black waters all in motion. You could hear the swing of the big waves and their clashing, but I could see hardly anything. I heard faintly, as if it were far-away, shrieking and crying and moaning. Oh, it was black, black; and the cries were terrible, terrible. I could not forget it. What was it Major? What was there?"

"It was hell," answered the Major in simple faith. "You stood right on the brink."

"It was hell," murmured Ada to herself. "It was hell black and horrible and deep and filled with those horrible cries. Oh, you are good," she cried with an involuntary movement to cling to the Major. "You are good to come to me. You and Miss Noel. That night I remember it well. Do you know she put me into her own bed that night, and slept beside me, I thought at first she would put me with the servants."

"Now," said the practical Major, "we must get a billet and tomorrow we go back to Kingston and to good friends. We have given the Devil a facer this time at anyrate."

XVII

Gleaning in the Wake of The Hunt—Liberta's Review and Foreview for Ada's Benefit—The Major's Counter-view Unexpressed—Rumours True And Untrue—Meffala Returns to Oblivion—And We Leave The Major at a Black Moment.

Well we won." The speaker was Liberta and she addressed the Major. They were sitting at night in the Passley drawing room. "What is the programme to be now for Ada?"

The Major sketched the virtuous career that she saw Ada pursuing.

"Undeceive yourself, my dear Major," was the discouraging response, "her adventures are not yet over. Two men control her fate, and will to the end of the chapter. Harold is one and the other is John Meffala. Harold cannot marry her, but he may leave her alone. Meffala will not marry her, and he will not leave her alone. As regards Harold, he is supposed to be dying, and that may mean that he is a negligible quantity in the matter, at anyrate, he will make a decent try to leave the girl alone; Harold is no worse stuff than men generally are, he turns his worse side outward of intent; but Meffala; that is gutter mud, my friend."

"The good God—"

"Will not take John Meffala from his place in the scheme of things—on the dung-hill. He belongs there."

Liberta noticed that the Major's eyes filled with tears.

"Don't worry about it, Major. 'Some to honour,' you know and 'some to shame.' She may keep straight; she will for some time yet; but I tell you the only way to end her amorous adventures is to get Meffala over the edge of things. If he would oblige by breaking his neck."

"Oh, don't," came from the Major.

"Well we won't," said Liberta cheerfully. "Take another cup of tea. Still, Major, the wicked do not die young, you know; and you must not depend on Heaven being your ally to the extent of cutting Meffala off in the flower of his vice. His death would be altogether too opportune, and artistic, as well as useful, to be expected. I don't even believe that Harold means to die, sick as he is. These men have such a way—but I see I am wounding that tender soul of yours. Only I must stick to the fact that John Meffala will have that pretty little doll yet."

"However, by all means let us carry on the battle for her soul. Do not men and women perform prodigies of skill and daring to kill a fox. The chase is everything, or almost everything, and the tail of the wretched animal you get at the end of it merely a good excuse. When I think of how I snatched the girl out of the Meffala's closing teeth, I feel as if I had taken the finest lump of raw meat from between the very jaws of a hungry tiger and I thrill at the recollection. Suppose I take Ada down to the Penn for a few weeks."

Here was ground on which the Major could stand in agreement with her friend; so they fashioned out their plans; and what time they talked the Major spared a thought for John Meffala.

Kind thoughts of us from the pure hearts of true women, they flutter forth and wing their way, like white doves speeding across black oceans, across distance, across time, towards him for whom they are sent on their sure journey. And they enter our hearts though we be unconscious of their arrival even as the roistering crowd in the hall may make merry, unwitting that in the moment of their drinking and song a meek dove, burdened with the cipher message whose import is worth more than gold and rubies, is alighting at some open lattice in the castle walls and is being taken in by the hand of some humble page boy with the word that is to change the fate of all there.

Was there any window open in Meffala's heart towards Jerusalem on that night through which the Major's thought of him flew forth, half tender, half kind?

Was there spiritual consciousness of its arrival?

Softly the starlight lit the unquiet waves. Far on the west, the dark mass of the Jamaica mountains still made the gloom on the sky line deeper. The steamer, cleaving her way northward, was treading the dark waves beneath her prow into white foam. And the man who loitered on the deck was but a few days out from the last agony; the final passionate struggle of life rebelling against death's dominion; the horrible battle in black, bitter waters as the steamer's light faded from view in the gloom-vagueness—but how little could he have thought of it then; as little as tonight, he remembered that strange and resistless strength that had once pushed him into the abyss of oblivion on a Sunday night in a Kingston Street. What did he think? What was his feeling? Who can tell the story of these days in his mind and heart, since he cannot.

ONE DAY IN KINGSTON A rumour crept abroad and spread from place to place in the busy streets. It came like the shadow of death and it was of death that it spoke.

Men told in their counting houses that Harold was dead.

The rumour progressed till Masters crossed its path.

"Not dead," he said. "Dying."

The first part of his correction was really a correction. For the rest, this also was a statement needing further correction. The correction belongs to another story, the name of which has been mentioned in these pages as THE DEAD MAN WHO LIVED.

Another rumour spread dark wings and swooped down on the certain he uses in Kingston. It was said that John Meffala was dead.

Where the first word of this came from no one seemed able to discover; and the rumour met on all sides with doubt; even with the naked sword of abrupt denial.

Meffala and Company knew nothing of it. Peter Passley knew nothing of it. The rumour slunk away from the lips of men. But after a day or so it returned; for this rumour was true. It came baldly, perhaps because there was so little to tell. There was mystery, because there was such absolute nakedness of outline.

John Meffala was seen on deck on a certain night, and never a sign of weakness or ailing showed in his jolly face and ready jocularity.

John Meffala was seen no more by human eye. That was all; and the work of post and to cable freely given in obedience to the imperious demands of wealth and anxiety could bring no one nearer to the core of the mystery.

"The unexpected. What a naked cliff of surprize," said Liberta abruptly when she was told; and not another comment passed her lips.

Mrs. Meffala felt it very much, people said, and who are we to say she did not; but this, at any rate, was a fact that we record without innuondo. A month later, she said to her husband: "Why on earth should the Insurance people hesitate to accept his death as certain? It is clear as the sun in the sky and it means £500 to us. Why should we have two losses?" Which is merely mentioned to show that even in the bitter waters of grief Mrs. Meffala was still a good business woman. Let us take it at that.

The Major told Ada.

"I cannot believe he is dead," she said a great number of times. Then 'Thank God, thank God."

She saw the Major's disapproving face and excused herself.

"The world was not big enough to make me safe from him, Major, while he lived. He himself said it. He would have come for me again.

　　　　　　　　　　　　　　　　　　THOMAS MACDERMOT

I am glad he is dead. I cannot tell lies about it. It makes me believe in God, and God did it to save me."

It was the pure heart of the Major that raised for John Meffala such mark in memory as we like to think of as erected over the names of the departed.

There was a fear that reached out and struck the Major's heart at times. It was the fear that there was creeping out from the bosom of the Army that meant so much to her, a spirit that she instinctively shrank from, a spirit of hard, calculating service. On the day that she heard of Meffala's death she had come face to face with her fear more directly than ever before. For the first time in her life she had felt relieved by putting off the Army uniform. She was free for two days to rest, and it seemed to her that without the uniform she could think better of the points that certain decisions and incidents had raised in her mind.

Gossip was in heavy leaf that day. She was standing at a street corner in unobtrusive brown linen when she overheard the name Meffala.

Two young men near at hand were talking of him.

"Quite a number of sweethearts he leaves, doesn't he?"

"Quite so. There was some scandal about a Salvationist wasn't there."

"Well, I saw her myself coming from his rooms, in broad daylight."

The Major had overheard it all without being conscious that hearing it could be avoided.

She walked up to the speaker.

"You spoke of Mr. Meffala just now."

"Yes, Madam," the young man uncovered his head politely; but astonishment broke from his face in waves.

"And of a Salvation Officer." The Major was as pale as ever.

"Yes."

"Well I am that officer; and I thought I should tell you I overheard what you said and; that it is untrue. I think you believed it; but it is a lie. And if all they say about him is no more true, then it is all false. It is not for myself, it is for him I want you to know. For me?" she said wearily "I belong elsewhere. I go back to England, what does it matter to me what is said of me here. I go back to my own people, to my father and mother and sister who will believe me. But this is his country and—"

"I beg your pardon most humbly—" the young man began.

"Do this," she said abruptly, "when you hear men saying anything like what you were just now, contradict them as I have contradicted you. Do that; if you are really sorry."

She turned aside and left the two without another word. Her face was pale as death; her eyes filled with slow tears.

The End

A Note About the Author

Started by Thomas MacDermot in 1903, the *All Jamaican Library* was Jamaica's first indigenous publishing house consisting of a series of short stories and novellas written *by* Jamaicans *about* Jamaica and reasonably priced in order to remain accessible. Ultimately he was only able to publish four works with two authored by himself—*Becka's Buckra Baby* (1904) and *One Brown Girl and ¼* (1909)—comprising "The Story of Noel"; E.A. Dodds' *Maroon Medicine* (1905) and W.A. Campbell's *Marguerite: A Story of the Earthquake* (1907). While short lived, the *All Jamaican Library* features the first collection of short stories by a Caribbean writer and marked the beginning of modern Caribbean writing as it is known today.

A Note from the Publisher

Spanning many genres, from non-fiction essays to literature classics to children's books and lyric poetry, Mint Edition books showcase the master works of our time in a modern new package. The text is freshly typeset, is clean and easy to read, and features a new note about the author in each volume. Many books also include exclusive new introductory material. Every book boasts a striking new cover, which makes it as appropriate for collecting as it is for gift giving. Mint Edition books are only printed when a reader orders them, so natural resources are not wasted. We're proud that our books are never manufactured in excess and exist only in the exact quantity they need to be read and enjoyed. To learn more and view our library, go to minteditionbooks.com